Pay Me, Bug!

A Space Opera

C. B. Wright

This is a work of fiction. Names, characters, places and incidents either are products of the author's imagination or are used fictitiously. Any resemblance to actual events, locales or persons, living or dead, is entirely coincidental.

...except for the one time when the book mentions Voltaire, but they get that wrong anyway (and there's passing mention of the Catholic church, but it's a **future** Catholic church so that really could be anything).

The point is, none of this is real. Don't get your dander up.

PAY ME, BUG!
Copyright © 2011 by Christopher Brennan Wright
Cover art Copyright © 2015 by Nick James

ISBN 978-1-939633-00-2

This publication is distributed under a Creative Commons Attribution-Noncommercial-Share Alike 4.0 (CC BY-NC-SA 4.0) license. The license allows this publication to be freely copied, distributed, transmitted, or adapted so long as:

1. Proper attribution is given to the author
2. The work is not used for commercial purposes
3. Any work derived from this publication is distributed under the same license

To view this license, visit:

http://creativecommons.org/licenses/by-nc-sa/4.0

or send a letter to:

Creative Commons
444 Castro Street
Suite 900
Mountain View, California 94140
USA

Aside from the specific permissions granted by this license, all rights are reserved by the author. Requests for permissions not covered by this license should be submitted online at:

https://www.eviscerati.org/contact

Table of Contents

This book would not have been possible without, and is therefore dedicated to, the following people:

Patricia, my wife, who puts up with all my mad schemes;

Jason and **Matt**, my partners in crime;

and (of course)

Captain Kaff Tagon.

Chapter 1

WHEREIN the Woods, Noting Our Hero's Sudden Departure, Resolve to Give Chase

There were two competing theories about the difficulties involved in superluminal navigation.

The first, popular in universities and laboratories, stated that all things were measurable, and as far as navigation was concerned, all measurable things could be measured to any required accuracy. It was, according to this theory, simply a matter of finding the numbers and entering them in the correct order. The second, popular on the bridge of most space-faring vehicles across the known galaxy, stated that every tool was finite in scope and fallible in operation, making any of those measurements prone to error.

Grif Vindh, captain of the *Fool's Errand*, was an experienced pilot; as such, he favored the latter theory.

It wasn't that he felt superluminal travel was inherently unsafe—it was unsafe in *theory*, but in *practice* he felt it was safer than anyone had a right to expect from an engineering end-run around the laws of physics that enveloped a ship in a field of artificial space and time, hurtling it through the galaxy at speeds the universe would just as soon pretend didn't exist. Of course, on those statistically rare occasions when something *did* go wrong, the results were usually catastrophic... and *catastrophic results* was one of Grif's three least favorite phrases, right up there with *honest government official* and *mandatory tax on imported goods*.

But the danger of a *catastrophic result* folding Grif and his crew into five or six more dimensions than they really ought to have was the kind of thing that could be monitored and avoided in most instances. What bothered him a little more was that from the time they jumped to tach to the time they dropped out they were flying blind. He had to trust his on-board instrumentation to keep track of their direction and relative speed. He had to trust that the superluminal beacon sitting at their destination was functioning properly, that it was sending them accurate drop coordinates, and that it wasn't sending another ship the same drop coordinates at the same time. He trusted his ship and his crew enough that he didn't expect a fumble on his end.

What really bothered him—and bothered him every trip he took, all the way back to his first jump as a stowaway—was that when a ship was in tach it was completely engulfed in a solid, uniform, mind-numbingly *dull* gray field. It was an effect that someone had once, in a fit of misguided poetry, called "The Gray Wake." Grif preferred "The Gray Wall of Infinite Boredom," but the other name was the one that took.

The gray was ever-present: the "Pilot's Nest," set forward from the rest of the bridge and sunk into the deck, was encased in a bubble of transparent alloy that provided the pilot a magnificent view... when the ship wasn't surrounded by endless gray nothing. That gray nothing gave Grif the impression that he was hanging in the middle of oblivion.

He sighed, then pushed his chair back along its guide rail until it locked into the far position, taking him out of the nest and into the bridge proper. Immediately he felt the bridge crew tense: the click of his chair entering the bridge meant their captain was going stir crazy.

Grif looked at his crew, the older, white-haired man sitting to his left, and the dark-haired beauty to his right—both trying their best to ignore him—and sighed again.

"Morgan."

The white-haired man sitting to his left shifted at the mention of his name, but didn't look up.

"Shouldn't we be getting a beacon signal right about now?"

"I don't know." Morgan made no effort to disguise his annoyance. "I'm a sensor tech. Ask your navigator."

Amys tensed slightly. Grif grinned and allowed himself to be momentarily distracted by the curve of her neck.

"Amys?" he asked hopefully.

Amys exhaled, letting the breath escape through her teeth in a slow hiss. "Grif," she said, "you are being a pest. More so than usual. It stopped being charming about five *are-we-there-yet's* ago."

"Er. Yes. Sorry," Grif said.

"Honestly, I'm on the verge of mutiny. And I think the crew will support me."

"Yeah..." Grif sighed again and leaned back in his chair, staring at the bulkhead ceiling as he scratched at the stubble on his face. "Mea culpa. Our daring escape was a little more daring than I would have liked. I'm a little on edge."

Amys laughed sharply. Morgan grunted in agreement.

"... and I'm looking forward to making that daring escape *official* so I can gloat and caper. With glee."

Amys relaxed, smiling slightly. "That will be fun to watch. Once we get there."

"Which brings me back to my original question. Morgan, shouldn't we be getting a—"

Morgan's station beeped.

"Hold on," Morgan said. He tapped a few keys at his station and hunched over his datascreen. "Superluminal beacon confirmed. Amys, I'm sending it to your station."

"An end to monotony!" Grif happily slid his chair forward until it had descended into the nest and was locked securely in front of the pilot station. "It'll be good to see stars again!"

"Thanks, Morgan..." Amys scanned through the list of available drop locations supplied by the beacon. "Selecting drop coordinates."

"Stars," Grif continued, "and planets. And, of course, centers of commerce. Never forget the centers of commerce."

"Got it," Amys said. "Sending drop location to communications."

"Sending coordinates," Morgan replied. And a second later: "drop location confirmed and reserved."

The SL beacon would no longer give out that location to other ships. In theory, at least: three years ago an SL Beacon in the Timur Barony began sending out the same drop location to every ship trying to enter the system, and the resulting unpleasantness took a year and a half to clean.

Grif figured it would be another ten to fifteen years before anyone would have to worry about that happening again.

"Sending drop location your way, Grif." Just after Amys said it, Grif heard his station beep, and information flashed across his screen. He began to make the adjustments needed to bring the *Fool's Errand* out of tach and into the spot his navigator had chosen.

As he worked he activated the ship's intercom. "Heads up, crew. We're coming out in... uh..."

"Twenty minutes," Amys said.

"Twenty minutes," Grif repeated. "Everyone get ready. Ktk, how are the engines?"

Ktk, a hyper-intelligent member of an unpronounceable race from an unpronounceable home world, was his chief engineer. In its clicking, grinding manner of speech it explained that the tachyon drive was damaged: they'd pushed it to go faster than it was designed to go, and while Ktk could keep it in tach at present they wouldn't be able to use it again unless it was repaired at a decent spaceport.

"No problem," Grif said. "We're going to Oasis. We'll have the best the Tylaris Shipyards can offer before we'll have to run her hot again. Smooth sailing, wind at our back, no worries from here on out."

His pronouncement was greeted with silence from the other end of the intercom. Eventually Ktk replied that it had heard such assurances in the past, and they'd often proven premature.

"Hey." Grif glanced up from his station and glared at the intercom. It was voice-only, but old habits died hard. "Where's the trust?"

Ktk described an occasion when a promise of smooth sailing led to a sudden firefight and desperate chase through the upper atmosphere of a gas giant.

"... yes," Grif admitted, "that was a little more interesting than I'd have liked, but we're dropping into *friendly* space this time."

Ktk described an occasion when entering into friendly space had resulted in their immediate arrest and arraignment for murder.

"Also an unfortunate incident," Grif agreed. "And a case of mistaken identity."

A booming laugh echoed over the intercom, as Cyrus Mak, Grif's chief gunner, joined the conversation. "That's because we were using a stolen signature key that matched his ruddy ship! That you *bought* from him."

"I still say that was a good deal. Anyway, prepare for drop in seventeen minutes. All hands, strap in: clean getaway is imminent."

A second later, almost reluctantly, he added: "Doma, get on the bridge."

Minutes later the bridge door opened. A gangly, sullen kid floated on deck, glaring at Amys and Morgan before gliding over to a station on the starboard side of the bridge.

Doma Enge was Grif's nephew, a fact Grif tried to not to dwell on overmuch. They bore a certain physical similarity: both were of similar height and build, both had dark hair and eyes, but in countenance they were very different. Grif looked disheveled; he sported a fine layer of stubble that never quite coaxed itself into a beard, and always appeared to need more sleep. Doma, on the other hand, obviously spent a great deal of time grooming himself, not always to his advantage.

Doma looked down at his station and frowned. "It's turned off."

Morgan ignored him. Amys frowned as she focused on her navigation panel. Grif gritted his teeth.

"The Comm station isn't on," Doma repeated.

"That's right," Grif said. "Sit down."

"But I'm supposed to be the Comm officer!" Doma's voice took on a slightly higher pitch. "I can't be the Comm officer if the Comm station is turned off."

"Just strap in," Grif said. "I re-routed communications to sensors. Morgan is taking care of it."

"You can't do that!" Doma screeched in a mixture of petulance and righteous indignation. "That's my job!" His voice carried a thin, whiny edge that burrowed into a spot right behind Grif's left eye and started kicking.

"It *was* your job," Morgan said, voice calm. "Until you accidentally broadcast our in-ship communications to the ship we were *trying to get away from at the time.*"

"That was an accident," Doma protested.

"... and now I'm doing your job *and* my job," Morgan finished.

"It was an *accident*!" Doma repeated, and his voice continued to *kick, kick, kick, kick, kick*...

"Yes," Grif agreed, "it was an accident. You'll notice that Morgan actually used the word *accidentally* when describing it. I don't really think it was a situation where you said to yourself 'hey, wouldn't it be really neat if I broadcast a conversation between my captain and his gunner discussing the best way to target the engines of a Radiant Throne corsair *directly* to the ship in question?' No, we're all *absolutely convinced* your incompetence is *undeniably* involuntary."

"I'm just saying," Doma muttered.

"If I thought you'd done it on purpose, I'd have spaced you on the spot.

Your mother be damned."

Doma's face reddened. He opened his mouth, ready to retort, when suddenly Grif launched his chair back along the rails; it emerged abruptly onto the bridge proper with a loud *crack*. He swiveled the chair around to face Doma and *glared* at him.

"Strap in, Doma. And don't touch anything."

Glowering fiercely, Doma pulled himself into the now-defunct Communications station and strapped himself in to counter the sometimes awkward effects of zero gravity.

"Ten minutes," Amys said.

"Don't see why I can't touch anything," Doma muttered. "It's turned off."

"Because," Grif said, "you might turn it back *on*."

With that he swiveled his chair back around to face front, and slid down the guides back into the depths of the pilot's nest.

Minutes passed in blissful silence. Doma shifted in his seat, staring at the dark, lifeless controls in the station before him, then turned to look at Amys and Morgan, each intently monitoring their controls. Craning his neck, he could peer down the track into the pilot's nest and just make out the top of Grif's head.

"If I'm not supposed to touch anything, I don't know why I should even be here," Doma complained.

Morgan chuckled. "Grif's probably got money in the 'Amys kills Doma before we reach Tylaris' pool."

Doma glared at the back of Morgan's head, and glanced nervously at Amys. She smiled like a predator, all teeth and no warmth.

Doma cleared his throat, and took a different tack. "We're going to get caught, you know."

Morgan snorted derisively. "If we are, then we'll have you to thank for it, won't we?"

"OK, sure, blame me," Doma said. "But that doesn't change anything. They almost had us in a gravlock before we hit tach."

"Which is what we *wanted*," Amys said in a businesslike, even-toned voice. Grif knew that voice: that was the voice of a very dangerous woman who wanted to hurt someone *very badly*, and was exercising all her self-control to prevent it.

"That's right," Grif said. "I wanted them powering up the damn thing so they'd have to take the time to power it *down* before they could follow us. You don't go firing those things in tach. Not unless you want to get crushed like a grape. Or turned into a fine layer of carbon paste spread out on a bulkhead wall. Or wind up a drooling vegetable with one too many corners. It gave us a head start, see? And we're dropping into neutral space, so even if they caught up to us there's not a damn thing they can do about it."

"If they do," Doma said gravely, "they'll probably kill us."

"Doma." Grif resisted the urge to push his chair back out into the bridge again. "As much as I personally admire your innate *optimism*, my executive officer is about two seconds away from tearing you to pieces." Grif heard a slow, even release of breath and revised that estimate downward. "Remember what I told you about self-fulfilling prophecies?"

Doma glanced at Amys nervously, then turned to look at the lifeless Communications screen, pouting.

"And for God's sake," Grif repeated, "*don't touch anything*."

After a minute of blissful silence, Amys reported they were eight minutes out.

"Right," Grif said. "Time to play captain." He reactivated the intercom. "Eight minutes to drop. All stations report."

Cyrus Mak was the first to report in. "Fine down here. Main cannon overheated, but we got it off line and secured. Cutter and Hari are looking into why... if we run into trouble we'll have to rely on the turrets."

"No trouble," Grif insisted. "Why does everyone always think there's going to be trouble? Don't you dare answer that question, Doma..."

Doma muttered something under his breath.

"Ktk? Status?"

The voice that replied was human and female: Vod Hallik, one of Ktk's engineers. "Everything's OK, Skip. Ktk's running a few last minute checks. It wasn't kidding about the Tach drive, though... we're kind of hoping you'll let us upgrade instead of patching this one up. Gurgan's even been going through old Tylaris catalogs..."

"We'll see. We have to sell our cargo first. All right, all hands stand by."

"Seven minutes," Amys reported.

Doma, Morgan and Grif sat in silence as Amys counted down the time. At 30 seconds, Grif began the sequence to disperse the tachyon field.

Space travel is the sublime art of hurtling through a nearly empty void, and narrowly missing everything in it.

Grif had no idea who was responsible for coining that phrase—the Earthies he knew insisted it was someone named Voltaire—but it always seemed appropriate at this point.

"Five, four, three, two... mark."

The gray field disappeared immediately, and stars burst into view as the real universe replaced the artificially generated one. Grif felt a slight sensation of vertigo as the tachyon field disappeared, and they dropped completely into reality.

"And we're in," Grif said. "Good work Amys."

"Of course it's good work," she said. "You worry too much."

"Uh... Skip..." Morgan was typing at his console furiously. "We're being hailed by the... ah... SL Beacon. General audio."

"Right." Grif straightened in his seat. "Patch that in, would you?"

"Unidentified ship, this is Superluminal Beacon 274, please identify yourself and state your purpose."

"Return channel open," Morgan said. "Wait—hold on—there. Return channel open."

"What's the matter, Morgan?" Doma sneered. "Having trouble with communications?"

Amys spun in her chair and glared at Doma furiously. Doma realized that he'd spoken while the channel was live. He shuddered.

"... unidentified ship, I didn't quite copy that. Is everything all right?"

"Everything's fine," Grif said. "Superluminal Beacon 274, this is Cargo Vessel *Fool's Errand*. We request entry into your system."

"Copy, *Fool's Errand*. Please transmit your Signature Key for authorization."

"Morgan," Grif prompted, and Morgan keyed in the transmit code that would send out the data key that uniquely identified their ship. A few seconds later, the voice said, with a bit more warmth, "*Fool's Errand*, system entry is granted. Welcome back, Captain Vindh."

"Acknowledged, Beacon," Grif replied. "And thank you. Morgan, kill feed."

"Feed is dead," Morgan announced.

Grif slid his chair back out into the bridge. "Doma, I'm getting tired of—"

In a blur of motion Amys propelled herself out of her chair, shot up to the bulkhead ceiling, and shot toward Doma. Doma, still strapped to his chair, squawked in alarm as her left arm lashed out and grabbed his neck, jerking his head back as she swung herself around behind him. A hum filled the air as a knife, blade vibrating thousands of times a second, hovered only inches from his now-exposed neck.

"Doma." She spoke softly, but the anger was plain in her voice. "When the captain opens a comm channel, only the captain speaks. Unless he's given you leave to do so. Nod if you understand."

Doma nodded.

"If you ever do that again, I will cut out your tongue with this knife. Nod if you understand."

Doma nodded.

Amys lowered the knife, patted him once on the cheek, then floated back to her station. Grif slid his chair back down into the pilot's nest without comment.

The next few minutes were devoted to restoring ship's gravity. After a general announcement from the captain, the crew set about securing anything that might shift when the gravity plates were activated. This largely consisted of taking sealed containers and placing them in larger containers, then strapping themselves back in to their chairs once more to make sure unexpected gravity spikes didn't cause injuries. The bridge crew was secured relatively quickly, then a report from Cyrus announced the gunnery crew was secure as well. It took a little longer for the engineering crew to report because, as Cyrus liked to say, "there's never a clean way to fix something proper." Eventually Ktk announced the engine room was secure.

"Right." Grif settled back into his chair. "Morgan, ready?"

"Grav plates online and ready. Nullifier plates online and ready."

"All right. Gravity on in five... four... three... two... mark."

The floors emitted a soft hum as the gravity plates came to life. The ceilings groaned slightly as the nullifer plates did the same, preventing the ship's gravity from extending beyond the hull. Grif felt a slight jerk as he pulled deeper into his chair, and heard a dull thud as Doma, who was apparently unable to pay attention to a countdown, wound up banging his head against the deactivated communications console.

Morgan and Amys laughed. Grif grinned, but didn't join in. That had happened to him his first time out.

Of course this wasn't Doma's first time out.

The grin disappeared. He would never have suffered this level of incompetence from another crew member. The only reason Doma was still alive at this point was because he was family. Grif, as a rule, hated family... but they were still family.

"Amys, set a course for Tylaris Prime," Grif said, removing the chair restraints and stretching. They'd been in zero gravity for more than a week, and while the calcilate supplements in their food negated any potential effects on bone density and muscle mass his muscles still ached for a while when gravity was restored.

"Nothing unusual on scanners," Morgan reported. "The only other ships in the vicinity are the warships guarding the SL Beacon."

Grif turned on the intercom. "This is your Captain speaking. Looks like we're in the clear. I need a drink."

Over the intercom Grif heard Cyrus shout "Pay me, Bug!"

Grif laughed. "Bet against me again, Ktk? You should know better than to—"

The entire ship lurched violently. Grif was thrown from his chair, his shoulder hitting the top of the pilot station as he landed face-first against the viewplate.

"What the hell?" he shouted.

"We are in a gravlock!" Morgan's voice was tight and animated, not quite shouting but definitely vigorous. "A ship just dropped from tach... I don't understand, it's right on top of us, and—holy hell, that's a *Battlecarrier*."

Grif choked. He pushed himself back over the pilot's station, climbing back into his seat, ignoring the throbbing in his shoulder. He noticed the intercom was still on.

"Battle stations!" He snapped the order as he strapped himself back into his chair. "I want gravity off and I want it off now. Ktk, we are in a gravlock. I need you to boost the fusion drive so we can wiggle out. Morgan I need tactical."

A flickering holographic display of the immediate region of space appeared in front of each station on the bridge, showing the *Fool's Errand* in the center. "Above" and "behind" their position was a ship so large that it completely filled the default view of the display.

"They found us," Doma whispered. Or he would have whispered, if the intercom hadn't been on.

"Shut up, Doma," Grif said.

"We're going to die," Doma continued.

"I said shut *up*, Doma. *Right now.*" In his mind Grif repeated *it's not him it can't be him this has nothing to do with him there's no reason he'd wind up being involved this has to be some kind of—*

"Dammit!" The tone of Morgan's voice escalated from 'animated' to 'alarmed.' "Grif, they just broadcast their signature key. It's the *Centurion.*"

—son of a bitch.

Chapter 2

WHEREIN Our Hero, Noting the Woods' Triumphant Return, Desperately Casts About for an Axe

"*Centurion* is hailing us," Morgan reported.

"Damn the *Centurion*!" Grif snarled. "Ktk, engines! Morgan, get me the SL Beacon. Better yet, get me one of those warships!"

Grif felt a sudden release as the grav plates deactivated, then a slight tug above and aft from the *Centurion's* gravlock. That cut away as the nullifier plates kicked in, preventing the gravitational pull of the beam from crossing the hull into the ship.

Over the intercom, Ktk reported that it was a bad idea to try and push the fusion drive at this point in time.

"I don't care if it's a bad idea," Grif said. "Until we're presented with a *good* idea, we're going to go with the only idea I have at the moment. Get on it!"

"This isn't fair," Doma whimpered.

"For once," Grif said, "I agree with you."

They no longer felt the initial jolt of the gravlock, but the tactical display showed that the *Fool's Errand* was slowly being pulled toward the much larger ship. Ktk announced, somewhat reluctantly, that it had managed to boost the fusion drive, and Grif wasted no time.

"Get ready for a rough ride," Grif said. "Amys, I need slingshot patterns *now*." He keyed in a command and the ship shuddered as her engines opened up.

Escaping a gravlock wasn't an easy process, but it was possible. Unlike planetary gravity, which came from a source so much larger than a ship that precision wasn't necessary, a gravlock was a single beam that was aimed at its target. When the target moved, the beam had to follow, and if the pilot was creative enough it was possible to use the gravlock as a slingshot to increase the force and speed of a ship to break free of the artificial gravity well. It was a difficult and risky maneuver, but the more power a ship had to put into it the better its chances.

Grif saw a flash of blinding white energy streak across his viewplate. "They just fired a warning shot," Morgan announced.

"How do you know it was a warning?" Grif was only half-aware of what he was saying as he set in the courses Amys fed him. "They could just be really bad at it..."

"No, they sent a message saying 'That was a warning shot. We encourage you to answer our hail.'"

"I don't want to talk to them! I want to talk to the Tylaris warships!" Grif uttered a few choice curses against the *Centurion* as he saw warning lights flash on his console. Ktk was right; pushing the fusion drives had been a bad idea. They wouldn't last long. He abandoned his attempt to escape the gravlock, and settled for resisting its pull just long enough think of something else.

Even if we got out of the gravlock we wouldn't be in any condition to fight. If those bastards from the Barony would just—

"One of the warships has responded to our hail," Morgan announced.

"Put it through!" Grif ordered.

I hereby rescind and apologize for any comments or insinuations I may have made concerning your familial status.

A small screen on Grif's station blinked, and the image of a heavyset man in the green-and-gold uniform of the Tylaris Royal Navy appeared.

"Captain Vindh, yes?" The man stared at Grif politely through the screen.

"Captain," Grif said, "we are in desperate need of assistance here."

The captain nodded gravely. "What is the nature of your emergency?"

Grif blinked. He heard Morgan swearing softly behind him.

"We're... uh... being *detained* by a Radiant Throne Battlecarrier. Perhaps you noticed it on your sensors."

"Yes," the captain replied politely. "I admit it startled us when it first appeared. Apparently it managed to hack into the beacon—we have no idea how it managed to do that from tach, mind you—and locate your drop point."

"That's all very interesting," Grif said, "but we're in a bit of a hurry... because we're being *detained*. By a *Radiant Throne Battlecarrier*. In *Tylaris Barony Space*. Maybe I'm old-fashioned, but I thought governments took a dim view when other governments *violated their sovereignty.*"

The captain shook his head. "I'm afraid you aren't in Tylaris Barony space yet, Captain."

"The hell we—" Grif interrupted himself, frowned, and muted the communication for a moment. "Morgan?"

"Of course we're in—wait." Morgan muttered something indistinct, then swore. "Technically he's right. But he's splitting an awfully fine hair."

Doma whimpered softly and began to hyperventilate.

Grif unmuted the channel. "Can we assume, then, that no help will be forthcoming?"

An expression of genuine regret appeared on the captain's face for a moment, then smoothed out into a mask of professional disinterest. "I'm afraid we are unable to interfere in the affairs of foreign powers," he said.

Son of a bitch.

Grif unceremoniously killed the channel.

"*Centurion* is hailing us again," Morgan said. "And she's powering her main weapons."

"All *right*!" Grif snarled. "Put the bastard on."

The display on his station blinked again, and another uniformed man appeared.

Grif tried his best to smile. "Commodore Mavis. What a *pleasant* surprise."

Commodore Mavis was a well-preserved, middle-aged man who carried himself with poise and confidence. He was arrogant, which Grif hated, but he was also very smart... which Grif hated more. Mavis stared out from the screen with a look of mild, polite disinterest.

"Captain Vindh," Mavis replied. "The pleasure is mine, I assure you. If you would be so kind as to deactivate your fusion drive and lock your ship's weapons, we'll pull you into our hold and search your ship very, very thoroughly."

As disinterested as the Commodore appeared to be, the smugness in his voice was infuriating.

"Well, Commodore..." Grif forced himself to sound unconcerned. "If you'll look at your charts, I believe you'll find we're solidly in Tylaris space.

The Radiant Throne has no jurisdiction here, and—"

"The Radiant Throne has jurisdiction *everywhere*," Mavis said. "That men hide from the truth that the Lord God burned into the very stars is regrettable, but ultimately irrelevant. And I think you'll find your claim of being 'solidly' in any kind of space is optimistic, even for you. My communications officer has already contacted Baron Tylaris and explained the nature of our operation. He has voiced no objection."

Grif heard Morgan swear, again, under his breath.

"At any rate, Captain Vindh, you are in no position to practice the finer arts of diplomacy."

Morgan swore one last time, and muted the communications feed. "*Centurion* has locked its main cannon on us," he reported. "Needless to say... that won't be a crippling shot."

Grif considered his options, then punched the intercom. "Ktk, take the fusion drive offline. Cyrus, take our guns offline, lock them down."

"Roger that." Cyrus was clearly unhappy with the development. Ktk emitted a series of untranslatable clicks and ticks—it was swearing, Grif decided, though he couldn't determine precisely who or what was being pilloried—then announced that the bet was still in play.

"Morgan, resume audio," Grif said. A moment later a message flashed beneath the image of Commodore Mavis, reporting that audio had been restored.

"Is everything all right, Captain?" Mavis asked politely. "We lost audio for a second, I was concerned you might be having some difficulty."

"Our engines are powering down, Commodore. We are also taking our guns offline. The entire process will take about an hour to do safely. I *insist* we be given that hour."

"Of course," Mavis agreed. "We will, naturally, be monitoring your progress with interest. Should you attempt to jettison anything during that time, please inform us of what and why... otherwise, we will be forced to assume it is contraband and act accordingly."

Grif scowled. "We have no intention of jettisoning any of our cargo."

"I am glad to hear it. When we have determined your engines are powered down and your guns locked in place, you will be brought into *Centurion's* primary flight bay. You will then be requested to exit your ship, which will be subject to a full search. Civility requires that I say I hope, when all is said and done, that I won't be forced to execute you on the spot. End communication."

The monitor went dark as *Centurion* killed the feed from their end.

"That... could have gone better," Grif said.

Amys and Morgan said nothing, patiently waiting for orders. Doma moaned hopelessly, sinking his head into his hands and rocking back and forth in his chair.

Grif took a moment to assess the situation. He examined a number of different possible actions and outcomes, looking for the best way out... when he made his decision he punched the intercom.

"We have about an hour before they pull us onto their ship," Grif said. "Cyrus, Ktk, get to Bay Two now."

"What about the guns?" Cyrus asked, confused.

"Cutter and Hari can manage," Grif said. "And Gurgan and Vod can bring the drive off line without Ktk. Go to Bay Two and unseal private storage."

"... *what*?"

"Then re-seal it. *Poorly*. Make the seam visible enough for the inevitable search party to find, if they put any effort into looking. Pile a bunch of crates on top of it, though. We don't want to make it too obvious."

"You're going to give up the cargo?" Morgan sounded puzzled.

"You want us to do *what*?" Cyrus was much more than puzzled, he was furious. "Grif, tell me you're not about to roll over and expose your belly to that—"

"The Captain gave you an order," Amys snapped.

Cyrus fell silent.

Ktk uneasily pointed out that Mavis and his men were going to search for smuggled cargo.

"I know," Grif said.

Ktk added that Mavis' men would very likely discover the bays if they were not fully sealed.

"I know."

Ktk stated that it was looking forward to making a profit from this venture, and it didn't see how that would happen if they effectively gave up their cargo to the Radiant Throne.

"Noted," Grif said. "*Trust me.*"

Ktk fell silent, considering. Eventually Grif heard Cyrus grunt, say "aye, Captain" in a bitter, angry tone, and that was the end of it.

Grif pushed his seat along the rail until he emerged into the bridge proper. He glanced at the others; the expressions on their faces were about what he expected. Amys was troubled and thoughtful, Morgan was confused and scowling, and Doma was gaping at Grif in mute wonder, as if someone had punched him in the face then kissed him square on the mouth.

"Hope you know what you're doing," Amys said.

"Me too," Grif said.

"You're insane," Doma whispered.

"As for *you*..." Grif turned in his seat and glowered at Doma. "You will say *nothing*. Nothing at all. Not a *single thing* to any Throne officials, soldiers, janitors, interns, *anyone*. If you do *anything* other than stutter, stammer, or look like you're going to have an accident in your shorts... I will tell your mother exactly what you did on Grenaris."

Doma's eyes widened slightly. He coughed, grinned meekly, and tried his best to look innocent. "Grenaris? What? I didn't—"

"And send her the pictures."

Doma's voice failed. He turned white as a sheet.

"Oh, yes, I found them." Grif said. "Actually, Cyrus found them. And showed them to Cutter and Hari, who gave them to Ktk, who showed them to Vod and Gurgan, and *then* gave them to Amys... who proceeded to *critique* them, rating each by creativity, poise, athleticism, and enthusiasm... and who then gave them to me."

"You scored high in enthusiasm," Amys said.

Doma looked from Grif to Amys. "I..." he hesitated, closed his eyes, and took a deep, ragged breath. "I'll keep quiet."

"Good." Grif nodded. "If you're a good boy and don't screw this up, you'll get 'em back."

Doma whimpered softly.

"Oh..." Grif grinned wickedly. "Pay attention to those critiques." He leered at his navigator, who smirked in spite of herself.

Doma blushed furiously.

Twenty minutes later Cyrus reported that they had successfully un-hidden the hidden cargo. Grif sent them back to their stations. Thirty minutes later, Cyrus reported in again, this time announcing that all three guns were locked down. Fifteen minutes after that Ktk reported that the fusion drive was powered down and off line.

"Right," Grif said. "Morgan, Get Mavis on the line and tell him that—"

The ship shuddered suddenly.

"*Centurion* is pulling us in," Morgan reported tersely.

"Well, never mind then. I guess he figured it out."

"Guess so," Morgan said. Grif noticed something unusually hostile in his tone.

"What's eating you?" Grif asked.

"Well I don't know," Morgan said, voice dripping with sarcasm. "We go to all this trouble to smuggle hootch out of Throne space and now we're about to hand it over to them without a fight. To Hu Mavis, of all people. We're a hair's breadth from friendly space and *why the hell didn't you show me those pictures*?"

Grif blinked in surprise. "What?"

"Everyone else on the ship got a chance to take a look," Morgan said. "What's the deal?"

"I... thought you wouldn't be interested," Grif said.

"In what? Ridiculing Doma?"

"Hey!" Doma protested.

"Point taken," Grif said, "but it was kind of childish. I figured you'd find it beneath you."

"Well I wouldn't!" Morgan snapped.

"Well I'll remember that next time!" Grif shouted.

"Good!" Morgan shouted back.

"And I'll make sure you look at them before I hand them back to Doma!"

"Fine!"

"Hey!" Doma protested again. "Don't I get a say in that?"

"No," Grif said.

"Not really," Morgan agreed.

The *Fool's Errand* was a large ship. Maximilian class frigates were originally designed to be naval gunboats and troop transport vessels. When they were first commissioned, they were the largest ships capable of flying through planetary atmosphere without having to rely on antigravity plates to withstand re-entry. Thirty years later they were still the third-largest ship capable of such.

The *RT Centurion*, a Radiant Throne Battlecarrier, made the *Fool's Errand* look like a small toy.

The gravlock pulled the *Fool's Errand* ever closer to the *Centurion*. Soon the bridge viewports were filled with the *Centurion's* hull—nothing distinct, just the dull gleam of alloy blocking out everything else.

"Damned big," Morgan muttered.

"Yeah," Grif said. "Ever been inside one?"

Morgan shook his head.

"Damned big inside, too."

"Funny thing to see in Trade Baron space," Amys noted. "Warship like that in an area they're not actually at war with. Seems a little wasteful."

"Mavis really hates Grif," Doma said. "A lot."

"Yes," Grif replied. "Thank you, Doma. Remember: stuttering, stammering, accident in your shorts. Nothing else."

Doma fell silent.

"Besides," Grif continued, "the fact that the Radiant Throne built a flotilla of those things tells me that they don't consider excess one of their Seven Deadly Sins. I mean, just look at it. It's bigger than most space stations. And it *moves*. With all the mass it transfers when it jumps to tach... hell, it could probably make it to the core in a month."

"Doubt it," Amys said.

"It'd be fast, that's all I'm saying. And they have *more than one*. Twenty or thirty, last I heard. I can't wrap my head around how much one of these things would cost."

"Well," Morgan observed, "they *are* the second largest government in known space."

"Yeah..." Grif stared at the ever-growing hull of the *Centurion* and frowned. "Here's a thought: when they pull us on board, and Mavis' men are pointing their guns at us, how about we not mention that the Throne is only in second place, hmm?"

Morgan thought it over. "Good point," he conceded. Something beeped on his station, and he turned his attention to one of his screens. "It's *Centurion*. Mavis wants to talk, I guess."

"Oh, for..." Grif closed his eyes and counted to three. "Put him on the big one."

A large tactical screen at the fore of the bridge, currently tracking the *Fool's Errand's* position in relation to *Centurion*, shifted to display Commodore Mavis looking on in smug satisfaction.

"Captain Vindh, I am launching a number of towships to guide your vessel into *Centurion's* main flight bay. We expect the process to take roughly half an hour. I must request that you and your crew exit your vessel as soon as I give the order. Come out unarmed, with your hands raised above your heads, and do so slowly."

"I know the drill, Commodore. And please remind your boys that Ktk has no hands that actually reach over its head. I'd hate to revisit that particular misunderstanding."

Mavis smiled slightly. "Of course. I would hate for anything to happen to your pet centipede."

Grif suppressed a scowl. "Right. Vindh out."

Morgan killed the channel as Grif punched the intercom. "As soon as we're secure in Centurion, go to Bay One. You know the drill. Cyrus, please leave all your weapons behind." He cut off the intercom before Cyrus had a chance to protest.

Four towships emerged from Centurion and quickly attached tow-lines to the hull of the *Fool's Errand*. It took longer than expected—forty-five minutes in all—before the *Fool's Errand* finally came to rest. Two minutes later the entire crew was assembled, waiting to disembark.

Cargo Bay One was cavernous and dimly-lit. Loading cranes hung from the ceiling, locked and secured in harnesses, and crates of cargo lined the walls. Grif looked around the bay in annoyance. While the bay was carrying more cargo than many of the smaller independent trading ships could hold, it still looked sadly empty compared to what it could manage.

They'd left in a hurry.

The crew gathered at the far end of the bay next to the fore lift, which would lower them out of the *Fool's Errand* and on to the *Centurion's* flight deck.

Amys stood to the left of the lift platform. Her long black hair, usually pulled back and wrapped into a bun when they were operating in zero gravity, had been let out and pulled back into a simple ponytail. She looked a little bored, but Grif noticed she'd pulled a strand of hair from her ponytail and was absently twirling it around her finger. He considered flashing her one of his "you worry too much" grins, but ultimately decided against it. She could usually tell when he was lying.

Standing next to her was Morgan, scratching his pepper-gray beard and trying not to look worried. Beside Morgan, Doma looked ready to faint.

Grif caught Doma's attention, mouthed the words *stuttering, stammering*, and *shorts*, then moved on.

Cyrus Mak stood to the right of the hatch, shifting his massive form impatiently and glowering at Grif as he approached. He was a giant of a man with long, dirty-blonde hair pulled back into a rough ponytail. His thick beard and twice-broken nose gave him a mean, thuggish appearance. Cutter and Hari stood to his left. Both were considerably shorter than Cyrus, but they looked no less disreputable: Cutter was a mass of stringy, knotty muscles, and had the distinction of being the ugliest man of any race Grif had ever met. Hari was Invagi, and like the rest of his race was a heavily-built humanoid with spiny ridges around his face and joints. At the moment the spines on his face were partially extended—he was nervous and trying to keep his emotions in check.

Grif looked at everyone and frowned. "Where's the bug?"

The faint hiss of the interior hatch opening announced the arrival of Ktk, Vod and Gurgan. Ktk didn't transmit anxiety the way other races did, but the constant staccato chitter coming out of its mandibles indicated it was unhappy, and its three prehensile tails twitched in agitation. Vod, a slim human woman with dark skin and practically no hair on her body, and Gurgan, a hulking man almost as large as Cyrus with olive skin and a single topknot of dark hair at the top of his head, followed their chief looking vaguely discontent.

"Well," Grif said, "here we all are."

Cyrus scowled and muttered something under his breath.

Grif ignored him. "Let's get this over with."

They all filed onto the lift platform, crowding to the edges to give Ktk enough room to scuttle in between them. Grif slid in next to the control pad and pressed a button. The lift shuddered a moment, then died.

Grif frowned and hit they key again. Again, the lift shuddered momentarily and died.

Doma whimpered.

Grif punched another key next to the lift—the key that controlled the external intercom—and cleared his throat nervously.

"We're all here," he said. "We're coming down now, with our hands over our heads. Please don't shoot us."

He pushed the first button again. This time, the lift didn't even shudder.

"Isn't it supposed to, you know..." Grif gestured vaguely.

"Unlock it first," Amys said.

Grif looked down at the control pad and noticed that the exterior locks were still in place. "Right." He keyed a short code into the control pad and with a click the locks smoothly retracted, allowing the lift to descend. "Thank you, Amys. Now... hands up, everyone. Let's try not to make them angry."

He raised his hands over his head; his crew, with varying degrees of reluctance, followed suit. Moments later they stepped onto *Centurion's* flight deck and into the line of fire.

Chapter 3

WHEREIN Our Hero, Axe in Hand, Discovers the Forest Brought Guns. Many, Many Guns.

Centurion's flight deck was immense.

As Grif stepped off the lift, onto the smooth alloyed floor, he didn't feel like he was on a ship; he felt like he was underground. The few times the *Fool's Errand* had berthed in an enclosed space, the facility had been underground, and *Centurion's* flight deck clearly borrowed from this design. The walls were a series of octagonal tiles—in an underground facility they would have been wedged into the surrounding rock itself. The ceiling, which cleared the top of Grif's ship with at least twenty meters to spare, housed long strips of lights to provide general lighting, and track-mounted lights to provide greater illumination where necessary.

It wasn't the first time Grif had been on this ship, and the initial feeling of disorientation passed, replaced with all the sights and sounds of a starship: the metallic taste of air pumped through recycling filters, the low hum of the gravity induction field, and the faint sheen of light reflecting off the Maxwells as they kept the atmosphere on one side of the launch port and the vacuum of space on the other.

A crisply spoken command drew his attention from the ship toward the two squads of heavily armed Radiant Throne Marines, and he was again reminded how very easy it was to be distracted from impressive feats of engineering.

Commodore Mavis stood behind the marines, staring at Grif intently. Grif waited patiently, adopting an air of casual disregard as a contingent of marines broke away from the main group, surrounded Grif and his crew, and marched them toward Mavis.

"Captain Vindh." Mavis was all business—whatever he was feeling, he didn't allow it to creep into his voice.

"Commodore," Grif answered.

"I am required, at this point, to ask for your cargo manifest."

Grif slowly lowered his right hand, revealing a small data chip. Mavis nodded to one of his officers, who retrieved the data chip, placed it in a reader, and handed it to the Commodore.

"Thank you, Captain," Mavis said. Then, turning back to the same officer: "search them for weapons."

The officer barked out an order and marines advanced on the crew, separating each and searching them thoroughly... but not excessively, Grif had to admit. They were completely professional about the job.

"Farming equipment?" Mavis looked up from the reader in surprise. "You're transporting farming equipment?"

Grif shrugged as best he could with his hands still raised above his head. "There's a market for it," he said. "And Varkav's equipment is almost as good as what you can get from Tyrelos. At half the price."

"I see." Mavis sounded unconvinced. "According to this manifest, you paid all cargo duties promptly and without complaint."

"That's because this is legitimate cargo," Grif said.

"It would seem to be..." Mavis nodded to another officer, who immediately ordered his men onto the lift and into the *Fool's Errand*. "And yet when one of our corsairs hailed you, you ran."

"Force of habit."

"They apparently intercepted onboard communications between you and one of your gunners concerning the best way to cripple them," Mavis continued.

"No, that's just a big misunderstanding," Grif said. "See, what happened was—"

"They're clean." The officer who supervised the search of the crew interrupted Grif in mid-sentence. "No weapons of any kind."

"Very good," Mavis said. "Captain, you and your crew may lower your arms. Including your... bug-friend's tentacles, I suppose."

Ktk replied that they were tails, not tentacles, but Mavis had no idea what it was saying. Grif didn't bother translating.

"So, Captain Vindh... your cargo is legitimate, your fees were paid in full... yet you ran at first contact from one of our military vessels. What am I to think? Is there anything else to declare? Perhaps you may have... omitted something from your manifest?" Mavis allowed himself a slight smile.

Oh, but he is enjoying this, Grif thought. *Bastard.*

"Yeah," Grif said. "Now that you mention it, I do have something to declare. This is an illegal search. This system isn't part of your empire, it's part of the Tylaris Barony—neutral territory, for your information, and declared so by your very own Emperor, who I think would be upset if some second-rate blanker—"

Something heavy smashed into the back of his head. He sank to his knees, gasping in pain. Marines grabbed his arms, keeping him from falling face-first on the floor.

"That is enough, Lieutenant." Mavis' voice sounded distant through the ringing in Grif's ears. "He is being impolite, but we mustn't overreact."

The marines hauled Grif to his feet and released him. He staggered slightly as he fought to regain his sense of equilibrium. As his vision cleared, he saw Mavis staring at him thoughtfully.

"It is true," Mavis admitted. "A crude word, even vulgar. But not *wrong*. God did not bless me with the divine telepath's gift. Then again, we are taught that the Apostle Paul, in his later years, found himself going blind... And though he prayed, God did not restore his sight. Even so, was he not one of the greatest of God's servants?"

"Couldn't tell you," Grif said. "That's something for you and the Earthies to talk about. Morgan and Cutter are Terran, they probably know more."

"I'm an atheist," Cutter drawled.

"And I'm a scientist," Morgan added. "I'll leave it to you to decide which one is worse."

"And astrology is really more my thing," Grif said.

"Indeed?" Mavis looked at Grif in mild surprise. "Disappointing. I was expecting a stalwart proclamation of atheism, like your crewman there." He gestured to Cutter with a wave of his hand. "And now I come to find that you are simply a star-worshipper."

"I didn't say that," Grif said. "I just happen to think it's a better con."

The lines around Mavis' mouth tightened. "I see. You seek to mock me, then. And not only me. Give a care, Captain Vindh: you mock a faith that sustains not only me, but nearly every man and woman that serves aboard my ship."

Grif's vision cleared just in time to see Mavis nod to someone behind him, and he felt a second sharp pain on the back of his head. He sank to his knees again, grunting in pain.

"Are you through, Captain Vindh?"

"Y... yes..." Grif's tongue felt heavy and swollen. He tasted blood in his mouth; he suspected he'd bitten it after that last blow. "No. This... this is not legal... Tylaris..."

"Yes, Tylaris," Mavis said. "Tylaris is under treaty with the Radiant Throne, its sovereignty momentarily secure. Yet you see, we are not quite in Tylaris space, Captain. If we were, your complaint might have more merit. As it stands, Baron Tylaris is fully aware of my presence here, and does not object to it. He knows the only reason we allow him his petty kingdom is because he has use to us. When that utility ends, we will retake what is ours. And it *is* ours, Captain Vindh. The Radiant Throne claims all. Everything falls under the shadow of our empire."

"Right..." Grif struggled to his feet, clutching the back of his head. "How does that work, exactly? Are you *subletting* some of that out to the Alliance of Free Worlds, or..."

Before he could finish the taunt he yelled in pain as the butt of a rifle smashed against the back of his head a third time. This time they didn't catch him; he fell forward, sprawling before Mavis' unmoving form. Before Grif could move, he felt the heel of a boot come down hard on the small of his back. Amys cried out in alarm, Cyrus bellowed with rage...

...and forty marines powered up their weapons in unison. Silence ruled the day.

Mavis knelt beside Grif's sprawled form, grabbed his hair, and forced his head up. Grif tried to focus and failed miserably.

"You should learn to hold your tongue, Captain Vindh." Mavis' voice was mild, almost soothing. "You shouldn't play the rooster when you're in no condition to crow." He let go of Grif's hair. Grif's head thumped loudly as it hit the deck.

Grif groaned and tried to get on his hands and knees. Someone grabbed his shoulder and offered a hand—Grif took it and struggled shakily to his feet.

It was Amys.

"I thought you said we shouldn't make them angry," she said softly.

"Tha' was the plan," Grif agreed, speech slurring slightly. "Apparently I'm improvising."

She grunted as she steadied his balance.

"I'm fine," Grif said.

"You're a liar," she murmured.

He leaned against Amys, waiting for his vision to clear. A minute later he heard the lift to the *Fool's Errand* descend. Amys tensed and swore softly.

"What?" Grif squinted. "Anything more than three meters away is a blur."

"They found something," Amys whispered. "One of the marines is waving Mavis over to the lift. They're talking about something—the marine seems pretty excited about it. And now... oh, *hell*. Grif, Mavis is *smiling*."

"Bring them here," Mavis called out.

The marines immediately separated Grif and Amys. Two marines grabbed Grif's shoulders and forced him over to the lift. They were lining up the crew as if they were participating in a revue.

Or a firing squad.

Mavis walked down the line, looking at each of Grif's crew in turn, before halting in front of Grif. Grif's vision had mostly returned at this point... there was a little halo of light around the peripheries, which gave Mavis the appearance of glowing ever so slightly.

"I'm afraid," Mavis said, "that my concerns regarding your cargo were wholly justified. I regret to inform you that you're carrying undeclared contraband on board your ship."

"I have no idea what you're talking about," Grif said, trying his best to look innocent while eyeing the marines apprehensively.

Mavis laughed. "I do admire this quality, Captain. Playing your role to hilt, right until the very end! You are very good at what you do, Captain Vindh, but even the best make mistakes. It seems I've come out ahead in this venture: my men report that your ship is carrying roughly twenty tons of Varkavian whiskey. As this was not included in your cargo manifest—and as you have no permit to transport liquor out of our territories—I'm afraid it qualifies as illegal contraband." He made a tsking sound as he shook his head in mock sadness. "Apparently your rather ingeniously hidden extra cargo bays were improperly sealed."

Grif whirled around, stepping out of the line to face the rest of his crew, and glared at Ktk. "I thought I told you to *seal those hatches*!" he snapped.

Ktk replied wordlessly, emitting a sound that could only be described as "infinite frustration."

Grif reacted as if Ktk *had* spoken, however, and looked away in stunned amazement.

Commodore Mavis looked at Grif curiously. "What did your centipede tell you?"

Grif made a show of struggling briefly before giving in and speaking. "It said... it said the plates must have buckled when we dropped out of tach. We were running the ATID pretty hard. It was a rough drop." Everything he said oozed *grudging defeat*.

His crew took the bald-faced lie in stride. The only visible reactions were from Cyrus, who looked annoyed, and—to Grif's alarm—Doma. Doma looked confused.

Doma opened his mouth to speak. Cyrus reached over and smacked him in the back of the head without even looking sideways.

"Ow!" Doma cried out indignantly. "What the hell was that for?"

"For pissing me off," Cyrus said casually.

"No," Mavis said. "No, that won't do." He walked over to Cyrus and Doma, eyeing them carefully. "What *was* that for, Mr. Mak?"

Cyrus said nothing, face stoic. Doma whimpered.

Mavis, sensing weakness, zeroed in on Grif's nephew. "Young man? Is there something you wanted to add to this conversation?"

Doma began to stutter. Mavis waited patiently.

Grif swore silently. Doma was trying not to speak, but he was completely out of his depth with Mavis. Sooner or later—probably sooner, based on his current level of panic—Doma would crack and start babbling every thought that came into his head.

Which, as always, would screw everything up.

"Hey!" Grif nearly shouted the word, and as everyone turned to face him, he looked livid with rage.

"Wait just a damned minute..." Grif scowled, glaring at the entire crew suspiciously. "Did you say *twenty* tons?"

Mavis turned his full attention to Grif.

"Twenty. That's what you said, right? Twenty tons of..."

"Varkavian whiskey," Mavis replied impatiently. "I assume there is a point to this?"

"Hell yes there's a point to this. We started out with *twenty-five*!"

Grif took a step back from the line so he could face his entire crew. The marines didn't react, more amused than alarmed. The crew looked back at him uncertainly, except for Cyrus, who nodded slightly.

"All right," Grif said quietly. "We seem to be missing five tons of Varkavian whiskey. Anyone have anything they'd like to confess?"

Nobody moved.

"I counted twenty-five tons when we loaded it on to the ship. There are twenty tons now. So *somebody* tell me what happened to *five tons of hootch*!"

Again there was no response. Then slowly, sheepishly, Cyrus stepped forward.

"*You!*" Grif lunged forward, hands outstretched, grasping for the big man's neck. Cyrus stepped back as Grif was restrained by four marines and clubbed over the head—again—by a fifth.

Grif cried out this time, and fell to the deck, covering his head.

"It was just before we left port," Cyrus said sheepishly. "I had to pay off a... pay off a... well, I had to pay someone."

"You..." Grif struggled to his feet once more, but this time Amys knelt beside him and pinned him to the ground.

I guess she thinks if I don't stand up I'm less likely to be clubbed, Grif thought. *All things considered... not a bad idea.*

"You..." Grif didn't try to shout; it hurt too much to even think of shouting. "You paid her with five metric tons of high-grade liquor?"

Cyrus stepped back into line, looking nervous. Some of the marines chuckled.

"Gentlemen," Commodore Mavis interrupted, "as interesting as this little drama of treachery and betrayal is, I'm afraid it will have to continue somewhere else."

Grif put on a show of calming down, and allowed Amys to help him stand.

"It is far more important," the Commodore continued, "to determine what, exactly, will be your *punishment*." He began to pace back and forth. Grif watched him very carefully.

"We can't kill you," Mavis said. "Smuggling whiskey, even the rather expensive kind you are carrying, isn't punishable by death. *Unfortunately.*"

Grif relaxed a little.

"And, alas, due to more pressing matters, the Radiant Throne can't afford to incarcerate you—especially when, as you have pointed out, there are delicate matters of diplomacy involved due to a treaty our Emperor has chosen, for the moment, to recognize.

Grif felt they were very nearly through this.

"I can, however, confiscate all cargo found on your ship, legitimate or otherwise. And I intend to do so." He nodded to a marine, who directed more soldiers into the cargo bay of the *Fool's Errand.*

"Hold on a second—"

Commodore Mavis cut off Grif with the wave of his hand. "I'm afraid I will not, Captain Vindh. Today you have lost. I suggest you come to grips with this unalterable truth, and carry it with you in your future endeavors. I fear it may harm your reputation somewhat... you can no longer claim to be the one smuggler in this region who has never lost cargo, I believe?"

Grif glared at him.

Mavis smiled. "I thought not." He turned to the marine standing on the lift, murmured a few words, then stepped away as the lift ascended into the *Fool's Errand.*

He strode purposefully towards Grif and stopped, regarding him silently. Grif stared back, biting his words. There was a lot he wanted to say, but in the end he decided he preferred not getting hit in the back of the head.

The corner of Mavis' mouth curled into a contemptuous smile. "I would be lying, Captain Vindh, if I claimed I'd never looked forward to this moment. And yet... now that it's here, I find it somewhat unsatisfying. Why do you think that is? Perhaps, in the end, I expected more from you..." he frowned slightly, then shrugged. "No matter. When my men finish their business you may return to your ship. If you attempt to restart your fusion drive before *Centurion* hits tach, your ship will be destroyed, no quarter will be given. Goodbye, Captain."

With that, Commodore Mavis walked off, leaving the crew of the *Fool's Errand* to watch as his men unloaded every piece of their cargo. They started with the legal cargo—the farm equipment was lowered using their own crane onto the deck, where it was carted off for impound. But the marines made sure to carry out the whiskey one crate at a time, and Cyrus seemed to wilt a little each time he saw another piece of precious cargo leave the ship.

When the last of the cargo had been carried out, they were permitted to return to their ship. It was a grim homecoming: Ktk, Gurgan and Vod went aft to the engine room, not saying a word, Cyrus glared at Grif then headed off with Cutter and Hari to their quarters, and Amys, Morgan, Doma and Grif headed up to the bridge.

At that point there was nothing to do but wait. The bridge crew sat at their posts in silence as *Centurion's* tugs towed the *Fool's Errand* out of the ship, deposited her a reasonable distance away, then returned in haste.

Shortly after the tugs returned, the *Centurion's* hull rippled slightly as her ATID began to generate the ship's tachyon bubble. Her engines fired, and she moved in a slow arc across their view ports, gathering velocity as the distortion around the ship's hull continued to increase dramatically. Finally the distortion exploded outward for a fraction of a second, and the ship vanished from view.

Grif watched the distortion fade from view in silence, then pushed his chair along the rail until he emerged from the pilot's nest and into the bridge proper. Doma sat sullenly in his chair, still shaken from his encounter with Mavis. Morgan reported tersely that *Centurion* had successfully jumped to tach, but said nothing else. Amys stared at Grif thoughtfully.

"Well," Grif said, "that was interesting."

No one bothered to reply. Grif unstrapped himself from his seat and floated over to an empty console, activating the intercom.

"Ktk, bring the fusion drive online, then restore gravity." He turned off the intercom before anyone had a chance to reply. He turned to Amys. "I'll be in the officer's mess, if anyone needs me."

He made it all the way off the bridge before he started laughing.

Chapter 4

WHEREIN Our Hero is Revealed to Have Pulled a Fast One

Amys watched the bridge hatch close on Grif as he doubled over with laughter. The laughter, muted but still audible, faded as the lift took him to the lower decks.

Morgan stared at the hatch as Grif's laughter faded, replaced by a largely uncomfortable silence. "Huh."

Amys frowned thoughtfully.

Morgan glanced at Amys, clearly perplexed. "Do you think he's all right?"

Amys hesitated, then shrugged.

"Of course he's not all right," Doma said, forgetting where he was, who he was talking to, and abandoning anything that could reasonably be attributed to a survival instinct. "He was clubbed in the back of the head with a gauss rifle at least five times..."

"Shut up, Doma." Amys reminded herself of the kind of trouble Grif would get into if she killed his nephew.

"Well he did," Doma protested. "And we just lost a fortune in cargo!"

"Shut up, Doma," Amys repeated, eyes glittering.

"But... he... hey, this isn't my fault! He's the one—"

"Doma." Morgan interrupted Doma in mid-stammer, voice calm and soothing. "While I personally think it would be wonderful if your lack of self-preservation provoked Amys into gutting you from stem to stern, Grif has this funny rule about us not killing you. So for God's sake... just shut up!"

Doma closed his mouth, turned around in his chair and sank into a deep pout.

A few minutes later Ktk announced it was restoring gravity. Much to Amys' disappointment, Doma remembered to brace himself properly.

Amys stood, testing her weight against the newly restored gravity, and tugged at her ponytail absently. Morgan and Doma looked up questioningly.

"I'll be right back," she said. "Morgan, monitor communications and contact Grif if anything important comes in."

Morgan nodded and returned his attention to his station. After an intense but brief internal struggle, Doma looked away without asking any questions. Amys smiled in spite of herself; for an instant Doma had looked exactly like Grif when his curiosity was killing him. She made a mental note never to tell Grif that.

Amys took the lift two decks down, and when it opened she stepped into a short hallway that ended at a door bearing the sign "Wardroom."

The *Fool's Errand* had originally been commissioned as a troop transport, and amidships above the cargo bays there was a large galley and general mess designed to feed a company of soldiers. The Wardroom was nicer, as it had been designed for use by the ship's officers, and the crew used it for all meals.

Amys opened the door and stepped into the room. It was well-kept, and still maintained much of its elegance from its service as an officer's mess. It was large, with a higher than average ceiling, and at the far end the bulkhead sported a panoramic viewport that could either display a projected image—very popular with the crew when they were in tach—or fade to transparency, as it currently was, providing a magnificent star-filled view.

The room was tiled, rather than sporting the standard monochrome metallic floorplates common in most of the ship, and tiles were dark colors intended to replicate the effect of a polished wood floor. The walls were also designed to resemble faux wood panels, and globe lights, rather than the ceiling mounted light panels, lit the room in a softer, more ambient light. There was a master table in the center of the room, smaller tables set against the wall, and to Amys' right there was a bar which Grif kept well-stocked. Behind the bar, Grif was preparing a drink: a glass was set on the bar in front of him, and he was wrestling to uncork a bottle of something.

He didn't look his best. The back of his head was puffed and swollen from the repeated beatings, giving his head a slightly misshapen appearance, and the front of his face was bruised from all the times he'd used it to stop his fall. When he looked up and saw her, he grinned—the grin she liked, not the other one—and immediately reached under the bar and set another glass beside his.

Amys shook her head. "You know I don't drink Stellis."

Grif laughed. "Not Stellis this time. This is a bottle of that whiskey Mavis thought he confiscated."

Amys shrugged, nodded, and walked up to the bar as Grif filled first her glass, then his own. He grinned again and raised his glass in a toast. She smiled slightly, returned the toast, and drank.

It was good whiskey. It was smoky with just a hint of wood. On Varkav they made their whiskey the old fashioned way, in real wood caskets and with real fire. Modern distilleries spent fortunes trying to mass-produce this natural taste quickly, some with more success than others, but the distilleries on Varkav had yet to be beaten.

Amys watched Grif closely. He was a masterful liar, but she'd known him long enough to figure out when he was playing an angle. At the moment he wasn't even trying: he was in a genuinely good mood, confirming something she'd suspected for a while.

"So," she said, "what did we *really* smuggle out of Throne space?"

Grif grinned wider. "I knew you'd sort it out. When?"

Amys smiled. "When you ordered Cyrus and Ktk to expose our cargo I thought maybe it was decoy. When you were winding up Mavis on *Centurion's* flight deck I was convinced. So are you going to let us in on the secret now, or will you wait till Cyrus loses his temper and tries to strangle you?"

Grif laughed. "Fair point. Once Ktk brings the fusion drive back on line, bring the crew here and I'll do the Big Reveal."

Amys sighed. "I suppose that means you're not going to bother telling me now," she said.

Grif just winked, and took another drink.

Two hours later, the crew assembled in the Wardroom to find that Grif had set out a glass for each them. Each glass was filled with Varkavian whiskey. It was one of their traditions: after each successful job their Captain would pour them a drink, and they'd toast to their victory.

Grif leaned against the bar, coldpak held to the back of his head with his left hand as he held aloft his glass in his right, and motioned for the others to take theirs. Nobody moved.

Finally Cyrus spoke. "If this is a joke, it's in pretty bad taste."

"No joke," Grif said. "Drink. You earned it. And good thinking on *Centurion*, Cyrus. 'Owed someone money' indeed!"

Cyrus scowled. "Fat lot of good it did," he snapped. "And really, the victory toast? We lost everything!"

"No we didn't," Grif replied, and winked. He set his cold pack and his drink down on the bartop, kneeled down behind the bar and started rummaging around.

"The hell we didn't!" Cyrus wasn't exactly shouting, but he was getting there. "Fifty thousand a ton—*fifty thousand*! That's a million standard we sank into that whiskey, plus another fifty thousand in legit cargo just to cover it up. And it got confiscated because, for some damned reason, you *wanted* them to find it!"

Grif popped his head up from behind the bar, expression grave.

"For the record," he said, "no one *ever* wants twenty tons of high quality whiskey forcibly removed from their ship. I had *plans* for that hootch—plans that involved *drinking*. I'm not saying I could actually drink twenty tons, I'm just saying that it would have been the greatest challenge of my career..."

Grif ducked his head back behind the bar and the rummaging sounds continued. "Now if I could just *find* it..."

Cyrus shook his head and turned to Amys, hoping for a more sympathetic ear. "We put a lot of our own money into that haul."

"I didn't," Doma said. "I didn't trust him."

Cyrus' scowl deepened. "Well, for once it looks like the boy was less abysmally stupid than usual."

"Yes, I—" Doma stopped in mid-sentence, working through what Cyrus had just said. "Hey!"

Grif ignored all of them. Boxes appeared on one side of the bar as he discarded them each in turn, muttering "no, not this one, this isn't it, what the *hell*, I know I put it here *somewhere*" as he did so.

Ktk suggested that it could have been worse, and they were probably lucky to still be alive.

Grif stopped his search and popped his head back up over the bar. "Oh, Mavis didn't want us *dead*. He wanted us very much alive. He wanted us to know he'd finally caught us, and we'd lost."

Grif paused.

"Too bad we didn't." He grinned, then ducked back behind the bar and resumed his search.

Cyrus opened his mouth to retort, hesitated, narrowed his eyes and frowned. "What's going on, Griff?"

Hari also frowned, the ridges across his face extending and retracting in confusion. "I feel pretty thoroughly beaten."

"Of course you do." Grif dragged a plastic foodstuffs container out from behind the bar, opened it, and began looking through the contents, examining their labels and discarding each in turn. "You should. It looks to you like he won. And if it looks to *you* like he won, Hari, you can *bet* it looks to *him* like he won, which was the important part. Now where the hell is it...?" Abandoning the container, Grif dove back behind the bar. The rummaging noises continued.

"What didn't he win?" Morgan asked, bewildered. "Was it the part where he took our cargo, or the part where he humiliated you and ended your streak? And exactly how do you manage to store so much hootch behind that bar when there's so much other crap back there as well?"

"Hold on a second," Grif said. "I just need to find... oh. Huh. I don't remember putting it there..."

Grif popped up from behind the bar carrying a green medium-sized container. He placed it on the far end of the bar and gestured toward it with a flourish, beaming.

The crew looked at the green container uneasily. Finally, Ktk asked what was in it.

Grif grinned. "I'll show you."

He wrenched off the lid. Inside it were a number of sealed gray packets, all neatly stacked on top of each other. He took one out and casually threw it to Cyrus, who caught it and looked at it suspiciously.

"Your bonus," Grif said. "About seven hundred thousand standard, if you can find the right contact. It's worth a hell of a lot more than that, but it's so ridiculously illegal I doubt you'll find too many people willing to fence it for what it's really worth. And one for you... and you... and you..."

Grif tossed a packet to everyone in the room. When he threw one to Doma, it bounced off his head and landed on the floor by his feet.

"Ow!" Doma rubbed his forehead furiously as if Grif had thrown a rock at it.

Grif rolled his eyes. "Don't be so dramatic. And pick that up. It's worth a lot of money."

Doma looked down at the packet and wrinkled his nose. "It's a food ration."

"See, that's what I'm talking about." Grif sighed and shook his head. "You'll never be any good at smuggling with that attitude."

"What? It's a food ration." Doma bent over to pick it up, and held it out for everyone to see. "Look—it even says on the front: 'Food Ration: One Meal, Standard Fare.'"

Cyrus didn't look angry now; he looked confused. "Hell, it *is* a food ration," he said. "What's going on, Grif?"

"Wealth," Grif replied. "*Wealth* is going on. We are all going to be *incredibly stinking rich* by the end of the week."

"... from food rations?" Cyrus looked at Grif like he'd sprouted wings out of his ears.

Vod leaned in to Gurgan. "He's gone and lost it," she muttered.

Gurgan nodded in agreement. "I always wondered when. Not 'if,' mind you, because it was only a matter of time—"

Amys sighed in exasperation. "Come on, people," she said, raising her voice slightly. "Think about this. Grif is a *smuggler*. Everyone here except Doma is a smuggler. Smugglers *lie*. *Connect the dots*."

Cyrus stared at his food packet, turning it over and over in his large hands, thinking. A moment later his eyes widened with surprise: when he looked up at Grif he was grinning with excitement. "This isn't a food ration, is it?"

Grif grinned back. "Nope."

"The whiskey was a damned decoy!"

Grif's grin widened. "Yep."

"It was the most expensive decoy we've ever used mind you," Cyrus said, "but you wanted to make Mavis think he'd found something worth confiscating... and then *stop looking*."

"Yes!" Grif's grin threatened to split his face in half. "And he fell for it *perfectly*."

Cyrus stared at his packet intently, as though he were trying to see through the wrapping by force of will alone. "Grif... what the hell is in this thing?"

"Ah, Cyrus, that's a good question. Bit of a story there..."

The crew relaxed. Some of them went to get their drinks, all of them settled in various chairs in the room. All except for Doma, who decided to try, without much success, to open his packet to see what was inside.

"You see," Grif said, "Varkav is a very interesting planet."

Cutter sprawled into one of the seats at the master table, then snatched Vod's arm as she drew near, pulling her into his lap. "I hope your story is a bit longer than that," he drawled.

"Hah. Yes." Grif leaned against the bar. "Very interesting planet: you know about the whiskey, you know about the underworld-run and wholly illegal 'entertainment network,' you know it's a port of call for a lot of the big ships in the Radiant Throne Navy..."

"Usually for the above-mentioned reasons," Gurgan chuckled.

"Well, yeah," Grif said. "I mean, they're all sailors, aren't they? Anyway, there's also Ur Voys."

The room fell silent. Doma, struggling to rip open the synthetic fiber packet with his teeth, stopped in mid-tug and stared at Grif in surprise.

"Yeah," Grif said, "*that* Ur Voys. The heavily-guarded, impregnable 'medical facility' that makes pharmaceuticals for the Emperor and her favorite children."

Cutter cocked his head to one side and raised an eyebrow. He was the ship's doctor, and had legitimate medical training. "Psi-drugs? Not much of a market for those..."

"No, not psi-drugs," Grif said. "Surely you don't think the Emperor and her psychic inquisition devote all their time to taking drugs that increase their psychic voodoo, do you? No, there are perks that come with that kind of power. Like access to WU-961."

Cutter lapsed into stunned silence. Everyone else looked at Grif in blank incomprehension.

Grif sighed. "Well, at least Cutter got it. What say, sawbones? Maybe you'd like to fill everyone else in?"

Vod turned in Cutter's lap and looked down at him questioningly. Cutter shrugged. "Anagathic," he said. When he saw the term didn't register, he added "it slows down your aging. Only works on humans, though; sorry, Hari, Ktk."

"Not just an anagathic," Grif said. "One of the most potent anagathics ever created."

Doma immediately spat the synthetic fiber packet on the floor and pointed to it. "That?"

Grif smirked.

"Oi!" Cyrus swore. "This packet has immortality pills in it?"

"No such thing," Grif said. "But each dose of this thing will slow the aging process for a very, very long time. I think you age a month per decade, so long as you get a regular injection every year or so. It's high-grade stuff. And we've got a hundred packets of it. *And* I've got a buyer willing to pay *five hundred thousand standard* per packet for a minimum of seventy, though he's willing to buy more."

Ktk observed that paying five hundred thousand standard per packet would total a sum of fifty million standard, assuming all of the packets were sold, which seemed unrealistic.

"Oh, this guy is for real all right. Why do you think I wanted to berth on Tylaris Prime? The Tylaris Barony is the richest of the Trade Baron systems, and our buyer oozes money wherever he goes. And he's *vain*—he definitely wants what we have. So here's the deal: each of you gets to keep one packet as a bonus. You can do whatever you want with it... use it yourself if you want, or sell it yourself, or throw it into the package for this buyer. If you do the latter, you keep all the profit from the sale of your packet. Everything else is divided the usual way: half between us, half back into the ship."

The crew sat in stunned silence, mouths agape, as the realization that they were all about to become filthy rich started to sink in. Finally Cyrus reached over and hit Ktk in its carapace, beaming widely.

"PAY ME, BUG!" he bellowed.

Ktk chittered in laughter.

"All of us?" Doma asked hopefully. "What, me too?"

"Oh yes," Grif said. "Especially you, Doma. Think of it as your severance package."

"Wow, that's... er... my what?"

"Severance package. Because you're fired."

"Fire—what? Wait... what?"

"Don't be so surprised," Grif said cheerfully. "You're a barely competent Comm Tech on a good day, and you don't have many of those. On a bad day you're a ruddy nightmare, and you have a *lot* of those. You hate this work, and we... well... fill in the blanks. But this way you get to leave with more than two million standard in a bank in the Tylaris system. You're set for the rest of your life, kid, assuming you don't piss it away... though I warn you that's a family trait."

Doma considered the situation. Finally, he shrugged. "OK."

Grif looked pleased. "Well, that's out of the way then."

"As long as I get my pictures back."

Grif laughed. "Oh, those. Well, all right, but I have to show them to Morgan first..."

"WHAT? NO, I—"

"Later, Doma," Grif said. "Right now we're reveling in wealth."

The reveling lasted a while. Grif had managed to conceal eight bottles of whiskey from the Radiant Throne, and the crew decided they were honor bound to ensure those bottles were never recovered. Grif leaned against the bar, grinning madly as he watched his crew celebrate their success.

Amys walked up to the bar, smiled, and kissed Grif on the cheek. "So why didn't you tell anyone?"

"Well..." Grif struggled between telling an obviously ridiculous but clever lie and telling the truth. "Three reasons. First, I wanted to see the expression on everyone's face. Priceless, by the way. Second, I didn't want everyone jumpy on Varkav, since I didn't know if any of those telepathic sociopaths who think they're God's Right Arm were hanging about. And third, even if telepathy weren't involved, if Doma had known about this he'd have found some way to screw the whole thing up."

"That's true," Amys agreed.

They both looked at Doma, slumped over in his chair, passed out from too much whiskey, and shook their heads.

"It was better to keep you all out of the loop," Grif continued. "Because of the telepath issue. They notice things. If we were all walking around with 'this is the big one' rolling around in our heads, one of those sons of bitches would have picked up on it, no matter how cool we were playing it. I wanted to minimize that."

"But how did you get your hands on them?" Amys asked.

Grif hesitated. "Well... that's complicated. Some other time?"

Amys let the matter drop and went through the container, counting ration packets.

"I'm pretty impressed with the disguise, though," Grif said. "If I do say so myself. Nobody pays attention to a box of one hundred food packets these days, especially not marines who have already uncovered a huge cache of illegally transported whiskey."

"Wait," Amys said. "How many did you say?"

"One hundred. Nice, even, metric number. Makes the math easier. I think that—"

"Ninety," she said.

"What? Oh, right, if you include the bonuses, but if you throw that in they—"

"I've already counted them," Amys said. "There are ninety in all."

Grif shook his head. "No, there are a hundred, dammit. Hold on a minute."

Grif sifted through the container, counting quickly.

"Well I'll be damned. Ninety."

A look of confusion settled on his face, which was then replaced by a look of concern, then of genuine alarm. "How would they...?"

"What?" Amys stared at Grif intently. "Are you saying that ten packages of one of the most illegal and highly-sought-after substances in known space are missing?"

"Yeah," Grif said. Then he frowned. Then he started to laugh. "Five million standard... talk about an expensive meal!"

"Please do tell," Amys said.

"This is rich," Grif said, still laughing. "I *knew* I hadn't put the container where I found it. Those marines... someone must have swiped a few rations, you know? For the road? Probably thought it would be a nice break from the food they serve in *Centurion's* mess.

He grinned. "Imagine his surprise when he opens the packet and realizes it's not food. Imagine Mavis' surprise when he finds out what it really is!"

Amys grinned in return.

"And hey," Grif added, "it's not like we'll be hurting for money. Ninety packets, if we sell 'em all to this guy... that's 45 million standard. From one job. I think that's a new record for independents."

"Bloody hell!" Cyrus swore, hitting the table as he overheard the last piece of that conversation. "Five hundred thousand for each of us, pure profit, and then half of 40 million between the lot of us."

Vod laughed, kicking her feet on the table as she rested her head on Cutter's shoulder. "That's 20 million to spend on the ship! You know what that means, Gurgan."

Gurgan blinked a few times through the haze of the whiskey that had built up around him, then slammed his fist down on the table, shaking his head so his topknot swung around the room. "UPGRADE!" he bellowed.

"That's right!" Vod said happily. "New tachyon drive!"

"New weapons!" Cutter chimed in.

"New fusion drives," Gurgan continued, "and maybe screens!"

Ktk, Cyrus, Vod, Gurgan, Cutter and Hari chattered excitedly about ways to upgrade the ship. Grif looked on, the throbbing in his head almost completely forgotten as he basked in the glow of victory. He and Amys stood at the bar drinking in silence as they watched everyone's plans unfold.

"I do have one regret," Grif said eventually.

"Oh?" Amys looked at him questioningly.

"I'm not going to be there when Mavis realizes my reputation is still intact."

Chapter 5

WHEREIN the Devil is Given His Due

Commodore Hu Mavis was not a man given to luxury or excess; he was, largely, a man of discipline and austerity. His office aboard the *Centurion*, however, was a concession to comfort. He had remodeled it after the den in his home on Nuris: everything but the fireplace, which was impractical even on a ship that size. His desk was wood; the bookshelves, while not wood, were a good facsimile, and the books, while not made of paper, were actually bound.

It calmed him. It helped him focus. More than once he'd hit upon the solution to a seemingly insurmountable problem simply by sitting in this office, staring at the pictures of his wife, children, and grandchildren, and drinking tea.

It was late, and under most circumstances Mavis would, if he were up, be drinking tea before turning in to sleep. Tonight, however, Mavis had no intention of sleeping. Nor was he drinking tea: tonight he was drinking whiskey.

Mavis leaned back in his leather-bound armchair—the one piece of furniture he actually took out of his den instead of trying to recreate it—and stared at the ten deceptively innocuous packets lined up on his desk.

WU-961. The chemical sniffers confirmed it, once they'd been set to actually look for it. Only one was open, unused: it was to the Marine's credit that he immediately reported what he'd found. The Marine's sense of duty saved his life and salvaged his career. Mavis was a just man, and his crew knew it. The Marine would recover from purification and continue to serve with distinction: in fact, in time the loyalty he displayed by willingly revealing his misdeeds might even serve to advance his career. The Radiant Throne recognized that all men were sinners before God; just as Christ had told the thief that he would be in paradise that day, so too were those who would willingly repent be shown mercy by the Throne.

At the end of it all, the Marine would be a better man for it.

"Quite unlike you, Captain Vindh."

Mavis raised his glass and toasted the smuggler's victory. It was, he was forced to admit, a brilliant deception, expertly played. He'd underestimated Vindh—a habit that he very much needed to break—and Vindh had prospered greatly from it.

Mavis sighed, sipped his drink, and frowned. Captain Vindh had deceived him, but more troubling than the deception was the original theft. Captain Vindh, a non-citizen, an unbeliever and a known criminal, had managed to enter one of the Radiant Throne's most secure facilities, steal a large quantity of one of the rarest gifts the Emperor had to bestow on her favored servants, and leave without the theft being detected.

He had no idea how.

Vindh couldn't have simply waltzed into the compound, grabbed the drugs and sauntered off into the sunset. He would have needed help from within the facility itself, and that possibility was troubling. The men and women at Ur Voys were placed there only after submitting to a vigilant screening process. Who had fallen through the cracks?

Mavis didn't know. Either someone had the ability to deceive a Servant of the Lord, or he (or she) had been coerced in some nefarious way. Perhaps the traitor had been loyal originally, turned only after entering the facility. Satan was ever-present, testing the faithful, looking for any opportunity to cause them to stumble.

The entire facility would have to be locked down. The thought made him deeply unhappy. He would need to bring in a Sword... a skilled one, capable of rooting out the tiniest traitorous thought in a strong-willed insurgent. Mavis wasn't a telepath, and as such had little authority in those matters, but he had some influence with those who did. If he requested aid, and explained why, he was confident he would be heard.

They would reach Varkav in a day. When they arrived, Mavis would set about determining how a common smuggler was able to break into a high security facility and make off with one of the Throne's most precious treasures. Until then, he would sit, and drink, and meditate on the subtlety of the devil's work.

Chapter 6

WHEREIN Our Hero, Having Reveled in His Success, is Faced With Certain Consequences

Grif Vindh, captain of the *Fool's Errand*, woke up to discover two things: first, his head felt as if a Nengit were jumping up and down on it with all four of its legs, and second, someone in the room was shrieking at the top of his lungs. The second item contributed greatly to the discomfort of the first, and it took nearly half a minute before Grif had regained enough of his wits to figure out who was shrieking and why.

"Oh, for the love of—Hari!" Grif tried to shout over the din but found the exertion of raising his voice was also painful, so he resorted to the largely impotent tactic of clutching his head and desperately wishing the alien would *stop*.

Drinking with other races was an uncertain proposition: while every sentient race in the known galaxy was familiar with the rituals surrounding the act of *getting drunk*, the specifics weren't always the same. The substances varied, for one, which meant that precautions needed to be taken when different races decided to *get drunk* together, lest someone inadvertently down a glass of something fatal. Another potentially less fatal detail, though in this specific instance it was difficult to keep that in mind, was that different races recovered from their rituals differently... and when they were all recovering at the same time, and in the same location, it often led to unintended conflict.

Invagi, for example, had very similar drinking customs to humans. They drank the same kind of alcohol humans did, got drunk from basically the same strengths and quantities, and when they woke up the next morning they felt generally the same level of discomfort. There were, however, two notable differences.

First, Invagi possessed a vestigial hive mind, the remnants of which allowed most Invagi to influence and be influenced by the emotions of other Invagi. This meant that when one Invagi woke up after a heavy night of drinking, the distress he or she felt would be sensed, very slightly, by any other Invagi in the room. If the other Invagi were feeling a similar level of distress, then that link would be increased, feeding back on itself, until either one of the Invagi was able to fully regain control of his faculties and break that link, or until someone else was able to break the link for him.

Second, and of more immediate importance, was that while Invagi did get hung over, they didn't experience discomfort from loud noises. This meant that, as far as hangovers were concerned, they had no cultural taboos against shrieking in agony at the top of their lungs.

"Damn it, Hari!" Grif gave up trying to *will* the sound away, and forced himself to pick his head off the table and look around the room. He was in the Starglow... thinking back, he dimly remembered being there the night before, celebrating with his crew. There were other people as well—people everywhere, he saw, people strewn about the large room as though they'd all succumbed to poison and died where they stood. This was not too far from the truth, in Grif's opinion: getting drunk was, when done properly, a process of intentionally poisoning yourself and just barely surviving. He rubbed his eyes, looked at the mass of people passed out over tables, in chairs, and slumped on the floor, trying to find Hari.

He found most of the rest of his crew: Cyrus was snoring peacefully, leaning back in a chair balanced precariously on two legs, his own legs propped up on a table and his head pressed up against the wall. Cutter and Vod had passed out in a corner by one of the gaming tables. Gurgan was lying on his back, spread-eagled on the floor. Ktk was draped over the bar, tails twitching slightly as its vocal plates ground ever so slowly in the bug equivalent of a snore. Amys was slumped over the table beside him, across from Dak Wallace, captain of the *Long Haul*, who had been trying to drink her under the table again.

No Hari.

The shrieking stopped abruptly, and Grif sighed in relief as the room grew silent... only to curse once more as the shrieking resumed, with three other voices joining in. There were other Invagi in the room, and that damned vestigial hive mind was making their hangover a group effort.

Four Invagi belting it out was almost too much to bear. Grif swore as loud as he could and staggered to his feet, knocking Amys out of her chair and on to the floor in the process. He squinted, trying desperately to find at least one of the Invagi in order to resolve the matter with a swift kick, but his vision was still a bit blurry.

The keening continued, and other people in the bar were starting to notice. Rather, they were waking up and gripping their heads in pain, some cursing, some screaming in their own right.

An energy weapon discharged. The screaming stopped abruptly, and the room was quiet once again. Unfortunately, it also smelled of ozone and burning flesh.

"Hari." Grif's voice was hoarse and ragged. "*Hari.*"

He heard someone grunt directly behind him. Turning around he saw the bar, and peering over the edge he saw Hari laying down behind it, staring up at the ceiling, the ridges on his face fully extended.

"Hari. Did someone just shoot you?"

Hari frowned, considering the question. "I don't think so."

"Good," Grif said. "Now get a grip, because we're all well-armed and our ability to make decisions is pretty poor at the moment."

"Right," Hari said. "Thanks for not shooting me, Grif."

"Uh, speaking of that..." a familiar voice, possibly one of Dak's crewmen, sounded equal parts sheepish and concerned. "We need to call a medic."

"Evory." Dak didn't bother to raise his head off the table, or even open his eyes, but his voice was loud enough to be heard throughout the room. "Did you shoot one of the Invagi?"

"It was Rost," the crewman Evory said, "and I only shot him in the leg." Dak sighed and pushed himself up into a sitting position. He was a slightly heavyset man with short, black hair and well-trimmed black beard dyed with streaks of white. He nodded at Grif, then turned around in his chair to face the room, hitching his elbows on the table to keep him upright.

"Captain Vindh," Dak said, "when you rented the Starglow for the night and morning you purchased the full package, didn't you?"

"Uh..." Grif didn't actually remember renting the Starglow. "Hold on a second." He reached into his vest pocket, pulled out a datacard, and started scrolling through its history.

"Yeah..." Grif read the contents of the ticket displayed on his datacard in mild astonishment. "Apparently I did. Full medical and everything. That was... unusually thoughtful of me."

"Yes it was," Dak agreed. "Emory, please stand." From the other side of the room a lanky, straw-haired human reluctantly staggered to his feet.

"Yes, si—" Emory's reply was cut short as Dak Wallace shot him in the leg. Dak favored slug throwers, and everyone howled in protest as the sound echoed through the room.

Everyone except for Amys, who eschewed protest in favor of kicking Dak's chair out from under him. Dak fell backwards, hitting his head on the edge of the table as he slid to the floor. She kicked his hand sharply, and his gun skittered across the floor.

"I'm trying to sleep," she said.

Dak swore, laughed, then swore again as he prodded the back of his head. "Damn it all, woman, I'm *bleeding*," he said.

"Don't shoot people," she replied.

"They weren't people, they were my *crew*," Dak said. He picked himself up off the floor, wincing as he probed his wound. "Kenner."

"Yessir." Another human stood up even more reluctantly than Emory.

"Captain Vindh has procured full services for everyone this morning," Dak said. "See to it that Rost and Emory get medical treatment, and then send the medic my way."

He picked up his chair and sat back in it, staring at Amys ruefully. She climbed back into her own chair and punched Grif in the arm.

"Ow." Grif rubbed his arm absentmindedly.

"That's for knocking me off the table," Amys said. "Did I win?"

"Win what?" Grif, still rubbing his arm.

"Drinking. With Dak." Amys pulled her fingers through her hair, trying to get it into some semblance of order.

"Oh." Grif thought back. He had a vague memory of blurry people doing blurry things. "I think... maybe a tie? I'm not sure whose head hit the table first, but..."

"A tie." Amys looked disappointed. "I'm slipping."

Grif grinned suddenly, eyes twinkling. "Old age," he suggested.

The room fell silent. Everyone near the table put aside their personal discomfort and gaped at Grif. Low, urgent whispering emerged from the silence as a number of the more coherent revelers exchanged bets as to how long Captain Vindh would live after Amys tore his throat out of his neck with her bare hands.

Captain Dak Wallace, the only other conscious person at the table, slowly rolled his chair away from the impending carnage.

Amys stared at Grif steadily, the way a snake might stare at a mouse it was about to swallow whole. Then she grinned, threw her head back and laughed loudly.

"You *bastard*," she said, still laughing. "I *hate* you *so much*."

The urgent whispers turned into confused mutters as the gamblers realized no one had actually bet on this particular outcome.

An hour later most of the revelers had recovered enough to drag themselves into chairs. They put themselves to work trying to solve their most pressing problem: figuring out exactly what had happened the night before.

A number of people complained they were missing money. A certain amount of this was expected, and in response someone called for the List. The List was a computer record of what possessions everyone had entered the party with, and what possessions had been lost in bets and contests. The List had been a standby of every serious celebration this group had thrown for years, and had prevented a number of potentially serious feuds as a result. The List provided everyone on record a summary of what they had lost, what they had won, and a brief description of why. Some of the bets were minor, and it had been mutually agreed when the List was instituted that no bet would go beyond a certain cap, so no one would wake up the next morning to find they'd lost their starship in a card game.

There had also been at least one gunfight. There was scoring on the walls, a number of people beyond the two Captain Wallace had just shot discovered they had been treated for wounds, and Wallace announced he had two empty clips of ammunition in his pocket.

Ktk reported that no one had been killed, but would say nothing more: it, like all bugs, did not get hangovers and never suffered memory loss from alcohol. It did, however, get drunk, and when it did its inhibitions disappeared and would behave in a manner it would later describe as "unreservedly silly." The crew of the *Fool's Errand* then turned to one of their favorite post-revelry games: trying to pry out of Ktk what embarrassing things it had done the night before. Ktk, as always, refused to play, but Morgan found a particularly interesting entry in the List that, when shared with Grif, forced the issue.

"Cutter," Grif said, "the List says you made a bet with Ktk last night. And that you won."

"Could be," Cutter said. "It ain't hard to win a bet against the bug." He scratched at the scars that scrawled across his face, frowning as he thought about it.

"Cutter, think carefully. Were you... riding Ktk around the room last night?"

There was a short silence.

"Think maybe I was, Skip."

Ktk pleaded for someone in the room to kill it.

The morning shift arrived, looking at the group of dirty, stained, and thoroughly hung over spacers with mild surprise, but they went about their business and left their patrons to rally themselves as best they could manage. Eventually everyone recovered enough to eat, and Grif discovered to his surprise that he had prepaid breakfast for everyone in the room. The crew gathered at Grif's table joined by Dak Wallace and two other captains: Piko Tan, human captain of the *Burly Forager*, and N'grash, g'grlsha captain of the *Grlashimargrak*.

Captain Tan was an impossibly thin man, nearly emaciated. Grif thought he looked like a dessicated corpse that, after having been brought back to life, disliked it so much it went on a hunger strike in protest. Captain N'grash, like the rest of her race, was hard to describe because they were only slightly visible in the spectrum of light humans could see. To Grif she looked like a short inky blot with rows of very sharp teeth.

"What I wish to know," Dak said, pushing a cup of coffee out of the way as he leaned forward for emphasis, "what I wish to know is exactly how you did it. How did you manage to get into that damned medical lab?"

Everyone at the table looked at Grif expectantly, and in a moment he noticed the rest of the room had quieted down and the others were staring at him as well.

Grif looked from Dak to the others at the table, then at the rest of the patrons in Starglow, and shrugged. "There was this girl..."

The room erupted in laughter, which he waved off good-naturedly.

"No, it wasn't like that..." Grif's explanation was interrupted by a wall of jeers and catcalls.

"All right, well, maybe it *was* a little like that." The catcalls turned into cheers and whistles.

"Well, if you must know, it was *exactly* like that!" Grif finished, and the crowd roared their approval—except for Amys, of course. She just frowned thoughtfully.

It was times like this, Grif thought, when her lack of gullibility was damned inconvenient.

"Anyway, it's not the most interesting story in the world, except for the part where we all got filthy stinking rich," Grif continued. "Rich enough to retire to a long life of comfort and lavish decadence."

"Is that what you're going to do?" Piko Tan's voice was deep and vaguely ominous. "Are you going to retire?"

"*Hell* no," Grif said. "You know me better than that. It's business as usual. We're going to refit the old girl first, but after that the *Fool's Errand* will be back to her usual tricks."

"Then what?" Dak Wallace looked at Grif appraisingly. "You made more money on this one job than most independents will make in their entire careers, Vindh. I expect even the big outfits will notice, eventually. What are you going to do with all that money?"

Grif looked around the Starglow, then pulled out the datacard that listed everything he'd purchased the night before.

"I'm going to piss it away on frivolous nonsense, apparently," Grif said.

Two hours later the revelers had recovered enough to head out. One by one they headed out into the bright sunlight, cursing as they did, until only Grif's crew were left. Finally Cyrus Mak shifted in his chair and turned to Grif. He looked troubled, and Grif thought he knew why.

"Grif..." Cyrus hesitated and frowned, looking for words. Cyrus had been wrestling with something most of the morning. Grif recognized it for what it was: loyalty struggling against ambition. It was something he'd struggled with himself, once.

"Cyrus," Grif said, keeping his voice light. "You don't seem too worn down by last night. Bastard."

Cyrus grinned nervously. "Yeah. Look, I want to talk to you about something."

The rest of his crew stopped what they were doing and listened intently.

"So talk," Grif said cheerfully. He tried to ignore how much he hated this moment.

"Well." Cyrus took a deep breath. "I guess it's no secret, I always wanted to captain my own ship."

Grif nodded. "You made it clear when you signed on."

"Yeah. Well..."

Grif smiled. "It's OK, Cyrus. I'm not going to be offended. You just pulled in two and half million standard from a once-in-a-lifetime run. That's enough for a down payment on a good ship."

Cyrus blinked rapidly.

"Oi, don't be such a *baby*," Grif laughed. "I knew it was going to happen sooner or later. You'll be welcome on the *Errand*, either as crew or a guest, but always a friend. Just make sure you get a good crew. If you need names, ask me first."

Cyrus nodded. He turned to the others and said his good-byes, one by one, clapping Ktk awkwardly on its carapace. Amys kissed him on the cheek, and he reddened slightly. That done, he sighed and turned back to Grif.

"Pleasure serving with you, Captain."

Grif nodded. "Free skies, Cyrus."

"Aye. Clear landings..."

With that, Cyrus turned, headed for the exit, and stepped through the door.

"Bloody hell! Who turned on the sun?"

The door closed behind him.

Everyone was silent for a moment. Grif sighed. "Well, Cutter, you came on after, so you've got his spot."

Cutter nodded grimly, not particularly happy with the idea. Vod, sitting to his right, leaned in a little and squeezed his arm. Cutter smiled a bit, then looked at Grif questioningly. "You want me to look for a third gunner, Skip?"

Grif sighed again. "I guess so. You'll also need to oversee the weapons refit."

Cutter made a sour face. "Guess I'll have to learn to shoot that damn gun. Cyrus was the only one of us who ever got the hang of that thing."

Ktk added that with Doma gone they might also be able to hire someone who actually knew how to use the Comm station.

"That would be nice," Morgan said. "It's a bit rough to handle the scanners and communications at the same time..."

"Sounds fine to me," Grif said agreeably. "And Ktk... you, Vod and Gurgan need to figure out exactly what new toys we're buying. Remember, we've got twenty million standard to spend on her. Spend it right."

Ktk chittered in agreement.

"Well," Morgan said slowly, "I guess I'll take a shower then. With real water, damn it, *hot* water." With that he got up and walked unsteadily to the door.

Cutter and Hari left next, discussing possible replacements for the guns and for Cyrus. Then Ktk, Vod and Gurgan left, arguing over which tach drive was a better investment. Amys and Grif sat alone in the bar.

"Well," Amys said.

"Well," Grif agreed.

"You *stink*," Amys added.

Grif frowned and sniffed at his clothing. He gagged. "I'm not even going to ask why," he said, "because I'm not sure I want to know. I swear, Amys, I'm going to almost remember last night for the rest of my life."

Amys smirked. "If you really want to know I expect we could check Starglow's cameras."

"Oh, no," Grif replied. "We can't." He held up his datacard. "This thing says I paid extra to have the cameras turned off. The official reason listed is 'to avoid unnecessary blackmail attempts.'"

Amys grinned. "Always thinking ahead." Then, sobering, she added "I think Cutter is going to have some difficulty replacing Cyrus. You know, I don't think he really wants the job."

"Yeah," Grif agreed. "I'm not real excited about it either. Nothing against Cutter, but I *hate* that Cyrus is leaving. I mean I wish him all the best, and every success, but... *dammit*. He's a good gunner, and a good technician too. And he *never* bet against me. Now who's going to keep the bug in check?"

Chapter 7

WHEREIN Things Appear to be Going Well Until It Is Too Late To Do Anything About It

Ktkt'tkkt'kktt'tkkk'tktk'ttkt'tkkk'kktt'kktk'tk—or Ktk to the bipeds it traveled with—waited impatiently as the technician from Tylaris Industries explained how the new Artificial Tachyon Induction Drive would be installed. The technician was describing the process using a level of detail Captain Vindh would probably have called "mind-numbing," and Ktk already knew the process. It probably knew how to install the drive better than the technician did, but it waited patiently while he droned on about the T-420 induction field and how it would be attached to the fusion drive to draw the power it needed, and how it would be linked to the ship sensors so it could cut off when a gravity spike was detected, and every other aspect of the installation.

Years of traveling had taught Ktk that other races, particularly humans, were rendered nearly useless when denied the opportunity to engage in exposition. It was a polite creature, and didn't wish to offend this human... and it decided there were likely social customs surrounding this need to explain things that were already known, so it waited patiently for the human to decide he was finished speaking. It was obviously very important to the technician that Ktk be kept informed of their progress, and Ktk decided this extended explanation was tied in to the human's sense of professionalism.

For the most part it didn't mind. The human was fairly pleasant to work with. His reaction to Ktk's appearance had been mild and quickly mastered. When he learned Ktk was in fact the chief engineer of the *Fool's Errand*, he accepted the information immediately and made a point to deal with it directly. This more than anything else did much to increase his esteem in Ktk's compound eyes, and when Captain Vindh had asked how things were going after the first week the bug was pleased to report that everything was quite satisfactory.

Ktk had only two complaints. The first was that the technician and his crew insisted on calling it "sir." Ktk's species had a complicated reproductive cycle, and gender was essentially a superfluous distinction. They didn't think of themselves as either "male" or "female," preferring the gender-neutral "it" as a more accurate description. Many other races found this disconcerting and tended to treat Ktk's species as though they were all male, especially when they were trying to be polite. It was a minor and inconsequential error, but Ktk always found the imprecision of the title annoying.

The other annoyance was that Ktk was forced to wear a translator when dealing with the refit crew. Other than the crew of the *Fool's Errand*, it had met few creatures who understood its native language... and it wasn't capable of producing the sounds necessary to speak any of theirs. The translator interpreted the clacks it produced with its mandible and translated them into other languages, which was very useful. Unfortunately, what the translator didn't do was factor in the sounds created by the two plates located just behind the mandible, so there was no way to introduce subtlety or emotion into what it was trying to say. The translator converted Ktk's speech in an even, carefully modulated tone that it found very aggravating, especially since it depended on the device for most of its social interaction.

When Vod and Gurgan were around, Ktk preferred to deactivate the translator and let them do the translating instead, but at present they were working with Cutter and Hari on the weapons upgrade. Ktk needed to stay in engineering because it was most qualified to calibrate and integrate the new equipment with the rest of the ship's systems. Ktk, like all its kind, had a nearly innate understanding of complex mathematics: they were unique among the sentient races in that they developed an understanding of binary mathematics before developing a written alphabet.

The technician finished explaining what he and his crew would do next, and looked at Ktk expectantly. Ktk moved its head in a manner that approximated a human nod, and chittered its approval. The translator interpreted this as "I am pleased," which the human apparently found acceptable. He barked out orders to his underlings, who seemed a bit more nervous around Ktk than their leader, and they set about actually installing the T-420 ATID.

The crew had wasted no time taking advantage of their new wealth, and set to the task of updating everything they could find. Grif's eyes lit up when Ktk, Gurgan, Vod, Hari and Cutter laid out their suggested improvements: new ATID, new fusion drive, upgrades to the screens and sensors, modifications to the guns... and of course they were gutting and redesigning the cargo bays, since the hidden bays were no longer hidden.

When they were finished, the *Fool's Errand* would "be a new girl," as Grif put it. As it was, they were nearly halfway finished.

Ktk found itself wishing the process could be sped up. It didn't like being in one place for extended periods of time. They'd already been on Tylaris Prime a month, and it would take another month, perhaps two before the ship would be ready for the test flights needed to get all systems working smoothly.

"Ktk."

Ktk broke out of its reverie and saw Captain Vindh standing at the top of the stairwell leading down to the engine pit. He looked a bit worse for wear from Ktk's perspective—drinking and gambling again, though Vindh preferred to call it "interviewing potential crew members."

"Everything all right?" The Captain asked.

Ktk replied that everything was going fine. It added they were about to install the ATID, and it didn't foresee any problems.

"Oh, right... the 420. Hey, did you hear they're coming out with a new model? The 450... apparently it's about two-thirds the size, but nearly twice as efficient. Can you believe it? We haven't even installed ours, and it's already obsolete..."

Ktk answered, somewhat crossly, that this wasn't the kind of thing the Captain needed to be telling it at that specific moment.

Vindh chuckled. "The curse of technology... there's always a better tool than the tool you have. Technology can't remain static, at least not in the Baronies. There no market for static. I bet right at this moment they're already working on the 470."

Ktk stated that irrespective of the truth it was impolite to tell an engineer that a replacement for an old part was anything less than perfect.

Grif ginned. "Sorry, bug. Didn't mean to burst your bubble. I suspect you'll wind up doing what you always do, and optimize the damn thing so that it works just as well as the newer model anyway."

"What?" The technician interrupted, looking alarmed. "No! No, you can't do that. You void the warranty if you do that!"

"Since when has Tylaris Industries ever honored a warranty? No, don't get upset, I was just leaving." Captain Vindh winked at Ktk, whose plates ground together in a brief burst of laughter. "Ktk, I'm going out to see about a replacement for Cyrus.... no, I really am. This isn't an excuse to drink in yet another dodgy bar. I think everyone else is off too, so keep an ear—ah... stalk, I guess—on the comm channels, OK?"

Ktk replied that it would, and wished the Captain luck.

Vindh nodded, grinned at the technician, shouted "take care of my baby!" and left.

Ktk watched the technicians work for a while. When it was satisfied that they needed no extra guidance, it excused itself and went to its cabin.

Ktk's cabin was sparse: it had no furniture other than a desk with a computer terminal and a second desk that served as a workbench. The room was comfortably large for a crewman's cabin, but it seemed smaller due to the clutter—the floor was littered with spare parts, discarded tools, and half-disassembled gadgets. Clutter was a luxury Ktk permitted itself when they were groundside: in space, everything had to be stored carefully so it wouldn't go flying about in zero gravity.

Ktk turned on the terminal and patched a comm channel to the bridge so it would be informed of any incoming messages. The terminal beeped softly: there was already a message in the queue. Ktk queued the message and saw it was from Cyrus Mak, addressed to itself. It selected the message, and Cyrus' shaggy head filled the terminal screen.

"Hey there, bug," Cyrus boomed, grinning good-naturedly. "Got your last message. Yeah, I found it! Saw it in the shipyards a few days ago. A refurbished scouting vessel... old-model Hummingbird, believe it or not. Tiny thing—crew of three or four, cargo bay good enough for private jobs but not for general commerce—and only one turret, currently without weapons. But I qualified for the loan, seeing as I was putting three million standard down... that's right, *three* million! Don't look so surprised, bug, I've been saving up for this.

"It needs a little work, and I was kind of hoping you might wander by the shipyards in a day or two and see what you think. I can handle most of it, but I'd a like a few pointers on the fine-tuning. The drive is a beaut—well it will be, as soon as I get a few parts. And I might have some leads on a crew! Grif's been helping me there, and I think I've found two lads I can trust. Well, if you can call a Ggrlsha a *lad*, at any rate.

"I sign the papers on it in a week." The image of Cyrus beamed. "After that, I need to get a line on a gun for the turret—I hear from Cutter an' Hari that you lot are upgrading yours, you think Grif would be partial to selling one of the old ones cheap? I didn't want to ask when I had the chance, since he was helping me with something else at the time... maybe you could put in a word, eh? Anyway.

"Oh, hey, a bit of news—an Alliance diplomatic ship and a fully-loaded battle cruiser just pulled up into orbit a few hours ago. Some higher up in the Alliance is talking to the Baron about something... probably trying to get the old man to join up again. The guy handling the red tape for my loan has a brother who works in the Baron's palace, and apparently the Tylaris diplomats are trying to figure out how to say 'stuff it' as politely as possible.

"Anyway, let me know if you can drop by and take a look. I'd be grateful... say 'hi' to everyone for me. I imagine the place is a lot more fun since that nit Doma left...

"So fill me in on the refit! Did Cutter and Hari find a decent upgrade to replace the old cannon? Hopefully it'll be something they can actually fire this time." Cyrus laughed. "They never could hit anything with the old one. And what about the engine room? Did you go for the T-420 like you were planning? You know, I hear they're coming out with a T-450..."

Ktk turned off the transmission, annoyed. That was the second time today someone had mentioned a new top-of-the-line item it didn't have. Ktk already found itself wondering about the 450. How could it possibly increase efficiency over the 420?

It was very pleased Cyrus had found himself a ship. That was what Cyrus had wanted to do, after all, ever since the first day Ktk had met him. On the other hand, it missed the man. There wasn't a member of the crew Ktk disliked, with the exception of Doma, who was thankfully no longer with them. They were all interesting people, and counted them all as friends, but it was especially fond of Cyrus. It had been tempted to leave when Cyrus had, but it considered the *Fool's Errand* home, and the chaos its captain created wherever he went was much too interesting to walk away from.

It buzzed with irritation and discontent, then distracted itself by scrolling through the ship's entertainment database. It chose a selection of music—actually, a recording of two E4 C#4 G4 A4 F4 F4/A#4/E4 males having a conversation about something that was most likely mundane, but to any other race it was exactly the same as music—and settled down to read up on the latest news.

Half an hour later, Ktk's terminal informed it that someone in orbit was trying to hail the ship.

Ktk ordered the comm station to acknowledge the hail and place the connection on standby, then made its way to the bridge, wondering who was trying to make contact. It had a vague image of Commodore Mavis circling Tylaris Prime in *Centurion*, trying to goad Griff into taking off. It wasn't a likely scenario, but Ktk couldn't think of any orbital communications they were expecting.

When it reached the bridge, Ktk scuttled over to the comm station and opened the channel with one of its tails. To its alarm, the main screen resolved into the official seal of the Alliance of Free Worlds Diplomatic Corps. The AFW seal faded, and in its place appeared the face of a vaguely familiar woman with grayish-blond hair.

"Where is he?" demanded the woman.

She had the air of someone who was used to getting what she wanted immediately, if not sooner, and the brusqueness of her question made Ktk uneasy. It replied that if she was referring to Captain Vindh, he was not currently on board.

The woman snorted. "The hell he isn't. I want to speak to him, and I want to speak to him now."

She dressed as a civilian, Ktk noted, but her bearing was distinctly no-nonsense military. Ktk replied again that Grif wasn't on board, that he'd gone into the city on business.

The woman was not convinced. "*Business*. He's never done an honest day's work in his life. I don't even want to know what—" she stopped, and stared out at Ktk as if seeing it for the first time. "What the hell are you?"

Ktk explained that it was the chief engineer of the *Fool's Errand*.

"That's not what I meant."

Ktk then explained that the name of its species was too complicated for humans to pronounce, but that many simply called them "bugs."

"Whatever. Look. I don't have time to keep playing these games with him. My brother might think he can dodge me forever, but he can't—I'll track him down sooner or later, and it'll be better for him if he just agrees to meet me outright."

The word *brother* set off an alarm in the back of Ktk's mind.

"I'm not joking, *bug*. I have no, zero, absolutely no patience. Please tell him that his sister demands he call her back, or she will do something to make him *very* unhappy."

The word *sister* caused Ktk's internal alarm to grow more urgent. It replied, as noncommittally as it could, that it would see that Captain Vindh received the message.

"He damn well better," the woman snarled, then cut off the transmission abruptly.

The main screen darkened, and all was quiet. Ktk wondered if Cyrus needed a full-time engineer.

Chapter 8

WHEREIN Our Hero, Confronted With the Threat of Impending Family, Reacts in a Measured and Appropriate Fashion

Captain Vindh took his sister's message the best he could: he panicked.

"She's *where*?" Vindh looked like an animal with a leg trapped in a snare—an animal, Ktk noted, that hadn't quite decided to chew off its own leg, but also hadn't ruled out the possibility of chewing off someone else's.

"*Here*?" The Captain began to pace up and down the Wardroom floor. "Good God, Ktk, are you sure that's what the woman said?"

Ktk retold the entire story, including Cyrus' message about the diplomatic vessel and battlecruiser in orbit around the planet, and the diplomatic seal Captain Vindh's sister used when transmitting her message.

Vindh slumped into a chair and leaned on the table, staring at his hands. "Amys."

"I know, Grif."

"Amys, we have to find a way to *get out of here*."

"I *know*, Grif."

Ktk noticed that Amys, though not as expressive as the Captain, was not doing anything to dismiss or downplay his reaction. Ktk explained to them both that the refit would take another month to finish, and the *Fool's Errand* was grounded until then.

"A month?" Captain Vindh stared at Ktk sharply.

Ktk clarified that it would take a month assuming everything went without incident.

"Oh, we have an incident right here," the Captain muttered. "My psychopathic sister is in orbit around this planet... *looking for me*."

He stood, clenched his fists, and began to pace the room again. "I need a stiff drink," he muttered. "A stiff drink, and a heavy gun. A stiff drink, a heavy gun, a new identity, and a *working ship*—"

Ktk suggested that perhaps it might be prudent to simply meet with her. Captain Vindh stopped pacing abruptly, and he and Amys both stared at Ktk as if it had suggested they go swimming in deep space stark naked.

"Are you crazy, bug?" Vindh's expression indicated he wasn't sure if Ktk was trying to make a joke. "I'm not going to meet with that woman! I have no idea what will turn up missing if I do!"

"Or *who*," Amys muttered. Vindh nodded vigorously.

Ktk expressed doubt that his sister could really be *that* bad, no matter how strained their relationship.

"*Strained*?" Captain Vindh looked up at Ktk in disbelief. "*Strained* suggests that with great amounts of time and energy it's possible to dance around any kind of substantive conversation that might provoke conflict. *Strained* implies that by walking on eggshells it's possible for two people to have a civilized, if chilly, conversation. *Strained* assumes a relationship where polite conversation is difficult, but still possible. Our relationship isn't *strained*, Ktk—it's the kind of relationship a man in an unshielded envirosuit has with a corrosive atmosphere. You breathe just fine for a while, and then suddenly your flesh is exposed... and it *burns*, Ktk, it *burns*..."

Ktk wasn't convinced.

"Dammit bug..." The Captain searched for words. "Dammit! She really is that bad. She's—well—Amys, tell it how bad she is! I'm too busy panicking."

Amys opened her mouth to speak. "She—"

"No, nevermind, I'll tell it," Captain Vindh interrupted. "Ktk, my sister may very well be the single most evil creature currently knocking about the galaxy." The plates behind Ktk's mandibles produced a sound that was the bug equivalent of a dubious snort.

"*Evil*," the Captain insisted. "Pure evil, extracted from the evil residue left behind by thousands of evil carcasses, distilled into its *purest essence* and then molded into the form of my dear sister. And by *dear* I mean *dear God, run away*!"

Ktk turned to Amys and asked her to give it a clearer, less obviously biased opinion.

Amys thought it over. "He's understating it a little," she said finally.

"Evil!" Vindh continued. "And not only evil, but she's got a position in the Alliance's Diplomatic Corps... at least, that's what they call it. 'Ministry of Dirty Tricks' is closer to the truth. Black ops, black bag missions, all the Alliance's dirty work done in secret to keep their reputation intact. You don't get where she is without having skeletons in your closet—skeletons, I might add, that you *seek out* in order to *add to your collection*. And sometimes you steal them from someone else's closet! Or, if you're feeling magnanimous, you look after them for a colleague who is sick. Or on sabbatical."

Ktk had never heard of the "Ministry of Dirty Tricks."

"Of course you haven't." Captain Vindh went to the bar, poured himself a glass of Stellis, and set the glass down on the bartop without so much as taking a drink. "They don't officially exist, after all. The Alliance are the good guys, right? They'd never have an elite corps of thugs who secretly disappear anyone the government finds too inconvenient to deal with openly. Officially they're just a branch of the Diplomatic Corps, called the 'Office of Information Management' or something ridiculous like that. *Unofficially* they do all the dirty work that needs doing. All on the dark, so the politicians can keep yammering on about the high-minded ideals of the Alliance without looking like pack of barking, bloodthirsty lunatics."

"She practically runs the place," Amys added. The Captain nodded in agreement.

Ktk wondered why she would be looking for Grif.

"Well I don't know that, do I? I haven't heard from her in years, except for the occasional message she'd send through Doma. And now she shows up—in Trade Baron space, no less—and *demands* to see me? I don't know. I *do* know that there's a little piece of my mind that is screaming *Danger! Run Away!* And it's a piece of my mind I usually listen to. Which means I've got to find a way to avoid it, or—"

The intercom beeped. Captain Vindh sighed in irritation and punched it on. "What?"

"Uh, Skip..." Cutter's usually easy drawl was slightly uneasy. "... some lady claiming to be your sister just hailed us, and is demanding to speak with you."

Captain Vindh's face drained of color. "Tell her I'm not here," he croaked.

A second later, Cutter's voice said "Uh... Skip..."

"What?" The Captain sounded like he might snap at any moment, and Ktk unconsciously skittered away from him.

"... your sister said if you don't talk to her right now she'll de-orbit the moon and crash it into the planet."

Ktk asked if that was an idle threat.

"Yes," Captain Vindh said. "She wouldn't actually cause a planetary catastrophe just to get my attention."

"Um, Griff..." Amys said, looking uncomfortable.

"*Unless* she'd already planned to cause a planetary catastrophe for some *other* reason, and decided to kill two birds with one stone." Captain Vindh swore at the top of his lungs and hit his head once against the paneling over the comm terminal, hard. Then he sighed. "Cutter, I'm on my way."

Amys followed after Vindh, and Ktk followed them both in a mixture of curiosity and dread. He had never seen Vindh act this way before, not even when hunted by Commodore Mavis.

When they arrived on the bridge, the grim face of the woman Ktk had seen earlier glowered out of the comm terminal. Cutter sat at the comm station, trying his best to look nondescript.

Captain Vindh's earlier agitation had all but vanished, replaced with a casual disdain. He smiled slightly as he looked at the image of his sister. "Velis. What a pleasant surprise."

"I'll bet."

The similarities between them were obvious, mostly around the eyes and cheekbones. There were differences: Velis was obviously older, and had a wider build. Her hair was lighter than the Captain's, nearly blond, while his was almost black. Her eyes were pale blue, his were dark. But they carried themselves the same way—aloof, confident, even cocky—and they stared at each other with exactly the same expression of caution and calculation.

"You and I have a few things to discuss," Velis said. Her clothes were simple in design but obviously expensive, and she wore the purple sash of the Alliance of Free Worlds Diplomatic Corps.

Captain Vindh stared at the purple sash and rolled his eyes. "Look, Sis, I'd love to talk, but I'm really busy. I'm in the middle of a ship refit, I'm trying to hire a new crewman... so let's get this over with. The sooner you tell me your demands, the sooner I can ignore you and go back to my business... and you can go do... whatever it is you do..."

Velis frowned. "I see you're still an idiot," she said, "which doesn't surprise me. What *does* surprise me is that you're still *alive*. Well, I take that back: it doesn't surprise me as much as it annoys the hell out of me."

Captain Vindh smirked. "Glad to know some things don't change. So you came all this way to tell me that I ought to be a good little brother and get myself killed to preserve the family name? I ought to point out that *you're* the black sheep of the family, not me."

"I'm the *white sheep*. The only one. But as much as it might please me to urge you to kill yourself to *try*, in some small way, to restore a tiny piece of our family's good name... that isn't why I'm here." Her frown deepened, as if she were about to say something she disliked very much. "I'm here... to hire you."

Captain Vindh blinked.

Amys' eyes widened. "What?"

Captain Vindh looked at Amys and then back at Velis. "I'm with Amys on this one. What?"

Velis did not smile. "I'm serious. I'm here to hire you."

"There it is again," the Captain said.

Ktk confirmed that it heard his sister say, twice, that she wanted to hire him.

Captain Vindh looked at his sister's image in disbelief. "You want to *hire* me?"

"I don't *want* to hire you." The look on Velis' face fully supported that statement. "I *am* hiring you. As soon as that ship of yours is ready to go..."

Amys sat in the navigator's station and swiveled her chair so that her back was to the main screen. Everyone in the room clearly saw her mouth the word "no."

Vindh nodded slightly in response. "Well," he said, "that's an interesting offer... but I'm going to have to tell you to get bent."

"I'm not surprised," Velis said. "But you're hired anyway."

"No, I'm not."

"We'll be by tomorrow to give you more details."

Captain Vindh allowed a hint of annoyance to creep into his voice. "Didn't you hear me? I said there's no way in hell that I'm—"

"There's a message coming your way," Velis interrupted. "Take it, and then we'll talk."

"What are you talking about? There's no—"

The comm station beeped.

"It's important," Velis said. Her previous agitation had vanished completely. "You really *must* take this call. I'll hold."

Cutter leaned over the comm station and looked up the ID of the caller, then swore. "It's from House Tylaris, Skip."

Captain Vindh's eyes widened slightly. Amys frowned. Vindh looked back up at the main screen, where his sister sat patiently, the faintest trace of a smile etched on her lips.

"Sis... I think I'm going to put you on hold now," he said.

Velis nodded.

"Cutter... put the other call through." The Captain's voice shook slightly. Ktk couldn't help but feel a little uneasy. The Barony never dealt directly with independent traders—there wasn't enough money in it. They were more than happy to act as a port of call to anyone who cared to use their facilities, of course, but their direct attention was reserved for the big trading units, the smuggling syndicates, and the crime lords. Not small timers, even ones who had pulled in score as staggeringly successful as theirs.

The main screen shimmered slightly as the picture changed from the figure of the Captain's sister to that of a thin, balding man with a wispy beard. "I must speak with Captain Vindh," the man said in a soft voice.

"Vindh here." The Captain cleared his throat nervously. "To what do we owe the distinction?"

"Ah, yes..." the man picked up a digital tablet bearing the official seal of House Tylaris and waved it in front of his face. "Captain Vindh, I am serving you notice that we have frozen all your assets in the Bank of Tylaris Prime, pending audit."

Cutter swore. Amys swore. Ktk ground its vocal plates together and swore. Captain Vindh stared at the comm screen, gaping. It took a great deal, Ktk noted, to render the Captain speechless; apparently freezing his assets and threatening an audit met and exceeded that standard.

"This isn't necessarily something to be concerned about," the man continued. "We conduct them from time to time, especially on our new accounts and larger accounts. Since you have both a new *and* a large account, it was only a matter of time..."

"I'm being *audited*?"

"As I said, this isn't necessarily something to be concerned about. We'll let you know in a week or two."

The Captain gripped the back of Cutter's chair so tightly his knuckles turned white. "A week or two?"

"Sometimes more," the man said. "But a week is about average. Your account will be suspended until the audit is finished, of course. By that time we'll let you know if your assets will remain. Your creditors have agreed to defer any payment you might owe until after the audit has completed."

"My credit—wait, what? You've already talked to my creditors?"

"It's standard practice to notify them first. At any rate, should we have any questions we insist you make yourself available."

"Of course," the Captain said in a hollow voice.

"Very well then. Thank you for your cooperation in this matter, and have a pleasant evening."

The screen went dark.

"What just happened here?" Cutter asked.

"Hold on," Amys said, and swiveled around in her chair to face her Navigation station. She called up a personal terminal and accessed a few files. "They're auditing my account too."

"What?" Cutter opened a private session on the comm station and followed suit. "Hell's Compass, they're auditing me too."

Ktk had already started accessing its account at a spare terminal on the other side of the room. It found that it, too, was being audited. It read through the various reasons given and after doing some quick calculations determined that none of the stated reasons made any sense.

There was absolutely no way the Tylaris Barony would ever consider auditing every account above a certain size just because it was new. The Bank of Tylaris Prime was specifically for people who wanted a Bank that didn't stick its nose into its customers business. Ktk said as much.

"Yeah," Captain Vindh said. "It's just their excuse. Damn her. *Damn* her! Well played, though. But *damn* her!"

"Yes," Amys agreed. "We're right in the middle of a refit. If they cancel that account, they'll take the ship. And probably throw you in jail."

Vindh shuddered. "Tylaris Penal Colonies... no thanks. Cutter, put my lovely sister—and by 'lovely sister,' I mean 'wouldn't it be lovely if something terrible happened to my sister?'—on screen."

Cutter hit a key. The main screen came back to life, with Velis once again looking down on all of them.

"All right, Sis," the Captain said. "You have my full, undivided attention."

"Good." Velis sounded quite satisfied. "So nice to have a little cooperation around here. If you keep being that helpful I'm sure we can smooth out any problems that may have come up in the last, oh, five minutes or so."

"Just tell me what's going on, Velis."

Velis laughed. "Oh no," she said. "Not on this channel. I'm coming planetside, and I'm bringing friends. We'll be by tomorrow night, 2100 hours. Don't bother coming to greet us, we know exactly where you parked." With that, the main screen went dark.

"That is one mean lady," Cutter observed.

"Bloody *hell*!" The Captain shouted, and stalked off the Bridge.

Ktk moved to follow, but Amys waved it off.

"Let him go," she said. "He... needs to be alone for a while."

Ktk asked if he was going to spend some time in quiet introspection as he tried to make sense of the tensions in his family dynamic.

"No," Amys said. "This is Grif we're talking about."

"He's going to get drunk," Cutter explained.

* * *

Grif stormed into the Wardroom, fuming. He saw the glass of Stellis he'd poured himself earlier, still sitting on the bartop, and downed it quickly. Stellis was cheap, strong, and hit hard: Grif poured himself another before the first glass even registered. That went down just as quickly, and by the third he was starting to calm down, just a little, as the tingling in his fingers began to numb.

He downed the fourth glass just as the door to the Wardroom opened. Cyrus Mak, face expressionless, strode into the room.

"Cyrus?"

"Grif."

Grif turned unsteadily and attempted a halfhearted grin. "Cyrus, you picked a hell of a time for a visit. You wouldn't believe what just—"

Cyrus' hand shot out and his fingers wrapped, vise-like, around Grif's throat.

"Urgk—"

Cyrus shoved. Grif flew across the room and hit the wall hard. Stars exploded around him.

Cyrus moved quickly, much faster than normal for a man his size, and grabbed Grif's neck once more. He lifted Grif easily, pinning him to the wall.

"Cyrus, I—urkgack—"

Cyrus' hand tightened until Grif could barely breathe.

"I trusted you," Cyrus said.

Grif tried to reply, but could manage no more than a desperate gurgle.

"I trusted you, Grif. You said we'd split half the take among the entire crew..."

"We... did..." Grif, gagging from the force of Cyrus' iron grip, tried desperately to struggle free.

"Aye, we did." Cyrus' eyes narrowed. "And then you had the balls to *report me to the Baron*!"

"I... didn't..."

"Oh, you didn't?" Cyrus' voice was harsh, his grip unrelenting. "Who knew I was saving up for my own ship? Who tipped off the authorities about my account and my record? Why did you *do* this to me?"

"I... didn't..." Grif gasped again.

"*Who then*?" Cyrus shouted. "Who did this to me?"

"My..." Grif clawed desperately at Cyrus' hands, gasping for breath. "My... sis... ter..."

Cyrus' eyes widened. He loosened his grip, and Grif slid to the floor, gasping and coughing.

"Your sister?" Cyrus asked, face blank.

Grif nodded, still coughing and gasping for air.

"Bloody hell."

Cyrus slumped down on the floor next to Grif.

"She got me too," Grif said.

"Bloody *hell*," Cyrus swore again.

"Yeah. And Cutter, and Amys, and Ktk. Vod, Hari, Gurgan and Morgan too, I'll bet."

Cyrus sat next to Grif in silence as Grif slowly recovered from this throttling.

"Why?" Cyrus asked plaintively.

"She... wants me to do something."

"What?" Cyrus looked at Grif in confusion.

Grif shrugged. "I don't get it either. She says she wants to hire me for some kind of job. I wouldn't trust her to save my life—hell, I wouldn't trust her to save *Doma's* life—but she's hinted that if I take it she'll stop the audits."

Cyrus mulled over that information. "I see," he said.

"She's coming by with some of her, ah, *associates* tomorrow night. 2100."

They sat against the wall in silence for a bit.

"Sorry I almost killed you," Cyrus said.

"Honest mistake," Grif replied. "There's Stellis on the bar."

Cyrus retrieved the bottle and came back to the wall, sitting down in the same spot. He took a swig directly from the bottle, and passed it to Grif. "You taking the job?"

Grif took the bottle and shrugged. "I guess I'll know tomorrow night."

Cyrus sighed. "Well, at least I know you didn't screw me out of that ship. I should have known. But I couldn't think of anyone else who could have... and it... damn it Grif, I was so close! I went a little crazy."

"What ship?" Grif asked.

"Hummingbird. Good condition, drive needed work. I was going to sign the papers soon. That's when I found out about the 'little problem...'"

"Right." Grif took another swig of Stellis and handed the bottle back to Cyrus. "Don't worry too much. The guy told me that during these things all creditors agree to wait until the audit clears up before moving on. So if I play nice with my sister and Velis is true to her word, you still might have a chance to sign those papers..."

Cyrus considered it, then shrugged. "All right. I won't write it off just yet. But what if you tell your sister to get stuffed?"

Grif grinned. "Then I guess you'll start choking me again."

Chapter 9

WHEREIN the Terms "Rock" and "Hard Place" are Given Due Consideration

All of the crew had been affected by the audit, and when Hari, Vod, Gurgan and Morgan came back, Captain Vindh filled them in as quickly as he could, starting with the all-important disclaimer "first of all, it's not my fault..."

They took the news stoically, except for Morgan who flinched at the mention of Velis' name.

"She's here?" Morgan kept his voice even, but he pulled at his beard nervously.

"Sorry old man," Vindh said. "She's not only here, but she's stopping by for a visit tomorrow night."

"Wonderful," Morgan said tonelessly. Ktk thought if he tugged at his beard any harder he would be in danger of actually pulling out tufts of hair.

They all agreed that the best course of action that night was to get as drunk as possible.

Cyrus decided to stay on board to commiserate, and to be on hand the next day "to help handle the trouble she's going to bring with her." They all gathered in the Wardroom and drowned their sorrows with a considerable amount of Stellis (in both the green and blue varieties), as well as some other more exotic and substantially more toxic concoctions that Hari and Gurgan brewed in a spare cabin near the engine room.

Ktk opted not to drink that night. The giddy silliness that inebriation inflicted on it seemed inappropriate to the situation, and it wanted to think... and, perhaps, get a little more information on Captain Vindh's sister. It scuttled over to Cyrus, whose infamous tolerance for alcohol made him only slightly drunk. Cyrus looked up from his glass, grinned half-heartedly, and toasted.

"Missed you, bug," he said, slurring his words slightly.

Ktk replied that it had missed Cyrus as well, and was sorry he wouldn't be able to buy his ship.

Cyrus waved his drink dismissively. "Grif says not to worry just yet. I figure I'll wait a day or two before I start mourning... If Grif does what Velis wants—whatever the hell that might be—I'm pretty sure we'll get our money back. I don't trust her, but she's absolutely reliable when it comes to blackmail and extortion."

Ktk looked at the others in the Wardroom. Gurgan was telling a story that had Grif, Amys and Hari in stitches. Cutter and Vod were sitting apart from the others, and it looked like they might head off somewhere more private soon. Ktk leaned in closer to Cyrus and asked him to explain the situation between Captain Vindh and his sister.

Cyrus frowned. "Right. You weren't with us back when all that started."

Ktk replied that it had never actually heard of Captain Vindh's sister directly. It knew Doma, of course, and as a result hadn't thought highly of Vindh's extended family, and had decided Vindh felt the same way.

Cyrus chuckled. "That's about right. But it wasn't always that way. He and his sister were close once."

Ktk observed that this was obviously no longer the case.

"No it isn't," Cyrus agreed. "I don't know exactly what it was that soured them. I never actually met her until after the falling out..."

Cyrus emptied the rest of his glass and tilted his head back, thinking. "Grif had just bought the *Fool's Errand*," he said. "He'd had her for not more than a year. I was the engineer then, and other than Amys it was a completely different crew. I don't think you ever met any of the others. Anyway, one day Grif tells us we're headed off to Allied space, to Kinnar. That's where he's from. His sister was getting married, and he was looking forward to seeing her. So we set down on Kinnar, and he and Amys go off together. They were quite the pair back then..."

Cyrus shrugged. "The rest of us, we settled down for some extended R&R. Imagine our surprise when a few days later they come back, Morgan in tow, and we immediately head out to Trade Baron space. He didn't talk about what happened. He just said his family could burn in hell for all he cared, and he never wanted anything to do with them again for as long as he lived."

Ktk asked if Amys or Morgan had ever talked about it, and Cyrus shook his head. "I asked Amys about it once and she said, and I quote, 'Cyrus, I like you, so don't ask me again.' Morgan just muttered something about trust. I couldn't get him to say anything else."

"After that," Cyrus continued, "Velis would show up from time to time to yell at Grif and make demands. Mostly he tells her to go to Hell. We thought when he took Doma on board she'd ease up, but he just left, didn't he?"

Ktk wondered if the trade-off was worth it.

"Hmph. Hard to say."

At that moment Captain Vindh and Amys erupted into howls of laughter as Gurgan began to impersonate Commodore Mavis on the flight deck of the *Centurion*. It was an uncanny impersonation, even though Gurgan was considerably larger. Ktk and Cyrus turned to watch, and the conversation ended.

* * *

The next morning a representative from the shipyard called to announce that, regrettably, technicians would *not* be arriving to continue their work on the refit. The shipyard was more than willing to work pending successful completion of the audit, she stated, but they would wait until then before continuing.

"These things have been known to take months," she explained. "And we have, unfortunately, found that some people are tempted to leave before we can be assured of payment."

"Of course," Grif said pleasantly. "Well let you know when that's taken care of."

The woman smiled indulgently. "No need, sir. The auditors will notify all your creditors when it's finished. I suspect we'll know before you do."

Grif forced himself to smile wider. "Outstanding," he said. When the viewscreen went dark, he let his smile fade into a scowl and turned to Amys. "Someday..."

"Kill her later," Amys said evenly. "Get our money back tonight."

"But I want to—"

"I know what you *want*," Amys said. "Get our money back *first*."

At 1900 the entire crew was sober, dressed, and armed to the teeth.

"I don't know what she wants," Grif said to his crew, "but she won't be coming alone, and the people she works with are dangerous. So we need to be dangerous too. Amys, you and Cyrus work out some contingency plans."

Amys nodded. Cyrus grunted in agreement.

Velis arrived at 2100 sharp.

The *Fool's Errand* was too large to fit in a traditional hanger, so it was berthed outside near the hangars. It was a well-lit area, and they saw Velis and her entourage as they emerged from the central hub of the spaceport complex. They were hard to miss: eleven humans traveling in a group, nine obviously armed.

"To the teeth," Morgan confirmed. "Weapons are secured but not concealed."

It wasn't a comforting thought.

"I don't think I like these odds, Skip," Cutter said.

Grif, Amys, Cyrus, Cutter, and Gurgan were standing in a small lounge fore of the cargo bays, watching Velis and her entourage through a video feed Morgan had routed to one of the monitors.

"Me either," Grif agreed. "Sure would like to know how she convinced the Baron to freeze a paying customer's assets."

Everyone nodded. Most people who lived in Trade Baron space preferred to have as few ties to the Alliance and the Radiant Throne as possible. Close alliances with either upset the balance of power, and it compromised markets: if a Trade Baron was *neutral* it could do business with the Alliance and the Throne alike. As soon as a Trade Baron chose a side, however, it had to give up one or the other... not to mention it hurt the home industries that catered to the smugglers, pirates, and other criminals who considered the Trade Baronies safe havens.

Baron Tylaris was the largest, richest, and most powerful of the Barons: if he chose a side, it would throw the other baronies into chaos as they struggled to adjust to the changes.

As Velis' entourage neared the ramp leading into the exposed underbelly of Bay One, she called out an order and they came to a stop. After a moment, Grif realized with some surprise that they were actually waiting to be invited in. Grif glanced at Amys in surprise and saw her staring at him in confusion.

"Is she being *polite*?" she asked.

"Can't be," Grif said. "She's my sister. This has to be some sort of trick."

"They're just standing there," Gurgan said. "And... who is that?" He pointed to a figure standing to the right and immediately behind Velis.

Grif studied the figure for a moment before answering. "He's the one in charge," he decided. "Look, he doesn't have the physique that the guards do—Hell, he looks much older than Velis—but he definitely has that 'I'm in charge' vibe. And you see how my sister is deliberately putting him behind her? She's ready to take a shot for him if it comes to that."

"Will it come to that?" Amys asked the question, but everyone looked at Grif.

"I hope not," Grif said. "I'm pretty sure you'd survive that fight, Amys, but I don't know if I would. Unless I ran away and hid—which, now that I've said it out loud, is actually a pretty good plan..."

Amys snorted. "You're many things, Grif, but you're not a coward."

"You know it hurts me when you say things like that," Grif said. "It really hurts. Right here." He tapped his chest solemly.

Amys sighed.

"Right," Grif said. I guess it's time to say hello."

The lounge connected to the cargo bays via a short, wide hallway. Grif walked down the hall, flanked by Cyrus and Gurgan, both carrying plasma rifles. He hesitated a moment at the door, then keyed it open, stepping into Bay One and into the warm, dry air.

Bay One was in the process of being rebuilt, and was missing half of its deck. Grif, Cyrus and Gurgan walked to the edge of the deck and looked down the ramp at Velis and the rest of her entourage. The armed men tensed slightly at Cyrus and Gurgan's weaponry, but made no move to their own.

"Hello, Sis," Grif said. His voice was casual and vaguely friendly.

"Grif," Velis replied. She didn't sound nearly as friendly, but she did manage to keep the greeting venom-free.

"I see you brought company."

Velis nodded. "I said I would."

She turned her head and gestured slightly to the older man standing behind her. "This is Alef Halge," she said. "My boss."

Grif looked at the older man. Alef nodded his head in greeting, and looked at Grif with as much interest as Grif had in him. Alef had gray eyes... cybernetic, Grif thought, though he wasn't completely certain.

"Good evening, Mr. Halge," Grif said. "And to the rest of you. Won't you all come in?"

The invitation extended, Velis relaxed slightly and turned to her guards. "Wait here," she ordered. "Alef and I will go in alone."

The guards stood down without protest. Velis and Alef walked up the ramp and into the cargo bay. Grif turned, gestured, and led them into the ship proper, Cyrus and Gurgan trailing Velis and Alef.

"There's a meeting room one deck up," Grif said. "We can talk there."

They walked down the corridor and re-entered the lounge. Amys and Cutter were no longer there. Grif crossed the room, opened the lift, and they all stepped inside.

Alef Halge looked around the lift and nodded to himself. "Large," he said. "Your ship is bigger than I thought it would be."

Alef's voice was strong and clear. He sounded far younger than his age, but other than that Grif couldn't pick up anything. He appeared to be interested in the size of his ship and that was it.

"She's about as big as a ship can get before you have to rely on antigravity and shields to fly in the atmosphere," he said. Despite his current situation and his predisposition to dislike the man, he couldn't resist talking about his pride and joy. "They originally designed her to be a troop transport, so the size of the lift and the hallways are a lot wider than you usually find."

"How large is the crew?" Alef asked. "If you don't mind me asking."

"She can hold up to sixty," Grif said. "We manage with less."

"Less?" Alef pressed.

Grif hesitated, wondering why Alef wanted to know, then shrugged. "Usually ten," he said. "We're down one at the moment."

"Nine crew," Alef said. "Remarkable."

"We multitask."

The lift stopped. Grif stepped out, and Velis and Alef did the same. Cyrus and Gurgan started to follow, but Grif shook his head. "I'll be fine. Just... stand by."

Cyrus nodded.

Grif led his guests down a hallway and stopped midway in front of a door. "Here we are." A moment later the door slid open and they emerged into a conference room.

It was fairly standard as far as such rooms went: one long table in the middle of the room, chairs placed around it, spaced evenly. A large screen was set into one wall, and computer terminals were placed between every pair of chairs.

The air was musty and stale. "We don't usually use this room," Grif explained. "We prefer the Wardroom. Usually everything in this level is turned off to save power."

Alef nodded as he entered, Velis following. Grif closed the door behind them, waited for them to sit, and chose a chair directly across the table, facing them. Then he waited.

Nobody spoke.

The silence stretched on for a few minutes. Alef Halge looked at Grif with an immense amount of interest, but seemed completely satisfied with the silence. Velis looked subdued, though Grif noticed her jaw was set determinedly.

Eventually Grif lost patience. "Come *on.* You went to a great deal of trouble to freeze my assets and put me and my crew in a great deal of financial peril. The least you can do is *tell me why.*"

Alef inclined his head in acknowledgment. "I'm sorry, Captain Vindh, but we felt—"

Grif snorted. "Sorry? Sorry my—well, I don't know, maybe you *are* sorry, Mr. Halge, though I'll bet my ship that Velis enjoyed every minute of it, and she's not one for *regrets*. But that's completely beside the point. It happened—whether you're sorry for it or not—and I want my money back. My sister promised to tell me how, so here we are. Please feel free to jump in with the specifics at any time."

"Tell me, Captain..." Alef leaned back in his chair, looking casually about the room. "How exactly did you break into Ur Voys? I'm very interested in the specifics of *that*."

Grif stared at Alef dumbly. "What?"

"Ur Voys. On Varkav. Of course, you know this, since you broke into it in order to steal a rather valuable quantity of WU-961, which you later managed to smuggle past one of the most brilliant tactical minds of the Radiant Throne Navy, and ultimately sold to someone here, becoming quite rich in the process.

Grif looked at Alef carefully. The old man folded his hands across his stomach, smiling slightly.

"What do you want?" Grif asked.

Alef shrugged. "We were very impressed when we caught word of your success, Captain. Specifically: when we heard that one man—you—had broken into one of the most secure medical facilities in the Radiant Throne territories and walked out with one of their most prized products we were *very deeply impressed* indeed. What we want, Captain, is for you to repeat your success."

Grif frowned. "You want anagathics? Doesn't the Alliance have its own facilities for that?"

"Captain Vindh, you are a perceptive and clever man. You are also, I believe, an extremely *intelligent* man, so understand me when I say that playing dumb will not work with me."

Grif's frown deepened. "All right. So what do you want, then?"

Alef leaned forward, placing his hands on the table, and peered into Grif's eyes with his strange, gray stare. "What we want, Captain, is for you to return to the Ur Voys medical facility on Varkav and *break into it again*."

Grif stared at Alef in disbelief: an unguarded, genuine reaction that Alef ignored completely.

"The Radiant Throne has something we want," Alef said. "We want it very much. And apparently you are the only person we know who seems to have any chance at all of getting it for us."

Chapter 10

WHEREIN Our Hero, Having Just Come Out of the Woods, is Pushed Back In

Grif shifted in his chair, looking from Velis, then to Alef, then back, trying to find some clue as to what they were thinking. Velis was, for the moment, unreadable. She sat still, gaze unfocused, as if she were only partially paying attention to the conversation. Alef, on the other hand, was watching Grif carefully... *very* carefully, with an intensity that made him shiver. Alef's eyes glinted in the light, and Grif thought, once again, that they had to be cybernetic. He wondered what it was like to view the world through the lens of a machine—for that to be the only reference available.

Alef watched, and waited.

"I..." Grif rubbed the back of his neck, trying to get the hairs to lie down. "I don't understand..."

"...what I mean?" Alef interrupted. "Surely you're not going to deny it. Not *here*. We've already heard the story at least four times—all slightly different, of course, but all essentially telling the same tale: Grif Vindh, Captain of the *Fool's Errand*, made off with a fortune in anagathics stolen from a planet fairly deep within the borders of the Radiant Throne. And not only that! He managed to outsmart—brilliantly, I might add, assuming that part of the story is accurate—one of the sharpest officers in their fleet."

"Actually," Grif replied, "I was going to say 'I don't understand how you found out about this so quickly.'"

Alef simply smiled.

"It's been a month! I mean, I expected the story to travel—I *wanted* the story to travel—but these things take time, and most of the people I know don't travel too deep into Alliance space..."

Grif suddenly realized who it was who had told them.

"Doma."

Velis allowed herself the faintest hint of a smile.

"Even when he's not here, he still manages to screw everything up. That little son of a—"

The smile vanished. Grif coughed nervously and let the sentence trail off.

Alef nodded agreeably. "Yes. Doma. He, ah, didn't exactly volunteer the information willingly, if that's what you were thinking. But his mother couldn't help but notice that he had, very suddenly, become a very rich young man. A bit too rich for his own safety, in fact. And once Velis learned exactly how the young man had become so dangerously rich, she realized we had a way in. You."

Grif scowled. "I'm not interested in being your spy or your thief," he said. "And besides, there's no way I'd make it in a second time."

Alef shrugged. "It's a better opportunity than we've had in some time," he said. "We tried sending our own agents. Very good ones. We believe they are all dead."

Grif rolled his eyes. "You have a funny way of selling this idiocy. Your super-spies get killed and you think I can help you? You're insane."

"There is the matter of all your money. One call from me and I can guarantee it won't be yours anymore. Which means, among other things, that they'll take your ship..." Alef looked around the conference room. "That would be a shame. It's a wonderful ship."

Grif narrowed his eyes.

"You're a hard worker, Captain Vindh," Alef continued. "Not an *honest* one, but a hard worker nonetheless... and this ship is the fruit of your labors..."

Grif clenched his fists under the table. It took every ounce of will not to attack the man right then and there.

If Alef noticed, he didn't show it. "If you are reasonable and cooperative, then you will be able to make this ship even more impressive. If not..."

"I get it," Grif said. "I do. I get it."

"Good." Alef settled back in his chair, watching.

The only sound in the room came from the air ducts circulating the air. Grif stared at a spot on the table, ignoring Alef and Velis as he tried to think things through.

It was a bad situation. The Alliance of Free Worlds, at least in theory, was a relatively benign organization: it was interested only in protecting its member worlds, and getting more worlds to join them. In practice, it mostly lived up to that reputation, but it was *huge*. There was too much to keep track of, so for the most part it didn't bother, giving each system enormous latitude in how it conducted its business. Alef's organization took advantage of that inattentiveness, and by keeping out of the government's eye was able to advance the Alliance's interests with a ruthlessness that would make the average despot squeamish.

This wasn't something Grif found morally offensive, but at the moment he did find it damned inconvenient.

Alef wasn't bluffing, Grif was certain of that. They would bankrupt him without hesitation, and Grif would be in serious trouble. Bankruptcy was a very serious crime in the Tylaris Barony; the *Fool's Errand* would be taken from him, and he'd very likely be imprisoned... probably shipped off to a penal colony.

Grif didn't want to go to prison, and he didn't want to lose his ship.

"You're going to have to sweeten the pot," Grif said.

Alef raised one eyebrow ever so slightly above the other. "Am I?"

"Yes. My options are either to go back into Throne space and probably get myself killed on a suicide mission, or go bankrupt and probably get myself killed on a penal colony. I'm damned if I do and damned if I don't... but if I don't, I'll have the satisfaction of *not doing what you're trying to make me do*. As I see it, you need to do two things: you need to explain to me exactly what you will do to help me and my crew survive, and you need to show me exactly how I'm going to *profit* from this."

Alef stared at Grif thoughtfully, then nodded. "Fair enough."

Grif chose not to comment on Alef's concept of fairness.

"First," Alef said, "you won't be expected to do this alone. We don't trust you to do it on your own, to be honest—it's more likely you'd make a run for the independent worlds."

"True," Grif agreed.

"You will be taking some of my agents with you," Alef continued. "A fair number of them, actually, as well as a complement of specialists who will want to see the item as soon as it's recovered. This will place a great deal of resources at your disposal, Captain. You will have doctors who can alter your appearance—even down to the genetic level, if necessary—as well as a full array of drugs tailored to resist the effects of Sword-rated telepathy. And, of course, a number of highly-trained agents who will be there to assist you in achieving your objective."

Grif considered this. The Ministry of Dirty Tricks excelled at dirty tricks; that might give him an edge.

"Also," Alef added, "Major Enge will be accompanying you... no, she won't be taking command of your ship. We're relying on you to get us there, get the item, and get everyone away. But she excels at this kind of work, and despite your obvious distaste for each other, I think you'll find her an asset."

Family again, Grif thought. *If we're lucky we'll kill each other before we get to Varkav.*

"As to your payment..." Alef hesitated. "We can't pay you directly. There is an ocean of red tape surrounding the exchange of currency to non-citizens, and it is... difficult to navigate, even for us. However, there are other means of compensation that a man in your position can find just as rewarding."

"Oh?" Grif asked. "Do tell."

"I am willing," Alef said, "to offer you a license, in perpetuity, to trade in the capital system."

Both Velis and Grif stared at Alef in amazement.

"Are you serious?" Grif asked.

"Are you *insane*?" Velis demanded.

Alef immediately focused on Velis. His expression did not change, but to Grif's astonishment Velis immediately backed down. She clenched her jaw in protest, but stared down at the table and remained silent.

"Yes," Alef said. "I am quite serious. And it's a relatively simple thing for me to do. This is not the first time I've had to rely on outside expertise to accomplish a goal, and we have developed a very robust system of rewarding our... *contract employees* without drawing undue attention to the transaction."

Grif whistled softly. Being granted a license to trade in the capital system also gave the merchant the right to trade at any federal port on any planet in the Alliance territories. It was an expensive license, but a lucrative one... most of the merchants who could afford such a license owned *fleets* of ships, not just one. And a license in perpetuity was, essentially, a charter—an officially recognized *right* to transport goods in the AFW that would never have to be renewed, and could even be passed on as inheritance, or given away as a gift.

A trader could get very, very rich with a license like that.

"Of course," Alef said, "you wouldn't be exempt from the laws of the Alliance... your ship would have to be cleared for entry into the Alliance core worlds, and if you were caught breaking any laws, your license would be revoked... which would be the *least* of your concerns. But that is my offer. If you accept, I will have it drawn up and properly registered before you depart for Varkav. I trust that will be acceptable?"

It was a hell of an enticement. The odds for success were *terrible*, of course... but if he managed to pull it off...

"You must think there's no way in hell I can pull this off," Grif said cheerfully. "If I were a betting man I'd put my money on this being an elaborate plan to get my sister killed before she qualifies for retirement."

Velis stiffened.

"Still," Grif said, "that's quite an offer." He stood up, leaned over the table, and stuck out his hand. "Guess we'll find out if I can pull it off."

Alef stood and shook his hand firmly. "Very good, Captain Vindh. I will see to it that this unfortunate audit is put behind you as quickly as possible. I suggest you continue with your repairs. As soon as they are complete, we'll contact you. Please... don't try and leave before we do."

"Right," Grif said. "While I understand your concern, I assure you: my greed is much stronger than my cowardice."

Alef smiled slightly.

"Well," Grif continued, "I'm sure you're a very busy man... assassinations to arrange, secrets to steal, small planetary governments to destabilize... if you could just tell me exactly what it is you want us to steal I'll be happy to brief my crew while you go off to slam the door on some other poor sod's balls..."

Alef shrugged. "I don't have that information."

Grif narrowed his eyes. "What do you mean, 'you don't have that information?' You don't know what you want me to steal?"

"You'll be given a full briefing on everything we know about it," Alef said. "But we don't know much."

"Because *usually*," Grif said, "people who want to steal something *specific* actually know what it is..."

"We do have some theories."

Grif closed his eyes and counted to three. "OK! No problem! We'll just... be flexible, or something..." He opened the door to the conference room and found Hari, Cutter and Vod trying to look casual.

"Can I help you?" Grif asked.

Hari and Vod looked down. Cutter adopted an expression of vague disinterest. "What do you mean, Skip?"

Grif snorted. "This is the most disappointing attempt at eavesdropping I've seen in a long time," he said. "If you really wanted to hear what was going on you should have hacked into the desk terminals, like Cyrus and Ktk did."

"Pay me, bug!" one of the terminals said.

Velis muttered something under her breath.

"As long as you're listening in, round everyone up so we can meet in half an hour," Grif shouted over his shoulder. "If you'll follow me," he added, indicating Velis and Alef, "I'll be *happy* to show you out."

He led them back to the cargo bay. Before he turned to leave, Alef shook his hand one last time.

"We'll contact you soon," Alef promised.

"Take your time," Grif said cheerfully. "The refit should take another month at least. Though you may want to have your team assembled by then, since after the refit we'll be integrating the systems, which means taking off and flying around a bit. I suspect you'll want your watchdog—I assume that's you, Sis—around for that."

Alef nodded. "Very well. In a month, then. Oh, and your financial situation should be cleared up in about half an hour."

"Outstanding. So long, then..." Grif waved them away, then watched as Alef and Velis walked off the cargo bay and down into the spaceport, where their escorts were still waiting patiently by the ship. He *continued* to watch as they made their way back to the central hub of the spaceport. It wasn't until the last of the guards had disappeared into the building that he allowed his cheerful demeanor to crack.

"Damn it all to hell," he muttered. He leaned against the bulkhead wall and forced himself to remain calm. Finally he stood, forced himself to grin, and made his way to the Wardroom.

The crew was waiting for him when he entered. Every one was grinning like a madman.

"You look like a pack of idiots," he said.

As if on cue, they bombarded him with questions:

"Is it true they're going to give you a charter?"

"Are we really going back to Varkav?"

"Are we working for the Alliance on this run?"

"Will we get our money back now?"

"Do you really think this is a good idea?"

Grif held up his hands, and the crew fell silent. "In order: I guess so, unfortunately, I'm trying not to think about it, soon, and hell no, it's a *terrible* idea. But... well. Penal colony."

Everyone murmured in agreement.

"All right... look. This mission is practically impossible. It was hard enough, ah, doing this the first time, and there's no way *that* trick is going to work a second time. If we get caught... we're dead. Especially if we're caught with a ship full of Alliance spies... which, apparently, we will in fact have. So if you want to bail out, do it now... with my blessing. You should be getting your money back in another ten, fifteen minutes or so."

No one said anything.

"Seriously. No hard feelings. *Seriously.*"

Cyrus shifted and looked around awkwardly. "It's decent of you, Grif," he said. "But... you know... a charter like that is worth as much to a crew as it is to a captain..."

Grif raised an eyebrow.

Cyrus coughed. "Ah, well, what I'm saying is... you've managed to pull this off once—and, well, sure, it's dangerous... but it's you. If it were anyone else, I think most of us would pull out... but it's *you.*"

"But Cyrus, you were about to buy a ship..."

Cyrus shrugged. "A few years working on a ship with a charter to the AFW Capital system and I'll be able to afford something much better than that Hummingbird," he said. "Think about it! How many independent traders have you heard about with one of those things? Hell, even the merchant fleets have to renew their licenses every ten years or so, and that's not cheap. That's good for a reputation..."

"Besides," Hari added, "we'll be the first choice for anyone in these parts trying to smuggle things into the Alliance."

"And besides," Cyrus said, "it's *you*."

Ktk chittered in agreement.

"Er... right." Grif looked at the group, decided they were serious, and shrugged. "Well, Cyrus, I'm happy to have you back... but I sort of gave Cutter your spot."

"He can have it, Skip," Cutter said. "I'll take my old spot back. I hate working that damn gun, and Cyrus is a much better engineer. He'll keep our guns in shape."

Hari nodded in agreement.

"Well... welcome back, Cyrus." Grif clasped the giant man's hand, and slapped him on the shoulder. "Cutter and Hari will bring you up to speed on what they've ordered to beef up the armaments. Get started on that in the morning. For now... get out of here. Go have fun."

There was a general cheer at the prospect of fun, then everyone shuffled out of the Wardroom as they went to confirm that their money—an integral part in their plans to have fun—was theirs once more.

Amys stayed behind, staring at Grif thoughtfully. Grif guessed where the conversation was going and reached for a glass and bottle.

"Maybe," Amys said, "you ought to tell me the story of how you managed to pull this off the first time."

"Ah," Grif said. "That." He pulled out a second glass and set it next to the first.

"Yes," Amys said. "That." She drew up to the table and watched as Grif poured.

"Eh, well." Both glasses full, he set the bottle aside and raised his in a toast. "I told you it was a long story."

"No," Amys said, "you told me it was complicated." She raised her glass in return.

"Oh! Well, that's much more accurate. It's not very long at all, to be completely honest."

"I'm really not going to like this," Amys muttered.

"Oh, that depends," Grif said, grinning the grin she *didn't* like. "How do you feel about irony?"

"I don't like irony," Amys said. "You like irony. I like you, so I *tolerate* irony. Up to a point."

"Yeah..." Grif frowned. "Well, due to the... specifics of how I managed to get the anagathics, this little venture is considerably more complicated."

"Oh, God." Amys downed her glass and reached for the bottle, filling it again. "How bad is it?"

"Well..." Grif put his glass back down on the table. Amys noted, with some concern, that it was not empty. "Look, there's a lot I did on that run that was, if I say so myself, absolutely brilliant. I mean, I played Mavis *perfectly*—he would still be completely clueless if one of his boys hadn't swiped a few 'rations.' And one of the things I've always believed is that a good smuggler takes his opportunities when he sees them, and that capitalizing on a situation that presents itself is as good as making it happen on your own..."

"Grif." Amys raised her voice slightly, impatience and concern rising. "What are you trying to tell me?"

Grif hesitated a moment. "I... may not have stolen the anagathics."

"You..." Amys frowned. "You may not have *stolen* them?"

"Well, no, I mean, I *stole* them. But, ah, not in the way everyone *thinks* I did."

"What are you talking about?" Amys asked in exasperation. "Nobody *knows* how you stole them. You won't give anyone a straight answer."

"But there are *assumptions*," Grif said. "Obviously. Otherwise we wouldn't be in this mess right now. And I didn't do anything to discourage those assumptions, because I figured it'd be good for our reputation, but the assumptions aren't *true*."

Amys said nothing.

Grif cleared his throat. "So... everyone *assumes* I found a way into and out of Ur Voys," he continued. "And that I stole the anagathics from the Ur Voys facility directly. That's... not the way it happened."

Amys' brow furrowed slightly. "Are you trying to tell me," Amys asked, "that you didn't actually break into Ur Voys? At all?"

Grif nodded. "That's right. I didn't have to."

Amys nodded slowly. "So... how *exactly* did you manage to come into possession of one of the most expensive and illegal substances in the civilized worlds?"

"Well," Grif said, "it's... hm. They sort of fell off a truck."

Amys blinked.

"Fell. Off a truck."

"Yeah. I stumbled onto one of the Ur Voys delivery routes, and I just happened to be standing there when it—"

"*Fell.* Off a *truck.*"

"Hard to believe, right? So you can see why I don't want Velis to know—"

"FELL OFF A TRUCK."

Grif noted, with some alarm, that the glass in her hand was trembling.

"Well, that's an oversimplification, really. The truck sort of flipped over two or three times then erupted into a white-hot ball of plasma and flame, and the boxes that weren't incinerated were thrown in every direction, so 'flew out the back' is probably more accurate. Calm down..."

Amys twitched, set her glass down on the bar, and started twirling a strand of her hair. "Calm down? Grif, I don't know whether to laugh at the insanity of it all or beat you senseless. You just got us hired by the Alliance's Black Ops division because you're the only person they know who's ever done this successfully, only you've *never actually done it!*"

"This wouldn't bother you nearly as much," Grif said, "if you only appreciated irony more."

Amys made an incoherent noise in the back of her throat, which Grif translated as "I am actively refraining from killing you now."

"Look," Grif said, "the actual story—that I just happened to stumble into a situation where I could walk off with ridiculously expensive contraband that everyone would assume had just been incinerated—*that* is unbelievable. That's the kind of story that makes people ask 'hey, Grif, what are you *hiding*?' and then resort to all kinds of unpleasant tactics to get an answer. As ridiculously implausible as it sounds, 'break into Ur Voys' was the most believable option, and if people believed I did that, the only thing they'd assume I was hiding was my explanation of *how*."

Amys thought it over. “I need another drink,” she said finally.

Grif relaxed a little. “You and me both,” he said.

“You are a bastard,” Amys added.

“Fair enough. But I promise you, if I’d known the Alliance was going to get wind of this, I’d have thought of a much less self-aggrandizing lie.”

“They wouldn’t have believed it,” Amys said. She filled both glasses. “Well, Grif... this is going to be one interesting run.”

Grif laughed sharply. “Interesting. Yes. Well, look on the bright side: you don’t actually have to do the break-in. If this little job goes bad—which, let’s be honest, it probably will—*you* have a shot at getting out alive.”

Amys handed Grif his glass. “Let’s not be honest,” she said. “it doesn’t suit you.”

Chapter 11

WHEREIN Gears Turn and Complicated Things Go Whirrrr

Grif Vindh, Captain of the *Fool's Errand*, peered over the navigation console display and frowned. "Damn it all," he said, "it did it *again*. What the hell is wrong with this thing? The screens don't even try to drop."

"Not a problem on my end." The frustration in Cyrus' voice was evident even over the intercom. "The gun is sending the drop code."

This was Grif's third refit. He remembered hating the first two—the first when he'd been the pilot on someone else's ship, the second shortly after he'd purchased the *Fool's Errand*—but he'd largely forgotten why. Now he remembered: buying and installing new technology was easy. Trying to get new technology to integrate properly was nearly impossible.

"That's all very nice," Grif said into the intercom, "but there *is* a problem down there, Cyrus, because your guns also keep sending the fire code at *exactly the same time*."

A storm of vulgarity erupted from the intercom as Cyrus investigated the problem.

Grif and Morgan were on the bridge running a simulation with Cyrus, who was in the main gunnery bay. They were trying to get their new screens and sensors to communicate properly with their new guns. This was important: firing an energy weapon into your own screens was not only tactically unsound, it was professionally embarrassing. At that moment *professional embarrassment* was winning by a wide margin.

"Oh, hell," Cyrus said, "this is a ruddy mess. It's just going down the checklist without waiting for a response from sensors. Morgan, are the sensors even working?"

"Don't be idiotic," Morgan snapped. They'd been at this for hours, and this was Morgan's first refit—his patience was badly frayed. "Shipboard sensors are working just fine. They are detecting that the screens are up and sending out the lock-flag just like they're supposed to. They're even receiving the drop code your idiotic guns keep sending... but they can't pass that on in time when your guns send a fire code at exactly the same time!"

"Well it's not *exactly* the same time," Cyrus said. "It's a hundredth of a second after. Like I said, it's going down a checklist."

"Does the checklist have an entry for 'wait for the sensors to tell us the screens have dropped before firing the gun?'" Morgan asked.

"Of *course* it—er..." Cyrus' voice trailed off. A moment later, in a more subdued tone: "let's try this again."

Grif grinned in spite of himself, and hunched over the Nav station once more. "Screens dropped! Fantastic! This calls for a drink. Or maybe ten... wait. Cyrus, are your guns still firing?"

"No." Morgan and Cyrus answered simultaneously.

Grif sighed. "The screens aren't coming back up."

Once again profanity erupted from the intercom.

Morgan pounded his console in frustration. "I can't believe we paid *money* for this! Technology is supposed to *work*."

"That's exactly the kind of nonsense I'd expect to hear from a scientist," Grif said. "Cyrus, do you figure you need to look at the screen code?"

"Maybe," Cyrus said reluctantly. "Ktk would get through it faster, though."

"Ktk is trying to bring our fusion drive online," Grif replied. "And I'd rather it focused on that. I like not exploding."

"I've been going through targeting code all morning," Cyrus complained. "We need another programmer on board."

"We need a comm specialist *first*," Morgan insisted.

"I know, I know," Grif said.

"I'm serious. I can't patch communications to sensors and do both any more. We've got a military-grade sensor array now. It's *complicated*."

"I *know*," Grif repeated. He turned his attention to a log of the last simulation and tried to determine what prevented the screens from coming back up. "It's not like I'm putting it off or anything. There just hasn't been a lot to work with around here over the last month. All the good people have already signed on to other ships, and I don't want another Doma."

"Well who would?" Morgan asked. "Except Velis... maybe."

"If you say so," Grif muttered. "I never understood what drove her to motherhood in the first place. But I guess we can ask her in a day or two. When I told Halge we were starting systems integration he said he'd send the team down soon."

"Ah... yes." Morgan looked uneasy.

"Nervous?" Grif tried not to grin.

Morgan didn't respond: he was staring at the data scrolling across his screen, tugging at his beard thoughtfully. "Grif, we're testing screen segmentation, right?"

"... yeah..." Grif glanced over at the summary display for the screens. "12 segments per axis. And we're trying to get segment 9-6 to drop, if that's what you're going to ask next."

"Wasn't going to," Morgan said. "I think I just figured out one of our problems. Sensors were reporting all segments were up—even 9-6—when you reported they'd dropped."

"But they dropped," Grif protested. "Well, the simulation reported they'd dropped."

"I believe you," Morgan said. "The simulation display reported it to you, but the segment didn't report its changed state to the internal sensors. As far as internals were concerned, all screens were up."

There was a short silence. "Are you saying that because the screen didn't report that it was down, it didn't know to bring itself back up?"

"That makes sense," Cyrus said. "The segment would wait till it was given an all clear before coming back up. And before you ask, Grif, yes. The gun sent the all clear properly."

"It did," Morgan said. "But internal sensors didn't send it to the screens."

"Well why not?" Grif asked irritably.

"Because the segment didn't report that it was down," Morgan said. "The sensors discarded the message as irrelevant, because the as far as it was concerned, all screens were up."

"I hate this," Grif said. "I hate hate hate hate hate hate hate hate this. I want to find the bastard in the Tylaris Shipyards who came up with this *idiotic*—"

The intercom buzzed. It was Hari.

"Grif, we have a slight problem in Bay One." Hari sounded quite upset.

Grif frowned. "What kind of problem is that?"

"Well. Your sister is here."

"That is a problem," Grif agreed, "but let her in anyway."

"With about thirty people," Hari added.

Grif sighed. "I'll be right down."

He stood, looked over at Morgan, and took a deep breath. "Here we go. Wish me luck."

"Keep your head down," Morgan said.

When Grif reached Bay one he saw Hari standing at the top of the loading ramp with his arms crossed, glaring down at Velis, who was glaring back. Behind Velis was a large group of humans, all dressed in dark, nondescript clothing.

Hari turned at Grif's approach. The ridges on his face and arms were quite extended.

"I'll handle it, Hari. Go up to the bridge and see if you can help Morgan figure out why the screens aren't working right."

Hari nodded, gave Velis a final venomous look, and stalked off to the bridge.

Grif looked out at the small army assembled in front of him. Along with Velis and her sizable contingent of *people*, there were also large bundles of gear and a number of sealed containers on grav carts.

"Sorry, Sis," Grif said. "We didn't expect your group to be so... elaborate."

Velis nodded coolly. "Permission to come aboard?"

Grif stepped to one side, clearing the entrance. "Permission granted."

Velis barked an order and the others began loading their cargo onto the ship. Grif watched the sealed containers curiously, wondering what was inside them. When the last container had been brought into the cargo bay and placed carefully on the floor, Velis walked over to Grif with one of her men in tow.

"This is Lieutenant Commander Bennet Jax," Velis said, indicating the man to her right. "He is my second-in-command for this mission, and will be acting as a liaison between your crew and my team. He will also be briefing you on the mission objectives, and assisting you as necessary."

Bennet Jax was a young man, not more than twenty-five. Grif thought he looked like a male version of Amys—slim, dark-haired, coiled and ready to strike. He did not, however, seem particularly dangerous at present.

Of course, that's the trick, isn't it? Grif thought. *A spy isn't very effective when the first thing you think when you see him is "gee, he looks really well-trained and rather dangerous..."*

"Hello, Captain," Bennet said, extending his hand. "A pleasure to meet you."

Grif shook his hand. "Welcome aboard the *Fool's Errand*. Let me know if you or your people need anything."

"Well," Bennet said, "we need an operations center, and a space to set up some equipment we brought along. Do you mind if we use this cargo bay?"

Grif shook his head. "Not a good idea. We're going to be searched when we get into Throne space, and I want to be carrying a full complement of cargo when we do. But there are plenty of empty rooms on the decks where your people will be berthed, and some are modular and can be made quite large. You can probably find something workable up there. How quickly can you break everything down once it's set up?"

"Why?" Bennet asked.

Grif shrugged. "Like I said, we *will* be searched when we get to Throne space, and Radiant Throne Marines are usually pretty thorough. They'll question anything that looks out of place, and they are particularly sensitive to anything that might look like Secret Spy Equipment."

Bennet chuckled. "Noted," he said. "Well, we can break everything down pretty quickly, and it looks very nondescript when we do. Any idea when we'll be leaving?"

Grif shook his head. "We're integrating systems now," he said. "We installed a new fusion drive and ATID a few weeks ago and today the fusion drive is going fully online. Finally. Some of our other systems are being... less cooperative."

"Can I help?" Bennet asked.

"Can you read integration code?"

"I can, actually," Bennet said.

Grif looked startled, then hopeful. "Velis, I'd like to borrow the Lieutenant. If you don't mind..."

Velis nodded. "Commander, please assist Captain Vindh in this matter. I will remain here and get everything set up." She looked at Grif questioningly. "Do you have an estimate as to when we'll actually be ready to leave?"

Grif shrugged. "Two weeks, maybe, if everything goes well. Month and a half if every single thing under the sun goes horribly wrong. And even if we can take off in two weeks, we'll probably still need to make adjustments before we actually head out. This thing you want stolen... please tell me there's not a ridiculous time frame that goes hand in hand with the sheer impossibility of the task."

"No," Velis said, "that will fit. I'll tell Halge. Once we get settled in, those of us who have shipboard experience will be made available to assist you, if you think that will be useful."

Grif blinked. "Yes," he said. "I'm pretty sure it would." He managed to keep the all-consuming paranoia and suspicion out of his voice.

"Meanwhile," Bennet said, "let's see if I can do anything useful now."

Grif turned back to look at Bennet, shrugged, and headed to the lift. "I hope you can," he said. "We've been running weapon simulations, and we finally got a screen segment to drop when the gun fires, but it won't come back up. Something's not talking to something else."

Bennet laughed. "Systems integration is hell for custom ships, and from what I hear this ship isn't even close to a standard configuration."

Grif grinned in spite of himself. "You won't find many Maximilians that are. These ships were made to be tweaked."

"I'm looking forward to seeing what you've done with her," Bennet said. "Well... not everything. I suspect there are parts of this ship neither one of us wants me to know about."

"Careful," Grif warned. "Keep talking like that and I'll be forced to like you."

Chapter 12

WHEREIN Enmity Is Formally Established, Bets Are Made, Money Is Lost, and the Terrans Find Vindication

In the end it took three weeks to bring the *Fool's Errand* completely back on line. Bennet proved to be an enormous help in that regard—even Ktk was impressed with his speed and skill. Meanwhile, Velis' people set up their command center in the general mess. All but one of the sealed containers were unsealed: according to Cutter, they were medical equipment.

When Grif asked Velis about them, she confirmed Cutter's guess. "You remember Halge said we could alter your appearance, right down to your DNA?"

"Nice," Grif said. "What about the one still in the box?"

"Not important," Velis said. Something in the way she said it convinced Grif to drop the matter.

Eventually Grif declared the integration a success. "We're going to have to take her up sooner or later to shake everything out," he said. "I don't think we're going to get much more out of these simulations."

Ktk agreed, stating the *Fool's Errand* was completely space worthy as far as it was concerned.

"Excellent," Grif said. "Bennet, please tell my sister that we plan to take off in a few hours."

"That reminds me..." Bennet shifted uneasily. "Ah... Major Enge has asked me to inform you that she will be on the bridge when we do."

"Of course she did," Grif said. "She was beginning to worry me, what with her respecting my position as captain, and talking to me in complete sentences and everything. I'm actually relieved."

"...if it's all right," Bennet added, "I'd like to be on the bridge as well. I've been working on your ship for weeks and I'd really like to see what she can do."

Grif considered it. "How are you with ship communications?"

"I'm all right," Bennet said. "Your comm station is pretty standard, I don't think I'd have any problems."

"Well, we're short a comm specialist for the trip. If you don't mind doing the work I don't mind you being up top."

Two hours later Grif, Amys and Morgan were at their stations, going through a pre-flight check. When Bennet and Velis arrived, Bennet sat at the comm station. Velis sat in an extra seat near the door, at the far end of the bridge.

"Hello Sis," Grif said, sliding his seat out of the nest and into the bridge proper, swiveling it around to face her. "Welcome to the bridge. Lots of familiar faces here today. You know Amys, of course. And Morgan."

Velis looked at Morgan and nearly smiled. Morgan sat rigid in his chair. He'd done his best to avoid Velis entirely; he'd been very successful up to this point.

"Hello Morgan," Velis said. "You look well."

"Velis," Morgan said. That was all he could manage; he abruptly turned in his seat and devoted his attention to his station.

"This is going to be the *best trip ever*," Grif muttered. Then, in a louder voice, he added "Bennet, we filed a flight plan with spaceport authority about an hour and a half ago. Let me know when they approve it." With that he descended back down into the Pilot's Nest.

Liftoff was a resounding success. The *Fool's Errand* left atmosphere without incident, all instrumentation responded perfectly, system-to-system sensors had no issues communicating with any of the shipboard systems. Only minor tweaks were needed once the ship reached orbit, and a few hours later Ktk announced it felt the *Fool's Errand* could forgo further flight tests, and actually make the jump to tach.

"All right," Grif said. "Amys, set a course for Tyrelos."

"Tyrelos?" Velis frowned and shook her head. "That's not in throne space."

"No it isn't," Grif said. "It's a Trade Barony. A small one, just outside Radiant Throne territories. We're making a side-stop: we need some supplies for our cover story, and we need information. Tyrelos Station is the perfect place for both."

"Course ready," Amys said. "Transferring."

Grif saw the coordinates flash across his screen, and punched in the first leg of their course. "Right. We'll be out of the system in a few hours, then we'll be in tach for a few days." Half an hour before the jump to tach, Grif asked Velis if her people were trained to handle zero gravity.

"Most of them," Velis said. "Why?"

"Oh, well. We turn off gravity before we jump to tach and don't turn it back on until we drop." The peculiar quality of the silence that followed prompted Grif to turn around in his seat and gaze up into the bridge proper. Velis stood at the end of the rail leading down to the Pilot's Nest, staring at Grif with no expression on her face whatsoever.

"Er..." Grif shifted uncomfortably. "Is there a problem?"

Velis continued to stare at Grif, not blinking.

"OK," Grif said, "I'm starting to get the feeling that you don't *approve*."

Velis didn't reply.

"Look," Grif said, "our ship's gravity is older tech, and we don't have any redundant systems for the nullifier plates. We don't want one of those plates failing in tach. Gravity spikes are *bad*."

"I know," Velis said. "What I want to know is why you didn't bother telling us this until *now*?"

"Well..." Grif started, but Velis cut him off.

"Never mind," she said. "We need some time to secure our equipment more... securely. I'll need Bennet."

Without another word she turned and left the bridge.

"Uh... Captain..." Bennet sounded a little sheepish. "If you don't need me for anything at the moment, I think I'd better—"

"Go," Grif said. "And God have mercy on your soul."

Bennet hurried off the bridge.

"That poor bastard," Grif said.

"He seems all right for a spook," Morgan observed.

Grif punched the intercom. "This is the Captain. Jump to tach has been delayed until further notice." Switching the intercom off, he pushed his chair back, entering the bridge proper.

"Sure," he said. "Bennet's great. Seriously, I like him a lot. And I expect I'll keep liking him right up to the point where he turns on us."

"Oh, come on," Morgan said. "I mean, sure, he works for Velis, but..."

"And Velis," Grif said, laughing. "What do you all think about her, eh? I mean, she's almost *polite*. You think her boss ordered her to play nice? I bet it's *killing* her. I'd almost enjoy it if I weren't waiting for the other shoe to drop."

"That other shoe is causing me a great deal of concern," Amys said.

"They outnumber us, you know. There are thirty of them."

"Five of them are scientists," Morgan noted.

"Oh, well, that's all right then," Amys shot back sarcastically. "Take away the five scientists, and we have *only* twenty-five of Velis' hand-picked agents. That'd be an *easy* fight. Grif, if Velis really wanted to, she could take the ship."

"Yeah." Grif frowned. "Not a happy thought. I don't think she wants to, though. She wants this... *thing*. Whatever it is. Hopefully we get some clarification on *that*. Anyway, you know how she works. She won't turn on us unless she thinks we're going to do something that keeps her from getting the *thing*. As long as she thinks we're cooperating we should be OK."

"Sure," Amys said, "but Velis' definition of 'cooperative' is quite a bit narrower than mine..."

"There is that," Grif admitted. "So... what do you guys know about these agents? I've been focused on integrating the damn computers and haven't had much chance to be social."

"It's just as well," Amys said. "They're not very friendly. They keep to Deck One, for the most part. Cyrus and Ktk convinced two of them to play a round of cards. Ktk says they aren't particularly good at cheating."

Grif chuckled. "Spies who can't cheat. I'm sure they'll go far."

Morgan snorted.

"They don't do anything," Amys continued. "They stay in the rooms Velis picked out... they don't even really try to snoop. Except for Bennet, and he's not technically snooping since he asks first."

"Eh. Not exactly," Grif said.

Amys raised an eyebrow. "What do you mean?"

"Ktk found a few things the other day," Grif said. "When Bennet was helping us integrate our systems, he... showed some initiative."

"Initiative?" Morgan said the word as if he were using the proper name for a deadly, quick-acting contact poison.

"He bugged the ship," Grif said. "Ktk was impressed. Bennet didn't even try to hide it—actually, according to Ktk the way it's set up he made it very easy to disable... but not without alerting someone first."

"Who?" Morgan asked.

Grif shrugged. "Bennet, I guess. Or whoever he's assigned to monitor what we're doing."

"He didn't try to hide it?" Amys was having trouble digesting the concept.

"Yeah. According to Ktk he did everything but provide us a printed manual on what it is, how it works, and how to disable it. If you look at it one way, it's actually very polite."

"I guess so," Amys said. "What if you look at it the other way?"

"Oh, well," Grif said. "When you look at it the other way, I'd like to throw him out the—"

"I'd much rather you looked at it the first way," Bennet said as he entered the bridge.

They all turned to stare at him. He smiled slightly.

"There are parts of my job that I don't really like," he said. "They're necessary, but they're not... how I'd *prefer* to do things. Necessity is a bitch, and sometimes you have to be Necessity's son."

"Clever," Amys said, body tense. Not tense, Grif corrected—*coiled*.

"Sorry," Bennet said. "I guess now is a bad time for humor. Before you try to shove me out the airlock, let me lay our cards out on the table."

Amys looked at Grif. Grif waved for Bennet to continue.

"Thank you." Bennet leaned against the bulkhead wall. "I don't know what your history is with the Major—I mean, I know you're family, and that you don't like each other, but I don't know the specifics. I do know that you got strong-armed into this, and if you're like her at *all*, you hate being strong-armed into *anything*. You got a raw deal, and everyone knows it. Hell, to be honest, a lot of us even feel bad about it. Sort of."

Grif smiled sardonically.

"No one expects you to like your situation," Bennet continued. "We'd be a little worried if you did, to be honest. But that also makes it hard to trust you. I mean, we did blackmail you into doing the impossible a second time, and even with your track record, the odds aren't promising."

Amys glanced at Grif. Grif waited for Bennet to continue.

"So we're monitoring you," Bennet said. "I made it easy to disable, because once this is over—assuming we all survive—you can take it out and go on your merry way. But if you disable it before we're done... we're going to assume you intend to do something we will find *very inconvenient*, and react accordingly. Don't think it hasn't occurred to us that if you wanted you could seal off Deck One, pump out all the oxygen, then dump our dead bodies and equipment out into space.

"We'd probably keep the equipment," Grif said.

Bennet shrugged. "I expect you would. Anyway, I hope we understand each other."

Grif nodded.

"Good." Bennet nodded, then sat at the comm station. "The Major wants you to know we've secured our equipment, and you can turn off gravity at any time. Also, once we're on our way I'd like to brief you on your objective."

"Wonderful," Grif muttered. He slid his chair back down into the Pilot's Nest, and turned on the intercom. "This is the Captain... after a fashion. We're killing ship gravity in one minute. This is your first and last warning..."

* * *

The jump to tach occurred without incident, and after a quick systems check Grif and Bennet made their way down to the conference room. Velis was waiting for them, already seated.

Grif floated up to the ceiling and pushed off to land next to an empty chair. He strapped himself in and wondered which of them would start the show.

"I understand you and Commander Bennet had a little chat," Velis said.

"Oh yes," Grif said. "Quite informative."

"Good. Then you know where things stand."

"Let's talk about what I *don't* know," Grif suggested. "For example, I don't know what you want me to steal. Knowing what you want me to steal actually improves my chances of stealing it. So let's all assume I'm suitably intimidated and move on to the matter at hand."

Velis narrowed her eyes. "Fine," she said. She nodded sharply to Bennet, who settled in the chair to her right.

Bennet reached into a vest pocket and retrieved a data card. He plugged it into the terminal; all terminals in the room activated, each screen showing a picture of the planet Varkav from orbit.

"Look familiar?" Bennet asked.

Grif nodded.

"The main planetside port is Ovorid Station," Bennet continued, "which I assume you are also familiar with. There are civilian and military sections."

"Yes," Grif said. "There's also a space station in orbit for the really big ships. The ones that aren't atmosphere capable."

Bennet nodded. "Varkav is a major economic center for the Radiant Throne. The population lives in reasonable comfort... as long as you ignore that they live in a dictatorship ruled by power-mad telepaths."

"Yes..." Grif said. "Ignoring that. Can we skip the history lesson and get to the useful information? Or, if you like, I could take over and discuss the elaborate underworld of sin-infested 'pleasure dens' that are technically illegal but mostly ignored by the church. Because, if I remember correctly, the planet's Bishop is a loyal customer."

"Fine," Bennet said, "I'll get to the point..."

The viewscreens blinked, and the image of Varkav was replaced with an image of a complex of buildings that disappeared into the side of a mountain. Grif looked at the picture closely.

"Ur Voys," Bennet prompted.

"Is it?" Grif asked. "Huh."

Bennet looked at Velis in confusion. Velis looked suspicious. Grif started laughing.

"What's so funny?" Velis snapped.

"I don't know what kind of reaction you were fishing for," Grif said, "but I'd never seen an overhead shot of it until now. I don't even really know where on the planet it is..."

"How did you manage to get in and out?" Bennet asked.

"Don't change the subject," Grif snapped.

"I'm not—fine." Bennet took a moment to collect his thoughts. "Ur Voys is more than a medical facility. It's *called* a medical facility because its most famous product, WU-961, is manufactured here. But it also has rather extensive research facilities, very sophisticated facilities. In one of those facilities—we're not sure which, but we suspect in one of the lower levels—is this."

The aerial image of Ur Voys dissolved into what looked like an artist's sketch of a strange coin.

Grif looked at the coin suspiciously. "That?"

"That," Bennet confirmed.

"It looks like a traintube token," Grif said.

"It's a little bigger than that." Bennet keyed something into the terminal and measurements appeared above the sketch. "It's very thin, three centimeters thick, but it's forty centimeters in diameter. Notice the markings on it..."

"Hey, yeah," Grif said, leaning closer to the viewscreen, peering at the patterns that splayed across the face of the image. "What language is that?"

"We don't know," Velis said.

"You don't—" Grif looked up from the screen and looked at Velis. "Uh... what is this thing?"

"We don't know," Velis repeated.

"You don't know, or you're not going to tell me?"

"We actually don't know," Velis said. "No idea. But it's important that we have it instead of the Radiant Throne. So you're going to steal it for us."

"Fine," Grif said. "How heavy is it? Forty centimeters in diameter, three centimeters thick... what's it made out of? Metal? Rock? Plastic?"

"We're not sure about its composition," Bennet said. "Most of the information we have was reported before it was transferred to this facility, and the reports were pretty brief. It's heavy, but we don't know how heavy exactly. Our contact reported it took four soldiers to lift it and place it on a grav plate. We brought something that can be used to transport it, once it's been acquired..."

"But what *is* it?" Grif persisted. "I mean, all right, you don't know *exactly* what it is, but you have to suspect *something*, or you wouldn't be interested. So what is it? Some kind of new technology? A new energy cell?"

"All speculation is classified," Velis said, "and not relevant to your job. Just steal it, Grif. Steal it, bring it back to us, and then we can both move on with our lives."

Grif sighed. "Fine. You don't want to tell me, you don't have to tell me. I'm going to need a few things, though."

"Of course," Bennet said. "What do you need?"

"First," Grif said, "I'm going to need every piece of intel you have about Ur Voys. The... er... method I used last time will probably not work this time around, and I'm going to have to approach this as if I'd never done this before. I need all the information I can get."

Bennet nodded. "Done. I'll get you a data card with our intelligence on Ur Voys and some of the other facilities it deals with regularly."

"Good," Grif said. "Second... Alef told us you guys could change our appearance, down to the genetic level. We're going to need that, too. I expect Captain Grif Vindh of the *Fool's Errand* is probably a wanted man in the Radiant Throne these days, and his crew is likely in danger as well... and I'm pretty sure they have my DNA at this point."

Bennet nodded again. "That's why we brought our medical equipment. We figured you'd need new identities. We're already working on new appearances for each of you... except for Ktk, I'm afraid. He's going to be a problem."

"*It*," Grif corrected. "It won't be a problem. We'll be able to keep Ktk out of the way. What about Hari?"

"Invagi aren't a problem," Bennet said.

"Good." Grif unbuckled himself from his seat and pushed gently, rising out of it and floating up to the ceiling. "I guess that's it then." He pushed off from the ceiling and propelled himself to the door. "We should be in tach for another few days. Bennet, I'll need you on the bridge in a day or so to start looking for the SL Beacon."

"All right, Captain," Bennet said. "Until then, we'll be attending to other matters."

"Fine." Grif opened the door and pulled himself out.

***

When he arrived back at the bridge, he found Morgan and Amys at their posts, radiating casual disinterest.

"Oh, hello Grif," Amys said innocently. "How did the meeting go?"

Grif snorted. "As if you didn't know," he said. "I guess Velis forgot to tell Bennet that Cyrus and Ktk had already hacked into those terminals. Or she didn't care."

Amys grinned. "Fair enough. Not very helpful, were they?"

Grif rolled his eyes. "'Here's what it looks like. It's heavy. We brought a suitcase.'"

"I especially liked the part where they admitted they didn't know what it was, but they wanted you to steal it anyway," Amys added.

"Oh yes," Grif agreed, "that was *brilliant*. This is the best the finest minds in Alliance Intelligence can come up with: 'we don't know, and all our guesses are classified. Now go get it for us.'" He shook his head. "At least I know what I'm looking for now."

"I think I know what it is," Morgan said.

Grif and Amys looked at Morgan in surprise.

"You do?" Grif asked.

Morgan nodded, scratching his beard thoughtfully. "I think it's a Promethean artifact."

Amys rolled her eyes. "Terrans... I swear. You have Prometheans on the *brain*..."

"I'm serious."

"Look, Morgan..." Grif shook his head, grinning. "No offense to your previous profession, but you've yet to convince me that these 'Prometheans' even existed. I mean, they're sort of the fairy godmother of astrophysicists and biologists, aren't they? Someone says the Invagi are too close to humans biologically to have actually developed that way, and suddenly they were 'engineered by the Prometheans.' Someone maps out a star system with five life-bearing planets all in perfectly stable orbits, and it's because the 'Prometheans engineered the system.' If I had one standard for every planet that was deemed 'Promethean-engineered' because it had too few climates, or too many, or not enough species, or not enough fossilized remains to suggest ancient life—"

"You call it the fairy godmother," Morgan interrupted, "but we call it a theory to explain something that needs explaining."

"The religious types have a similar explanation," Grif replied, "but they're honest enough to call it *God* and not try to turn *magic* into *engineering*. I swear, you Earthies find the remains of one long-dead alien civilization on one of the planets in your main system, and you think you've uncovered an intergalactic conspiracy as old as time..."

Morgan sighed. "Well it predates human life on Earth, for one thing. And so far no other civilization has found one. And there are only a few racial home worlds that have any evidence of serious evolutionary activity..."

"I'm too sober to have this argument again," Amys said.

Grif winked at Amys. "How drunk would you have to be to have that argument again?"

Amys laughed and didn't answer.

"All right," Morgan said amiably. "I know, it's a crackpot theory to everyone who isn't Terran, and it makes us look like a bunch of arrogant sons of bitches because we're claiming to be one of the origin worlds for most of the sentient life in the galaxy. I get that. I still think it's a Promethean artifact... and I'd be willing to place a wager on it."

That caught Grif's interest. "Oh *really*."

"You never bet," Amys said.

Morgan shrugged. "I'm willing to bet now. And because I'm such a rich man, I'm willing to bet quite a bit. Five hundred thousand standard."

Grif blinked. "That's a hefty bet over something you can't prove."

"Shows what you know," Morgan said cheerfully. "When a scientist says 'Promethean' we're just using a placeholder to refer to something we don't know anything about. All I have to do is prove the artifact predates the earliest space faring civilizations. A few tests will determine that. If it does, then I collect."

"You're on," Amys said.

"I'm in, too," Grif said.

The intercom crackled to life. "I want in on that bet," Cyrus said. "Though Hari and Cutter here are too chicken. Well... Cutter is Terran. I think he actually agrees with Morgan."

The intercom crackled to life again, and this time Ktk chittered that it would not take the bet, since it agreed that Morgan's theory was plausible.

"And, uh, me and Vod aren't willing to bet against Ktk," Gurgan chimed in. "The only guy who ever has any luck with that is Cyrus."

Grif laughed. "Is there anyone on the ship not listening in on this conversation? All right... well, Morgan, the stake is fixed at one and a half million standard."

"I can cover it," Morgan said, grinning.

"Right... you're one of the thrifty ones. A terrible trait for a ne'er-do-well, I might add. Oh..." Grif looked around the bridge warily. "For those of you who may be listening in... This bet is restricted to CREW ONLY. Bastards."

Morgan laughed. "I will be vindicated," he said.

"We'll see," Amys said, and returned to her station.

Morgan nodded. "That we will. It's going to feel good taking your money, Amys. And yours, skipper."

"Quiet, you. You're just guessing. The Prometheans were your life's work. You see them everywhere. As far as I'm concerned you have absolutely no proof—"

"Well... not quite." Morgan looked smug. "I do have one small bit of proof."

Once again, Amys and Grif looked at him in surprise. "Well now," Grif said. "This changes the odds a bit. Spill."

Morgan shrugged. "The markings on that thing they want you to steal? It just so happens that I've seen one of those symbols before..."

Grif and Amys gaped at Morgan.

"Where?" Grif demanded.

Morgan grinned from ear to ear. "Just outside of New Berlin," he said. "On Mars. The remains of that long-dead alien civilization you mentioned earlier."

Grif allowed this new piece of information to sink in. "If this is true," he said slowly, "then I've just lost a lot of money."

Morgan chuckled.

Grif grinned. "Fair enough," he said. "This could prove to be the best bet I ever lost."

"Odd that you noticed that," Amys observed. "I wonder if Velis' people have made the connection..."

The bridge door opened, and Velis Enge stood in the doorway, face white. "Morgan, I need you to come with me," she said. "Right *now*."

Amys looked from Velis to Morgan, and then turned to Grif.

"I guess not," she said.

Chapter 13

WHEREIN Things Get Worse

Commodore Hu Mavis stared down at the motionless body of the broken man lying at his feet. The room no longer echoed with the sound of screaming; the man was now mostly silent.

Standing across from Mavis, also looking down at the broken man on the floor, was a servant of God. He was a Sword, chosen by God and the Emperor to defend the Radiant Throne from her enemies. No two Swords were alike, save only in their dedication to the Throne: some kept their names when taking on their new life, others abandoned their names altogether. This Sword's name was Kyas, but he was known only as the Viceroy.

"He isn't the one," the Viceroy said.

The Viceroy was, from what Mavis knew of him, extremely powerful. He was blessed with the ability to read the deepest hidden thoughts of men: it was a painful process, and occasionally fatal to the subject, but it was reliable. Few Swords had this gift with the precision and power the Viceroy had. That the Viceroy had come to oversee the investigation of the Ur Voys break-in meant the Emperor herself was deeply concerned by the breach.

"He isn't the one," the Viceroy repeated. "He is loyal to the Emperor."

Mavis nodded and knelt by the broken man's side. "You have been a faithful servant to the Emperor this day," he said, placing a hand on the man's shoulder. "You submitted willingly, and your innocence has been proven beyond all doubt. Your strength will return, in time, and this will not be forgotten. You and your family will be rewarded for your service."

The broken man couldn't speak, but he managed to nod.

Mavis stood. "Take him."

The door opened. Two men entered, pushing in a medical bed on a grav plate.

"Handle him with care," Mavis ordered. "Today he proved himself a true servant of the Throne."

The men lifted the broken man off the floor and laid him gently on the bed. The door opened again, and the men left with him.

"He had a good mind," the Viceroy said. "Well ordered. I hope it recovers. It may."

The Viceroy stood unmoving, staring intently at a point on the floor a meter from his feet. This, Mavis had come to learn, was what the Viceroy did when he was troubled.

"I am confused, Mavis," the Viceroy said. "I know you are telling me the truth. I read your soul."

Mavis suppressed a shudder at the memory. The Viceroy's gift was agony itself. The presence of the Viceroy's mind in his had felt like a searing flame of holy vengeance. Mavis was a sinner, like all men, and he nearly lost himself in his suffering.

"I know you speak the truth," the Viceroy repeated, "and I know the crime has occurred. But not a single person I've questioned has any knowledge of it. Even if their memories were altered, I'd detect traces of the alteration. And yet it seems that this... what is his name?"

"Vindh," Mavis said. "Grif Vindh."

"This 'Vindh' has managed to enter Ur Voys without being detected by any of our sentries, our sensors... nothing. There is no record of unauthorized life entering the facility. And yet... the drugs are missing." The Viceroy fell silent, gazing thoughtfully at the spot where the broken man had lain just moments before.

"If I may be permitted to ask..." Mavis chided himself for his impertinence, but pressed on. "What do you plan to do?"

The Viceroy considered the question. "I can find no evidence of this crime," he said, "yet I know the crime exists... so I will find the criminal. There is only one man who knows exactly how the Emperor's gift was stolen: Grif Vindh."

Mavis thought of Captain Vindh being forced to bare his soul to one of God's chosen.

"May God have mercy on his soul," Mavis said.

"He will not," the Viceroy said, "because I will not."

Mavis smiled.

Chapter 14

WHEREIN Our Hero discovers the Perils of Driving Too Fast

Grif shifted in his seat, glancing at the tactical display nervously. It was blank. *It shouldn't be blank*, he thought.

"Anything on the sensors, Morgan?" Grif tried to keep the concern out of his voice.

"Big rocks, floating through space," Morgan answered gruffly.

Grif grinned. Since he'd been commandeered by Velis, Morgan had been in a foul mood.

He has no one to blame but himself, Grif decided. *That's what happens when you notice a detail that all of the resources of a major galactic spy organization have managed to overlook.*

"Stupid spies," Morgan muttered.

Bennet, manning the communications station on the other side of the bridge, ignored him.

"Right," Grif said. "Well... please let me know if any of those rocks float in our direction. Ever been to Tyrelos, Bennet?"

"No," Bennet said. "Haven't done much in Trade Baron space. What's it like?"

"Nice place," Grif said. "Lots of interesting people... Morgan, pay attention."

A piece of rock about half the size of the *Fool's Errand* could be seen off the starboard side. It wasn't in danger of crossing the ship's path, but it also hadn't shown up on the tactical screens.

"What? Damn. Sorry." Morgan bent over the sensor station, frowning.

Grif sighed. This wasn't the time for him to be missing important data. Tyrelos Station was located in the middle of what once had been a moon of Obin, the system's gas giant. It had been torn apart by Obin's gravity relatively recently—"relatively" in terms of astronomical events, not human history—and the debris was in the process of forming a ring. The proto-ring was classified as "heavily concentrated," which meant that if you could see it through a view port it was probably too late to alter course to avoid it. It was a difficult area to navigate.

On the other hand, it was an excellent area to set up a mining operation, and ore extraction was one of Tylaris Industries' strong suits.

"Keep your eyes on the rocks, Morgan, that's all I'm asking right now," Grif said.

Morgan nodded. "Sorry Grif. I haven't quite figured out how to filter out all the extraneous information. It's a little crowded on my screen..."

They continued on in silence for a few minutes.

"The one thing I do know about Tyrelos," Bennet said, "though only because I just looked it up... there are no habitable planets in this system."

"Yeah," Grif said.

"Isn't that unusual, in this day and age?" Bennet asked.

"A little," Grif said. "Most people prefer to settle in systems that are easy. But Tyrelos Industries, they don't do easy. They specialize in hostile and exotic environments, ore extraction, mineral processing, and ridiculous feats of engineering. Wait till you see the capital..."

"You'd think a Trade Baron would find a more profitable system to claim as their own," Bennet said.

"I think House Tyrelos considers it a long-term project," Grif said. "Apparently there are minerals and gasses they extract from Obin that go into their more exotic alloys that they can't find anywhere else. At least, not easily... but you're right. This system is a bit of a money pit."

If Baron Tylaris was the richest and most powerful of the Trade Barons, Baron Tyrelos was the poorest. Tylaris owned four planetary systems, all with multiple life-bearing planets rich in natural resources; Tyrelos claimed one system only, with merely two colonized planets, neither of which could sustain life. While the Tyrelos system was rich in resources—perhaps, some speculated, one of the richest areas in known space, particularly for rare alloys and minerals—those resources were found in very inhospitable places: asteroid belts, planets with corrosive atmospheres, planets too close to the sun to sustain any permanent settlement, and frozen comets with temperatures nearing absolute zero.

The difference in fortune between the two Baronies was so pronounced, and their names were so similar, it was inevitable that Baron Tylaris and Baron Tyrelos would become the object of some sport. Tylaris was known as the man who had more than he deserved: he was rich because it was easy for him to be rich. It required little work to prosper on his nearly perfect worlds, some said, so his wealth came with little effort or risk. Baron Tyrelos, on the other hand, was thought of as someone who had to work very hard to earn what measure of profit she could... perhaps harder than what was warranted or fair. Thus Tylaris was known as the indolent layabout who did nothing and was rewarded for it, and Tyrelos as the hard worker who barely managed to eke out a profit at the end of the year. They were the embodiments of unearned success and undeserved struggle. As a result the Trade Baron systems had a saying: "the distance between luxury and hardship can be measured in two vowels."

In other words: life, by and large, wasn't fair.

Grif muttered a frustrated curse as his tactical screen blinked and a number of new objects appeared—far enough to compensate for their presence, but close enough to suggest they'd initially slipped Morgan's notice. "Amys..."

"Got 'em," Amys said. "Course adjusted." The tone of her voice suggested she wasn't happy with the last minute update either.

"Sorry..." Morgan muttered.

The bridge door opened. "Whoever you are," Grif said, keeping his eyes on his station, "you've picked a bad time to talk."

There was a brief pause, then someone said "right... sorry, I was just—"

"Do I know you?" Grif interrupted.

"Um, well Captain, we sort of met—"

"Evard, what are you doing on the bridge?" Bennet asked.

"Evard." Grif repeated. "That's a Terran name, isn't it?"

"Yes sir," Evard said. "Ganymede, born and bred."

"Bennet, is everyone in your group an Earthie but my sister?" Morgan chuckled. *Earthie* was a mildly derogatory term for Terrans. It was specifically used to describe Terrans who believed the Sol system was the birthplace of the entire galaxy minus four, but since most of the rest of the galaxy believed every Terran held that view, it was often used to describe the whole lot.

"Evard is from Ganymede," Bennet replied cooly.

"Planet Po*tay*to?" Grif asked. "Why no, it's planet Po*tah*to, thank you very much. Evard! What do you want? We're sort of busy."

"I... er... wanted to talk to Doctor Todd."

Grif frowned. "Who?"

Morgan grinned. "he means me, Grif. Remember? My previous life, back to bite me on the ass."

"Oh yes," Grif said. "Well—rocks, Morgan, you need to tag the rocks—well, uh... Evard..."

"Lyle," Evard said. "Dr. Evard Lyle."

"I wasn't fishing for you *name*, Evard," Grif said, punching in a new course to avoid a five hundred metric ton asteroid that was closing rapidly. "I was distracted by my attempt to avert the imminent destruction of my ship."

"Oh..." Evard sounded embarrassed. "I'm sorry Captai..."

"Look, Evard, I'm sure 'Doctor Todd' will be happy to talk to you after we've reached port, but right now he is *supposed to be looking for rocks*."

"I'm working on it!" Morgan protested.

"Well I know they're out there," Grif said, "because I keep seeing them FLY BY MY WINDOW. Of course, if I relied on my *tactical display*, I'd think I was flying through *deep space*. Silly of me to expect *technology* to assist me in this particularly *difficult*—"

Grif heard Amys swear, then swore himself as he received a new burst of navigation data that forced him to alter course very suddenly. The ship shuddered as her nullifer plates tried and failed to compensate for the extra inertia. Evard cried out in alarm, and Grif heard something hit the wall.

Grif punched the intercom, gritting his teeth. "This is your captain speaking," he said. "Sorry about that last bit, but you see, my sensor tech is BEING AN IDIOT."

He heard Morgan cursing under his breath.

"You all right there, Evard?" Grif asked.

"Uh. Ow." Evard sounded a little dazed. "I think I'll just... look for Dr. Todd later..."

"Good idea," Grif agreed.

"Look, Grif," Morgan said, "sorry about that, but these sensors—"

"Are still new," Grif said. "Yeah. I get that."

"So maybe if we slowed down a little—"

"Slowed down?" Grif asked.

"Yeah, just a little, and—"

"Slow down," Grif repeated. "now there's a thought. Amys, what is the slowest we've ever traveled through the proto-ring?"

"About this speed," Amys said. "But—"

"And was there ever a time when we went slower than this? In the *Fool's Errand*, I mean?"

"No," Amys said, "but I think Morgan has a—"

"And, let me ask you all this... is the speed and generally fearless nature of our approach to Tyrelos Station a topic of pleasant conversation every time we berth?"

"Grif," Amys said, clearly annoyed, "our reputation will mean nothing if we wind up—"

"Smashed into atoms, yes, I very much agree," Grif said. "Which is why I'd like Morgan to concentrate just *a little bit more* on the—"

"Rock!" Amys shouted.

Grif saw a rock out his view port. A moment later it appeared on tactical. *Too damn close.*

Grif yelped, then punched the intercom. "Cyrus!"

From the forward view port, the bridge crew could see a lance of brilliant yellow energy slam into the rock, breaking it up into thousands of smaller pieces.

"Screens, Amys!" Grif shouted, and a moment later the view ports went dark as the screens came up to full power.

The *Fool's Errand* shook as the screens were pounded by rock fragments moving at very high speed... but the screens held, and the ship managed to avoid the larger bits of rock that might have been a more serious threat.

Grif slowed the *Fool's Errand* down to a quarter its original speed. "You win," he said, shaken. "Morgan, take all the time you need."

Cyrus' voice came in through the intercom. "Grif, did we actually slow down?"

"Yes," Grif said. "It's Morgan's fault."

Ktk announced over the intercom that Cyrus owed it.

"Damn," Cyrus swore ruefully. "Grif, how could you do this to me?"

Amys laughed. "How many times has Ktk won betting against the Captain? Four, maybe five?"

"Every bug has its day, I guess," Grif said. "Uh... Amys... better check to see if anyone had a claim on that rock."

"Right." Amys accessed the navigation logs and waited. "No claim reported as of one month ago. That's the last time we updated the charts."

Grif sighed. "We'll have to report it, then, and hope for the best."

"What are you talking about?" Bennet asked.

"If you destroy a claim to avoid hitting a rock you have to reimburse the claim holder," Amys said.

"Yeah," Grif said, "and they usually inflate the worth of the rock quite a bit."

For the next twenty minutes they traveled in silence. The slower speed was, apparently, exactly what Morgan needed: there were no more issues with rocks. Grif relaxed slightly.

"Morgan, are we close enough to get a visual of Tyrelos Station?"

"Should be," Morgan said. "Especially with this new rig."

"Put it on the main display," Grif said. "Bennet's never seen it."

"Sure," Morgan said. A moment later: "Bennet, welcome to Tyrelos Station."

The display shifted, and Bennet gaped. "Ridiculous feats of engineering indeed..."

Tyrelos Station was huge. There was no other word to describe it.

It was a city built on one of the largest remaining rocks in the Obin proto-ring. It covered roughly a third of the rock, making the word "city" seem somehow inadequate. If it had been built on a planet it might have been mistaken as a land mass from orbit. The metropolis was everything you expected to see in a city, but cubed: towering buildings, sprawling urban complexes, elaborately designed parks, streets, houses, monorails, shops, offices... all enclosed in a transparent dome that glinted from Obin's reflected light.

The dome was a marvel of engineering, and one of the crown jewels of Tyrelos Industries. It was a transparent alloy that was strong enough to deflect the inevitable proto-ring rock collisions without, it seemed, so much as leaving a scratch. That alloy was in high demand for military-grade starcraft; even the Tylaris Shipyards preferred it when they could get it.

Apart from the city, but connected to it through a series of transport tunnels half-burrowed, half-engineered into the rock, were the Docks. These served as the landing, refueling, loading and unloading platforms for visiting ships. The transport tunnels gave the Docks direct access to the city. Ships that couldn't afford them had to simply float in space, accessing the city via a fleet of ferries that shuttled passengers to and fro daily.

Grif pushed his chair back along the rail just far enough to catch a glimpse at the look of amazement on Bennet's face, grinned, and slid back into his station. "Told you the capital was impressive."

"How do they get the dome to stay up?" Bennet asked.

"Beats the hell out of me," Morgan replied. "Ktk has a theory. It tried to explain it to me once, but I couldn't keep up with the math. It's impressive, though."

Bennet nodded in wordless agreement.

A short while later Bennet reported Tyrelos Station was hailing the *Fool's Errand*.

"Audio please," Grif said.

"*Fool's Errand*, this is Tyrelos Station Authority. Captain Vindh, good to see you in Tyrelos again."

"Thank you Authority, I'm here for supplies and will berth a few days. I can arrange to pay four days in advance. I authorize the transfer of funds from my standard account."

"Please wait while we verify the transaction." A second later the voice continued, "your transaction has been approved, Captain Vindh. Please follow the flight path we are sending your way. Your ship will be berthed at Dock 78. Enjoy your stay, Authority out."

"Always so professional," Grif said. "You'd never know half those guys were on the sauce."

Chapter 15

WHEREIN Our Hero Learns Of Yet Another Complication

When Amys, Grif, Morgan and Bennet entered Bay One they saw Cyrus and Ktk standing by the lift, arguing.

"Six hours," Cyrus insisted.

Ktk chittered in disagreement, insisting it would be at least twelve.

"All right then," Cyrus said. "That's the wager—six hours or less, I win. Twelve or more, you win. Anything in between is a draw."

Ktk agreed.

"What are they betting on?" Bennet asked.

Grif shrugged and looked at the group. "Only six of us? I expected more enthusiasm. This is as close to shore leave as we'll get in a while..."

"It's Hari's turn to stay on board," Cyrus said. "Cutter, Gurgan and Vod are keeping him company."

"OK," Grif said. "Let's go."

Tyrelos Station was actually two separate cities sharing the same location. The first city, built before the dome was erected, was tunneled into the rock itself and consisted of sealed, airtight buildings leading to an underground complex that delved deep into the rock. The second city appeared after the dome had been built and there was no longer a need for self-contained environments. The second city was more traditional in design, with buildings that rose high into the air instead of deep into the ground.

Most of the city infrastructure was located in the first city. Everything Grif found interesting was located in the second.

Grif, Cyrus, Amys, Ktk, Morgan and Bennet were in the second city, slowly making their way out of the transport hub that serviced Docks 71-80 and into the city proper. The view was spectacular. The dome provided a clear view of Obin, including some of its more prominent storms, and a swath of what appeared to be stars (but were actually fragments from the proto-ring) spread across the sky like a shining belt. The second city had no true day or night cycle: light that came through the dome was reflected off Obin, which was always visible, and bathed the city in a state of perpetual twilight. Most of the city supplemented this natural light with light fixtures, but some parts did not. Those were dangerous neighbourhoods, and people who had to walk through them didn't do so alone or unarmed.

The second city was filled with noise: noise from business storefronts advertising their goods, noises from tinned music pumped in through speakers outside of bars, noises from the air cars and grav sleds racing through the air, and noise from the citizens and visitors all talking, laughing, arguing, and occasionally spilling blood.

They made their way to a Metroline terminal and waited for the bus to appear. It did, eventually, floating a few meters over the ground traffic and slowly coming to rest on the loading platform. It was only partially full, and they were all able to sit together in the middle of the bus.

"Where are we going?" Bennet asked. He looked dazed, apparently overwhelmed by the chaotic nature of the city.

"Bar," Grif said. "Good place to relax. And do business."

"Relax *and* do business?" Bennet asked, raising an eyebrow. "Odd combination."

Ktk replied that perhaps Bennet needed to find more enjoyable work.

Bennet stared at it blankly.

Grif smirked.

Bennet looked at the others for a moment, then shrugged apologetically. "We don't run into too many of them in Alliance space, and when we do they're wearing voxes. Perhaps if Ktk would agree to wear one for the rest of this trip, my people could—"

Ktk chittered angrily.

"Ktk doesn't like them too much," Cyrus said. "Says they make it sound too cheerful all the time. Besides, we understand it just fine."

"Ah, so you all speak, ah, 'bug' then, do you?"

"Well... we understand it," Grif said. "Bugtalk is pretty tedious when it comes to sentence construction. It's a binary language that starts with the total sum of all knowledge and drills down through it until it isolates the specific thought or concept the bug is trying to say."

The Metroline bus settled down onto a boarding platform and opened its doors. Grif, Amys, Morgan, Cyrus, Bennet and Ktk left the bus and headed down the street.

Dyorbid's Tavern sat near one of the poorer ports in the city. The port didn't offer dedicated umbilical connections to starships: it employed a number of ferries that went back and forth between the ships berthed in the area, picking up and depositing travellers as necessary. Grif looked up through the dome and saw perhaps 30 or 40 ships docked there.

"Hey," he said, squinting at one of the ships floating beyond the dome, "does that look like the *Dominion* to anyone else?"

Amys looked up. "Where?"

Grif pointed. "Just to the right of Obin's third band. See? Three engines."

"Hell," Amys said. "I think you're right. It does look like the *Dominion*."

Cyrus looked up, squinted, and nodded in agreement.

"What are you looking at?" Bennet asked.

"Kung frigate," Cyrus muttered. "That means slavers."

"Come on," Grif said, and entered the bar.

Dyorbid's was dark, crowded, humid, and seedy. A constant murmur of voices filled the air as people talked to each other hunched over small tables. Dim glow-globes dotted the tables, weakly illuminating the tables they rested on but going no further. The music was canned, of course—Dyorbid was too stingy to pay live musicians, and none of the patrons were interested in that kind of entertainment, anyway—and the drink, while potent, was cheaply made. It was the kind of place, Grif was fond of saying, where a glass of Stellis was considered a "classy drink."

Dyorbid was tending bar, his four, thick yellow arms all moving, all apparently engaged in performing completely separate tasks. He looked up when Grif and his crew entered and nodded briefly, blue-gray eyes atop long yellow stalks swaying gently as he did. A few other regulars noticed them as well, and one or two raised a glass in greeting.

"All right. Cyrus, Ktk, find someone with cargo to sell," Grif said. "*Legit* cargo. I'll find a table."

Cyrus nodded, and followed Ktk as it scuttled up to the bar to ask Dyorbid what he knew. Grif threaded his way through the crowd of patrons until he came across a table that a waitress—human—was just beginning to clear. Grif sat down hastily, grinning at the woman as she finished wiping down the table. She smiled back.

"What can I get you, handsome?" The waitress asked.

Amys sat next to Grif, smirking. Morgan chuckled and took the chair to Grif's left, leaving Bennet to sit in the chair facing him.

"A glass of something that won't kill me outright," Grif said. "Dyorbid still have any of that god-awful gin?"

"I don't know," the waitress said. "I'm pretty new. But I'll be happy to check. What about the rest of you?"

Amys ordered whiskey—the only thing she was willing to drink here, she claimed—and Bennet, apprehensive, did the same.

"Carumjak," Morgan said when it was his turn. "I'll take the bottle."

The waitress shuddered. "Your funeral, pops." Then, turning back to Grif, she said "I'll check on that gin for you." She winked, smiled slyly, then made her way back to the bar.

"It's about time Dyorbid actually hired an attractive waitress," Morgan said. Grif laughed.

"Well, hold on," Grif said, "let's be fair. The Murdec who worked here a few months back was very attractive... to other Murdecs."

"She had a thing for you too," Amys said, still smirking. "I think that's why you like it here—all the waitresses swoon over you."

"If they all looked like her," Grif replied, "that would be the only reason I'd need."

Morgan laughed at that. Bennet smiled slightly.

"The problem," Grif said, "is that Nengit like their females big-armed. And they tend to assume everyone else does too..."

"Speaking of that," Morgan said, looking around, "where is Hilda?"

"Got married." The new waitress had returned with a glass of whiskey for Amys and Bennet, a bottle and a glass for Morgan, and a glass of gin for Grif. "She's on her honeymoon... that's why I got hired, I guess. Dyorbid was a little short-handed." She laughed at her own joke.

"Hilda got married?" Morgan asked, surprised. "Who's the lucky groom?"

The waitress shrugged. "I never met her, how would I know him? Anyway, they're taking a honeymoon. Back in a month, I hear. Hope I can keep this job when she comes back..."

Grif smiled. "Well, I'll put in a good word for you," he said. "Miss, uh..."

"Velis," the waitress said. "Velis Sark."

Grif's smile froze on his face. Morgan blinked. Amys choked on her Whiskey.

"What was that?" Bennet asked.

"Velis," the waitress said again. "Hey, are you all right?" She peered at Grif closely. "You look a little ill..."

"I'm... fine..." Grif said with a pained expression on his face. "It's just the gin..."

"I'm not surprised," the waitress said. Leaning closer, she whispered, "just between you and me, the drinks here aren't very good."

She smiled, straightened, winked at Grif again, and then went to check on another table.

Morgan snickered.

"Shut up," Grif said.

Amys burst out laughing.

"Oh, for..." Grif looked from Amys to Morgan, who was now red-faced and wheezing, and then at Bennet, who was grinning broadly.

He sighed. "Of all the possible names in known space..."

"Aw." Amys patted Grif on the cheek in mock sympathy.

"For some reason," Morgan said, still wheezing, "I don't see the rest of the night going quite the way Grif was planning."

"Drink your poison," Grif growled.

Morgan continued to snicker as he opened the bottle and poured a brackish-colored liquid into his glass. "To Grif and Velis," he said, raising his glass. Amys raised hers in response, and they both toasted their scowling captain.

Morgan drained his glass without so much as wincing. "How can you drink that?" Grif asked, looking for a chance to change the subject. "It'll kill you, you know."

"Yes," Morgan said agreeably. "It's vile, and if you drink more than a glass or two—well, four or five, in my case—you'll die on the spot. But it grows on you."

"Well keep it away from me," Grif said. "I don't understand why everyone calls me the crazy one when you drink that stuff like it was water."

"Well, that's easy. You're the one who—" Morgan stopped in mid-sentence as he focused on something behind Grif. He frowned.

"Grif," he said, gesturing with this glass. "The news..."

Grif turned in his seat and found that a wall screen had been activated. It was a news program, and as an Invagi woman stared out from the screen with a grave expression on her face, an overlay read "SPECIAL NEWS REPORT—TYLARIS PRIME." A picture of Baron Mogra Tylaris and his son Rolis were displayed in the upper right-hand corner of the screen.

"Died today at the age of sixty-eight," the Invagi woman was saying. "Official cause of death is reported to be a fast-acting blood infection as the result of eating improperly prepared food. Baron Tylaris was known to be particularly fond of exotic foods, specifically vokh intestines. Tylaris officials reacted with shock and dismay to the announcement."

Grif was stunned. "Baron Tylaris is dead?"

The Invagi news anchor continued talking. "The Tylaris Barony is the largest of all Trade Baron empires, and is famous for its advanced shipbuilding facilities. At this time it isn't known whether the industries that make the Tylaris Barony so powerful will be affected by his death—"

There was an uneasy murmur as the patrons in the bar considered the prospect of upheaval in the Tylaris systems.

"—but in a short statement made earlier today, Rolis Tylaris, heir to the Tylaris Barony, claimed there would be no immediate changes to the day-to-day operations of his father's holdings."

The screen cut to a picture of Rolis, a thin, foppish man with a weak chin and watery eyes. "My father did much to secure the success and prosperity of this Barony," he said in a clear, thin voice.

Amys snorted. Baron Tylaris wasn't thought of as a particularly driven man—very canny, but he'd preferred to set things up once and leave them to run themselves, while he indulged himself with various vices.

"I intend," Rolis continued, "to see to it that the Tylaris Barony becomes even greater than the one my father built. In his name and in his memory, I can do no less."

The image of Rolis disappeared, replaced by the Invagi anchorwoman behind her desk.

"Other than that statement, delivered a short time ago in front of the

Tylaris estate, the only other comment from the new Baron Tylaris was an expression of shock and dismay that his father was taken at such a comparatively young age."

Grif looked around the room. Everyone looked shocked and a little worried. Whenever a Barony went through a succession of power, even under the most benign circumstances, there was almost always an attempted coup. These things were usually done as discreetly as possible. The source of a Trade Baron's power was business, after all, and disrupting that business in order to gain power was counter-productive—but the independents, not directly tied to any of the Trade Baron businesses, were usually in danger of getting caught in the middle of such things.

The only person who didn't look concerned, Grif noticed, was Bennet. In fact, he thought, Bennet didn't even look particularly surprised: he was watching the newscast with an expression that might be considered casual to most, but to Grif screamed "poker face."

Grif frowned. Bennet looked at him for a moment, then looked away quickly, examining the room in apparent bored disinterest.

The newscast switched to a short biography of Baron Tylaris' life, and the patrons turned their attention back to their tables, each table buzzing excitedly.

"Improperly prepared food," Morgan said, turning his gaze back to his companions. "I can't believe it."

"No?" Grif asked. "Why?"

"Well..." Morgan frowned. "The Baron always hired the best, didn't he? That was his thing. I can't believe he'd hire a cook who didn't know how to prepare his food properly."

"Accidents happen," Amys said. "If you're going to eat something that kills you—or drink it, for that matter," she added, gesturing to Morgan's bottle of Carumjak, "sooner or later you'll pay for it."

Morgan looked at his bottle dubiously. Then he shrugged, grinned and filled another glass, raising it into the air. "To the Baron," he said.

Grif and Amys raised their glasses. "Hear, hear," Grif said. "To the Baron."

Bennet, Grif noticed, did not join in the toast.

"Still," Grif said slowly, "it seems kind of strange, don't you think? A man in his sixties isn't particularly old—especially when you're one of the richest men who ever lived and can afford the best doctors in the—"

"Tester," said a gravelly voice by his ear.

Grif turned and saw a black, indistinct shape standing in front of him. His eyes slid around the edges of the creature. The only noticeable feature on it was the slightly luminescent set of goggles it wore somewhere near its head. Grif grinned.

"N'grash," he said. "Captain N'grash—good to see you. Come and join us."

"No, Tester," N'Grash said, "we must talk. In private. It is important."

N'grash was the captain of the *Grlashimargrak*, a vessel that engaged mostly in piracy, though she also dabbled in smuggling from time to time. She and Grif had been friends for years, and if she said she needed to talk to him privately, he was certain it was important.

Grif looked at the others. "I'll be right back," he said. "Go check on Cyrus and Ktk, see if they've found us any cargo."

Grif followed N'grash deeper into the bar.

N'grash was Ggrlshan, a carnivore race from a high-gravity world that was nearly always dark to the human eye. Their fur partially absorbed most light, which made them very hard to see clearly in a dimly lit room. Short and powerfully built, they had evolved from a race of predators and still displayed many of the same instincts and mannerisms.

There were many back rooms in Dyorbid's. N'grash had reserved one in advance and stepped inside, motioning for Grif to follow. She closed the door behind them and pulled herself up on a chair next to a table. Grif sat down across from her.

"What's up?" Grif asked. "I have to say, this isn't very encouraging..."

"It is not, Tester..." N'grash's expression was unreadable in this light, but she sounded concerned. "It is bad news. Very, very bad news."

Grif felt a twinge of uneasiness.

"You are being hunted," N'grash said. "By a Sword."

Chapter 16

WHEREIN A Previous Disagreement Is Finally Resolved

Grif leaned back and stared at N'grash doubtfully. "Really. A Sword."

"A Sword," N'grash repeated. "He is known as the Viceroy. You are in danger, Tester."

N'grash's people had a tradition of *labeling* everyone they knew. It was, N'grash claimed, an attempt to know the essence of another's soul. Grif's soul, it seemed, was hard to label—or was non-existent, as N'grash occasionally claimed—because she was never satisfied with any label she chose. When they'd first met she called him "Trickster," then "Jester." She found neither label satisfactory, and would occasionally replace it with a new one: "Mocker." "Liar." "Madman." "Fool." Lately she had taken to calling him "Tester," because, she said, he insisted on testing the boundaries of everything and everyone he met.

"The Viceroy?" Grif frowned. "Never heard of him. Name's a bit ostentatious, though, isn't it? Nothing like a little hubris to start off your day..."

A low growl of frustration escaped N'grash's throat as she leaned forward, half-rising out of her chair. "This is not a joke, Tester. I know of this one—not personally, but by reputation."

Grif fell silent. N'grash had surprisingly accurate sources of information, and her sense of humor didn't lend itself to pranks along these lines. If N'grash was telling him this, it was because she had a strong reason to believe it was true: and if she had a strong reason to believe it was true, it probably was.

"The Viceroy..." N'grash made a growling, gurgling sound deep in her throat. "He is very dangerous."

"That was implied when you said he was a Sword," Grif said.

"He is dangerous, even among Swords," N'grash snapped. "He is rumored to report directly to their Emperor. Very powerful. His sorcery is very strong."

Ggrlsha were not, as a rule, psionically gifted, and tended to view the trait as a form of dream-magic. Which, as far as Grif was concerned, wasn't really too far off the mark.

"All right," Grif said. "I believe you. But why me?"

N'grash's laughter sounded like a hundred dogs barking at the same time. "Your recent success, Tester. They wish to know how you broke into Ur Voys, and the Viceroy plans to... *extract* the information."

"Well," Grif said, "that's... just... *perfect*."

N'grash stared at Grif silently, trying to work out what he meant. Finally she added, "there is a rumor that he will arrive here."

Grif closed his eyes and swore softly. "When?"

"Soon," N'grash said. "Surely you expected this?"

"No, not really." Grif stood, stretched, and started to pace the small room, agitated. "I figured Mavis would want to kill me, but honestly I didn't think much farther than all that damn money falling into my lap."

N'grash laughed again. "Foolish," she said. "But understandable. The lure of that wealth would make many throw caution to the wind." The way she said it implied that she did not consider herself part of that group.

Grif sighed. This was the last thing he needed right now. If he could put it off until this current mess was over and done with, he'd deal with it then. Or he'd be dead, which would also solve the problem.

"You need to run," N'grash said. "To Alliance space, where it will be easier for you to move than it will be for a Sword. Perhaps he will give up. Perhaps you can fake your death. I do not know. I know I would regret to see you killed."

"Me too," Grif muttered. "Unfortunately, I'm otherwise..." he let the sentence trail off, then shrugged. "I just can't."

N'grash snorted in frustration. "Do not think you can *fight* him," she said. "Even the Amazon would fall against him in a fight."

"I've never seen Amys lose a fight," Grif said.

"She would lose this fight," N'grash insisted.

"Well, look, I don't want to fight him." Grif threw up his hands in frustration. "I... look, do me a favor. Spread it around that I'm going into Alliance space to follow a big score. If anyone asks what, just tell them you have no idea, but add that I'm pretty excited about it."

N'grash stared at Grif thoughtfully. "You are planning to return to Throne Space," she said finally.

Grif didn't reply.

N'grash shook her head slowly. "I suppose you will refuse to tell me why."

"I'd love to tell you why," Grif said. "Can't. If I get back alive it'll be one hell of a story."

N'grash said nothing. Grif fidgeted.

Finally N'grash nodded. "Very well, Tester. I will tell your lie."

Grif sighed in relief. "Thanks," he said. "That should buy me a little time..."

N'grash nodded again, stood, and turned to leave.

"Hold on a minute," Grif said. "I want to tell you something else. Unrelated, but important."

N'grash turned back to look at Grif.

Grif closed his eyes and, for a second, felt uneasy about what he was going to say. When he opened his eyes, uncertainty was replaced with resolve.

"The Alliance killed Baron Tylaris."

N'grash went rigid, her ears standing on end. "If you jest, Tester, it is in poor taste..."

"Not joking," Grif said.

"They claim he died from tainted meat," N'grash replied.

"The meat had help," Grif insisted. "Look, N'grash, I don't have any proof. None. But I'm almost one hundred percent certain. And if I'm right Tylaris isn't going to be a particularly friendly place for people like you and me. More you than me, though..."

"Yes," N'grash agreed. "I will think on what you say, Tester. I will think on it very carefully."

"All right," Grif said. "Thanks for the warning. I'll be careful."

N'grash snorted. "You will not," she said. "But perhaps now you will at least be *watchful*."

Grif grinned. Together they stepped back out into the main room.

Morgan, Amys and Bennet had moved to a larger table in the middle of the room, joined by Cyrus and Ktk and some of the crew of the *Grlashimargrak*. N'grash's crew were mostly non-humans from high gravity worlds. One of them, a Nengit, was arm-wrestling Cyrus. To Cryus' credit, he wasn't losing too badly.

When Grif and N'grash reached the table, Cyrus relented. The Nengit, Rask, raised one arm in victory as the other three flexed.

"You're a showoff," Cyrus said, grinning.

"And you are buying the next round!" Rask rumbled.

Grif sat down to join them, trying to put N'grash's warning out of his mind for the moment. He waived the waitress down for a drink.

"Stellis," he said, ignoring the way Amys wrinkled her nose in distaste. "A strong one."

"OK handsome," the waitress replied. Grif shifted uncomfortably. Amys, Morgan, Bennet and Cyrus laughed, while Ktk chittered its amusement.

The waitress looked to Cyrus. "Can I tell him now?"

Cyrus nodded, grinning.

"Tell me?" Grif looked from Cyrus to the waitress, then back to Cyrus. "Tell me *what*?"

"My name," the waitress said. "Your big friend offered me a hundred standard if I flirted with you and told you my name was Velis. My real name is Ela."

The entire table roared. Grif, caught between a grin and a glare, fixed his eyes on Cyrus. Cyrus laughed so hard his face turned bright red.

"Oh, Cyrus," Grif said, smiling broadly, "you are going to *pay* for that."

"Sorry Grif," Cyrus said, wiping tears from his eyes as he gasped for breath. "The minute I saw her, I couldn't resist. It was... beautiful."

"Brilliant," Amys agreed. "Absolutely brilliant."

Ela looked at them in confusion. Grif stood, turned to her, and bowed.

"I'm sorry, my dear," he said. "It seems my friends have used you as an unwitting pawn in their mind games. Perhaps at some point in the future I can make it up to you—"

"It will have to be at some point in the *very near* future." A loud voice cut through the din of the bar. "Because after that, Captain Vindh, you won't have much of a future to speak of."

Grif flinched. Everyone at the table stared at something behind him. He turned around.

Standing at the entrance was a group of roughly twenty humans. The term "human," in this case, was used loosely. The Kung were known for three things: their skill at robotics, their enthusiastic embrace of slavery as a commercial venture, and their tendency to replace parts of their body with machinery. The man who called Grif's name was very tall, nearly as tall as Cyrus, and half metal. He had a slightly oversized, nasty looking metal arm protruding from his right shoulder socket, and a sensor mount where his left eye should have been.

"Slavers," Cyrus muttered in disgust.

"Ah," Grif said. "Captain Orrith. How wonderful to see you."

"You've got a lot of nerve, coming back here," Orrith said. His right eye narrowed.

Grif looked around the room. The other patrons in the bar were slowly moving back against the walls.

"Nerve is sort of what I'm known for," Grif said. "How's the *Dominion* running these days? Hope you got it fixed up after that little—"

One of the other men—Burek, the *Dominion's* engineer—started forward angrily. Orrith held him back.

"You got lucky," Orrith growled. "For some reason, I didn't expect you to play pirate *on my ship*!"

"Funny," Grif answered cooly, "for some reason I didn't expect you to believe I'd hang about and do nothing when you tried to *sell my nephew into slavery*."

"I was going to sell him back to you," Orrith spat. "I'd no quarrel with you, Vindh. It was just business. Then you attacked my ship and made off with my cargo."

"Well, that was the difference," Grif explained. "For me, it wasn't business at all. It was just personal."

"Now it's personal for me," Orrith said. "I want your blood, Vindh. After your blood, maybe I'll take your ship. Or your woman," he added, leering at Amys.

"Oh, *please*." Grif rolled his eyes. "Amys hasn't been 'my woman' for years, and if you really feel like losing that other eye, by all means try—I think it would be *fascinating* to hear a man your size *shriek like a little girl*."

Amys sauntered up to Grif's left. She made a slight motion with her hand, and a vibroknife appeared at her side, buzzing softly.

N'grash padded up to Grif's right and growled in a low tone. "Leave, Orrith. I cannot afford what it will cost to clean this bar of your blood."

The low hum Grif heard behind him meant Dyorbid had activated the old-model plasma rifle he kept behind his bar. "Get out of here, Orrith," Dyorbid boomed. "I told you before—you and your crew are no longer welcome here."

Orrith smiled contemptuously and made no effort to leave.

"Right..." Grif's hand moved slowly to his holster.

"Three hours, fifty minutes," Cyrus said. "Pay me, bug!"

A flash of silver arced across the room over the top of Grif's head. Another flash of silver, this time in the other direction, as Amys threw her knife. Then the room exploded into a frenzy.

Grif smelled the telltale scent of ozone and threw himself to the ground as heat seared across the back of his neck. The table to his right erupted in a white-hot ball of plasma, and Grif rolled away, desperately trying to avoid the splash.

"Dammit, Dyorbid!" Grif backed up against another table and struggled to get his pistol out of its holster. The latch was caught.

Orrith swore in pain as Amys' knife tore through his shoulder, then swore again as the knife burrowed deep into the man behind him. Tables overturned, and beams of energy streaked across the room, hitting other overturned tables. The crowd not directly involved with the fighting panicked and surged for the exits.

Amys crouched low, two more knives in her hands. N'grash leaped halfway across the room and landed on a Kung slaver, ripping into his face with her claws. Grif worked his pistol out of its holster and started in surprise as the table he'd been leaning against shattered, crushed by the now-limp form of a slaver. Grif thought he heard Cyrus say "sorry."

Grif crawled across the floor, looking for another table. He saw Ktk leap across the room, heedless of enemy fire, and land behind the tables the slavers had erected as barriers. It grabbed three of the slavers by the neck with its tails and swung them around, nearly effortlessly, using them as clubs against their comrades.

Grif saw Orrith fighting four of Dyorbid's bouncers. He got up into a crouch and raised his weapon.

"Get down!" Bennet shouted.

Something heavy hit Grif from behind, knocking him back to the ground. Another blast of plasma lanced past, destroying yet another table and spraying semi-molten alloy throughout the room.

Bennet pulled himself off Griff and grimaced. "Sorry."

Griff rolled to the side as a chair crashed on to the floor between them, then bounced away. "That's OK," he said, checking his gun to make sure it wasn't damaged. "Thanks."

"Don't thank me," Bennet said, lashing out with his foot. A slaver grunted in surprise and fell to the floor. Without hesitating, Bennet jabbed an elbow to the slaver's exposed neck. "Your sister will kill me if you die early."

Grif laughed, then yelped as one of Ktk's makeshift clubs landed on top of the slaver Bennet had just incapacitated. Grif noticed he was still alive; his gaze shifted from the fallen man to his pistol, then he shrugged and pulled the trigger. The pulse hit the side of the slaver's head, killing him instantly.

"Not sporting," Bennet said. "Not very sporting at—"

An alloyed boot smashed down on the small of his back. Bennet's eyes widened in pain, mouth working wordlessly. The alloyed boot kicked Bennet in the side, then stepped over him toward Grif.

Grif looked up and saw a slaver, skin mottled with splotches of chromed metal.

"Er... hi, Patch," Grif said. "Long time."

Patch didn't reply. Grif scuttled backward across the floor, raised his gun, and fired. He missed; a light fixture on the ceiling exploded in a shower of sparks. He fired again, and the shot went wide, burning into the wall with a hiss. The third shot missed Patch's head by a matter of centimeters. Patch didn't so much as flinch.

"Steady," Grif muttered, forced himself not to panic, took aim, and pulled the trigger.

Nothing happened.

Son of a bitch.

Grif tried to roll away, but Patch was faster: he leaped through the air, and an alloyed boot landed directly on Grif's left elbow. Grif heard something crunch. Ice cold pain rushed through his arm.

Patch laughed. Grif heard something whistling through the air, then felt a crushing pain in his side as something hit him. Turning onto his back, Grif saw Patch holding a heavy, chromed baton in his hand.

Patch raised the baton again, then grunted in surprise as another one of Ktk's discarded clubs smashed into him. Grif scrambled to his feet, bending his left arm gingerly. He could use it, but it hurt like hell. He expected it would be pretty useless as soon as the adrenaline wore off.

Patch shoved the body off him and got to his feet. Grif stepped back and stumbled over the remains of a chair. He kept to his feet, and jumped to the side as Patch swung his baton, narrowly missing Vindh's head. Grabbing the baton at both ends, Patch charged: Grif felt the air leave his body as Patch slammed him against a wall. Grif was pinned against the wall by his neck.

He clawed at the baton, but Patch was too strong. He kicked. His foot hit something solid: not Patch, but Dyorbid's bar. A few bottles still stood upright on the counter top.

Patch laughed. "You're turnin' blue, Vindh."

It was getting hard to see. Grif reached out with his left arm, trying to ignore the pain. His fingers closed around the neck of a bottle, and he swung it at the slaver's head with all his strength.

The bottle didn't break. It bounced out of Grif's hand and fell to the floor, bouncing two or three more times before resting under a barstool. Patch swore and dropped his baton as he bent over, clutching his head. Grif picked up the baton and swung it overhead, bringing it down on the back of Patch's skull. Patch fell.

Grif bent over, coughing up blood, and tried to remember how to breathe.

He was out of the main fight for the moment. The firefight had ended and turned into a huge, chaotic melee. Grif saw Amys, briefly, dancing between two slavers as one fell, a look of mute surprise frozen on his face. He didn't see N'grash, but he heard her: she was howling, a fierce, feral sound, and cries of fear and alarm followed wherever the sound went. Cyrus towered over the melee, bleeding from gashes in his arms and face, but showing no signs of tiring.

"Oh, good," Grif said. "Everyone is doing well but me."

"Very true, Captain Vindh," Orrith said.

Grif looked up. The slaver captain stood behind the bar. One arm hung uselessly at his side, but the other arm—the cybernetic one—held Dyorbid's plasma rifle.

He could easily fire that thing one-handed, Grif realized.

"I thought Amys killed you," Grif said.

Orrith sneered. "You wish."

"Yes," Grif said. "I really do." He felt his legs buckle, and he slumped back against the wall, sliding slowly down to the floor.

Orrith fired once into the air, scarring the ceiling with a bolt of plasma. The room quieted as he re-trained the rifle on Grif.

"I have Captain Vindh in my sights," Orrith warned. " I suggest you stand down."

Ktk released its last club, body falling to the floor with a wet thud. Cyrus glowered, but didn't move. Amys dropped her knives on the floor, expressionless, and N'grash remained perfectly still, watching. Other crew from the *Grlashimargrak* reluctantly threw various weapons to the ground. Rask folded both sets of arms and glared.

"Good," Orrith said. He smiled at Grif, revealing chromed teeth. "Captain Vindh, I find myself facing something of a moral dilemma."

"Shocking," Grif said. "And by 'shocking,' I mean 'isn't it shocking that you know words with more than one syllable?'"

Orrith's smile froze in place. "Perhaps I could allow pleasure to overcome my business ethics. Just this once. I'm not convinced you'd draw much of a price, at any rate. Perhaps, after your mind was wiped, you could be sold as a plaything. Or might be set up to stud a merchant's private stock..."

The slaver's gaze drifted to Amys. "She, however... she will fetch a *fortune*. The reconditioning process will be expensive, but worth every standard. She will be highly sought after as a bodyguard..."

Grif noticed the plasma rifle dip slightly.

Orrith glanced at Cyrus and Ktk. "The rest of your crew is something of a mystery. Cyrus might fetch a fair price as a laborer. The bug, however... there is no market for bugs. We might as well kill it now."

The plasma rifle dipped even lower.

"Get bent," Bennet said.

Orrith frowned as he tried to locate the unfamiliar voice. "Who said that?" The sensor in place of his left eye glowed blue in the dim light as he scanned the crowd. The plasma rifle shifted a little to the left.

Bennet lifted his head off the spot where he'd fallen. "Over here... Orrith, is it? And I said 'get bent.'" Bennet glanced at Grif and gestured slightly to his left. Grif nodded.

"Who are you?" Orrith demanded. The plasma rifle drifted even further left.

"That's not important," Bennet said. "At least, it isn't important right now..."

On the word "now," Grif dove to his right, trying to reach a table. Orrith's attention snapped back to Grif, firing hastily. The table exploded, and Grif screamed as plasma and metal shrapnel tore through his left side.

A dark object shot away from Bennet, slid across the floor, and landed in Grif's good hand. It was a pistol. As Orrith brought the plasma rifle to bear, Grif gritted his teeth, sat upright, and shot first.

The pulse hit Orrith in his damaged shoulder, staggering him. Orrith's shot went wild. Grif forced himself to stand as he fired again, hitting Orrith in the chest. Orrith roared in pain; he tried to re-aim his rifle but his metal arm twitched erratically.

Shouting in a mixture of agony and rage, Grif ran toward the slaver captain, pulling the trigger of his pistol over and over again, as fast as he could manage. Orrith fell back, disappearing behind the bar, and with a final rush of adrenaline Grif leaped over the top of the bar, firing into the slaver's motionless body the entire time.

He didn't stop shooting until the gun was empty. He fired pulse after pulse until the only sound in the bar was the "charge depleted" buzz the gun emitted each time he pulled the trigger. When he finally came to his senses he realized the entire bar was watching him in stunned silence.

Breathing heavily, he fumbled with the gun as he tried to put it in his holster. He missed the holster entirely, and the gun clattered uselessly to the ground.

"I think he's dead," Grif said.

"I think so," Bennet said, gingerly picking himself off the floor.

Grif looked at what was left of the *Dominion's* crew. "We win," he said. "Get out."

A wave of pain and nausea washed over him. The next thing he knew he was staring at the ceiling. Bennet, Amys, and Cyrus stood over him, looking concerned.

"I don't feel very well," Grif mumbled.

"That's all right," Bennet said, "you look *terrible.*" Grif tried to laugh, and wound up gagging instead. "Am I on fire? I feel like I'm on fire..."

Someone said "plasma." Amys frowned.

"Grif," she said, "we need you to stand up. *Now.*"

Amys' face blurred slightly. Grif squinted. "Yeah? Uh, no thanks..."

"Grif." Amys' voice grew sharp. "This is important. *Stand up.*" There was something in her voice Grif couldn't place. She sounded... *worried.* Something in the back of his head reminded him he usually paid attention when she sounded like that. He tried to sit, but the attempt made him gag. He rolled over on to his side and vomited.

"No," he said, "I really don't like that plan. At all."

"Grif..." Amys sounded more than worried, now. The part of Grif that wasn't numb from pain was surprised to discover that she actually sounded frightened. "Grif, we have to get you out of here..."

"Right..." Grif took a deep breath. "Well, I'm pretty sure that's a good idea... but if you don't mind, I think I'll pass out first."

Then he passed out.

Chapter 17

WHEREIN Our Hero Awakens in a Strange Place, to Familiar Circumstances

When Grif regained consciousness he realized two things:

First, the smell told him he was in some kind of medical bay. Second, the smell also told him it wasn't the medical bay on board the *Fool's Errand.*

He tried to sit up, but couldn't. He was strapped down to something: first he thought he'd been tied to a bed, but a moment later he realized he was actually attached to a device that ran down the side of his bed, covering his left arm and part of his chest. He panicked as he realized he couldn't feel his left arm.

"Don't move," someone said.

Grif lifted his head and tried to focus on the direction of the voice. He saw a white blurry figure to his right, in a moment the blurry figure sharpened into a man in a medical uniform looking at a monitor at the foot of his bed. He looked up at Grif and smiled politely.

"Moving your head is still moving," the man said, a hint of amusement in his voice.

Grif sank back into his pillow and stared up at the ceiling. The white light panels set in gleaming white tiles filled the room with bright, white light.

"Disorientation is normal," the man said. "Especially considering how long you've been under. We had to immobilize parts of your body to speed the healing process along. You probably feel a little numb over there right now—that's normal. We're re-growing your shoulder, and we haven't unblocked the nerves yet."

"Re-growing?" Grif's voice was cracked and hoarse. He wanted a drink.

The man nodded. "You were pretty banged up when they brought you in here... plasma eating through what was left of your arm and shoulder. Seeping into your side, too; you were lucky you got here when you did. We also had to extract a fair amount of shrapnel out of your body. Someone wasn't fond of you."

Grif thought back. "Yeah."

"It was easier to re-grow the shoulder than try and put it back together." The man looked at Grif, then the monitor, then at his watch. "I guess I'll let your friend know you're awake. She's been here a while."

The doctor turned to leave. As he reached the door, he stopped and looked over his shoulder. "Don't try to get up," he warned. "Regrowing an arm is complicated, and you've only been credited for one."

With that, the man left.

Only credited for one? Grif wondered who had credited him for it in the first place. Re-growing bones, muscle and skin was expensive.

The door opened again. Grif lifted his head and saw Amys walk into the room, smiling slightly.

"You don't look dead," she said. "I guess that's a good thing."

Grif grinned. "Matter of opinion I guess. I expect Mavis would disagree. How long have I been here?" His voice was still hoarse but getting stronger.

"About a week," Amys said. Seeing the look of alarm on his face, she added, "it was because they were re-growing your shoulder. It's almost finished now."

"They?" Grif asked. "Who is 'they,' exactly? I assume it's not 'us,' because this doesn't look like a hospital we could afford..."

Amys didn't answer.

"You know, Amys, whenever you don't answer I tend to assume you're trying to find a way to put bad news in the best possible light."

"I am."

"Oh, good." Grif leaned his head back on his pillow and steeled himself. "So where are we, exactly?"

"We're in one of the restricted access recovery wards in the first city... it's a MediCorp facility. Fairly close to the Tyrelos estate..."

Grif whistled. "Fancy."

"Yes."

"And expensive..."

"Yes..."

"So who exactly made the decision to take me here?" Grif asked. "Instead of taking me to MedCommons, or getting an indie to show up at the *Fool's Errand*... either one could fix me with a little Plastall. I mean really, re-growing bone is expensive..."

"I'm not paying for this," Amys said.

"I didn't think you were. I just want to know who is..."

Amys looked nervous.

"Amys? It's not Velis is it? Please tell me it's not—"

"It's not Velis," Amys said quickly.

"Good, because—"

"It's Baron Tyrelos."

Grif blinked. "Um... what?"

"Yeah," Amys said. "We dropped you and Cyrus off at MedCommons... Cyrus had his arm cut up in the fight, but it wasn't that bad. You were in pretty bad shape, though. I was waiting in the lobby..."

"So I was, originally, at MedCommons?" Grif asked.

Amys nodded. "For about a day. They'd stabilized you and were getting ready to take you in to surgery. I looked out the window and I saw some MediCorp techs loading you into a transport. Naturally I was curious: I ran out and asked them what the hell they thought they were doing, and they said someone had paid to have you transferred to their facility in the first city. They wouldn't say who, but they agreed to let me come along."

"They agreed, just like that?"

Amys shrugged casually. "I explained to them that I was your first officer. When that didn't work, I offered to help them explore exactly how comprehensive their medical coverage was."

Grif smirked. Amys was a very persuasive woman.

"Later on," she continued, "I overheard one of the doctors in a conference call. He kept saying 'milady,' and 'Baron' once or twice. He was talking about your condition... not hard to figure out..."

Grif tried to sit up, then remembered what the doctor said about his shoulder and forced himself to relax. "I've got to get out of here," he said. "I don't know why Baron Tyrelos would want to pay my medical bill, but..."

Grif saw Amys tense as the door opened. Raising his head, he saw four armed Station Authority guards enter the room. A guard stood at either side of the door, the remaining two leveled their weapons at Amys.

"Stand away from the prisoner," one ordered.

Amys glanced at Grif in alarm—alarm that Grif wholeheartedly shared—and backed away from Grif's bed.

"What's going on?" Grif asked. The guards didn't answer.

The door opened again, and another guard—a sergeant—entered the room. Grif's doctor entered with him, looking very unhappy.

"It's still too early," the doctor protested.

The sergeant shrugged. "We're on a schedule. If the arm will finish healing on its own then we're taking him."

The doctor sighed, exasperated. He moved over to the machine attached to Grif's bed and did something Grif couldn't see. Grif immediately felt a mild sensation of warmth spread up and down his left arm.

"This is going to hurt a bit," the doctor said.

Grif frowned. "A *bit*?"

The doctor hesitated. "A lot, probably." He pressed a button, and a series of lights running down the length of the machine turned green.

Intense pain shot down Grif's left arm, from his shoulder to the tips of his fingers and into his side. His eyes bulged from the overwhelming rush of sensation returning to his arm; it hurt so much that he couldn't even yell. All he could do was gasp in shallow breaths as the pain washed over him.

Grif was dimly aware of the sound of a pulse rifle powering up. Someone shouted a command to stay back. Amys shouted something in return, but Grif couldn't tell what it was. His head was pounding, a rushing sound filled his ears and drowned out everything else. He thought he heard the doctor saying that the arm would be weak and tender for a few days, and there was something about prescribed drugs, and possible side effects. None of it made any sense.

He felt his left side vibrate four times, as if he were a tuning fork struck four times in succession, then felt his left arm drop to the bed. He was free of the machine, and the fresh air hitting his skin felt like open flame. Rough hands forced him to sit, provoking another spasm of pain from his shoulder. This time both Amys and the doctor shouted angrily at the guards, and the rough hands were replaced by a gentler grip.

He was very dizzy. His vision blurred in and out of focus, and the room was spinning... no, he realized, he was being turned around. They removed his hospital gown. Grif heard a wall panel slide open. A moment later he was shoved unceremoniously into a small, squarish room not much bigger than he was. His shoulder hit the corner of the entrance on his way in, causing him to cry out and double over.

"Be CAREFUL!" the doctor shouted. "She's not going to be pleased if you undo all the work she paid—"

The panel closed, and Grif could hear only muffled sounds.

He looked up. The panel was transparent. In the other room the doctor was arguing with the sergeant. Two of the guards stood next to the panel, watching him with bored disinterest. Two other guards leveled their weapons at Amys, who glared at them, quivering with rage.

The doctor threw up his hands in exasperation, shouted something Grif couldn't hear, and stormed out of the room. The sergeant turned his attention to Grif. He said something indistinct, and one of the guards near him reached over to fiddle with something to the right of the panel. Grif shook his head and turned, trying to figure out exactly where he was.

A second later hot water sprayed down from the ceiling, scalding him. He was in a medical shower for the infirm, apparently, and the temperature was not to his taste. The water adjusted itself quickly, and Grif stood patiently, waiting for the shower to finish. He touched his left shoulder gingerly; it throbbed fiercely, but seemed intact. It hurt when he moved it, but not in a way that said "this limb is no longer functional."

The water stopped and a vent opened, blowing hot air into the shower. Grif stood there as patiently as he could manage, waiting to dry. A sonic shower would've been more practical, Grif thought. Apparently rich invalids preferred impractical and expensive water for bathing.

A few minutes later, Grif was dry... damp, at least. The panel opened, and he shivered as the chilly air of the recovery room forced its way into the small, humid chamber.

The sergeant crossed the room and threw a bundle of clothing at him. "Put these on."

Still shivering, Grif stared at the sergeant, then looked over at the bed. "Can I put these on over there, or do you want me to change in here?"

The sergeant looked surprised, not expecting Grif to speak, then shrugged. "Use the bed if you want," he said, and walked back to the door.

Grif staggered into the room and rotated his left arm, wincing. It worked, but it didn't have much strength—the slightest amount of pressure caused intense pain.

"You OK, Grif?" Amys' voice was taut with worry and anger.

Grif tried to grin and nearly succeeded. "Fine... just a little, uh, surprised by our visitors..."

He looked at the five guards. Two were watching Amys warily, though they no longer pointed guns at her. The other two were standing by the shower, obviously bored.

"Get dressed," the sergeant snapped. "We're pressed for time."

"We are?" Grif fumbled with the bundle of clothes as he set it on the bed. "Where are we going?"

The sergeant didn't reply.

"Well," Grif said, unrolling a shirt and setting it aside, "This isn't a prison uniform—I've seen those—so I guess I'm not going to jail. On the other hand it's pretty cheap, so I guess I'm not going to meet the Baron, either. Which is a shame... I hear she paid my bill. I was hoping to thank her personally..."

"Just get dressed," the sergeant repeated.

Grif dressed slowly, awkwardly working his way into the briefs and trousers, trying to minimize the use of his left arm. He was worried. The armed guards were treating him like a prisoner, but this wasn't prison garb. They weren't dressed like prison guards, either... they didn't have shock sticks, for one thing, and they weren't wearing the traditional body armor...

Then Grif noticed they were wearing earpieces. Very specialized earpieces. He swore.

The guards looked at him sharply. The sergeant frowned suspiciously. Grif winced, and grinned awkwardly. "Damn arm," he said. "Still hurts. I'm not used to how weak it is."

The sergeant relaxed. The other guards resumed their half-attentive vigil.

Grif continued to dress, watching the guards furtively. He thought he knew where they were planning to take him, and he didn't want to go there.

He'd been given no shoes. That annoyed him. He looked at the shirt—it used buttons. This gave him an idea.

He managed to put the shirt on, making a great show of barely being able to move his left arm, and then fumbled with the buttons as he tried to fasten them with one hand. Finally he sighed in frustration, and looked at the sergeant, resignation on his face.

The sergeant snorted in disgust and gestured for a guard to help him. Grif angled himself so that the guard helping him was directly between him and the guard by the shower.

"Stand still," the guard said, annoyed.

"Sorry," Grif said. He grinned at Amys. "I feel like I'm four. Hey, remember when I was four?"

Amys raised an eyebrow.

"Well of course you wouldn't," Grif said. He looked at the guard and grinned wider. "Of course she wouldn't. I mean, *she* was four... er... three."

"I was two," Amys said.

Grif nodded. "That's the one..."

Amys kicked. A guard cried out in pain, gripping his wrist, as his rifle struck the ground and slid across the floor. The hum of a vibroknife filled the room as Amys slashed, and a second guard staggered back, clutching his neck. The vibroknife deactivated and disappeared into Amys' sleeve as she caught his rifle before it fell to the floor.

The guard buttoning Grif's shirt frowned and looked over his shoulder. When he saw Amys he tensed, whirled around and reached for his pistol—only to close his hand around Grif's wrist.

"Oops." Grif grinned up at the guard sheepishly. "This is awkward." He kicked the back of the guard's leg with his knee. The guard's leg buckled, and he stumbled forward, letting go of Grif's wrist as his arms flailed in an attempt to keep his balance. Grif slid the pistol out of the guard's holster, deactivated the safety, and fired a single shot into the guard's back.

The guard by the shower stall yelled in alarm and raised his rifle. Grif fired at the guard, missed, and dove behind the machine that had regrown his arm. Energy exploded against the computer paneling.

I hope I'm not here when the doctor sees that, Grif thought.

Grif heard two more shots, then silence.

"You can get up now," Amys said.

Grif got to his feet. All five guards were down.

"The sergeant tried to go for his comm link," Amys said, "but I dropped him before he could turn it on."

"Good," Grif said. "That might buy us a little time. But not a lot. Someone had to have heard that."

"Maybe not..." Amys started rummaging through the sergeant's pockets for ammunition. "This is a restricted ward. There's another door down the hall that takes you out of the ward, and it's sealed. I didn't see any patients in any of the other rooms. I don't think we've attracted any attention yet."

"Well, that's something..." Griff leaned over the guard he shot and pulled a few energy cells out of his holster. "Let's get out of here."

Amys nodded. "Mind telling me why we killed them?"

"They were going to hand me over to a Sword," Grif said.

Amys frowned.

Grif leaned over the guard he shot and started pulling off a boot with his good arm. "I'm serious. Look at their earpieces. They don't actually fit into the ears."

Amys peered down at the sergeant. Her eyes widened. "Attached to the temple. Damn. Psi-blockers."

"Not standard equipment for prisoner transport." Grif started tugging on the other boot. "I'd probably want one if I was paranoid about the guy I was delivering a prisoner to. Not that it would matter against a Sword. Especially this one. Assuming N'grash's information is right."

The second boot pulled free, and Grif hastily slipped into the pair.

"N'grash?" Amys finished scavenging the bodies and turn to face Grif, frowning deeply.

"That's what she wanted to talk to me about. She heard a Sword was after me to try and figure out how I 'broke in' to Ur Voys. She also said that one was on his way here. If I've been out for a week, the timing could line up."

"Charming," Amys said. "And you didn't mention this because...?"

"Because we were fighting a bunch of goddamned cyborg slavers is why!"

"OK," Amys said, "sorry. It's just, you know, we never *talk* any more..."

Grif laughed.

Amys opened the exit hatch and looked out. "Clear," she said. "This area is sort of removed from the rest of the complex. Lots of empty recovery rooms."

"Good." Grif walked over to the door slowly, getting used to the fit of the boots. They were a little small.

"How's your arm?" Amys asked.

Grif grimaced. "Hurts like hell. I'll manage."

He straightened, and shifted uncomfortably. The clothes were too thin, practically pajamas, and the boots were too thick and a size too small. "I feel like an idiot."

Amys looked him over. "You look like an idiot."

"Excellent." Grif checked the charge on his pulse pistol. "Dignity above all. Let's get out of here."

Chapter 18

WHEREIN Our Hero Attempts a Graceful Exit

The ward was sealed, as Amys had said, and every other room in the ward was empty. While convenient, it wasn't something Grif found particularly reassuring: empty rooms were rooms that didn't make money, and Grif was fairly certain MediCorp could fill the rooms with little difficulty. If a ward was empty of everyone but one patient, it was done so deliberately. The important question was "why?" The first answer that sprang to mind wasn't one Grif liked very much.

They slipped into a room near the sealed door. Grif could see the nurse's station through the door's window, and a bit of the bustling hallway beyond. He sighed.

"We really need to get out of here."

Amys' mouth curled into a crooked half-smile. "Brilliant. That's why you're the captain."

"That and my sterling moral character," Grif said. "Where's the nearest exit? Where's the *easiest* exit?"

Amys thought. "Hangar one floor up. That's where they brought you in. Exit to the first city is ten floors down."

"Ten floors down is easy?"

"Easier than the hangar," Amys said. "Unless you have access to an official hospital transport. Or Station Authority credentials."

Grif shook his head. "First city exit it is. If we can get down there. Steal me some clothes, will you? There's no way I'll make it wearing pajamas and boots."

"You do sort of stand out," Amys agreed, handing Grif her rifle. "I'll be back soon."

Grif heard the ward door unseal and reseal as she left, then all was silent.

Grif slung Amys' rifle across his good shoulder, leaned against a wall, and rubbed his weak arm gingerly. It almost felt normal until he tried to do anything with it, then his arm erupted into spasms of pain. He could almost, but not quite, raise his arm level with his chest before the pain became too much to bear.

The ward door hissed as the seal broke and the door opened once more.

"Grif?" Amys called softly.

"Here," Grif said.

Amys poked her head into the room. "We've got help," she said, and threw him a bundle of clothes. She stepped into the room, followed by a very perplexed Bennet Jax.

"Bennet!" Grif placed the bundle of clothing on the empty patient's bed, unslung the rifle, and handed it back to Amys. "Welcome to the part where we seriously piss off a corporate barony."

Bennet stared at Grif blankly. "Exactly what the hell is going on?"

"Long story," Grif said, and kicked off his boots.

"Station Authority wants to hand Grif over to a Sword," Amys said.

"OK," Grif said, disrobing and reaching for the bundled clothes, "apparently not a long story. It *feels* like a long story, though..."

"A Sword." Bennet stared at Grif, no expression on his face whatsoever. "You're sure?"

"Yep." Grif slipped on a pair of pants. "They do show up in Trade Baron space from time to time. Not very often. Barons get twitchy around them, because... well. You know. They're insane telepaths."

"So this Baron has seen fit to overcome her innate twitchiness to hand you over to a Sword?"

"Sounds stupid, I know, but we've got five dead men in a back room laid out as a testament to the willingness of governments to do stupid things."

"Right..." Bennet nodded. "Well, that won't do. We've got to get you back to the *Fool's Errand* and get the hell out of here. I better contact the Major..."

"First of all, *no*." Grif pulled a shirt over his head. "Second, comm links can't get out of the first city without tying into their comm network—we are underground, after all. And I wouldn't count on the comm network being a secure line. And third? *Hell* no. I'd almost rather get caught by the Sword..."

He tucked his pulse pistol into his waistband at the small of his back, and pulled the shirt down so it fell to his hips, concealing the weapon nicely. The clothing was more expensive than he preferred, but it was infinitely preferable to the thin material the guards had given him, and it fit well—especially the shoes, which was a relief.

"Better," Grif said.

"Much better," Amys agreed.

The ward door hissed as its seal broke, and it slid open. Grif, Amys, and Bennet pressed themselves up against the wall, out of the line of sight of the hallway. Grif gripped his pulse pistol with his good hand, and Amys readied her rifle. Bennet, Grif noticed, was now armed as well. He wondered how Bennet had smuggled it past hospital security.

"Well all I can say is it was very irregular." It was the doctor who'd treated Grif. "Station Authority never acted like this before, even with prisoners. There are protocols and guidelines, and the hospital is supposed to be notified in advance..." The voice grew softer as the doctor and whoever he was with continued down the hall.

"I know I'm the new guy," Bennet said, "but I think we should leave."

Grif nodded sharply. "Amys, you better leave the rifle behind. It's going to attract attention."

Amys nodded and set the rile against the wall. Bennet offered her a second pistol, which he had pulled from... somewhere. She took it, nodding her thanks, and tucked it under her waistband. A few clothing adjustments later, it was hidden from view.

"Come on then." Grif stepped into the hallway, unsealed the ward door, and walked into the reception area.

It was a spacious room, rectangular in design, and opened into wide hallways on the left and the right. The nurses' station was set up next to the door, a u-shaped station with two terminals built into the desk. Chairs, couches, and small tables were arranged in the room so that people could move from one hallway to the other without obstruction. A wall on the far wall displayed a Tyrelos Barony newscast.

A few people sat in the reception area, half-watching the news, or reading. One nurse was at the nurse's station. He didn't bother looking up. The hallways were fairly busy, but there was little crossover traffic from one hallway to the other.

Directions and arrows were stamped into the floor in various places. On the right hallway floor, the word EXIT was stamped in large red letters. Grif walked quickly but casually down the right hall, Amys and Bennet in tow, following the EXIT marks until the hallway ended. At the end of a hall was a door, the right and left walls had three lifts each. Over the door a sign read STAIRS.

"Ten floors down," Amys murmured.

Grif nodded, went to a lift, and pushed the down button.

The door opened almost immediately. Grif stepped back, startled, as four Station Authority guards stepped out and rushed in the direction of the waiting room.

"Not reassuring," Bennet said.

"No," Amys agreed.

"Let's not take the lifts," Bennet suggested. "If there's trouble they might cut the power."

Grif nodded reluctantly. They hurred to the door at the end of the hall. Amys pushed a button to the right of the door, and it slid open with a soft "whoosh."

"You there," a voice commanded. "Stop!"

"Running now," Grif said, and rushed through the door.

"Stop!" the voice called again.

"Running now!" Grif shouted, and ran down the stairs.

The whine of a pulse rifle cut through the air; energy burned into the arch above the door. Grif ran down the stairs two at a time, pulling out the pulse pistol he'd tucked under his shirt. Amys, her own pistol in hand, ducked behind the door frame and returned fire. Someone down the hall shouted in alarm.

"Shoot later!" Grif shouted. "Run now!"

Half a flight down they heard Station Authority enter the stairwell above them. Someone shouted an order, and bolts of energy burst over their heads.

Grif grabbed the rail with his left arm and vaulted over the side, aiming to land on the stairs below. He shrieked as his arm collapsed, and he toppled forward, tumbling headlong down the stairs onto the next landing.

Amys and Bennet crouched behind the rails and fired back. The guards fell back behind the door, and Amys leaped over the rail, reaching the landing as Grif picked himself up off the floor.

Amys helped him up. "You OK?"

"No." Grif grimaced and picked up his gun. "But I'm getting used to the agony." The door opened. Grif and Amys immediately opened fire as a group of Station Authority guards backed out of view. Bennet appeared above them, firing up the stairs as he retreated.

Grif closed the door and shot the control panel, stepping back to avoid the sparks. "This isn't good."

Amys looked over the rail. "It's about to get worse."

Grif heard the sound of booted feet below them.

"They're coming up," Amys said.

"They're not coming down," Bennet said. "I think I got 'em all."

Amys fired a few shots over the rail. Grif heard cursing, and a shouted order to pull back.

"A plan would be good right now," Bennet said.

"I'm thinking," Grif said. The door on their level shuddered.

"That door won't stay closed forever." Bennet sounded slightly impatient.

"I know!" Grif shouted. "You're the super-spy, right? Think of something?"

"This isn't the kind of thing we plan for," Bennet snapped. "This is the kind of thing we plan on *avoiding*."

Amys fired a few more shots down the stairs, then stepped back. Energy slammed into the railing and the stairs above them.

"This isn't going to get any better," Grif said. "Back up the stairs. Hurry!"

They sprinted back up the stairs. Halfway up they found the bodies of five Station Authority guards. Amys took one of the rifles. Bennet took another.

They nearly reached the landing when the door to the hall opened: a guard stepped through, with more behind. Amys and Bennet fired in unison, and the first guard fell. Grif fired and missed, shooting through the doorway and hitting the ceiling. The other guards pulled back.

Grif heard something moving behind him. He turned and saw the barrel of a rifle peeking up over the edge of the stairs.

"They're coming up!" Grif pointed his pistol over the rail and fired blindly into the stairs below. He heard cursing and the sound of people scattering. Amys and Bennet were at the stairwell now, shooting into the hall.

A piece of the door frame exploded, and the lights in the stairwell flickered as the conduits along the ceiling began to overheat.

Grif saw another barrel and fired over the railing again. This time the rifle returned fire. Grif pulled back.

"Hurry up!"

"We're working on it," Bennet said. "It's not as easy as it looks..."

"Well I can't hold these guys off much longer." Grif tried to peer over the lip of the stairwell without exposing himself. "Sooner or later they'll realize it's just one pistol..."

From below someone shouted "it's just one pistol!"

"Damn it all to *hell*," Grif muttered.

Amys rolled her eyes. "Nice work."

"You know," Bennet said, trying to sound calm, "I didn't really think we'd run into any trouble until we actually tried to get into Ur Voys."

"Oh yeah," Grif said. "About that..."

Bennet narrowed his eyes. "About what?"

A guard popped up from under the stair. Grif opened fire and hit her in the shoulder, knocking her back down.

"Hall is clear," Amys said. "Come on."

Grif shot down the stairs again, turned, and ran for the door. At that moment, the guards decided to rush en masse.

Part of the wall melted as Grif, Amys and Bennet ran through the doorway, out of the stairwell, and into the hall. Amys and Bennet positioned themselves on either side of what was left of the wall and returned fire. Grif started searching the bodies of the dead guards in the hall.

"Now is not the time to loot corpses!" Amys shouted.

"I'm not looting!" Grif shouted back. "This has nothing to do with money whatsoever!"

"What was the misunderstanding?" Bennet asked. A terminal next to the doorway exploded in a shower of sparks over his head.

"What?" Energy smashed into a set of lift doors, scoring them.

"Misunderstanding!" Bennet snaked around the doorframe and fired two quick shots. "You said there was a misunderstanding!"

"Yes!" Grif cried, and pulled three oval objects off of a dead guard's belt. "I knew one of them would have these! Amys! Crowd control!"

He threw one of the ovals to Amys, who caught it, twisted it, and pushed both ends together. The oval beeped and she threw it down the stairs. Grif heard a panicked shout, and an instant later the stairwell shuddered.

Silence.

"Compression grenade," Amys said. "Technically non-lethal."

"We were lucky," Grif said. "He was getting ready to use one when Bennet shot him." He handed the other two ovals to Amys.

Bennet turned to look at Grif. "You were saying?"

"Not right now, sorry," Grif said. "Priorities. Avoid death by armed guards now, awkward confessions later."

Bennet narrowed his eyes but said nothing.

"What are we going to do?" Amys asked.

Grif's mind raced. "You said there was a hangar one level up?"

Amys nodded. "That's where the medical transport dropped you off."

"We'll give that a shot. If we can get to something that flies I can try and get us some place safe."

"This way," Amys said, and ran toward the recovery ward.

As they raced through the lobby, more guards appeared from the other hallway. Grif and Bennet managed to get behind the nurse's station as the guards opened fire. Amys took cover behind the sliding door that led to the recovery rooms.

"One... two... three..." On three, Grif and Bennet each popped up over the nurse's station and opened fire. Grif missed completely, Bennet felled a guard. As they drew back, the guards returned fire, obliterating a good fourth of the nurses' station.

Grif started to laugh.

"Is now a good time for confessions?" Bennet asked. "I don't like to die curious."

Amys opened fire from the doorway. Bennet and Grif rolled to the edges of the nurses' station—-now somewhat narrower than it had been moments before—and opened fire. Three guards fell that time, but more were coming to take their place.

Grif and Bennet crawled back behind the nurses' station. It shuddered as energy tore off the ends even further.

"Oh, all right," Grif said. "As it happens, I never actually..."

Another piece of the nurses' station disintegrated near Grif's left hand. He yelped and moved a bit to his right.

"I never actually broke into Ur Voys, per se..."

Bennet was so surprised Grif had to pull him back as the nurses' station continued to diminish in size.

"Per se? You didn't break in per se? Define per se."

"Not so much 'per se' as 'at all...'"

Another chunk of the nurses' station blew away, and Grif and Bennet rolled out to return fire.

When they rolled back behind the station—now barely wider than the two of them shoulder-to-shoulder—Bennet asked "anything else I need to know?"

Grif considered the question.

"I'm a lousy shot," he admitted.

"Heads down!" Amys shouted. Grif and Bennet covered their heads as something beeped. Amys threw an oval object over the nurses' station and into the room.

There was a shuddering boom. Bits of chairs flew across the room. When the dust cleared, the room was quiet.

"Took you long enough," Grif said.

"I was waiting for a decent crowd," Amys replied. "Didn't want to waste it."

Grif stood and looked around cautiously. The guards were lying on the ground, moaning and twitching. "Let's go," he said. "Amys... after you."

Amys nodded, and helped Bennet to his feet.

"Grif says he never broke in to Ur Voys," Bennet said, bewildered.

"I know," Amys said. "That's what you get for trusting a smuggler."

Grif grinned.

"You realize," Amys continued, "that Bennet is going to have to tell your sister exactly what you told him."

Grif's grin widened. "You're assuming we survive this. You big softy."

"You're both crazy," Bennet muttered.

Amys moved carefully across the waiting room to the other hall. Grif followed.

"We're crazy?" Grif shook his head. "You're the one working for a top-secret Alliance organization that hired an infamous liar to break into a place you had no proof he'd ever been."

"So how did you get the anagathics?" Bennet asked.

"Luck," Grif said.

Bennet shook his head. "She's going kill me right along with you," he muttered.

"Uh... let's table that discussion for another day," Grif said, looking around suspiciously. "Has anyone else noticed anything strange?"

"What," Amys asked, "Like people shooting at us in a hospital?"

"No," Grif answered. "Like people *not* shooting at us in a hospital... and no doctors in the hospital... or nurses..."

"Or patients," Amys added, frowning.

Grif's eyes stung. Bennet coughed. Grif felt his lungs burn.

"To the recovery rooms!" Grif choked.

Station Authority was flooding the hospital with gas—from the smell of it, a particularly nasty crowd pacifier.

Trying not to breathe, Grif ran through the door into the recovery room hallway. He rushed into the first room he found and started opening wall panels at random. Finally his eyes locked onto a small white canister with the words OXYGEN stamped on it. It was a quick breather, used by first aid and trauma teams.

Or, as circumstances warranted, when a hospital was being flooded with gas.

Grif twisted the face mask to the "on" position and placed it over his nose and mouth. He waited a second and then took a deep breath, coughing as he did so.

Amys staggered into the room, clutching the wall. He pushed the quick breather over her face and held it steady as she took a breath. He left the quick breather with her as he went back into the hallway and ducked into the next room down to get another. He found two. When he returned, Amys and Bennet were sharing the first.

He handed a fresh breather to Bennet, who quickly turned it on and placed it over his face. Grif did the same with his, and realized that he was now completely useless. Quick breathers didn't come with straps: they were held over the patient by a nurse or an orderly. Grif's good arm was stuck holding the oxygen... he couldn't fire his gun.

"Let's try and make it to the hangar," Grif said, voice muffled through the mask. He suspected they had a little time before Station Authority came back in force.

Amys nodded and headed back into the hall. She walked as quickly as she could—not daring to run, half-blinded as she was by the gas—down the opposite hall.

Tears streaming down his face, Grif stumbled after her, dimly aware of Bennet stumbling behind him, coughing behind his mask. Eventually they came to a lift door. It was deactivated.

Amys opened a door to the right of the lift. Before them was another set of stairs. Amys pointed up. Grif and Bennet nodded.

At the top of the stairs they found a door and a ladder that led up to a closed maintenance hatch. Amys pointed up at the hatch. Grif looked at it in frustration.

How was he supposed to climb up there with only one good arm?

Amys took a deep breath, set her quick breather on the floor, and climbed the ladder to the hatch. It was an old-style mechanical hatch, with a wheel in the center that set and released the seal. Amys needed both hands to move the wheel. Eventually it turned, and the hatch cracked open a few centimeters.

Amys peered through the crack cautiously, waiting. Then she climbed back down and grabbed the breather, inhaling deeply. She walked over to Grif, and put her head close to his so he could hear her through the mask. "I didn't see anything," she said.

Grif shrugged. "How am I supposed to climb that ladder?" He asked. He raised his left arm and winced from the effort.

"Don't worry," she said. "We'll help."

Tucking the breather under her arm, she quickly scaled the ladder. She reached up for the hatch, hesitated, then pushed the hatch completely open and climbed up.

Peering up through the hatch, Grif saw that the room beyond was dimly lit and filled with thick, insulated cabling. When he saw Amys again, he noticed she wasn't using the quick breather.

"There's good air up here," she said. "Grif, you next. Bennet, try and keep him steady down there, if we can get him up a third of the way I'll pull him up the rest of it."

Bennet nodded.

It was an awkward process, but eventually Grif made it up the ladder and into a small room filled with machinery. Bennet came up soon after, gasping for breath, and Amys quickly closed and sealed the hatch behind him.

"Air," Bennet gasped. "Good."

Grif nodded, wiping his face with his sleeve, waiting for his eyes to stop stinging.

Amys grinned. "That was almost fun. What's next?"

Bennet looked from Grif to Amys and shook his head. "I'm not sure which of you is crazier," he said.

Amys pointed at Grif. Grif shrugged modestly.

Chapter 19

WHEREIN A Message is Constructed and Sent On Its Way

They took a moment to rest and recover from the effects of the gas. As they lay on the ground, coughing up phlegm and breathing in the clean air, Grif closed his eyes and forced himself to think.

"Well." Grif drew in a ragged breath after a final spasm of coughing. "With any luck they think we're still in the hospital, incapacitated and helpless. We're lucky they didn't use a proper nerve gas."

"MediCorp is going to be mighty pissed anyway," Amys said. "I bet that gas contaminated a lot of medicine."

"Where are we?" Bennet asked. "And if this is a way out of the hospital, why wasn't Station Authority sitting on top of it, waiting for us to come out?"

Grif looked around. The room was crowded with cables. At one end, a large generator hummed softly. "It's a backup generator, I think. Doesn't look like it's been used much, but it's on..."

Grif pointed with his good arm at a door on the far end of the room. "And that," he said, "appears to be the only way out. I bet we find a few Station Authority guards out there..."

Amys sighed. "What do we do? We can't go back down there and wander around in the gas, waiting for Station Authority to take us down."

"No," Grif agreed. "That would be a bad idea."

"But if we go out that door—hell, if Station Authority is waiting for us out there... bad idea number two."

"Yes, but here's the thing," Grif said. "Now that I've had half a second to think about it, I don't understand what the hell the Baron is doing handing me over to a Sword in the first place."

Bennet shrugged. "Why not? I mean, from her perspective. I know why not from your perspective."

"Because," Grif said, "the Trade Baronies are *neutral*. Tyrelos is a place where... *entrepreneurs* regularly come to roost. They wouldn't roost if she started handing them over to the Alliance or the Radiant Throne any time a high-ranking official asked nicely... or even asked not-so-nicely."

"Maybe the Baron and the Radiant Throne have some kind of deal they're not telling anyone about," Bennet suggested. "That would explain why she tried to do it on the sly."

"Yeah..." Grif stared at Bennet thoughtfully.

Bennet frowned. "What?"

"Nothing," Grif said. "I just wonder if any other Baronies have arrangements like that..."

Bennet didn't reply.

"Well, that's a conversation for another day," Grif said. "Right now I have an idea. Bennet, exactly how good are you with computers?"

"Pretty good," Bennet said.

"I assume they taught you how to do all the complicated stuff in spy school... breaking through computer security, accessing that which is not meant to be seen, that kind of stuff."

"Yes," Bennet said. "But usually I have tools for that. Tools I don't have with me, because for some reason I thought going to visit you in a hospital would be a simple and straightforward experience."

Grif grinned. "Now you know better. I hope you're not completely helpless without your tools, because this..." Grif stood, walked over to the generator, and pointed. "...is attached to this." Grif pointed to a dusty terminal set into the wall beside the generator. "Diagnostic equipment, I expect. It's hooked up to the generator here... and the generator is wired to the hospital's main power supply, so it'll know to turn itself on if the power goes out."

Bennet got up and crouched next to the terminal, studying it carefully.

"The main power supply," Grif continued, "is—if we're lucky—hooked into a lot of monitoring equipment in the main office, or the security room, or a data center or something."

"So you want to use the terminal to get into the hospital systems," Bennet said.

"If you can manage it," Grif said. "If you can get me into the hospital systems, I can get a message to the *Fool's Errand* without letting anyone know we're doing it."

"Well..." Bennet touched the terminal and the keypad lit up in response. "Maybe. It isn't a full keypad, which might be a problem... but..."

The terminal display blinked on, displaying a schematic of the power generator. A moment later the schematic disappeared, and data scrolled up the display.

"I can get us in," Bennet said. "Someone logged in to the terminal last month to do something routine and they were very sloppy when they logged out..."

"Great," Grif said. "Try to get to the hospital comm relay."

"Why is it you know this stuff can be done, but you don't actually know how to do it?" Bennet sounded annoyed.

Grif shrugged. "Can you fly a starship?"

Bennet shook his head.

"But you know that people do fly them, right?"

Bennet grumbled quietly to himself as he worked. A few minutes later he turned to Grif and Amys and smiled. "I'm in. The generator sends a signal to something when it needs maintenance. The something looks like a comm relay address."

"Excellent!" Grif grinned. "Get me there and I'll do the rest."

"Hold on a minute," Bennet said. "If we use that address we'll probably wind up activating the maintenance message. That might alert Station Authority."

"Er... right. Don't do that."

Bennet stared at the screen intently. "If I were designing this relay network, I would number the relays sequentially. At the very least, I would adopt some kind of naming convention that would make all the addresses consistent..."

"Liar," Grif said. "If you were designing this system you would make it as confusing as possible to prevent enemies of the state from doing what we're trying to do now."

"...yes," Bennet admitted. "You're probably right. Luckily, whoever designed this wasn't that paranoid. Here's the main system." Bennet moved so Grif and Amys could get a look at the terminal screen. Sure enough, it was displaying a primary system menu.

"Excellent." Grif moved up to the terminal. "Excuse me."

Bennet stepped back and Grif crouched in front of the terminal. He gingerly moved his left arm—it hurt even to move for simple tasks, but he persevered—so both hands rested over the keypad.

"I thought you couldn't program," Bennet said.

"This isn't programming." Grif began to type. "This is communication."

Amys and Bennet watched what he was doing intently. After a minute,

Amys laughed, nodding approvingly. Bennet looked at her in confusion.

"What's he doing?" Bennet asked.

"What he said he would," Amys said. "He's sending a message to the *Fool's Errand*. That's the navigation protocol SL beacons use to give ships positioning information before they drop out of tach."

Bennet looked at her in disbelief. "He's writing a message in the SL beacon protocol?"

"I am," Grif said. "And despite my *enviable* focus and determination, I'm quite capable of hearing everything you say when you're less than half a meter behind me."

"Well, what's the point?" Bennet sounded a little defensive. "SL beacons don't actually send messages. Just the positions of things in space."

"Yes," Grif agreed, "but those things have *names*. And those names are created manually, because it's easier to do that than to have a database entry for every single damn thing floating around in the galaxy. So I'm sending... hold on... seventeen dummy locations, and in each of the identifying fields I've got a piece of the message I want to send. The bulk of the data is just a bunch of zeroed coordinates and distances, with only the text field changing every time. Unless you can read SL protocol—which takes a while, unless you're a navigation terminal the message isn't going to make a lot of sense. I'm pretty sure Station Authority won't be watching for it."

"Clever," Bennet admitted. "How do you plan on sending it to your ship?"

"Dispatch relay."

The dispatch relay was a network every hospital in the city used to coordinate the availability of medical facilities in case of an emergency. It usually listed how many beds were available for various types of injuries, and was updated as the figure changed. Even when no beds were available—which, Grif guessed, was probably the case with the MediCorp facility at present—it would still send the message "no facilities available at present." Grif planned to piggyback his own message on the transmitter. It would scramble the data being transmitted by the relay for a moment, but would be almost immediately corrected.

"Sneaky," Bennet said, impressed. "Must run in the family."

"No need to be rude." Grif sent a final command through the terminal and smiled. "There. Message sent. Now we need to try and get out of here."

Chapter 20

WHEREIN A Message is Received and a Decision is Made

Cyrus sat at the Sensor station on the bridge of the *Fool's Errand*, sighed, and took another drink from the bottle of Stellis he'd placed on Morgan's console. He wondered when Grif would get out of the hospital; he wondered when they would leave. He worried, vaguely, about what they would do when they finally did, and how they would get out of Varkav alive for the second time. He occupied himself with "busy work" in an attempt to distract himself. At present he was going over the official ship's inventory, making sure the declared items looked like a reasonable load of cargo for a merchant's first run in an unknown port.

He was also trying to avoid Velis. Velis was, in polite language, a formidable woman. Other more pointed words sprang to mind before that—Cyrus wasn't a particularly polite man—but he was trying to show restraint. Velis had all but accused Grif of trying to get himself killed in order to "weasel out of their arrangement." He took another swig of Stellis and swore.

He pushed the problem of Velis to the back of his mind, only to find another problem had clawed its way to the front: the problem of what would happen if the Radiant Throne exercised its prerogative to board them, which it would.

At this point, Cyrus had no doubt that Grif was a wanted man in much of that part of space. They took precautions to disguise the *Fool's Errand*, and the disguise would hold up under scrutiny. A fake paper trail and a false ship identifier claimed that the ship was called the *Alo Minh*—named, Grif claimed, after a girl he knew on some planet somewhere—and that Grif himself was a Captain Jobin Tax, duly registered with the merchant marines of the Nyst Barony. Baron Nyst didn't pay much attention to the bookkeeping involved in maintaining his fleet, and was willing to let anyone use his name so long as they paid him for the privilege.

That only solved part of the problem, however. Every ship entering Radiant Throne space was boarded eventually. Once that happened, Cyrus figured, the presence of Velis and her people could prove to be something of a problem. It was obvious they weren't ship crew, but they might pass as hired guards, if they hid their gadgets.

He considered trying to get in touch with Amys for more information on Grif, and decided against it. Amys' message after they'd moved Grif to the MediCorp facility confused him. Grif was having his shoulder *re-grown*? And MediCorp refused to name the person footing the bill. Cyrus wondered if it was Velis using Alliance currency, but he couldn't imagine why Velis wouldn't mention it. Did Grif have any rich friends? It's not the kind of thing Grif would spend money on, when prosthetic parts worked just as well—sometimes better—and were far cheaper.

The only part of himself Grif would ever pay to have re-grown was his liver, Cyrus thought, and he might not be able to afford what it would cost, at this point. He grinned, and toasted his captain before taking another drink.

Cyrus was sure this would come back to haunt them. Ktk had disagreed and put money on the line. So far, it looked like the bug would win. Cyrus didn't mind. Money well lost...

The comm station beeped.

He hurried over to the station and looked at the incoming queue excitedly, hoping it was news of Grif. When he saw the message identifier, he frowned. It looked like a burst of data from a superluminal beacon.

"But there aren't any..."

SL Beacons were placed at the edge of systems, just outside the system gravity wells, where ships were most likely to drop from tach. They didn't send messages to ships sitting in port...

Curious, Cyrus forwarded the message to the nav station and hurried over, leaning into the terminal as he punched in the commands to display the data. It was a string of empty coordinates, he saw, and his confusion increased. Empty coordinates, and the object identifiers were full of meaningless...

Cyrus caught his breath. He read over each of the SL Beacon messages again, carefully, piecing together the object identifiers.

"That bitch," he muttered. "That ruthless, sorry..."

Cyrus moved over to the comm station and keyed up the hailing sequence to the *Grlashimargrak*. He needed to start telling other independents what was going on.

The orange-yellow eye stalks and flattened head of Rask appeared on the station's monitor.

"Cyrus," he said. His voice was slower than usual, and looked like he was still recovering from the fight. "What's going on?"

"Rask, I need to speak with captain N'grash. Right now."

Something in Cyrus' voice convinced Rask that no further questions were necessary. "She's in her cabin. I'll patch you through."

"Thanks," Cyrus said.

For a moment the screen went black, then N'grash's face—what could be seen of it in the dim light of her cabin—appeared on screen. The image was mostly indistinct, but her eyes glowed red from the light reflected off the terminal screen.

"Cyrus," N'grash rumbled. "Why have you called?"

"We have a problem," Cyrus said. "Grif is in trouble." N'grash laughed gruffly. "This is not new information."

"Baron Tyrelos is trying to hand him over to the Radiant Throne."

N'grash froze. "Tyrelos?"

"I know," Cyrus growled. "Hard to believe, isn't it?"

"Nearly impossible," N'grash said. "Tell me what you know."

"Grif just sent us a message," Cyrus said. "He used the identifier fields in the SL Beacon protocol to send a message to our navigator's station."

"What did this message say?" N'grash asked.

"It said 'this – is – Grif – Tyrelos – sold – us – out – hunting – me – for – Throne – MediCorp – facility – first – city – tell – others.'"

N'grash shook her head slowly as a deep, low growl emerged from her throat. "You are certain this message is legitimate?"

Cyrus nodded. "Can you think of anyone else who would send a message directly to the *Fool's Errand* using SL protocol?"

"No." N'grash growled again, louder than before. "I find it hard to believe she would do this!" Her eyes narrowed in the monitor, and her ears flattened into the sides of her head. "Still, I do not believe you lie, Cyrus Mak."

"Er... yeah, look," Cyrus said, "you ought to know I wouldn't joke about something like this."

N'grash shook her head. "You are a liar and thief, Cyrus. Just like the rest of us. But no, you would not lie about this... and I have known Tester for too long to believe he would allow you to deceive me. I believe you." She made a ragged, rasping sound that might have been a sigh. "It is difficult to accept that the Baron would violate her neutrality in such a fashion, however."

"We've got to get the word out to other independents," Cyrus said. "If we can get enough of them yelling for blood—"

"Wait," N'grash said. "Wait before you warn the others. I must try something first."

"Try what?" Cyrus asked.

N'grash hesitated. "I fear this is my doing. I must try to put it right."

Cyrus frowned. "How is this your fault?"

"It is complicated, Cyrus Mak. It is very complicated. Stand by. I will contact you again." The screen went dark as N'grash killed the link.

Cyrus stared at the darkened screen, sighed in frustration, then activated the intercom. "Ktk. Come on up to the bridge. I just won another bet..."

Chapter 21

WHEREIN a Conspiracy is Uncovered, and Needs Reupholstering

Baron Minerva Tyrelos was very young for a Trade Baron. Because common medicine was able to extend the lifespan of humans by decades—and uncommon medicines were able to extend it far longer than that—that youth frequently worked against her. When her father died, and she assumed the title of Baron in his place, it was accepted by the corporations and holdings of Tyrelos Industries on a procedural level... but she quickly learned that many of her father's closest allies within the barony had difficulty thinking of her as anything other than a child. It didn't help that many of those allies remembered when she had actually *been* a child, or that she was considered beautiful... and therefore, for some reason no one could explain to her satisfaction, weak and malleable. In less than a month, the new Baron Tyrelos realized that her board of directors intended her to be a figurehead only and were maneuvering to effectively dismantle the organization her father had built.

The board was very surprised to discover that she had other ideas. It took years, but in the end opposition gave way to grudging respect, and eventually most of her enemies became her most outspoken admirers. She was a very hands-on baron, had learned the ins and outs of the businesses she controlled and kept abreast of the latest developments in the corporations and research and development firms working within the barony. She knew what her barony was doing, and she knew where it was going. She kept on cautiously polite terms with the larger crime families that operated in her space, and maintained polite but distant relations with the Radiant Throne and the Alliance of Free Worlds.

At any given time she usually knew more about what was happening in her space—especially in her city—than anyone else.

This, however, was not one of those times.

Baron Tyrelos stood in the middle of the Tyrelos Station Operations Center, listening to one of her officers update her on the status of a fugitive who had gone on a killing spree in one of the city hospitals.

"Why is this happening?" She demanded again.

The Baron didn't like losing her temper. Under most circumstances she tried to maintain a crisp, businesslike demeanor. At the moment her demeanor was slipping.

The officer shifted uncomfortably in place. "Reports are inconsistent. Apparently not all of the Station Authority units were using the proper comm channels. We evacuated the hospital and are pumping it full of gas."

The Baron narrowed her eyes. "Do we have an updated body count?"

"It is still holding at eighteen dead, another twenty wounded," the officer answered. "We expect another report any minute..."

"I want that man caught," she seethed, "and then I want him executed. Immediately."

"Perhaps I might make a better suggestion, my lady?"

The Baron turned to see her Chancellor, flanked by two Station Authority officers, approaching.

Chancellor Muringyne was Vage: a mottled icthyoid, complete with webbed feet, webbed hands, and a set of vestigial gills. They evolved from aquatic creatures (or, if you believed the Terran scientists, were *engineered* out of an aquatic species) but were now an oxygen-breathing race. His eyes glistened with excitement.

"I have, yes, I have hit upon an interesting piece of information about our fugitive," Chancellor Muringyne said, beaming happily. "It appears the Radiant Throne has an interest in this one, yes, and is willing to pay a bounty to have him handed over."

"Not interested," the Baron said brusquely. "That bastard attacked my men without provocation, and I will send a message that such actions will be dealt with immediately and without hesitation or mercy."

"I understand," the chancellor said soothingly—as soothingly as he could manage in the strange tones of his race—"but handing him over to the Radiant Throne would not be an act of mercy."

"Oh? What is their interest in Vindh?"

"I do not know the specifics of their interest, but I do know that it is a Sword who has offered this bounty."

The Baron shuddered. "A Sword? What the hell did Vindh do?"

The chancellor shrugged. "Who can say what terrible things a man capable of murdering in a hospital would commit in other places? But it must have been something big, to attract this Sword's interest. He is... known in some circles..."

That information made the Baron uneasy. She began to pace across the floor, thinking hard. "I don't know, Mur... we're neutral in the affairs of other governments. If people learned I was extraditing—"

"This one violated your laws, Baron... he certainly has no expectation of protection now, nor would any expect you to protect him, after what he has done."

Baron Tyrelos nodded slowly. "That's true. But—"

Just then the door to the operations center opened, and Baron Tyrelos' brother ambled in.

Lord Raphael Tyrelos was her younger brother by a space of five minutes. While they bore striking physical similarities, he was her opposite in almost every respect. Where she was severe, he was opulent; where she practiced restraint, he indulged in nearly every excess he could find. He was also completely uninterested in having her job, which meant that—unlike other members of her family—he was completely trustworthy. They were close, as twins commonly were, and he refused to use her titles in public, which she found infuriating.

"Ah. Min." He jogged over to her, nodding a greeting to Chancellor Muringyne as he approached. "You have a message on a private channel, and I think you need to hear it."

Baron Tyrelos looked up at her brother in annoyance. "I'm busy, Raphe, or didn't you—"

"I think it is very important you talk to *Captain N'grash*," he insisted, looking at her meaningfully. "She was quite... *agitated*."

Baron Tyrelos frowned at her brother, thinking.

"Who is this 'N'grash,' my baron?" The chancellor asked politely.

"An independent," Raphael said, still smiling. "Does a bit of reporting for us from time to time. A good contact... with *good information*." He looked at his sister expectantly.

"Fine," she snarled. "If you'll excuse me, Chancellor, I've been meaning to have a few 'words' with this one anyway... I'll be back in a moment."

She whirled and stalked toward one of the conference rooms. "I want ABSOLUTE PRIVACY!" She yelled, and sealed the door behind her.

"It is a very good thing," the chancellor observed, "that these doors do not slam."

"We should get her at least one," Raphael said. "Poor dear. She so desperately wants to slam them."

Minerva Tyrelos growled in anger as she sat in front of one of the terminals and keyed in the commands needed to access her private, secure feed. Finally the terminal screen shifted, and the barely visible head on Captain N'grash glared out at her.

"You have got a lot of nerve, Captain," the Baron snapped.

"And you are showing your true colors at last," N'grash growled menacingly.

"Your source of information seems to have turned into a homicidal—"

"When the independents learn that you violate your own neutrality for profit—"

"What?" Baron Tyrelos drew back, stung by the remark. "How *dare* you threaten—"

"This is not a *threat*, Baron. It is not safe to berth in a place that claims neutrality but is on the take from the Radiant Throne!"

"I am *not*—"

"Or perhaps it is both? Perhaps you decided to hand Vindh over to the Sword because you already knew about the conspiracy to kill Baron Tylaris. Am I next then? I warn you, others are already hearing of this betrayal—"

"But I didn't—"

"*No*!" Captain N'grash roared in rage—a frightening sound, even on the other end of a terminal, and the Baron edged back unconsciously. "Captain Vindh is a trusted colleague, Baron, and he managed to send us a message after avoiding your first attempt to hand him off to the Throne. Do not expect me to take your word over his... that will not happen."

"Wait!" Baron Tyrelos' gruff demeanor vanished, and was replaced with an air of bewilderment and confusion. "Captain N'grash... I don't know what you're talking about."

N'grash hesitated. "Baron, very recently Captain Vindh's crew received a message from him."

"Oh really?" The Baron wasn't sure how to react to that claim. "My people are monitoring all communications out of that hospital, N'grash. I seriously doubt he could have—"

"You would not detect this transmission unless you were specifically looking for it, and would not understand the specifics of how the message was transmitted unless you have crewed on a ship."

"All right," the Baron said. "Assuming he did send a message. What did it say?"

"That you'd sent your guards to hand him over to the Radiant Throne, and that we should tell others. I assume he means to tell others you are violating your own neutrality."

"But I haven't," Baron Tyrelos protested. "I didn't even know the Throne wanted him until a few minutes ago!"

"Then you deny sending your guards to hand him over?"

"My only interest in Captain Vindh was in regards to the information you gave me. And if I'd known he would start killing my men—"

"He would not have killed your men," N'grash snarled, "if you had not tried to hand him over to the Throne!"

"I did no such thing!"

"Then someone else *did*," N'grash pressed. "Someone with the *knowledge* and *authority* to do so."

Baron Tyrelos shook her head. It didn't make any sense. It just wasn't possible...

N'grash stared out from the terminal in silence, then made a gurgling *hrmgh* sound in the back of her throat. "Baron." The Ggrlsha was no longer angry, her voice was calm and thoughtful. "If you did not order Grif handed over to the Throne... who did?"

Baron Tyrelos stared at N'grash's image for a long time as she thought about everything the Ggrlsha captain had said. "N'grash, I need to look into this. If what you say is true, someone is working against me."

N'grash nodded. "I will wait," she said. "But if this is a trick—"

"No trick, N'grash. I will be in touch."

She ended the transmission and angrily slammed her fist down on the table. "What the hell is going on?" N'grash's accusation didn't make sense, and that bothered her. The captain had done work for her in the past, and she was, in the Baron's opinion, a reliable source. The idea that Baron Tyrelos had been murdered by the Alliance was preposterous—at least, it was until N'grash had mentioned it, at which point it became worth looking into. N'grash had a good head for these things.

Was this worth looking into as well? If the Ggrlsha was right, and someone in her organization was making deals with foreign governments without her authorization... that would be an act of treason. And if the deal involved Captain Vindh, the traitor was very high in her organization.

Baron Tyrelos shook her head. What was she thinking? She knew her people, and they were loyal. Perhaps N'grash didn't know her friend as well as she thought...

The terminal beeped. Baron Tyrelos looked up and saw that she had a saved message in her account. It was from Dr. Faron, her physician—the physician she'd assigned to look after Captain Vindh.

She pressed play, and Dr. Faron's face appeared on the terminal screen. He looked very annoyed.

"Minerva." He sounded as annoyed as he looked, she thought. She looked at the time of transmission—approximately thirty minutes ago. "I don't pretend to tell you how to govern, but I must protest the mistreatment of a patient while under my care."

Baron Tyrelos felt her heart sink.

"Captain Vindh only had three hours left in his treatment—was it really so important to unhook him now?"

"Damn," she muttered. "Damn, damn, damn, damn, damn..."

"And another thing," he continued, voice getting a bit sharper. "You didn't tell me he was a prisoner. If we had known we never would've allowed his friends the opportunity to visit, and we would've insisted on armed guards the entire time we were treating him, for our protection. That's pretty standard. Again, I don't want to tell you how to govern, but your guards were being pretty rough with the man... and with me."

The image of Dr. Faron sighed. "At any rate, I want to lodge a protest at his treatment. He looked pretty confused, and his arm is in terrible shape. It's regrown, but it was still knitting—it can very easily be broken, bruised or sprained. It's your money, Minerva, but it seems like a waste to me. If you wanted to treat a prisoner you should have taken him to your prison facilities. They do have a pretty good medical bay there..."

The image of Dr. Faron disappeared.

"Dammit." Baron Tyrelos dismissed her account with an angry press of a button, and then stalked over to the door, waiting impatiently while it opened.

The door hissed open, revealing the operations center. "Pull back your men," she commanded, stepping into the room. "If Vindh is spotted, keep tabs on his location, but do not move in, do not apprehend. And do not kill."

"What?" The chancellor looked at her in surprise. "Are you serious, my Baron?"

"Yes I'm serious. Raphe, get your ass in the conference room. We need to talk. You too, Muringyne. Now."

The Chancellor blinked, looked at Raphael, and shrugged elaborately. "As you wish, my Baron. "

"I'll... just... be in the conference room then," Raphael said.

Baron Tyrelos looked at the rest of the people in the operations center. "Remember—*do not engage*. Stand by for my next order."

"Yes milady," the communications officer said, and began transmitting the orders to the guards in pursuit.

She didn't speak again until the Chancellor and her brother had entered the room and she had closed and secured the door behind her. Then she swore so loudly and fiercely that Raphael jumped in surprise.

"I smell a rat," the Baron seethed.

The chancellor's gills twitched in confusion. "A rat?"

"She means a traitor," Raphael said. "At least, I assume she means a traitor, unless we've branched out into some kind of unpleasant genetic research that—"

"I mean a traitor," the Baron said impatiently. "Someone has seen fit to violate the neutrality of this Barony in my name, without my authorization."

Raphael and Muringyne looked at each other doubtfully.

"How do you come to know this?" Muringyne asked. His vestigial gills worked rapidly—a sign of agitation on his part.

"From my personal physician, is how..."

Baron Tyrelos told the two of them of her conversation with N'grash, and then about Dr. Faron's message. When she finished, the chancellor looked stricken.

"This is not good at all," the Chancellor said. "If what the doctor has reported is true, then we are in grave danger. Someone among us has no compunction about violating our declaration of neutrality. If this becomes common knowledge, many of the independents will refuse to do business here."

"And we get a fair amount of business from the independents," the Baron finished. "I know. More importantly, I had already taken an interest in Vindh."

Raphael raised an eyebrow. "Sis?"

"Not that kind of interest, oaf. You're the libido in our family. My interest is irrelevant at the moment, however—Captain Vindh is wanted for questioning by the Radiant Throne, they put a bounty on him, and it seems someone I know has decided to collect on this bounty in my name."

"Hold on a moment," Raphael said, looking at Muringyne suspiciously. "Weren't you trying to convince Min to hand the man over to this Sword when I walked in?"

Chancellor Muringyne held up his hands in a placating manner. "It is reasonable to have suspicion," he said, "but I advised taking Captain Vindh alive only after I learned of the bounty... and I believed, at the time, that he'd attacked our guards without provocation."

"Relax, Raphe, it's not Muringyne," the baron said. "He has no authority to command the guards."

"Hmmm." Raphael looked at the chancellor thoughtfully. "All right, then. Who?"

"Someone with the authority to command the guard in my name, obviously."

Raphael nodded and grinned slightly. "That puts me on your list."

"It would, if you ever displayed any interest in anything other than wine, women, and song."

"And gambling," he added. "Don't forget the gambling."

"It is unfortunate," the chancellor said, "that we cannot trust the ones who are armed." The room fell silent as the realization of what he said set in. Finally, Baron Tyrelos broke the silence, asking the question the others wouldn't say aloud.

"Is this a coup?"

Raphael looked down at his hands and said nothing.

The chancellor, however, shook his head. "I do not think so," he said. "Not yet. I believe it is a sign that one will come, perhaps soon. But because this was done in secrecy, I feel they are not yet ready."

"A deal in secret... with the Radiant Throne... good God, is the Throne backing this?"

"Perhaps," the Chancellor said. "Or the traitor is simply trying to foster good relations with the Throne. It's hard to tell. I suggest we spend more time trying to discover who the traitor is."

"Lord Sonim." Raphael smacked his forehead in disbelief. "It's got to be Lord Sonim."

Baron Tyrelos shook her head. Lord Sonim was the High Commander of Station Authority, and had been a good friend of their father's. "What reason would he have? He was a friend of father's, a good friend..."

"He has the authority to do it," Raphael pointed out. "He can go up to a guard and bark an order and it will be followed. No one would even question by whose authorization—who would believe the two of you were working at cross purposes?"

"But motive! What motive would he have?"

"He's not the Baron." Raphael peered at his sister, judging her reaction. "Look, Min, not everyone is like me. Some people actually want to be the one calling the shots. I don't pretend to understand it, but it's true. And Sonim... well, he's a man with big dreams, strong opinions, and a general sense of entitlement. And, if I may say so, he never quite adjusted to you being Baron, instead of just the Baron's little girl."

Baron Tyrelos flushed. It was true... Sonim had always treated her the way an uncle might treat a favorite niece, and hadn't been comfortable when that relationship changed.

"Raphael has a good point," the Chancellor said, "but I would caution, my Baron, against leaping to any conclusions at this point. We do not know that it is Lord Sonim, and if it were not, we would lose a powerful ally if we made a false accusation. And we have no idea who else might be involved. If we were to say the wrong things in front of the wrong people—"

"I see your point," the Baron said, sighing heavily. "But what do we do about the current situation?"

Chancellor Muringyne hesitated. "The wisest course would be to leave Captain Vindh to his fate."

The baron looked repulsed by the idea. "No. Absolutely not."

"Consider, my Baron... if we work to save the man, your enemies will suspect that you have uncovered their plans. We do not yet know who is involved, and whether they have gained the loyalty of your men. It is safer for you if—"

"I said no." Baron Tyrelos' voice was firm. "Ignoring for the moment my immediate distaste for the idea of letting him be a patsy... if Vindh dies, N'grash will tell the independents that we have violated our neutrality, and they will be less inclined to stay."

Muringyne blinked rapidly, and his gills pulsed with discomfort. "Yes, that is true."

"Well, what then?" Raphael looked at both of them expectantly. "I mean, we can't just tell Sonim to call off the guards—we do that and he can use it to turn the guards against you..."

"You're assuming he's the one behind it," the Baron said. "And you don't know that, Raphe."

"Whoever it is—whether Lord Sonim or someone else entirely—it does not matter. They would use such a thing against you without hesitation," Muringyne said. "They would whisper in the ears of your men that you care nothing for their safety, that you allow murderers to go unpunished, that their spouses and orphaned children have no recourse under your rule. Without the loyalty of your guards, you would be vulnerable to a great many dangers, and it would make their play for power, when the time came, that much more effective."

Baron Tyrelos leaned back in her chair and closed her eyes while she massaged her temples slowly. Her life was getting more complicated with each passing minute. "So what do we do?"

"We do what we must," the Chancellor replied. "We must find a way to resolve this quietly, in a way that leaves all sides beyond reproach. We must look as though we responded to this crisis appropriately, and we must also look as though we are unaware of treachery within our ranks. The best scenario would be one where we preserve our neutrality of the independents as well, though I'm not sure how we can manage all three."

The three sat in silence.

"Oh hey," Raphael said. "Here's a thought."

The other two looked at him curiously.

"What if you didn't uncover the conspiracy that they're running—but you uncovered another conspiracy altogether?"

Chapter 22

WHEREIN Our Hero Struggles with Probing Questions

Grif, Amys and Bennet crowded around the terminal display, studying a schematic of the hospital.

"Looks like we're here," Amys said, pointing to an area on the map, then at a door at the end of the room. "And it also looks like that door will take us out into the hangar. Grif, if I got you into one of the hospital's grav sleds could you fly it with one arm?"

"Yes." Grif didn't hesitate.

Bennet looked at Grif doubtfully. "We'd still need to get past the Station Authority guards. If I were giving the orders I'd have every exit under heavy guard."

"Yeah," Grif agreed. "It'd be nice to be able to convince them to go somewhere else..."

They thought in silence.

"I have an idea," Bennet said. "Assuming they're monitoring all hospital communications." He entered a few commands into the terminal, and the map disappeared from the screen.

"Care to elaborate?" Amys asked.

"Well..." Bennet entered a few more commands into the terminal, and a list of data scrolled down the terminal screen. "If we can convince them we're in another part of the hospital, we can probably convince most of the guards to go *there* instead of hanging around *here*. I just need to find a convincing place... there."

"There what?" Grif looked at the screen and shook his head. "Looks like gibberish to me."

Bennet pointed to a line of characters on the screen. "I *think* this is the address to an isolation chamber in another wing. It has its own self-regulated atmosphere, which makes it a plausible location to hide from the gas. We just need to figure out how to convince Station Authority that we're there instead of here."

"Just turn it on," Amys said. Bennet and Grif looked at her curiously.

"You can't unseal an isolation chamber from the inside," Amys said.

"Cutter has a funny story about that. When an isolation chamber on a ship is active, it sends a message to the bridge so life support knows not to unseal it or mix environments unless it's given the all-clear. I assume it's the same with a hospital. If they're monitoring hospital systems, they'll notice when an isolation chamber turns itself on."

"OK," Bennet said. "There. Done."

Almost immediately they heard faint shouting.

"Promising," Bennet said.

"Yeah..." Grif crept over to the door. "Right then. Here's the plan..."

"Steal something fast and run for it?" Amys asked.

"I see you're familiar with my plans," Grif said. "Are we ready?"

Bennet and Amys nodded.

"OK." Grif took a deep breath, then flipped the electronic release on the door. The bolts released on the door and Grif winced as it slid open in a loud, grinding fashion.

"Not my favorite door..." he muttered. He poked his head out the door as Amys and Bennet moved past him, weapons ready.

The hangar was empty.

"Huh," Amys said.

It was a large, cavernous space. The entrance to the second city was a massive iris on the hangar ceiling. Usually it would be open, allowing traffic to easily drop in or exit as needed, but at the moment it was sealed shut. There were no people, only rows of vehicles sitting silently and unused.

Grif walked deeper into the hangar, past a few support columns, and looked around nervously. The place was empty. Deserted.

"Odd," Bennet said. "I thought there would be at least a few guards left."

"Yeah," Grif agreed. "It doesn't make sense for this place to be deserted. The hangar has too many vehicles, you'd think there would be *someone*..."

Something in the back of Grif's mind shouted *it's a trap*. Then he went blind.

Amys shouted in alarm, then Bennet, their pulse rifles firing in tandem. He groped for something to use as a guide. His hand touched a support column. He felt his way around it, blinking rapidly, trying to clear his vision.

The gunfire continued without pause, Amys and Bennet shouting information to each other as they fired.

"Main entrance, right column!"

"What?" Grif shouted.

"He's moving left! Second column!"

"*Who*?" Grif shouted again.

"Look out, he's..."

Bennet cried out in pain. One of the guns stopped firing.

Grif heard someone running. He shook his head, trying to clear his vision. Why couldn't he see?

"Amys, are you... ?"

A pulse rifle started firing again. Not focused like before, but wildly: a shot here, two shots there. At one point Grif heard and felt a shower of sparks as a pulse of energy exploded next to him.

Suddenly the gun stopped firing. Grif heard Amys grunt in pain, and a rifle clatter onto the ground. Then there was a smack, and a thud, then silence.

"Amys." Grif's voice sounded hoarse to his own ears, barely a whisper. He coughed and tried to clear his throat. "Amys? Amys, can you hear me?"

Someone laughed. Grif suddenly realized why he was blind.

"Yes," someone said. "You understand now."

Grif felt a crushing blow to the side of his head. He sprawled on the ground, falling on his left arm, and shrieked in pain.

"Poor child..." the voice muttered.

Grif gasped for breath and struggled to his knees. "I don't believe we've met," he said, trying to sound nonchalant.

There was no answer.

"Let me guess," he continued. "You must be the Sword they call 'The Viceroy...'"

He heard footsteps approach him, circle around him, but no one replied.

"A bit much, don't you think?" Grif was on his knees now. He wondered where his gun was; he dropped it when he fell. "I mean, it is grandiose, I'll give you that, but there's pretension and then there's—"

Someone kicked him in the stomach, hard. Grif collapsed again as the air rushed out of his body.

"Impudent," the voice said. "Impudent, arrogant, ignorant. You know me, or claim to, and yet you try to mock me. No matter..."

Strong hands dragged Grif to his feet and forced him to walk... where, Grif couldn't tell.

"You are a problem, Captain Vindh. You are, in fact, *the* problem... the problem at the beginning of all this. The serpent invading Eden. But I didn't truly comprehend its scope."

"Eden?" Grif did his best to sound unimpressed. "Didn't know you were from that hellho—"

Another swift kick, and Grif flew back, landing hard. This time he couldn't rally himself to struggle to his feet. He lay on his back, heaving, trying to breathe, cursing his blindness.

"Frustration." The man—the Viceroy—kneeled by Grif's side. Grif could feel his breath. "Yes... I am doing this to you. I've robbed you of your sight. I have also, in a way, robbed everyone else in the world of theirs..."

The Viceroy lifted Grif, seemingly without effort, and placed him on something cold and flat. "It is simple enough. You simply tell people that they can't see you, and they won't. God has many gifts, and one is to shroud His angels from the eyes of men."

Grif laughed weakly. "Angels..."

The Viceroy's voice became considerably colder. "Do not mock me, Captain. You will not survive if you do."

Grif coughed, and continued laughing. "I won't survive either way, you bastard." A hand struck him on the cheek, and his head spun.

"Such defiance. Stupidity in the face of peril. I ought to kill you regardless... you made this far more difficult than it needed to be."

Grif tried to collect his wits as his assailant dragged him across the ground.

"I didn't expect you to run, you know. I didn't expect you to know where you were being taken. Gossip is the devil's instrument, and he used it to help you... but he failed."

Grif felt himself being pushed down onto his knees.

"Let the scales fall from your eyes," the Viceroy said.

Light returned. Grif squinted. What had previously seemed like dim light from glow panels on the hangar ceiling now appeared to be bright light from rows of rectangular suns. The Viceroy knelt in front of him. He was a tall, thin man with almost no hair at all on his head, save for dark, thin eyebrows. He was smiling, revealing rows of perfectly white teeth.

"You can see," the Viceroy said. "And now *I* will see..."

The Viceroy reached across and placed a hand on the top of Grif's head. "Open your thoughts to me, sinner," he said, voice gentle. "Open your soul, that I may judge thee..."

Searing pain cut through Grif's head, and his vision faded again. He felt something force its way into his mind, as if it were tearing away tiny pieces of his brain and reattaching them when finished.

Memories came unbidden into his conscious mind. A child on Kinnar, a young man on his first pirate vessel, buying the *Fool's Errand*, meeting Amys...

"No," the Sword muttered. "Not those. Too far back."

The pressure increased tenfold. Grif whimpered softly as the Sword forced his memory forward in time.

Meeting Mavis. Avoiding his trap. Traveling to Varkav...

Grif stood, helpless, as the entire story was revealed.

The Sword laughed. "This is the secret? That you stumbled across your bounty by *accident*? *That* is what you would have me believe? Stop fighting me, boy, or I will destroy your mind completely."

"It's... it's true," Grif gasped. "It was all... luck... I just... made it up..."

"Perhaps," the Sword said. "But I think there is more, Captain. I think there is more you aren't telling me. Something you don't want me to see..."

The image of the alien object came unbidden to his mind.

Anger flooded into Grif's brain like a white-hot poker. The Sword's voice was icy calm. "What is this picture, Captain Vindh? What is this secret?"

More memories. Documents Grif had read but didn't remember came back into his mind, all the details right there in front of him. Things that had scrolled by on terminals for the barest of moments during the meeting on the *Fool's Errand*, things he'd told himself he'd study in detail later—all there in complete clarity, as if he'd studied them for years. He was reading through it all because the Sword was reading through it all.

An aerial view of Ur Voys. Estimated troop numbers and known employees. Transport routes, and suspected cargo. Service centers that supplied the facility...

And suddenly, Grif saw the weak link.

"What?" The calm malice of the Viceroy evaporated, replaced by startled uncertainty. "What is this?"

Grif tried to back away from the thought in his mind and focus something else.

"No," the Viceroy snarled, voice shaking with rage. "You do not decide. *I* decide. Show me what you saw!"

Grif whimpered softly as he tried desperately to fight against the weight of the Viceroy's mind.

"Break," the Sword muttered. "Break!"

Grif screamed as the pressure on his mind increased beyond the point that he could bear. Something wet and salty ran down his lips; his nose was bleeding. He felt himself start to black out. He clawed at his sanity, but it was too much: he felt himself slipping away, as though he were about to fall into a dark well that he would never be able to climb out of.

Using the very last of his strength, he shoved his knee into the Viceroy's groin.

The Viceory grunted in surprise and pain. The crushing weight in Grif's head disappeared, replaced by the weight of the Viceroy as he fell on top of Grif.

The Viceroy rolled up to his feet quickly—almost instantly—and stood before Grif could do anything. A single foot lashed out as Grif tried to roll to his side, and caught him in the side.

The Viceroy kicked again, face twisted into a mask of feral rage. Grif tried to turn to the side, but the Viceroy was too fast: Grif's eyes glazed over with pain as his head snapped back, and he collapsed back on the floor.

"Enough games, Captain Vindh." The Viceroy stood over him and pulled out a long, slender knife. "Now it is time to—"

Energy arced through the air, and three short bursts slammed into the Viceroy's side. He spun, surprise etched on his face, and shuddered as three more bursts hit him square in the chest. He crumpled to the ground, motionless.

Grif looked at the Viceroy sprawled on the ground. He was lying on his back, glassy lifeless eyes staring up at the ceiling. Slowly, painfully, Grif looked in the direction of the pulse fire. Amys stood, leaning against a column, pulse rifle dangling from one arm. Bruises covered one side of her face, and she bled from one ear.

"Hi," Grif said. "I was hoping you'd show."

"Hey." Amys forced herself to stand upright and dragged herself over to Grif. "You all right?"

"No," Grif said.

Amys laughed.

Grif grinned. "Is Bennet..."

"Still breathing," Amys said. "Out cold though."

"Oh."

Amys slumped down beside Grif and let out a soft groan.

"You don't look so good," Grif observed.

"You look worse," Amys said.

"I'll bet," Grif replied. "Thanks for the save. Maybe someday I'll get a chance to return the favor. Be nice if I could save you for a change."

Amys laughed again. "Dream on, Grif."

An alarm sounded as the hangar iris began to open. Grif heard men shouting in the distance.

"I guess Station Authority will be here any minute now," Amys said, sighing regretfully.

"Yeah," Grif said. "It's a shame. I figured out how to do it."

"Do what?"

"Ur Voys... I figured out how to get in."

Amys looked at him, raised an eyebrow, and said "when?"

"When what?"

"When did you figure out how to get in?"

"Oh," Grif said. "When that guy was tearing my mind apart to figure out how I broke in last time." Amys shook her head, confused.

"Ironic, isn't it? I don't think I could have done it without him." Grif grinned, then winced.

"So what is it?"

Grif thought. “Complicated,” he said.

Amys snorted.

“I can’t talk about it right now. There’s something else I need to do first, and I want to make sure I do it before Station Authority arrives.”

“What?” Amys asked. “Planning on passing out?”

“Thank you,” Grif said. “I think I will.”

And with that, Grif passed out. Again.

Chapter 23

WHEREIN Our Hero Talks Too Much

Grif opened his eyes to see a hauntingly familiar white ceiling.

"Dream?"

He tried to sit up and was stopped, once again, by something gripping his left side. He looked to his left and saw a machine completely covering his left arm and side.

"Deja vu, Captain Vindh?"

Grif looked up to see a very familiar doctor standing in a disturbingly familiar doorway.

"What the hell?" Grif croaked, and struggled to free himself.

"No!" The doctor hurried forward in alarm and gently pushed Grif back down on the bed. "It's all right, Captain. Just let the machine work. This time we won't be interrupted."

"What the hell?" Grif repeated, grabbing the doctor by his coat.

"Yes, I can imagine it's a little confusing." The doctor looked down at Grif's hand and sighed. "But everything is all right. You're no longer wanted by Station Authority. The Baron herself pardoned you and your friends. All very unfortunate... it seems you were caught in the middle of some kind of coup."

Grif's eyes widened in alarm.

"Which failed. And hopefully this time I'll be able to fix you up without any interruptions."

Grif released the doctor and looked around the room. "Amys," he said. Once again, his throat felt very dry.

"Your lady-friend? Very resilient woman. I think she's waiting in the lobby, if you'll hold on a moment." The doctor studied the monitor at the foot of Grif's bed, checking his vital signs for anything out of the ordinary.

Grif waited in silence, trying to be patient. Then a very distressing notion occurred to him.

"Please," he said, looking around apprehensively, "tell me... this isn't the... same room, is it?"

"What?" The doctor looked up, distracted. "What? Oh. Oh, no... no, this is a different room. Yes, that would be disturbing..."

The doctor turned and left the room. Grif lay on his back and stared at the ceiling, trying to relax. The door opened again, and Grif looked up to see Amys, face slightly swollen and bruised, arm in a sling.

"Amys!"

Amys smiled. "You don't look as bad as I thought. Feel like you've been here before?"

Grif chuckled nervously. "I'm not sure how paranoid I should be right now."

"Only your standard level. They dropped all the charges. We were apparently caught in the middle of something."

"As usual."

"A bit above standard, actually," Amys said. "We chose the wrong week to visit."

"What about Bennet?" Grif asked. "Is he—"

"He's fine, recovering back on the *Fool's Errand*. He said to tell you he thought he'd sit this visit out, and hoped you wouldn't take it the wrong way."

Grif laughed weakly.

"He also said," Amys added, "that he would sit on your 'confession' for a while."

"Oh yes," Grif said. "That's... uhhh... good. Very good."

"I told him what you told me," Amys said. "That you found a way in. Remember?"

Grif nodded.

"Well he wants to hear your plan, and if he likes it he'll play ball."

Grif sighed in relief. "Better than I expected."

"Yeah," Amys said. "Surprised me. I guess he's only half a bastard."

"And the Sword?" Grif asked. "What happened to him?"

Amys started to reply, hesitated, then shrugged.

"Amys? The Sword..."

"I heard, you," Amys said. "They couldn't find the body. At least, that's what they told me."

"They couldn't find it? It was lying on the ground next to me."

"Well, I thought it was, too, but now that I think of it I don't remember it after you passed out."

"Well," Grif said, "that's a shame. I prefer confirmed kills."

"Yeah," Amys said. "Me too. I never saw anyone fight like that before. Bennet and I didn't really have a chance... and, you know... we're good."

"Yeah..." Grif stared at the ceiling, starting to worry. "Hey, as long as we're on the subject of bad news, what's the deal with Station Authority? I gather they dropped the charges, but still... if they're going to hold a grudge we'll probably have to find another place to—"

Before Grif could finish, the door opened and three people entered the room—two human, male and female, and a Vage. Grif thought the Vage was male, but it was tough to tell for certain.

"Hello Amys," the woman said.

Grif looked at the three newcomers suspiciously. The male human was an older man, thin with gray hair and a distinguished air. He wore a Station Authority uniform, but Grif didn't recognize the insignia on the shoulder. The woman was dressed simply and somewhat severely—which did little to disguise the fact that she was at least half a decade younger than Grif and stunningly attractive. The Vage, standing behind the other two with a deferential air about him, was taller than the woman and shorter than the man. He looked like a bipedal fish in a suit.

Amys saw the expression on Grif's face and cleared her throat cautiously. "Grif... this is Baron Minerva Tyrelos, Lord Sonim Makar, and Chancellor Muringyne."

Grif blinked.

"Captain Vindh," the Baron said, "I'd like to start off by saying..." She hesitated, peered at him curiously, and then turned to Amys. "Is he all right? He seems... is he on medication?"

Amys frowned. "He's all right. Just confused. Grif, snap out of it."

Grif blinked again. "Sorry," he said. "I... I'm sorry, Baron, I just—ah..."

Grif steadied himself, took a deep breath, and smiled. "Hello Baron, lovely to meet you. I'm sorry it had to be under such awkward circumstances."

The corners of the baron's mouth twitched slightly. "Captain Vindh, I'd like to start off by saying that on behalf of Tyrelos Station, we would like to offer our apologies for the dangerous situation you found yourself in earlier. We take our declaration of neutrality seriously, and the breach of security that nearly ended that declaration has wounded us grievously."

"Thank you," Grif said. "I was a little... er... that is to say, at the time I wasn't very—did you say breach of security?"

The man—Lord Sonim, Grif supposed—nodded gravely. "Someone attempted to hand you over to the Radiant Throne and make it appear as though the Baron herself had authorized it. I myself was unaware of this treachery until the Baron discovered it. It's quite unfortunate that you were an unwitting pawn in their game."

Grif looked from Lord Sonim to Baron Tyrelos, expression blank. "I'm confused," he said. "Are you telling me you had no intention of ever handing me over to the Throne?"

The Baron shook her head. "That was never my intention."

"Then why did you pay to have me transferred from MedCommons to MediCorp? And pay to have my shoulder reconstructed?"

"That..." The Baron hesitated. "We'll discuss that in a moment. Suffice to say that I wanted to talk to you, and it seemed best that I speed our meeting along."

Grif frowned.

"Unfortunately," the Baron continued, "someone very close to me used his access to forge an order to Station Authority, authorizing you to be handed over to the Radiant Throne. In a way I am in your debt, Captain. If you hadn't escaped when you did, the traitor would've leaked news of your fate after the fact—and our reputation as a neutral system would be ruined."

"We thought that was uncharacteristic," Grif said dryly. Amys nodded.

"Well, it's behind us now," Baron Tyrelos said.

Grif stared at her, fascinated. She tried awfully hard to make herself look older and less attractive than she really was, but she was obviously striking...

Amys coughed. Grif realized he was on the verge of undressing the Baron of the Tyrelos System with his eyes, and suddenly found the machine connected to his left arm immensely interesting.

"So if it's not top secret information, or anything," Grif said, forcing himself to sound only mildly interested, "who was the traitor? Who do I have to thank for all this fun we've been having?"

Nobody answered. Baron Tyrelos looked at the floor, lost in thought.

"Uhhh... sorry," Grif said. "It's not really my place, I was just—"

"The traitor was Lord Raphael Tyrelos," the Baron said softly, still looking down at the floor. "My brother."

Lord Sonim placed his hand on the baron's shoulder and squeezed it gently. The baron clasped his hand, apparently grateful. Grif saw her stiffen slightly.

"I see," Grif said, voice neutral. "Well. I'm sorry to hear that."

"Don't apologize," the Baron said. "It wasn't your fault."

There was an awkward silence.

Finally, the Baron turned to Lord Sonim and smiled. "Sonim," she said, "I'd like to speak to these two in private. Would you be so kind?"

Lord Sonim bowed stiffly. "Of course, my Baron. I will try to determine exactly where your brother went." He turned to Grif and Amys, bowing slightly to each in turn. "My apologies for your travails. I hope the rest of your stay is more pleasant."

"I will accompany you," the Chancellor said. It was the first time Grif heard the Vage speak. He found the voice slightly unsettling.

Lord Sonim nodded, turned and left the room. The chancellor bowed to the Baron, nodded at Grif and Amys, and left.

The Baron waited a moment after the chancellor left the room, then turned back to Grif. "Now we can talk without interruption."

"Oh?" Grif looked at the Baron warily. "So this is something important?"

Baron Tyrelos laughed sharply. "You are a pain in the ass, Captain."

Grif relaxed slightly. He felt he was on more familiar ground.

The Baron walked over to Grif's table, looking at him and frowning thoughtfully. "This entire mess started," she said, "because you—"

She stopped and her frown deepened as she glanced at Amys.

"Anything you need to say to me, you can say in front of her," Grif said. "We're thick as thieves."

"Hey," Amys protested.

"Independents, then. Thick as independents."

The Baron frowned, studied Amys for a moment, then shrugged. "Very well. But I warn you both not to repeat this conversation. This entire mess started because you said something very interesting to Captain N'grash, who passed it on to me."

Grif frowned. "What did I say to—" His eyes widened. "She told you *that*?"

"She tells me a lot," the Baron said. "I find it useful to know what's going on in the world of the... 'Independents.' When she told me one of her colleagues was claiming that Baron Tylaris was murdered by the Alliance—"

"What?" Amys looked at Grif sharply.

The Baron smiled slightly. "Thick as thieves, are you?"

"And when were you going to tell me *this*?" Amys snapped.

"The same time I was going to tell you about that damn Sword," Grif snapped back. "When we were in a private place, where certain parties wouldn't *overhear*."

Amys frowned. "You're sure?"

"I'm sure."

"But that's insane."

"Pretty insane," Grif agreed. "But I'm pretty sure."

"What makes you so sure?" the Baron asked sharply. "N'grash said the same thing, that you were absolutely convinced of it. And that when you were like that, you were usually right. Do you have any proof?"

Grif grinned. "No proof. But I'm pretty sure. Just like I'm sure you're lying about your brother."

The baron gripped the side of Grif's bed tightly. "Please explain yourself," she said.

Grif half-shrugged. "You're not a bad liar, Baron, but I'm *much* better. You were putting on a show. Not just for us, but for... what's his name? Sonim. I don't know about the fish, Vage are hard to read."

The way Baron Tyrelos stared at Grif made him wish he'd kept his mouth shut. He wondered if the medicine being pumped in through his arm was making him stupid.

"We'll talk about that next," the Baron said. "For the moment, tell me about Baron Tylaris. What about his death made you suspicious?"

"What didn't?" Grif replied. "I mean, he's the single richest man in known space—sorry, he *was* the single richest man in known space. He can afford the best... and suddenly he's accidentally poisoned by improperly prepared food?"

"Circumstantial," the Baron said dismissively.

"There were Alliance operatives on the planet just before his death," Grif continued. "Not just diplomats, but the kind that play for keeps."

Baron Tyrelos looked confused. "How do you know—"

"Not important right now," Grif said. "I also know that one of those operatives was sitting in the same bar I was when the news of Baron Tylaris' death showed up on vid. And unlike any other person in the bar, he was completely uninterested in the broadcast. Like it was old news..."

The Baron stared at him thoughtfully. "That's still circumstantial."

"Sure," Grif agreed. "I said I can't prove it. But I put it all together, and it screams 'externally enabled transfer of power.' Everyone knows the old Baron wasn't interested in joining the Alliance, but everyone knows the Alliance was trying to court him just the same. If he wasn't going to budge, well, what about his son? Comes across as a weasel to me. Maybe easier to convince? I don't have proof, but I'm right."

Baron Tyrelos sighed, then nodded reluctantly. "You might be right. I received word today that the *new* Baron Tylaris reached a tentative accord with the Alliance of Free Worlds."

Grif blinked. "Well. I thought it would take a little more time than that."

"It's true. They will be joining the Alliance as an autonomous member."

Grif shook his head. This was a coup for the Alliance. The Tylaris Shipyards were considered the best in the known worlds, and that alone was a boon to any government. Add the natural resources of the Tylaris planets, and the other corporations that made their home in Tylaris space... the Alliance had increased its economic power enormously.

"I can't believe it," Amys said.

"Believe it," Baron Tyrelos said bitterly. "Mogra would never have considered such a thing—what would he get from the Alliance that he didn't already have? He liked his independence. But Rolis..."

The disdain in her voice for the Baron's heir was plain for all to hear. "He has never had a taste for power. The trappings of it, yes, but not the care and nurture required to maintain it... 'indolent' and 'lazy' are the words I'd use to describe him."

"The Tylaris Trade Barony, part of the Alliance," Grif murmured. "Well... that's sure going to shake up the Independents." Even as he said it, he wondered exactly what would happen. The Independents—smugglers, pirates, and legitimate businessmen not tied to any particular trade company—favored Tylaris Prime as their home port. It had been a free port in the truest sense of the word, and a haven for all sorts of transactions that would almost certainly be forbidden by any kind of Alliance membership. Even autonomous membership, which allowed a local governing authority the most independence from the Alliance, carried with it some mandatory laws governing interstellar trade that had to be enforced. Most of the Independents—Grif included—would no longer consider Tylaris Prime their home.

"What do you think will happen?" the Baron asked.

Grif looked at her curiously. She was staring at him with a very neutral, guarded expression—an expression, he decided, of someone trying to determine whether to call or raise the stakes.

"Dunno," he said. "Independents will be looking for a new place to congregate. Baron Cedoris, maybe, though he's a little too enthusiastic about slavery for my taste—drink too much, run out of money, wake up God knows where—"

"What about here?" Baron Tyrelos still wore a guarded expression, but her eyes gleamed.

"Tyrelos?"

The Baron nodded.

"Well," Grif said, "I, personally, am very fond of the Tyrelos system—when I'm not a pawn in some unseen political game, that is—but I don't know how well it would go over with the Independents as a whole."

"Why not?" The Baron asked. "We already get some of that traffic."

"Yes," Grif said, "but it's a very specific subset. Miners, mostly. People looking to shop the exotics market. Slavers who don't want to give Cedoris a cut. But it takes a certain amount of trouble to get here, and your shipyard facilities are... well..."

"... not so good," Amys said.

Grif nodded. "They're all right for what you do, but they're a bit sparse for most needs."

“Not to mention,” Amys added, “that you don’t have a single planet in your system that could be considered habitable without environmental controls. A lot of the Independents who flocked to Tylaris did so because they could sell their goods and enjoy a little R&R.”

“The shipyards can be improved,” the Baron countered.

“And the planets?” Amys asked. “‘Come relax in our highly corrosive atmosphere’ is not exactly a compelling lure...”

“Are you serious about this?” Grif asked. “You really want to become the new watering hole for the Independents in the Baron systems?”

Baron Tyrelos nodded. “The Barony needs to expand its interests.”

Grif glanced at Amys. She was openly skeptical.

“But you seem hesitant, Captain Vindh,” the Baron noted. “And you have something of a reputation among the Independents—certainly N’grash seems to think highly of you, which I consider both unusual and telling. If I can convince you...”

“Well, you don’t need to convince me,” Grif said. “I already come here, fairly regularly. But as I said earlier, Tyrelos attracts a certain element, an element which I’ve been accused of belonging to. A scurrilous accusation, and wholly without merit, of course.”

Amys rolled her eyes.

“There are two big things working against you right now,” Grif said.

“I’d like to know what they are.”

“Well, first... you’re right on the edge of Throne space. That makes a lot of Independents nervous. Tylaris was right on the edge of Alliance space, and they’re usually considered the lesser evil. If the Throne suddenly decided it was time to annex the Trade Baronies, yours is the first they’d move in on. And because you’re, well, I’m sorry, but it’s true—because you’re considered the weak Baron, people sort of think it’s bound to happen any year now.”

Baron Tyrelos digested this news without appearing too offended. “I see. And the other reason?”

“Well... your recent political troubles are sort of going to feed into that general perception.”

“But the troubles are over, Captain Vindh,” the Baron replied. “I certainly hope you aren't carrying a grudge. My brother has fled the system, and he certainly won't be allowed back in..."

"Right," Grif said. "OK."

"Why Captain Vindh," the Baron said, smiling a little more noticeably, "if I didn't know better I'd say you didn't believe a word I was saying."

Grif sighed. "We've already been through this, Baron. If you want me to go along with the story that your brother tried to depose you, that's fine. But you're lying, through your teeth, and to be *completely* honest the fact that you've either framed your brother or—and here's an interesting idea—that you and your brother are working some angle together doesn't do much to convince me that this is a *politically stable environment*."

The Baron didn't reply.

"It just doesn't fit," Grif continued. "I've actually met Lord Raphael—of course he calls himself 'Dannig' when he's slumming—and if ever there was a man who was *thoroughly disinterested* in power, it's him. He's a lot like Rolis Tylaris... Though... not in the insulting way you're obviously taking it right now—"

The Baron's body stiffened, and her face was tight with anger. "My brother is not an idiot."

"No," Grif agreed. "Not an idiot. Let me rephrase. Your brother enjoys the good life a little too much to want the work involved in running this place. And might I add that you defending a man who, according to you, tried to *depose* you only makes it more obvious that you're making the whole thing up."

Baron Tyrelos relaxed slowly.

"If I had to guess, I'd say that you suspect Lord Sonim."

The mask fell from her face completely. "How—"

Grif grinned. "Well there you go," he said to Amys. "I seem to be on a roll."

"Grif," Amys said, "shut *up*."

Baron Tyrelos looked from Amys to Grif and shook her head in exasperation. "You are too perceptive for your own good, Captain. If I didn't want you on my side as badly as I did, I'd probably try and have you spaced, just to keep you quiet."

"Er..."

"Oh, don't worry," she said. "I've no intention of actually doing it. Like I said, I want you on my side."

"Your... side?" Grif asked suspiciously. "Look, I try not to get involved in—"

"Too late." The Baron discarded her severe demeanor for an instant and smiled. "Captain Vindh, you know entirely too much not to be involved."

The expression on Amys' face alternated between "I told you so" and "if she doesn't kill you, I will."

"There are people in Station Authority who still want you dead," Baron Tyrelos said. "Whether you were set up or not. You killed friends and colleagues of theirs, after all. They aren't coming after you because I ordered them not to. If I am usurped, the person who takes my place will certainly not be as disposed to keeping you alive."

Once again, Grif felt as if he were on familiar ground—this time, it was *not* comforting. "You know," he said, feeling the walls close in around him, "you are much better at threatening people than you are at lying."

"Much better," Amys agreed, voice tight.

Baron Tyrelos smiled, looking radiant. "Why thank you, Captain Vindh. I'm so glad we understand each other."

Chapter 24

WHEREIN Our Hero Goes Home

A few hours later Grif's arm was completely healed—it wasn't even sore, a far cry from the mostly useless thing he'd been dragging about the last time it was taken out of the machine. Aside from discovering his bill was paid in full, he and Amys learned the Baron had also arranged for transportation to take them back to the *Fool's Errand:* a high-end transport, the height of comfort in Tyrelos Station. Completely separated from their driver, they had absolute privacy.

For half the trip they said nothing, each staring out their own windows. Finally Grif sighed, shook his head, and looked at Amys ruefully.

"I'm an idiot."

"Not usually," Amys said. "Which is why it's so goddamn frustrating when you are."

"I'm just not sure what *happened,*" Grif said.

Amys snorted in disgust. "You were showing off in front of a pretty girl. Only she wasn't a girl, she was the Baron of Tyrelos Industries. What the hell is wrong with you?"

"I...hell, I don't know, Amys." Grif shrugged defensively. "There's a part of my brain that tells me I need to shut up, and there's another part of my brain that *pantses* the first part, then goes on to get me in trouble while the first part is getting itself all sorted out."

Amys sighed, and stared out the window again.

"Besides," Grif added, face breaking into a grin, "you didn't complain back when I was showing off for *you.*"

Amys smiled slightly. "Another act of idiocy on your part."

"Without question," Grif agreed solemnly. "Worst decision I ever made."

Amys barked a laugh and elbowed him in the arm. Grif grunted good-naturedly.

"The fact that you're *charming* doesn't change the fact that you screwed up," Amys said.

"Yeah..." Grif admitted. "Well, let's review. The Throne hates us... wants to arrest all of us and apparently kill me. The Alliance is sending us on a suicide mission. And now the weakest of the Trade Baronies, caught in the middle of a coup, is trying to force me to be their spokesman for the Independents Tourism Board."

"That sums it up," Amys said.

"On the other hand," Grif said, "Baron Tyrelos is *stunningly attractive*."

Amys shot him a look.

"Well did you *see* her?" Grif asked. "I mean, up close. You saw her, right?"

Amys narrowed her eyes. "You're baiting me."

"Nevermind," Grif said. "It's not as much fun when you figure it out."

The second city raced below them, gradually changing from the gleaming, well-to-do neighborhoods to the industrial districts. They were getting to close to the transport hub that connected to Dock 78.

"It could work. I think." Amys sounded reluctant. "Her idea."

Grif looked at Amys curiously. "Making Tyrelos the new home for the Independents? You didn't sound convinced back in the hospital."

"I wasn't," Amys said. "I'm still not. I said it could work, but I'm not sure if she'd be willing to do what it would take."

"What would it take?"

"She'd have to improve her shipyards," Amys said. "Drastically, and quickly. And it'd have to be on one of the planets. Tyrelos Station is too difficult to get to."

"It's not so bad," Grif countered. "We'd never have any troubles if I didn't insist on going in so fast all the time. And I don't think there are many independent ships as big as the *Fool's Errand*."

"Tyrelos Station isn't big enough," Amys said. "It's huge, but it's not large enough to handle the bulk of the independents, assuming they decided to come. It's already pretty full..."

"Fair point," Grif said. "It's harder to expand an artificial dwelling floating in space in the middle of a proto-ring than it is to expand an artificial dwelling sitting on solid ground. So it'd have to be one of the planets."

"Moji," Amys said. "Selur's atmosphere is too corrosive for a shipyard of any decent size."

Grif laughed. "Yes, Moji would be quite the hot spot for independents.

'Gimmie the respirator, Cyrus, I have a yen to see the moons rise over the lovely billowing chlorine clouds!'"

Amys smiled slightly. "I seem to remember you didn't mind that much."

Grif smirked. "Entirely different circumstances. And I wasn't paying much attention to the moons or the clouds—though I did feel like I needed that respirator once or twice."

Amys laughed. "You bastard."

"I am at that. So who's next in your sights? It's Bennet, isn't it?"

Amys wrinkled her nose. "Hardly."

"But he seems so *dreamy*..."

Amys shook her head, grinning. "Quiet, you. And he did agree to keep quiet about your... er... moment of honesty."

"Remind me to avoid honesty in the future. Bad decision on my part. But yes, that goes a long way toward lessening my general desire to kill him."

"Do you really have a plan?" Amys asked, trying not to sound anxious. "I mean, you're not kidding about that, or stalling for time, are you?"

"No," Grif said. "I swear, Amys—it all fell into my lap in the hangar back there. It's risky, but it can actually work."

"Define risky."

Grif shook his head. "Not yet," he said. "We need to get back to the ship and I need to make a call or two. Gotta track someone down before I know if we can even try it."

"Oh," Amys said. "One of *those* plans..."

Grif sighed. "You have no idea..."

The return was uneventful. Morgan, Cyrus, Ktk, Cutter, Hari, Vod and Gurgan were all very happy and relieved to see Grif and Amys, as was Bennet, though in a reserved way. Velis appeared briefly, scowled, and returned to her quarters.

The welcoming committee was threatening to turn into a welcoming party, but Grif regretfully derailed it. "I've got to take care of some things," he said, ignoring the protests of his crew. "I've got people to call, and I've got to pull an astoundingly brilliant miracle out of thin air."

"Or somewhere else," Amys muttered, causing Cyrus to burst out laughing.

"Hold on a sec, Grif," Cyrus said before Grif could leave. "You need to tell us, since none of us have ever been in a MediCorp building before—what's it like? Are the walls paved with gold? Is it more of a hospital or more of a spa?"

"It's fascinating," Grif said. "And by fascinating, I mean 'isn't it fascinating how little I want to go back?' Now if anyone needs me, I'll be in my cabin."

The Captain's Cabin of the *Fool's Errand* was spacious. It consisted of five rooms: a medium-sized living area, a bathroom and shower, a small kitchen area, a medium-sized bedroom, and a private office. Some might have called such extensive quarters "extravagant," and for starship quarters it was, but it was Grif's home. It was the only home he'd ever needed, and he rarely took lodgings planetside. The quarters were meticulously clean and free of clutter, a result of years of traveling in zero gravity. The living area had an entertainment terminal that included a holographic projector, and the office had both a terminal wired to the rest of the ship and a computer that could interface with the ship but also had its own private storage.

Grif stepped into the cabin and sighed in relief: it felt good to be home. He tugged off the clothes the hospital had given him, took a quick shower—sonic, he was too practical to store water on a ship solely for the purpose of bathing—and changed out of the hospital-donated attire into his own clothes. He felt much better.

He wandered into his office and sat at his desk, activating the terminal with a wave of his hand. He patched into the communication system, and sent a message to the Captain of the *Grlashimargrak*.

"N'grash, hey, it's Grif—just wanted to let you know I'm still alive. From what I can gather, I have you to thank for a great deal of that. I owe you one—again—just let me know when you need to collect. Vindh out."

A moment later, something occurred to Grif that prompted him to send N'grash another message:

"N'grash, Grif again... it just occurred to me that if you hadn't told the Baron what I told you I wouldn't have been put in this mess to begin with. What the hell is that all about, anyway? I don't recommend working for the government... seriously. I really don't. Anyway, I still owe you one, but for the record? It's a much *smaller* one. Vindh out."

That done, Grif patched into the city communications grid and called up directory services.

"You have reached Tyrelos Station Directory Services," a pleasantly artificial voice said.

"Ebur Tosk," he said. "He's in my short list."

"Please hold while we connect you to Ebur Tosk."

Grif drummed his fingers on his desk as the terminal screen displayed the word "STANDBY" in front of a blue test pattern. Finally, the terminal beeped, and the screen switched to show a thin man with wispy red hair peering out from the monitor.

"Hello?"

"Ebur!" Grif grinned at the terminal screen. "It's Grif."

"Grif?" The man peered back, squinting. "Hold on a moment, there's something wrong with my display..." The man turned away, fiddling with some controls, and then smacked the monitor in frustration. "OK, that's better. Oh, Grif! Hell, funny you should call. I just saw you on the news. Something about you shooting up a hospital?"

"Yeah... well, it's been an interesting few days," Grif said. "Look, I need to get to the point—you still hiring out?"

Ebur nodded. "Not as often, but yeah, if the price is right. Why? You looking to hire?"

"Yes," Grif said. "And it's incredibly inconvenient and dangerous, so it will most likely pay quite well."

A mixture of annoyance, intrigue and dread flitted across Ebur's face. "Could you, uh, be a little more specific about that?"

"All right," Grif said. "First, the job is in Throne space..."

Ebur didn't look happy about that. "You're going to put me in a crate, aren't you?"

"Well, a cylinder... but yes, same idea. Also, the job is... tricky. So I'm estimating we'll need to use you for a month."

Ebur looked even less thrilled. "A month? Are you serious? And how are you going to, you know..."

"Ktk," Grif said. "With the stick."

Ebur sighed. "This is going to cost you an arm and a leg."

"Hey, after this, I can practically guarantee you'll be able to retire in style."

There was a long silence. "One month, eh? What the hell are we doing, exactly?"

Grif grinned. "We're doing the impossible, Ebur. And if we succeed, the Throne is going to look pretty damned stupid."

"That's a nice thought," Ebur said. "Well, all right, but I'm serious—it's still going to cost you. A lot."

"Name a price, Ebur."

The red-haired man thought. "Two million standard."

"Uh... wow, that's not just an arm and a leg, Ebur. It's at least two arms, a leg and I think what's left of my liver."

Ebur smirked. "No great loss there. Look, Grif, this sounds like a big deal, and you know what those damn drugs do to me."

"OK, OK," Grif said, "tell you what. I'll float it by the lady footing the bill and I'll get back to you. Don't go anywhere, I'll get back to you in six hours or so."

Ebur nodded. "All right, Grif. I'll wait."

"Vindh out."

The screen went dark. Grif turned off the terminal feed, then punched into the intercom. "If Velis Enge and Bennet Jax would be so kind as to meet the Captain in the conference room in one hour. Thank you very much."

The intercom came to life again, and Velis' voice came through clear and sharp. "What the hell is this about, Grif?"

"It's about how we're going to get you that little trinket sitting in Ur Voys," Grif said. "One hour, please."

With that, Grif got up and wandered over to his kitchen, where he poured himself a stiff drink.

Chapter 25

WHEREIN It Is Decided It Just Might Work

When Grif walked in to the conference room, Velis and Bennet were waiting for him.

"You've been drinking," Velis said.

"A bit," Grif admitted.

He sat down on the opposite side of the table—their natural positions, he thought with some amusement—and studied them carefully. Bennet was openly curious, and slightly anxious. Velis didn't look curious, she looked as if she were just barely controlling the urge to kill.

"All right," Grif said. "I'll come straight to the point. I found a way in... sort of."

Velis snorted in disgust. "'Sort of' doesn't cut it."

"At least *hear* the plan before you reject it out of hand," Grif said. "We're going to have to get a little a creative. There's no way we're going to get in and out of that place carrying that damn thing in a sack."

Velis looked annoyed, but continued to listen.

"Ur Voys is too well guarded on most days," Grif continued, "and now that they're dealing with the mystery of their missing anagathics it's going to be locked down tighter than ever."

"So what do you suggest?" Bennet asked.

"Glad you asked." Grif grinned at both of them. "It just so happens that Ur Voys isn't a self-sufficient installation. It has regular shipments of supplies going into it, and it ships out what it produces in its labs. It also ships out any equipment that needs major repairs."

"We already tried that," Bennet said. "We thought we could infiltrate one of the maintenance crews that repairs their equipment. Ur Voys might use other facilities, but they transport everything themselves. They ship out all the equipment they need fixed, drop it off, and then pick up the equipment when it's ready to go. And all equipment is scanned to make sure there aren't people hiding in any of it."

"That won't be an issue," Grif said. "We won't be sending people into Ur Voys."

Velis frowned. "Grif, you're not going to be able to fast-talk your way out of doing this."

"I'm not talking my way out of anything," Grif insisted. "If we're going to have any chance of pulling this off, we can't send people into Ur Voys. People attract attention. Even if we could successfully smuggle someone in to Ur Voys—even if we could get someone in there *legitimately*—they'd be under observation the entire time, and they'd get noticed."

Velis nodded reluctantly. "That was our problem in previous attempts. There's a specific culture in the facility that requires a fair amount of indoctrination to adopt. We couldn't fake it." She narrowed her eyes. "How did you pull it off?"

Grif waved his hand dismissively. "Not important. Like I said, this time we won't be sending people."

"What then?"

"A thing, Velis. Rather, *things*. Specifically, *robots*. Robots are mobile. People don't bother looking at them twice." Grif punched in a command in front of his terminal, and the picture of a high security military complex appeared on each of the terminals in the conference room.

"This is Ur Ados," he said. "It's a facility that, among other things, does most of the repair work for any Ur Voys robots that need maintenance. It was mentioned in one of the files you sent me, Bennet. A brief footnote. It's listed in the public record of Varkav, so it's public knowledge... though it is high security and restricted."

Velis nodded again. "We tried to use that facility as a staging area for an infiltration. As far as we can tell, all agents died before the operation could get underway."

"Ah... Well." Grif frowned. "That's not encouraging. But we're not going to be infiltrating. I was thinking more of a stealth operation."

"You want to try and break in," Bennet said.

Grif hesitated. "Well... actually, I want *you* to try and break in. This needs to be completely undetected."

"What are we breaking in to do?" Bennet asked.

"Essentially," Grif said, "I want your people to break into Ur Ados and find a shipment of robots that are ready to be sent back to Ur Voys."

"You want to modify them, I guess," Bennet said, nodding thoughtfully. "So when they're reactivated inside Ur Voys, they'll be working for us."

"Well, sort of, but—"

"Won't work," Velis interrupted. "All items taken off-site are scanned before they are returned to Ur Voys, and are compared to the expected configuration. Any significant deviations result in the immediate destruction of the item. That includes programming... even robotic programming."

"What about devices?" Grif asked. "Could you conceal a *device* somewhere in the robot chassis?"

Velis looked at Bennet questioningly. Bennet thought a moment, then shrugged. "Maybe. Depending what it was made of, we could implant something inside the robot chassis that wouldn't be detected by the normal scans—essentially you'd have to rip the robot apart to find it. That's assuming it's not emitting anything. If it were a monitoring device, or some kind of remote control, they'd detect it as soon as you turned it on..."

Grif grinned. "That won't be a problem. The hard part will be getting into Ur Ados. Once you do that, you just find a few robots and conceal one of these on each of them..." Grif keyed in a command into his terminal and the picture changed. The item on the screen looked like a smooth, black stone no larger than three finger widths.

Velis looked at the object and raised an eyebrow. "Interesting."

"Yes," Grif said, grin widening. "I thought that might get your attention ."

Velis nodded thoughtfully. "You have someone who can use this?"

Grif nodded. "If we agree to his price. Which is, er, exorbitantly high... but understandable given the circumstances. And there are a few issues..."

"I'm sorry," Bennet said, "but what the hell is that?"

"It is a remote operator receptor," Velis said.

Bennet nodded politely. "Thanks for clearing that up. That means absolutely nothing to me."

"It's a way for a particularly rare breed of telepath to control technology," Grif said. "Mentally. I'm surprised you don't know about it—I thought it was the kind of thing spy organizations would go nuts over."

"Not really," Velis said, "since there aren't many telepaths that are actually able to use the damn things. Perhaps one percent of one percent—and they'd have to be relatively powerful to do anything useful with it."

"Oh, my guy is pretty powerful," Grif said. "That's actually a bit of a problem—"

"I want to know the whole plan," Velis said. "Now."

"Uh... OK." Grif took a deep breath. "Beyond a certain point, it's pretty simple. We get to Varkav. A team of your agents breaks into Ur Ados, and puts our receptors on a few key robots waiting to be shipped back to Ur Voys. You'll have to do what you do best to keep them from being detected in the initial scan." Velis nodded.

"Then," Grif continued, "we wait for them to be delivered and set up. Then we activate the receptors, at which point we'll be in direct control of those robots, and we can use them to locate your toy. And because these receptors are passive—they only work when the remote operator is actually using them—they don't get detected by the usual methods, or even by most of the unusual ones."

"Neat," Bennet said. "So you put robots in the facility and they find the... *toy*. What next?"

"Then... well, then we convince them to move it for us."

Velis and Bennet sat silently, looking at the picture of the remote receptor.

"We'll never be able to get to where it is—robots stop being unobtrusive when they start doing strange things, and if we tried to use them to get to the thing directly, then I expect people will notice."

Velis nodded in agreement.

"If, however, we manage to convince them that Ur Voys security had been breached—which shouldn't be too hard, because it will, in fact, have been breached—and they can't tell exactly how extensive the breach is..."

"They'll start moving their important things to more secure locations," Velis finished.

Grif nodded.

"And that will give us our opportunity to acquire the object."

Grif nodded again.

"Sorry," Bennet said, "But I'm still a bit lost. How many of those receptors do you have? How exactly do you plan to use them to convince Ur Voys personnel that the security breach is so extensive? As soon as they discover one they'll be able to scan for the rest of them—what we do to mask the scans won't work if they know specifically what to look for."

"We'll have four," Grif said. "But by the time we're ready to go, I plan to have many more robots at my disposal. You ever use a neural link?"

"Sure," Bennet said. "They're great for computer diagnostics, programming, playing with remote-controlled toys..."

"Right." Grif leaned back in his chair. "These receptors are like that, only a telepath can use them without being connected to anything. Which means we can use the telepath to make modifications to a robot's programming *after* they've been delivered to Ur Voys... and if we can find some kind of data link that the robots use—to set their work schedules, make log entries, dump the day's information into station records, that kind of thing—then we can affect the programming of other robots sharing the same link."

Grif waited for that sink in. "With enough time and a little luck, we could have an army of robots working for us."

"Tell me about your man," Velis said. "What are the logistics involved there?"

Grif sighed. "Well, it's going to be complicated," he said. "And expensive. But he's our best shot."

Velis frowned. "Be more specific."

"Well..." Grif tried to look unconcerned. "Well, his name is Ebur Tosk, and when he's on his meds he's a great guy."

Velis looked at him steadily. Grif shifted his weight nervously.

"It's not quite like that," he said. "OK, here's the whole story. Ebur just so happens to be a pretty highly rated telepath—you have to be to develop this, ah, I don't know what they call it, but the telepathic link that he can establish requires a high degree of ability."

Velis waited.

"Well... Where Ebur grew up, they don't really test for that kind of stuff, and most of the people who manifest telepathic abilities... you know what happens to a telepath who doesn't, ah, know how much is too much."

"They go crazy," Bennet said.

"Right. Well Ebur went crazy. Fortunately for him, he is one of the very few people who can be pulled back with treatment. Most of the time he takes, uh, I can't remember the name, but it kills his telepathic ability and alters his brain chemistry, and he's a normal, peaceful guy. Fun to be around. Good sense of humor."

"Ah." Velis made the connection. "He hires himself out as a slave circuit."

"That's right," Grif said. "You wait for his meds to wear off—that's the unpleasant part—and then you dope him up on something else. He sits there and does pretty much whatever you tell him. You can link a machine on your end to a machine on the other end by using him as a bridge. Alter programming, operate via remote, all sorts of things. He's got incredible range and bandwidth."

"As to the logistics," Grif continued, "it's tricky. First we'll have to put him in stasis and smuggle him in. From what I understand telepathy doesn't exactly radiate—I mean, you can't detect someone using it—but telepaths still manage to notice other telepaths, somehow. Even on meds he registers as a telepath, and if a Sword decided to try and read him on a whim... well, whims are bad. Next, we need to baby-sit him while he comes off his meds and then give him the slave circuit drug. Unfortunately they... they don't mix well. So we need to give him about a week after stopping his meds before dosing him with the other stuff."

"How do you manage that?" Velis asked. "Have you done it before?"

Grif nodded. "Yeah, we stick Ktk in a room with him. Bugs are dead zones as far as telepaths are concerned. It's not even a matter of not being able to understand the alien mind, Ebur says telepaths just don't sense anything at all from them. So Ktk sits on him—literally if necessary—and has a shock stick that it uses when Ebur starts messing around with our heads. Using psi blockers generally is usually a good idea at that point, but it's risky to have those in Throne space. Telepaths notice those almost instantly, and they stay in your blood for weeks after they wear off..."

Velis nodded in agreement. "But you've done this before? He is manageable?"

"Yeah, we've worked with him before, and he can be managed. It's not fun for anyone involved, and I guarantee at least one particularly nasty moment. The good news is that as powerful as he is, he's kind of clumsy with anything that's not a receptor... so you get fair warning before he does anything dangerous. It gives us time to tell Ktk, who then puts the stick to him."

Bennet shook his head. "He agrees to this kind of treatment?"

Grif shrugged. "He's *very* expensive. I mean, don't get me wrong—he's worth every standard. If I had to go through all that I'd charge a lot, too..."

"How much does he want for this job?" Velis asked.

"Well, I haven't told him the specifics," Grif said, "only the distances and projected time involved. He wants two million standard."

Velis didn't flinch. "I can't agree to that on my own," she said. "But if everything you say is true, I think I can get Alef to agree to it."

Grif hadn't expected her to agree so easily. "Well, he's expecting a call back. So I'll tell him you've tentatively agreed to his terms?"

Velis nodded.

"All right." Grif stood and stretched his legs. "Then I'll tell him to come on by... give you a chance to ask him any questions you want, brief him, whatever."

"And I will prepare a short message to Alef," Velis said. "Telling him we just might be making progress here. Congratulations, Grif. I didn't think you could do it... but it looks like you've come up with something that just might work."

"Hear that, Cyrus?" Grif called out. "She said it might work."

"Pay me, bug!" the terminal said.

Chapter 26

WHEREIN Our Hero Undergoes a Transformation

Ebur Tosk arrived at the *Fool's Errand* carrying nothing but two bags: one for his clothing and medicine, and one for the tools of his trade. The clothing he stashed in his cabin, the medicine in the medibay, and the equipment he handed off to Velis' people. He had four receptors with him, which were promptly examined in order to find the best way to hide them.

He was greeted with hearty enthusiasm by the crew and polite aversion by their passengers. The crew knew him, and they were quite happy to associate with him (when he was on his medication), but the passengers—all Alliance government officials—didn't trust rogue telepaths. The only officially recognized telepathic organization in Alliance space was the Order of Charlemagne, and they didn't associate with criminals.

The *Fool's Errand* left Tyrelos Station as soon as Velis received approval from Alef. Morgan, now familiar with the sensors, had no difficulty guiding them out of the proto-ring. After that it was a matter of waiting for them to get far enough out of the system to safely make the jump to tach.

And, of course, to anticipate and plan for unwanted attention.

Grif was in the Wardroom, staring out through the now-transparent panoramic viewport when Bennet came in carrying a digital slate.

"How attached are you to your appearance?" Bennet asked Grif.

Grif frowned. "Moderately?"

"Well I've had my people come up with new physical and DNA profiles for you," Bennet said. "It won't be permanent, but while it lasts the Radiant Throne won't know who the hell you are. You won't match any of your current DNA records. I assume they have DNA samples of you somewhere."

"Safe assumption," Grif said. "Tell me more. What do you mean 'while it lasts?'"

Bennet shrugged. "The procedure isn't permanent. We don't completely replace your DNA, just the types of DNA that are normally collected by law enforcement. It takes a while for your body to notice, but as soon as it does it'll replace the artificial chains with your real genetic code. And of course if they decided to do something *invasive* they'd probably bypass all our hard work and find your real DNA immediately."

"Comforting," Grif said.

"Yeah," Bennet agreed. "The good news is, that's the hard part. Altering your appearance is easy. They won't even be able to detect a surgical procedure. I've got a list of recommended changes for you and your crew, if you're interested."

"I am," Grif said.

Bennet handed Grif the slate. Staring at the screen, he saw the names of crew. Tapping each name in turn, he saw a before and "projected after" image of each.

"You're making Amys a blonde," Grif said. "You're going to pay for that. She's incredibly vain about her hair."

"That's why she's going to be a blonde," Bennet said. "With extremely *short* hair."

"And Cutter!" Grif exclaimed. "No scars! He's almost attractive."

"We didn't actually do too much to his appearance," Bennet said. "We just took the scars away."

"He's going to want them back, after."

"Why?" Bennet asked.

Grif shrugged. "I don't actually know. I think he likes them. He's a real doctor, you know; he could get rid of them himself, if he really wanted to. Cyrus will still stand out. I guess you can't make him a foot and a half shorter?"

Bennet laughed. "Not on a temporary basis," he said. "But look at yours. I think you'll appreciate it."

Grif tapped his name and examined the after picture.

"Odd," Grif said. "It looks like..."

His voice trailed off, then he burst out laughing. The "after" picture bore an uncanny resemblance to Hu Mavis.

"Not a joke," Bennet said, grinning in spite of himself. "Actually our analysts think that if you run into him—which is entirely possible, considering where we're going—this will give you an edge."

"Looking like him will give me an edge?"

"You won't actually look like him," Bennet said. "If you stand side to side, you'll look like completely different people. What we did was give you a strong family resemblance. People who know him will think you're related to him. They'll wonder if he has family outside the Imperial Throne. And according to the workup we did on him, he'll respond, on some level, the same way. He'll be predisposed to like you, assuming you play it right."

Grif thought about it. "I could do that," he said. "It'd be a hell of a good con. I think I know how to play it. But Bennet... don't show this to anyone. I want to see their faces when they see mine..."

***

"All right, sit still. I'm taking the bandages off now."

Grif's face started to itch immediately after the bandages were first applied. He'd coped with the torment the best way he knew—he got drunk—but the next morning he was faced with the combined torment of itching and hangover. Now he was waiting as patiently as he could manage while Bennet unwrapped layer after layer of medicated bandages, as most of his crew stood by waiting to see what he would look like.

His face felt cool air and the itch grew maddeningly stronger. The only thing he could think about was scratching. It was driving him crazy...

"There," Bennet said, removing the last bandage. "Let's take a look."

Everyone was staring at Grif in amazement. "So it took?"

Bennet nodded.

"It's creepy," Cutter said.

Grif grinned. "Let me see!"

Bennet handed him a small mirror, and Grif peered into it intently. Staring back at him was a thin-faced man, with an aristocratic bearing and a high forehead.

He *did* look like Mavis... like a brother, or a cousin.

Grif laughed. "Well, I'm a lot uglier than I used to be," he said. "But I'll be damned if that's not a great job. Thanks Bennet. I'm pretty sure Mavis himself wouldn't recognize me."

"It's incredible," Cyrus said, voice muffled under his bandages. He'd just finished being wrapped. "Bit spooky though. How does it feel?"

Grif suddenly remembered the itching, and started to scratch. "It itches like hell." He stopped in mid-scratch and looked at Bennet worriedly. "It's OK if I scratch now, right? I mean, I won't reshape it or anything?"

Bennet shook his head. "It should be fine."

"Good," Grif said, relieved, and scratched furiously.

"Oh, hell," Cyrus muttered. "Now *my* face itches."

"Drink," Grif said. "Drink a lot."

"Good idea," Cyrus muttered, and wandered off.

Morgan looked at Grif apprehensively. "Do I have to do this, Grif? I'd really rather keep my face."

"Everyone who has ever come into contact with Hu Mavis has to do this," Grif said.

"Ktk isn't doing it."

"That's because Ktk is going to be locked in a box with a stark raving mad telepath."

Morgan grumbled.

"Oh, don't be such a baby," Grif said. "You'll get it back. "

Grif strolled out of the medibay and traveled up the lift to the bridge. Amys sat in the pilot's nest, back to him.

"Hey," Grif said, grinning. "Turn around. You gotta see this."

"Do you feel like a new man?" Amys asked sardonically. She slid the chair full back, turned around, and yelped when she saw his face.

Grif grinned. "I'm officially my own worst enemy."

"That's..." Amys struggled between alarm, distaste, and amusement. "That's just... wrong."

"Wait till you see what he has planned for you."

Amys frowned. "I've seen it. I'm going to kill him."

"Wait till this is over," Grif said. "I don't want to look like this for the rest of my life."

"Fine," she said reluctantly. "He lives. Are you going to look like this the whole time we're in Throne space?"

"'Fraid so," Grif said, grinning again. "Anyway, I'm here to relieve you. Scat."

Amys left the bridge, shaking her head.

The next day, Cyrus had his bandages taken off, and Morgan had his put on. Cyrus' new face was decidedly uglier—thicker features and more thuggish in general. Or, as Gurgan put it, "even more like him."

The day after that, Morgan took *his* bandages off, which provoked quite a different reaction. He'd shaved his beard for the surgery, and that plus the new face made him look much, much younger.

"He's a child!" Grif exclaimed, gaping.

"Funny," Morgan said, "I still feel too damn old..." He looked into the hand mirror and sighed.

"I miss my beard," he said finally. "My face is cold."

One by one the entire crew except Ktk was subjected to the same treatment, each bearing it with varying levels of stoicism and grace.

They made the jump to tach without incident. After the jump, they set about changing the ship identifier. When they were done, the *Fool's Errand* was temporarily gone: in her place was the *Alo Minh*, registered trading vessel of the Nyst Barony, captained by one Jobin Tax. After that, the only thing left was to secure Ebur.

Grif, Cyrus, Cutter, Hari and Ebur gathered in Bay Three and set up the stasis cylinder that would house Ebur until they reached Varkav. Ebur looked at the cylinder apprehensively.

"Come on," Grif said. "You know it has to happen. Suck it up and get inside. The sooner you do it, the sooner you'll be coming out the other end—two million standard richer, I might add."

Ebur shook his head. "I don't want to wake up in this thing," he said. "I'll go crazy."

"You won't wake up in it," Grif promised. "We turn the stasis field on before we close the top. Next thing you know, we're there and Ktk is leading you to the room. *Then* you get to go crazy!"

"You are not helping."

"In," Grif commanded. "Just think of the money. The money, Ebur."

"All right," Ebur sighed. "Apologies in advance, for when I'm... you know..."

"Batty?" Cyrus suggested.

"Nuts," Cutter added.

"Trying to get us all killed," Hari offered.

"Yeah," Ebur said. "Nothing personal."

"It's OK," Grif said. "We'll all laugh about it later. Get in the damn can."

Ebur lay down in the cylinder, trying to get comfortable. "I'm ready," he said.

Grif reached down and activated the stasis field. Ebur's body shimmered as the field engulfed it, freezing it in time.

Cutter performed a quick diagnostic. "He's OK, Skip," he drawled.

"Thanks, Doc," Grif said. "How's the new face? Itching stop yet?"

Cutter frowned, passing a hand over his now-smooth face. "Never itched for me," he said. "Vod hates it. She says I'm ugly now."

Cyrus guffawed and slapped Cutter on the back. "I'll trade you."

"Right," Grif said. "Let's secure this thing and stow it."

They closed the top, locking it down for good measure. Cyrus, Grif and Hari placed it in the concealed hold.

"Well," Cyrus said. "That's that."

Grif nodded. "Time to do the impossible. That SL beacon should be coming in any minute now."

As if on cue, the intercom crackled to life.

"Captain Vindh, we're getting a message from the SL Beacon," Bennet's voice said. "You're needed on the bridge."

"Well," Cyrus said.

"Right..." Grif took a deep breath, walked over to the wall, and activated the intercom. "Acknowledged. All hands, prepare to drop from Tach... right into the middle of Throne space."

Chapter 27

WHEREIN Our Hero, Having Returned to the Woods, Pretends He is a Tree

"It shouldn't matter," Grif muttered to himself. "Space is space, right?"

He stared out from the Pilot's Nest into the region of space where they'd dropped and tried to remind himself that some of the stars he was looking at weren't even in Throne space.

"Morgan, you're a scientist."

"Was," Morgan corrected. "*Was* a scientist."

"Right. In your formerly scientific opinion, how would you define space?"

"How would I define *space*?" Morgan had, apparently, been expecting the conversation to go in a completely different direction.

"Right. Space."

"It's the big empty thing with all the stars in it."

Grif grinned. "Thanks for clearing that up, old man."

Morgan grumbled to himself.

"How long have you been doing this?" Amys asked teasingly. "Fifteen years at least. And you still need someone to explain space to you?"

"Just thinking, is all," Grif said. "I mean... space is pretty much the same wherever you go. A little more radiation here, a stronger gravity well there... and the stars you see aren't actually where you are. I mean, I *know* this. But... still. It feels *different*."

No one replied.

It was, Grif knew, a completely irrational feeling... but from the second they dropped from Tach, everything around him felt... oppressive. It was a trick of the mind, but a distinctly successful one.

"We have bogeys," Morgan said. "Closing fast."

Grif's focus snapped on the tactical display in front of him as Morgan transferred the information to his station. Three ships on an intercept course. "Are we being hailed?"

"Negative," Bennet said. "Not yet."

"I have a visual on the ships," Morgan said. "One Radiant Throne frigate, two short-range warships. All well armed, no big surprise there."

Grif punched the intercom. "We have contact," he said. "All personnel to stations. Ktk, time to hide. Velis, are your people ready?"

A moment later Velis' voice came through the intercom speakers, brisk and businesslike. "All personnel in position. Our gear is broken down and stowed. They'll find it, but they won't know what it is, and they won't care."

Grif hoped she was right. "Good. All hands: when I give the order we switch to our cover identities and we refer to each other by those names at all times until I give the all clear. The Radiant Throne is very good at what they do. Never assume they're not paying attention to you. Out." He turned off the intercom and slid his chair out of the Pilot's Nest, into the Bridge proper.

"Amys, take the wheel."

He unbuckled himself from the chair and pushed off toward the Navigation station as a blond-haired, apple-cheeked Amys floated toward him. Grif forced himself not to grin at her appearance. She detested that face, and while that amused Grif to no end there was little to gain in provoking her.

Grif strapped himself into the Navigation station and waited, staring at the distorted reflection of his own altered face off the console in front of him. He heard the click of the pilot's chair as Amys slid down into the Pilot's Nest. Then everyone waited.

A moment later Ktk reported that it was secure in the hidden compartment in Bay Three and would wait for the all clear before communicating again.

"I'm getting the signature beacon of the frigate," Morgan reported. "It's called the *Redemption*."

"Of course it is," Grif muttered.

"They're hailing us," Bennet reported.

"Patch them through to my station. Tight shot, my face only."

A screen on the navigation console blinked on. Grif saw a young Throne officer staring at him from the other side. Grif suppressed a grin as the officer's eyes widened in surprise when he saw the similarity between Grif's new face and one Commodore Hu Mavis.

"This is Jobin Tax, Captain of the *Alo Minh*," he said, affecting a bored but polite and slightly aristocratic tone. "We are a merchant vessel from the

Nyst Barony, and have all proper papers. Our ship and crew are at your disposal."

He smiled slightly.

The officer cleared his throat and collected himself. "Captain—Tax, is it? Lieutenant Gannet, Captain of the *RTS Redemption*. We don't have a record of your ship."

Grif nodded slightly. "This is our first trip into Throne space. We hope to make many more."

Lieutenant Gannet shook off the last vestiges of shock and nodded crisply. "Your ship identifier lists you as a merchant vessel."

"Yes," Grif replied. "My communications officer is transmitting our declaration of cargo to you now. We are at your disposal, captain."

Grif made a point of identifying the man by his title instead of his rank—it was exactly the kind of thing, he thought, that would improve the officer's disposition toward him. It worked: Lieutenant Gannet relaxed slightly and smiled politely.

"Thank you, Captain Tax," Gannet said. "Always nice to see cooperative outsiders. So long as you follow our protocols and don't resist our attempts to ensure you're following them, you should have no difficulties in the Empire of the Radiant Throne. There is, however, one bit of unpleasantness, which I apologize for in advance. I'm afraid I must insist upon searching your vessel."

Grif nodded without hesitation. "Of course. As I said, we are at your disposal."

Lieutenant Gannet nodded again. "Very good, Captain. We don't insist that your crew assemble, but make it clear to them they are not to interfere with our search. During the search, if you are so inclined, I'd like to invite you on board."

"Thank you captain," Grif replied. "I'd be honored to accept."

The Lieutenant smiled warmly. "Very good. Docking should commence in five minutes. We will use the apex lock. Gannet out."

The terminal screen blinked out.

"That seemed to go well," Bennet said.

"Sure," Grif said. "They'll have the captain separated from his ship if anything goes wrong. It's perfect. And by 'perfect,' I mean 'this is the perfect time for something to go horribly wrong.'"

"They're moving in," Morgan said. "Hope this works."

"Me too." Grif stood up from the Navigation station and stretched. "Good news is, if we get through this with flying colors we'll be searched less in the future, and those searches will be less thorough. Until we get to Varkav, anyway." He clicked on the intercom. "This is your Captain speaking. I want gravity back on before they dock, which is soon, so do it now. Put on the new faces and don't interfere with their search. If they ask you questions, answer the way you rehearsed it. And don't panic."

"You know," Bennet said, amused in spite of himself, "my people have had to lie before."

Grif laughed. "I suppose they have. But I'm being paranoid." He punched the intercom again. "Welcoming party at the apex lock."

The *Fool's Errand* had four primary airlocks: the apex lock, located at the top of the main section of the ship, the nadir lock, located in Bay One at the bottom of the ship, and port and starboard locks. Grif and Morgan arrived on the top deck to find Cyrus standing next to the apex lock, nervously stroking the contours of his new face.

"Everyone mind your manners," Grif said. "Let's greet our guests."

The apex lock consisted of two rooms. The outer room contained lockers with vacuum suits and monitors that reported on the status of the inner room, which was a sealed, cylindrical enclosure. The walls of the inner room consisted of reinforced plasteel windows, allowing the three to look into the currently empty space. A light over the reinforced sliding doors that led into the inner room radiated a solid green.

Cyrus walked over to one of the monitors and looked at the controls. "Nothing yet," he said.

Grif nodded. "Turn on the intercom."

Cyrus flipped a switch on the monitoring station.

"What's the status on the *Redemption*?" Grif asked.

A moment later Amys replied. "They've matched our position and are extending a boarding tube from their nadir lock. I estimate another minute."

"Thanks."

Grif, Cyrus and Morgan waited in silence until they felt a faint vibration shake the ship.

"The tube has connected," Cyrus reported. "Creating a seal now."

"Raise the platform," Grif ordered.

"Right," Cyrus said. "Depressurizing."

Ship-to-ship boarding was a complicated affair, even when both parties were willing participants. It was theoretically possible for the *Redemption* to fill their boarding tube with atmosphere, and for the *Fool's Errand* to open the entrance to the apex lock and let them in. In practice, this could be dangerous—if the *Fool's Errand's* setting for one standard atmosphere was even slightly mismatched with the *Redemption's*, the change in pressure could break the seal of the boarding tube. It was safer, and considered standard practice, for ship-to-ship transfer of personnel to be handled in vacuum, with the people involved properly suited. Most airlock software wouldn't allow the outer hatch to open unless the inner chamber had been decompressed first.

The solid green light over the doors began to flash yellow. The monitors showed the air pressure in the inner room drop, and when the room was a vacuum the flashing yellow light became a flashing red light.

"Please tell the *Redemption* that we are ready to receive them."

Moments passed, then the intercom crackled to life. "*Redemption* reports that they are ready to board," Bennet reported.

Grif nodded to Cyrus. "Open the top," he said.

Cyrus keyed in another command and the flashing red light became a solid red light. Looking through the windows, Grif saw the ceiling of the inner chamber slowly slide open.

Surrounding the opening was the boarding tube—a thick, translucent tube rising up and away from the chamber. Encircling the opening were armed soldiers, all in armored vacuum suits bearing the insignia of the Radiant Throne.

"Raise the platform," Grif said.

The floor of the inner chamber began to rise. Grif watched it rise past the window, obscuring more and more of the room until the only thing he could see was the hydraulic lift that supported it.

"They're lowering it," Cyrus said.

Grif saw the lift descend, and as the platform lowered, he could see the Radiant Throne marines—rifles ready—waiting patiently. One of the suits bore the insignia of a sergeant.

When the platform returned to its normal position, Cyrus closed and resealed the ceiling, and then began the sequence that slowly restored atmosphere to the room. The solid red light began to blink, then blinked yellow, then turned to a solid green.

"Here we go," Grif muttered. He nodded, and the double doors separating the outer and inner chamber opened with a hiss.

Grif, Morgan and Cyrus stepped back as the soldiers entered the outer chamber. There were fifteen in all, Grif noticed, and while ten stood watch, five began to remove their gear. The sergeant reached up and removed his helmet. He was an older man with short, gray hair. He looked at Grif and nodded politely.

"Captain Tax," he said in a gravelly voice, "If you'll suit up I'll take you up to the Lieutenant."

Grif nodded and turned to Cyrus. "See that the crew cooperates with these men completely and without hesitation," he said.

Cyrus nodded once. Grif walked over to a locker and began to climb into a vacuum suit. Unlike the military grade equipment the Radiant Throne marines had, his suit wasn't armored, nor did it have servo-assisted motors in its joints. It was a little large and a bit too heavy for his comfort, but after running a brief check he found it was working properly.

Grif motioned to the sergeant and stepped into the inner chamber. The sergeant nodded, replaced his helmet, and followed. Cyrus closed the hatch with a hiss, and the solid green light over the door blinked yellow, then red, then turned solid red. The ceiling opened up, and Grif stared up into the translucent lining of the tube. Far above him he saw the *Redemption's* airlock.

The floor rose silently up to lock into the exterior of the ship. The sergeant motioned to Grif and walked over to the side of the boarding tube. Lining the tube was a row of man-sized platforms locked into guides that ran up toward the other ship. The sergeant stepped onto one, grabbed a handhold, and motioned for Grif to do the same. Grif stepped onto the platform next to the sergeant's and grabbed a handhold that rose up from the platform's base.

As if on cue, the two platforms rose slowly up the tube. Grif saw the nadir lock of the *Redemption* grow larger above him.

The nadir lock of the *Redemption* was similar to the apex lock of the *Fool's Errand*, but considerably larger. Grif and the sergeant stepped off of their lifts and onto the nadir lock platform, which raised them into the room. The room filled with oxygen, and eventually the red light filling the room changed to a normal color. The sergeant immediately took off his helmet as a door on one side of the room opened. The sergeant moved toward the door and Grif followed, fumbling with the locks on his vacuum suit.

They emerged into the outer chamber, filled with rows and rows of armored vacuum suits. Two armed guards in Radiant Throne marine uniforms stood at attention.

Grif removed his vacuum suit and stood patiently as one of the marines searched him for weapons. Satisfied, the marine nodded to the other.

"Please follow us," the marine said. "Lieutenant Gannet is waiting for you in his office."

The other said, "Sergeant, the Lieutenant wants you back down on the *Alo Minh*, overseeing the search."

The sergeant nodded and put the helmet back on his suit.

Grif followed the two guards down a long corridor and into a lift. They didn't speak, and he waited in silence as the lift opened into another long hall. At the end of the hall, they stopped, and one buzzed a control to the right of a closed door.

The door slid open, revealing a small, orderly office. At the end of the office was a small, metal desk, and on the other side of the desk was Lieutenant Gannet.

"Come in," the Lieutenant said.

Grif stepped into the room. The marines started to follow, but Gannet motioned them to stay where they were. "We'll be fine," he said briskly. He waited until the door had closed, and then motioned to a chair. "Please have a seat."

Grif sat, trying not to look concerned. Lieutenant Gannet reached underneath his desk and pulled out a bottle and two glasses.

"Would you care for a drink, Captain? I have some Varkavian whiskey, I understand many in the Trade Baronies are quite fond of it."

"Please," Grif replied, trying his best to sound well bred.

The Lieutenant filled both glasses and offered him one. Grif took the glass and sipped politely.

"I was looking at your crew list," Gannet said, indicating a small stack of papers to his left. "You have an unusually large crew for a trading ship."

"Yes," Grif said, and he allowed a hint of regret to creep into his voice. "There are certain... events in the Baronies that made it necessary to supplement our standard crew with armed guards. I don't know if you've heard, but Baron Tylaris is dead."

Lieutenant Gannet nodded. "I believe I heard something about it. But you are from the Nyst Barony, are you not? I don't see how it affects you..."

"It is complicated to people who don't live there," Grif said. "When someone that powerful dies, everything in Trade Baron space shifts. We expect an increase in piracy in that region, eventually, but even now there are... instabilities. The guards are mostly to protect our goods while we are in port, sadly. They are professionals and will give you no trouble. I've already told them to allow you to inspect all their equipment, including weaponry, if you so order."

The Lieutenant nodded thoughtfully. "I'm afraid I may have to do that, Captain. But I do find your explanation satisfactory."

It was, in fact, a wholly reasonable explanation. Just before they had left Tylaris Station they'd heard about a cargo ship that was waylaid by thugs while in port. Station Authority intervened to drive them off, but two of the ship's crew died in the fight.

"We are under orders to search every Maximilian-class vessel that enters the system," the Lieutenant said apologetically.

"Oh?" Grif asked, unsurprised. "Problems with pirates?"

Lieutenant Gannet looked at him sharply for a moment. "Why do you ask?"

Grif shrugged. "The Maximilian class is popular among pirates and smugglers for the same reason that it is popular with traders. It is easy to modify. The *Alo Minh*, for example, was recently refitted with a tachyon drive that takes up significantly less space than the one she came with."

Grif sighed, smiling tiredly. "Unfortunately, the trade-off for captaining a Maximilian is that you come under closer scrutiny from governments. When you said you were under orders to search Maximilian-class vessels, I assumed it was pirates."

"Smugglers, actually," the Lieutenant said, obviously satisfied with Grif's answer. "One, to be specific."

"Ah," Grif said. "I ask, only because I've not been here before... does this mean we are likely to be searched often? I will certainly comply, but I'm concerned with the delay..."

"It is the duty of the military, in service to our Emperor, to ensure the safety of our Empire," the Lieutenant said. "I'm afraid that it may be necessary, yes. But I'll report that you cooperated with us fully, and that may speed you along."

"Thank you, Captain," Grif said.

At that moment something on the Lieutenant's desk beeped. Gannet touched something next to the monitor sitting to his right and said "report."

"The search is complete, sir. Nothing to report."

"Understood. Assemble your men and return to *Redemption*." The Lieutenant stood. "Well. That is good news for you, Captain. We'll uncouple our ship and allow you to continue to Varkav. Welcome to the Glory of the Throne. I hope your trip is profitable."

Grif stood and bowed slightly. "Thank you, Captain," he said courteously.

Grif was escorted back to the nadir lock, put on his vacuum suit, and made the long trip back to the *Fool's Errand*. When he emerged into the outer chamber of the apex lock, he found Bennet and Morgan waiting for him. Grif pulled off his helmet and grinned.

"That went well," Bennet said.

"Yeah," Grif said. "Kinda makes you want to get overconfident."

"So their captain isn't suspicious?" Morgan asked anxiously.

"No," Grif said. "Nice man. I hope they don't demote him when they inevitably learn the truth."

"Or kill him," Bennet added.

"Yeah... that would be a shame. He's a very courteous Lieutenant. Guess they haven't ground his spirit to dust just yet."

Chapter 28

WHEREIN an Unexpected Detour Requires Frenetic Adaptation

Varkav was an ugly planet.

The planet was, geologically speaking, very young. Plate tectonics had not yet separated the single land mass into multiple continents, but when it eventually did no one was certain exactly where those continents would go. There was only one ocean, and the pangea-like land mass covered so much of the planet that there was a debate in some circles as to whether it actually qualified as an ocean, or if it was a vastly oversized sea. The concentration of land gave the planet, in Grif's eyes, a misshapen and unbalanced appearance, as though it were teetering in space, liable to tip over at any point. The continent was riddled with muddy rivers and brackish lakes, giving it the appearance of being covered in blemishes and cobwebs. The final indignity, Grif decided, was that some particulate in the atmosphere filtered out bits of the spectrum of light, giving everything on it a drab, brownish tint.

"Ugly, ugly, planet," Grif said. "Best whiskey anywhere."

"Amen," Amys agreed.

Amys had just guided the *Fool's Errand* into a long-range orbit around the planet. It would be a long-range orbit until the Radiant Throne permitted them to descend into a standard orbit, and then—hopefully—to land on the planet itself. Each step of the way would require they be searched. Each search would be thorough.

Grif wanted a drink.

"It really isn't very pretty at all," Bennet said finally. "Is it as dreary as it looks?"

"Actually," Grif said, "most of the people who live there seem rather happy."

Bennet frowned. "Some kind of telepathic mind control? I knew Swords were powerful, but—"

"Don't be idiotic," Morgan said, glancing up from his station to glare at Bennet. "No telepath can control a planet."

"Cut him a little slack, Morgan," Grif said, grinning. "Remember back when *you* were part of the Alliance? You thought the Radiant Throne was a land of misery, with men and women in chains, and weekly hymn-filled torture sessions."

"So it's not like that?" Bennet asked.

"Well. Sometimes." Grif turned his attention back to the planet. "I mean, when the Throne decides it's time to make their displeasure known, then yes, there can be quite a bit of that sort of thing. But Varkav isn't exactly a rebellious planet. It has its criminal underground and illicit entertainments, but that doesn't make the population more likely to rebel. In fact I think it has the opposite effect. And, of course, the bloody *fantastic* whiskey. That's a source of planetary pride, and rightly so."

"So they're *actually* happy?" Bennet shook his head. "The reports I read tend to omit that fact."

"They don't dance in the streets," Grif said. "But it's a prosperous planet, there's not a lot of poverty, and one thing I'll grant the Throne is that they take care of their poor, so even the poor aren't all that bad off. Religious duty and all that."

Bennet shook his head again. "It sounds like some Alliance worlds, actually. I still don't know why none of this is in our reports."

Grif laughed. "They probably thought it was politically inconvenient to admit that there are worlds in the Radiant Throne that aren't depressing shitholes. Of course, all that comfort comes at a pretty hefty price. Ruled by telepathic religious zealots, immediate execution for daring to say anything that might be construed as treasonous... church on Sundays..." Grif shuddered.

"But the whiskey is *fabulous*," Amys said.

"Amen," Grif agreed.

"Still, it just doesn't seem right that—" Bennet trailed off and turned his attention to his console. "We're getting a message from Varkav Orbital Command. Instructions for standard orbit."

Grif frowned. "Interesting. I thought they'd search us first. No matter, send them to Amys so we can get that part over with. Assuming everything goes well we should be able to land in a few days."

Bennet forwarded the instructions to Amys' console. "What if things *don't* go well?" he asked.

"Well," Grif said, "in that case I won't have to bother coming up with an exit strategy. They'll just blow us out of the sky."

At that moment Morgan looked up from the sensors and turned in his chair to face them. "Grif."

Grif looked at Morgan. "What's wrong?"

"We have a problem," Morgan said. "*Centurion* is in standard orbit around Varkav."

Grif sighed. "Well, we knew it was possible, that's why they gave me this face..."

"There's another battlecarrier in orbit as well. The *Sentinel.*" Grif's eyes widened. "*Two* of those things? Damn it all to *hell.*"

"It gets better," Bennet said. "*Centurion* is hailing us."

The bridge fell silent.

Grif gritted his teeth. "Put him on screen at my station. This is going to be *so much fun.*"

The terminal screen at Grif's station flickered. The image of Commodore Hu Mavis stared cooly out at him.

Grif cleared his throat. "This is Jobin Tax, Captain of..."

"Captain of the *Alo Minh,*" Mavis cut in smoothly. "Yes, I know. I also know that you are registered as a merchant in the Nyst Barony and that your Maximilian-class starship has passed through one thorough search and one superficial follow-up. I'm afraid, Captain, that I will need to take up more of your time."

Grif slid smoothly into character and nodded in a polite and unconcerned fashion. "Of course," Grif said. "My ship, my crew and I are at your disposal."

Mavis raised an eyebrow. "Well, I see you are courteous," he said. "That is encouraging."

Time stretched out uncomfortably as Grif watched Mavis think.

"Well then," Mavis said, "I see you have entered standard orbit. That means, if I am not mistaken, that Varkav Orbital Command is arranging another search of your ship. A thorough one, I believe, that will require all hands assembled. A dreary situation, to be sure, but unavoidable I think. Pardon me a moment."

Mavis disappeared from the viewscreen, and Grif heard Mavis speaking—he couldn't quite make out the words, only that it was a question followed by a series of commands. A moment later, Mavis returned, looking pleased.

"I have learned," Mavis said, "that your ship was scheduled for a search in fifteen hours, but I believe I can expedite matters for you. I have spoken to Varkav Orbital Command and arranged to have my own men search your vessel in six. I hope that is acceptable."

Grif swore silently, but forced himself to show no expression. "Of course," he said. "Thank you for taking an interest. I would like to reach the surface as soon as possible."

"I'm happy to oblige," Mavis said. "Have your crew assemble in the cargo bay where the Nadir lock is located. All crew unarmed, of course."

"Of course."

"These things are inconvenient, I know," Mavis said. "And this search could take a while. Since I am interceding on your behalf, Varkav Orbital Command will want assurances, so this search will be... thorough."

Grif heard Amys shift uneasily from the pilot's nest.

"Good," Grif said. "I am eager to satisfy any concerns the Radiant Throne may have."

"I'm sure all concerns will be satisfied." Commodore Mavis smiled slightly. "These searches are tedious," he added. "That's regrettable for your crew, but I see no reason you should be expected to join in it. The search will take place roughly the same time that dinner is served for command staff on the *Centurion*. Would you care to join us?"

Grif bowed his head. "I would be honored," he said.

"Then it's settled. Our transport will see to it that you are delivered safely here, and you will be taken back after dinner. Everything should be settled by then. Mavis out, I look forward to your company." The image of Mavis blinked out.

"End of transmission," Bennet said.

"Damn it all to *hell!*" Grif shouted.

"Do you think he knows?" Morgan asked.

Grif punched the intercom. "All staff not currently locked in a closet to the Wardroom, *now*. You too Velis." He turned off the intercom and hit the console in frustration.

"What's wrong?" Bennet asked.

Grif forced himself to calm down. "We're humped, is what. Amys, once our orbit is stable and you're sure nothing's going to crash into us join us in the Wardroom, OK?"

"Sure thing," Amys said. He could hear the worry in her voice. "Won't be long."

"Good." Grif stared out the bridge viewport into the starry sky. He didn't see *Centurion* in that part of space, but he could feel Mavis breathing down his neck. "Morgan, let's go. You too, Bennet."

He stalked off into the lift without bothering to wait.

* * *

When Amys stepped in to the Wardroom she found the rest of the crew staring at Grif as he wandered around muttering to himself. Gurgan glanced at her and shrugged his massive shoulders—he had no idea why they were there. He looked worried. Actually, every person in the wardroom looked worried except for Velis, who looked impatient.

Amys cleared her throat softly. Grif didn't respond, but Velis looked up and sighed in relief.

"She's here," Velis said. "Mind telling me why the rest of us are?"

Grif didn't break his stride. "Velis, how good are your people at remodeling?"

Velis frowned. "What kind of question is that?"

Grif stopped and turned to face her. "I'm not kidding. Just imagine, hypothetically, that you had to... remove someone. And it was messy. You can clean up after yourself, yes? Make it look like it never happened?"

Velis frowned. Amys could see the reluctance on her face—she didn't like revealing any information at any time, she never had. But Velis also knew Grif, had known him longer than anyone else on the ship, and could tell Grif wasn't asking the question just for the hell of it.

"Yes," Velis admitted.

"Well we need some of that," Grif said. "Sort of. Cyrus, we need to figure out how to make the *Fool's Errand* disappear."

Cyrus looked at Grif blankly. "We already did that. She's not the *Errand*, she's the *Alo Minh*."

"Not on the outside!" Grif snapped. "On the inside. Five and a half hours from now, Hu Mavis is sending his men to search this ship from top to bottom. *His* men. And if he doesn't send men who have already been on board the *Fool's Errand*, then he's a goddamn fool. And while Mavis is many things, he is not a goddamn fool..."

Cyrus looked around the Wardroom, eyes wide. "Oh *hell.*"

"He has people who have been on your ship before," Velis said.

Grif nodded. "All that trouble to create a new signature key and it didn't occur to me to disguise her on the inside."

Amys caught her breath. She hadn't thought of that either.

"They're going to have to expect a certain amount of similarity," Cyrus said. "A Maximilian is a Maximilian is a Maximilian when it comes to floor plans. The cargo bays are different, but all the things they might use to identify her—type of guns, make and model of fusion or tach drive—those have all been replaced. And we've already switched over to the dummy crew manifest and cargo manifest, so when they access the ship records they won't find anything suspicious there either."

"They don't need to," Grif said. "All they need to do is see this room."

"They searched the entire ship?" Velis looked at Grif. Grif nodded. "So they've been in each cabin. They've been in here. They've been in all the places where the crew decorated. And you're afraid someone will remember something."

"I'm afraid of it," Grif said. "Mavis is *counting* on it. We need to tear the Wardroom down..." his voice trailed off. Amys could see how much it pained him to say that. "We need to tear it down. They came in here and actually removed some of the WU-961 from behind the bar... if *those* guys are involved in the search they will definitely remember this room."

"I can do that," Cyrus said. "Some of the luxury cargo we took on at Tyrelos could be swapped out for some of this stuff. Hari and Cutter can help me with that."

"I can handle the rest of it," Velis said briskly. "We're going to have to move you all around for a while, trade out some of your belongings. Redecorate. When we're done none of your rooms will look the same."

Grif sighed. "OK," he said. He turned to the crew. "You heard her. Whatever she says goes. If she says that Cyrus and Amys are an item, then God help us all, but—"

Amys laughed. "We get it, Grif. But you're going to have to do something to your quarters, too."

"Do what?" Velis asked.

Amys shrugged. "It needs dressing up. His quarters are pretty spartan."

"Oi," Grif protested. "They're *clean*."

"I'll have someone add things that are more suitable for Captain Tax," Velis said.

Grif sighed. "All right then. If anyone needs me I'll be sitting in my cabin, sobbing like a small, helpless child." He left the wardroom, still muttering to himself about Mavis and cons. Amys thought she heard him say "we are all going to die" before the door closed behind him.

Velis looked around the room. "Cyrus, you're going to take care of this room?"

Cyrus nodded.

"All right. The rest of you go back to keeping the ship from crashing into the planet," Velis said. Amys tried not to think about how much she sounded like Grif when she said it. "We'll take care of your cabins and the other public rooms. It should only take a few hours, you'll have some time before the Throne arrives to acclimate yourself to your new environment. Bennet, round up our people. We have work to do."

* * *

A few hours later Amys left Morgan in charge of the bridge and stopped by Grif's cabin to see how he was doing. She found him sprawled out on his couch, lights dimmed, drink in hand, staring at the ceiling. Amys frowned—Grif couldn't afford to be drunk right now.

"I'm not drunk," Grif said. In the dim light he looked even more like Mavis than usual. "I've had a sip. Maybe two."

"OK," Amys said. She looked around the room. "Have they done anything to the cabin yet?"

"Not yet." Grif gestured with his drink-hand to the kitchen. "The bottle's mostly full. No reason *you* can't have a drink. Unless you're still on duty."

"No," Amys said. "Morgan's driving."

"God help us all," Grif muttered.

Amys grinned, walked over to the kitchen and saw the bottle on a counter-top. She found a glass and poured herself a drink. "So," she said cheerfully. "Worried about this dinner?"

Grif laughed, a hint of hysteria seeping through. "A bit. He's got to be suspicious. He has to be. He wouldn't go out of his way to personally search a ship if he didn't think it was me. He's going to try something to trip me up."

"You'll be fine," Amys said.

Grif laughed again.

Amys sighed and walked back into the living room. "Lights full," she said.

The lights in the room increased. Grif shouted incoherently in protest and flung an arm over his eyes.

"That's your fault for not removing my voice from the control list," Amys said. She pulled Grif's legs off the couch, forcing him to sit, and plopped down at the end. "Isn't it time you did that?"

"I'm not holding a torch," Grif grumbled. "I'm just lazy."

"How long have you been sitting in the dark?"

Grif dropped his arm slightly and peeked over his elbow. "Since I left the Wardroom?"

"Jesus, Grif." Amys hit him in the side, hard enough to hurt. "Get over it."

"Ow!" Grif twisted in an attempt to avoid the blow, then rubbed his side furiously—without, Amys noticed, spilling the drink in his other hand. "What the hell was that for?"

"I'm trying to be nice," Amys said. "But we don't have a lot of time."

"You can say that again," Grif muttered.

"I get it," Amys said. "Really. I get it. This is a lousy situation, easily the worst we've been in, and you're going to have to pull off the con of all cons to keep us all alive. But putting aside that this is at least *partially* your fault—"

"Hey now—"

"Putting it *aside*... we can't afford to have you crack up now. Pull yourself together and do what you do best."

"Sneak out before she wakes up?"

Amys laughed. "No, the other thing."

"I'm not going to seduce Mavis."

Amys laughed harder. "Get cleaned up. You have a dinner

engagement."

Grif sighed, nodded, and put his drink down on an end table. "I hate this damn face."

"Yeah?" Amys grinned. "I hate this hair. You don't hear me crying about it."

"You don't have to cry. You can kill anyone you want just by moving your little finger."

Amys grinned wider, and wagged her little finger in Grif's direction.

"Fine, fine," Grif grumbled. "Time for Jobin Tax to charm Hu Mavis and the command staff of the *RTS Centurion* with his manners and superior breeding."

"That's the spirit."

Grif walked into his bathroom. A moment later he re-entered the living room to say "lying!"

"What?"

"Lying," Grif repeated. "That's what you meant. When you said I needed to do what I did best. You were talking about lying."

"Yes," Amys said. "I was."

"Ah, well, there you are," Grif said. "I thought you were talking about seduction. Lying makes a lot more sense in this context. Still, it's essentially the same thing in the end..."

"I'm leaving now," Amys said.

Chapter 29

WHEREIN Our Hero Enjoys the Company of Proper Society

When the *Centurion's* boarding party arrived through the nadir lock, Captain Jobin Tax and the rest of the crew of the *Alo Minh* were waiting for them in Bay One.

Captain Tax, a calm man of considerable discipline, sternly instructed his crew to cooperate with the marines in every way. He spoke with an air of both authority and unconcern, absolutely convinced that his instructions would be followed to the letter. After a brief exchange with the Lieutenant in charge of the search, he suited up, descended the nadir lock, and entered the transport ship that would take him to the *RTS Centurion*.

He asked and was given permission to stand on the bridge of the transport so he could watch the approach to the *Centurion*. He was, to the satisfaction of the pilot and his escorts, suitably impressed, and asked many questions about what it was like to serve aboard a ship that size. By the time the transport ship had passed through the Maxwell into the landing bay, everyone on board decided they liked him. Any initial suspicions they may have had were dispelled by his open admiration for the battlecarrier.

Grif planned this part out carefully: he wanted Tax to marvel at the *Centurion* while at the same time be completely unconcerned by it. Jobin Tax had nothing to hide; he was there legitimately. As far as he was concerned, the Commodore was doing him a favor by speeding up his timetable, and would result in him reaching the planet's surface ahead of schedule. Whatever plans Mavis may have in store for Tax on the *Centurion*, Tax saw only an opportunity to make an ally... and he fully intended to enjoy the experience.

Tax displayed none of the stress Grif felt. The nervous, ragged hysteria Grif had nearly succumbed to earlier was now channeled into the task at hand: the more agitated Grif felt, the calmer and more relaxed Jobin Tax looked. In Tax's mind, everything was going well. Grif didn't bother dwelling on the state of his own mind. Introspection was a sure-fire way to wreck a con.

As he descended from the transport onto the flight deck, he was greeted by Commodore Hu Mavis himself. Grif made a point of having Jobin Tax bow—it was the preferred formal greeting in the Nyst Barony, where physical contact of any sort was confined to family members and moments of intimacy. Captain Tax asked permission to come board, and Mavis, smiling slightly, bowed in return and gave his assent. An aide stepped forward holding a data slate and held it forward out to Captain Tax.

"All visitors must be logged," Mavis explained apologetically.

Grif nodded and placed his thumb on the slate. The device recorded Grif's altered thumbprint—and, Grif suspected, also took a quick scan of his altered DNA—then blipped softly. Mavis took the slate from his aide, scanned it briefly, then nodded slightly and handed it back.

"Dinner awaits," Mavis said. He dismissed his aide with a wave of his hand, then gestured for Grif to follow. A single armed marine followed them.

They traveled by transit tube—due to the size of the ship, traveling on foot was impractical—and Grif felt a moment of vertigo as he was confronted by the sheer enormity of the *Centurion*. It was a small, moving city, and it required a public transportation system to allow the crew to move from one area to the other. They were traveling via a smaller transit system reserved for officers, but as they did Grif saw larger cars filled with enlisted rush past them on other lines.

"This ship must be very challenging to manage," Grif said.

Mavis laughed—a genuinely warm laugh that Grif found unnerving. "Some days it doesn't feel like captaining a ship," he said. "From time to time I feel as though I were imposing military law on a city. The *Centurion* is a city, in a many ways. She has to be, considering the role she is intended to play."

Grif looked at Mavis questioningly.

"If she is needed in a fleet action," Mavis explained, "she will be the primary base of operations for repair and refueling. She will be the primary hospital where crew are treated for serious injury, the tactical command center where all actions are planned. She is, essentially, a flying military base, rather than a warship. Though she is of course heavily armed..."

As Mavis continued to talk about the *Centurion*, Grif was struck with the uncomfortable realization that Mavis genuinely loved his ship. It wasn't merely pride in what the ship represented to the Throne, or the prestige that came from captaining it: the Commodore clearly believed that this was where he was meant to be, that the *Centurion* was *his*—exactly the way Grif felt about the *Fool's Errand*. In Grif's mind there were two types of ship captains: the ones who viewed what they were doing as a means to an end, and the ones who were serious about the life—honest-to-God "spacers" who would never feel comfortable unless they were on *their* ship. Grif thought little of the former. All of his closest friends were the latter.

Commodore Hu Mavis, personal nemesis, eternal thorn in Grif's side, was a genuine spacer.

"So unfair," Grif muttered.

"What's that?" Mavis asked sharply.

Grif mentally kicked himself, and forced Jobin Tax, captain of the *Alo Minh*, to smile sympathetically. "I said 'it seems so unfair,'" he said. "This ship is magnificent, make no mistake, but... I see you are married." Grif nodded toward a ring on Mavis' hand. "To be separated from one's family for so long... it seems unfair."

"Ah." Mavis frowned slightly as he regarded 'Jobin Tax' in a new light. Grif suddenly realized that Mavis had the same opinion about starship captains that he did, and he'd just decided Tax was a man who viewed captaining a ship as a *means to an end* rather than the end itself. That was lucky—while Tax would surely fall somewhat in Mavis' esteem, he would also not be as readily associated with a certain smuggler named 'Grif Vindh.'"

"My wife knew the kind of man I was when we were wed," Mavis said simply.

They lapsed into minutes of awkward silence. Finally the transport slowed down, then came to a stop. Mavis stood.

"Here we are," he said. "Dinner awaits."

The Wardroom of the *Centurion* looked like a posh, private restaurant or club. It was carpeted, with vaulted ceilings, and while the light fixtures were rigidly mounted to the ceiling they were designed to look as if they were ornate, hanging chandeliers. The entire outer bulkhead wall of the main room was transparent, giving them a magnificent view—which was marred, much to Grif's disappointment, by the brown squalid surface of Varkav itself.

Grif was surprised by the sheer size of it.

"One of the disadvantages of a ship this size," Mavis said, as he led Grif and their escort across the vast room. "The officer complement of the *Centurion* exceeds the total crew population of most ships, which tends to make the officer areas crowded. Fortunately we have access to more intimate facilities..."

They entered a stateroom set to the side of the main floor. It looked like a miniature replica of the main Wardroom—high ceilings, thick carpet, faux hanging chandeliers, and a completely transparent outer bulkhead. A single long table was set in the center of the room, where two men and a woman were already seated. They stood as soon as Mavis entered the room.

Mavis turned to Grif. "Captain Tax, allow me to introduce Ando Fargus, my XO, and Ubin Malvier and Katryn Valdyrs, both on my command staff."

Each officer nodded in turn. Ando Fargus was a heavy-set man with dark skin that gleamed under the light in the room. He exuded an easygoing confidence that filled the room, and grinned rather than smiled at him. Ubin Malvier was Ando's opposite—rail-thin, pale, almost translucent skin, and a tendency to tug nervously at the cuff of his left sleeve. He smiled politely at Grif, but the tightness around his eyes suggested no real warmth. Katryn Valdyrs was a slim, attractive woman who reminded him a little of Amys. Grif forced himself to pay as little attention to her as possible.

Grif bowed slightly to each in the room. Mavis moved to the head of the table—the captain's chair—and gestured for Grif to sit at his right. Ando Fargus sat immediately to Mavis' left, then Katryn Valdyrs. Ubin Malvier took the chair immediately to Grif's right.

Grif forced back the feeling of being surrounded and waited patiently as attendants set food and drink in front of them. He smelled roast beef and realized he was very hungry.

"It is synthetic of course," Mavis said. "I'm afraid we can't afford the real thing on an officer's salary. Still, it is a cut above the norm."

"It's well above the stock aboard the *Alo Minh*," Grif said, which was true. The color was a little too uniform for genuine meat, but it smelled exactly like roast beef, and the gravy was almost perfect. He looked up at the others, and realized they were all watching him intently.

Grif fought back alarm as he tried to figure out what they were waiting for him to do. He pretended not to notice, and examined his food more closely. Mavis was trying to catch him at something, but what? He quickly reviewed everything he knew about merchants in Baron Nyst's service. Finally he realized the trick, and almost grinned in admiration. He'd nearly missed it.

"Is there a problem, Captain Tax?" Mavis asked. Grif allowed himself to look slightly uncomfortable.

"I'm afraid I find myself in something of a difficult position," Grif said, trying to sound as diplomatic as possible. "It is customary to toast the Baron's health before dining, but I fear it may be considered something of an affront to your Emperor."

Grif had guessed correctly. Mavis nodded to himself, apparently satisfied.

"Perhaps," Grif continued, hit by sudden inspiration, "if we could drink a toast to your Emperor's health first, you might forgive me if I raised a glass to my Baron afterwards?"

Mavis smiled. "Of course," he said. "In honor of your courtesy, I believe that can be forgiven. Yes?" He looked at his officers, who all agreed politely. "Very well."

Mavis stood, raising his glass. His officers stood in kind, and Grif followed, raising his glass with the rest of them.

"To our Divine Emperor," Mavis said, "chosen by God Himself to ascend the Radiant Throne in glory, to lead us in wisdom, to guide us in victory, and unite the stars under divine providence and manifest destiny. May she live long and in glory."

"Amen," the others intoned.

Grif uttered a hasty amen, and drank. It was Varkavian whiskey, and a particularly good batch of it—he would have to be careful to moderate his drinking. He raised his glass again. "To Baron Nyst," he said. "May long life and prosperity visit his house, that it may visit our own."

It was the simplest and least potentially offensive of the toasts Grif knew. The officers nodded politely and drank.

Everyone sat back down and began to eat. Grif joined them, careful to eat slowly and solemnly. The faux beef was delicious.

Mavis was apparently satisfied—for the time being—that Grif was who he claimed to be. He began to pepper "Captain Tax" with questions about recent events in the Baronies.

"We all heard of the death of Mogra Tylaris with some surprise," Mavis said. "How is that affecting the region?"

Grif wiped the corner of his mouth with a folded napkin and set it neatly folded on the table. "Things will be more dangerous for some time," he said in a disapproving tone. "I had to hire a complement of guards to protect my cargo while we were in port, and I fear I will continue to need them."

"Piracy is on the rise then?"

"Not yet," Grif said. "Thuggery in the ports. When I left, there were no reports of ships being attacked in transit. But it's simply a matter of time..." On a hunch, Grif added, "especially with the rumors."

Mavis raised an eyebrow. "Rumors?"

"I hesitate to say, since I don't know for certain," Grif replied, "but it comes from sources that give me reason to worry. There's a rumor that Rolis Tylaris will apply for—and receive—autonomous membership in the Alliance of Free Worlds."

The statement provoked exactly the reaction Grif was hoping for. Mavis' face drained of color, and he spilled a bit of his brandy on the table. Ando Fargus frowned, his normally cheerful expression turned to one of alarmed disapproval, and Katryn Valdyrs gasped alarm. Ubin Malvier simply increased the rate at which he tugged on the cuff of his sleeve.

Mavis smoothly mopped up his spilled whiskey with the corner of his napkin. "Are you sure of this?" Mavis asked. The tone of his voice was steady and unconcerned, and he betrayed no trace of the concern he showed the second before.

Grif shook his head. "As I said, it's only a rumor... but it's plausible. The new Baron isn't much like his father. He has no great love for work."

"And yet," Mavis said, "from what I hear, Mogra wasn't fond of work either."

Grif smiled. "True. But he didn't seem to consider politics work."

"That would be... a very bad thing," Ando Fargus said, speaking up for the first time. "Very bad news, if the Alliance were to gain the Tylaris Barony."

"It would be disastrous," Grif agreed, and it was a moment when Captain Tax and Grif Vindh were in complete agreement. "If true, business in the region will be destabilized for years to come. But at present it's a rumor only."

"Rumor or not, I may have to report it..." Mavis stared at Grif thoughtfully. "I am unexpectedly thankful I invited you to dinner this evening, Captain Tax."

Grif bowed his head. "I'm happy to have been of service."

They ate and talked more freely then, and Grif began to relax. He was still careful in what he said and how he said it, but he now believed that Mavis had accepted that Jobin Tax was who he claimed to be. That one piece of information had tipped the scales in his favor.

Halfway through the meal the stateroom door opened, and a junior officer entered the room. He handed Mavis a data slate. Mavis reviewed it carefully, nodded in satisfaction, tapped the slate once and handed it back.

"Congratulations, Captain. Your ship has passed inspection."

Grif felt relief wash over him. He smiled, unconcerned, as though he'd expected no other outcome. "I am very glad to hear it. Does this mean we'll be given clearance to land?"

Mavis nodded. "We're sending our report now. I fully expect permission to be given in the next one or two days."

The conversation became less formal after that, with the others joining in—except for Malvier, who ate silently, tugging at his sleeve the entire time. At one point Mavis asked about Captain Tax's family, trying to determine if there were a distant family connection, just as Bennet's people had predicted. Griff shrugged and suggested their similarities were nothing more than a strange genetic coincidence.

"Ah, but there are no coincidences in evolution, Captain," Mavis said. "Evolution is the Divine map of progress. It is creation reaching out toward its Creator. To remain static is to fall away and fall behind, so everything must move forward. There is purpose behind it all."

"I'd... never thought of it that way," Grif said.

Mavis smiled. "That is because you are, alas, an unbeliever. But don't fret—our reputation toward those who lack faith is undeserved. Mr. Malvier, here, is also an unbeliever, yet he serves the Radiant Throne with distinction, and we hope that some day he will come to know the divine light of truth."

Mr. Malvier nodded solemnly, and continued to tug at his sleeve.

"He accepts the reality of the world around him," Mavis said, "and has sworn fealty to our Emperor. For that, he is permitted his unbelief. We believe that in time he will come to see truth."

"I see," Grif said carefully.

"But enough of such things. I hope we will have many opportunities for such talks in the future. In fact I hope—"

A chime rang, and the stateroom door slid open. Another junior officer stepped into the room, looking very agitated.

Mavis looked at the officer and frowned in concern. "What's wrong?"

They found something, Grif thought, forcing himself to take a drink of whiskey instead of trying to bolt for the door. *Maybe they found Ktk.*

The junior officer hurried over to the Commodore and handed him a data slate. Mavis glanced at it, and his eyes widened in shock.

"Here?" he asked. "Now?"

The junior officer nodded mutely.

Mavis stood, wiping his mouth with his napkin. His officers, startled, stood as well. Grif hastily followed.

"Is something wrong?" Grif asked.

"My apologies," Mavis said, bowing slightly to Grif. "Something has come up, and duty demands I leave immediately. I apologize."

Grif felt relief—whatever it was, it had nothing to do with him. "Not at all. I thank you for your hospitality."

Mavis nodded. "I trust your stay on Varkav will be profitable. I hope we shall meet again. But for now, I—"

"Mavis!" The voice calling from the Wardroom was cold and demanding. It was a familiar voice, and the sound of it sent a chill down Grif's spine.

Mavis and his officers stood at attention. A moment later a figure wrapped in the robes of the Radiant Throne priesthood stepped through the door—a tall, thin man with almost no hair at all on his head, save for dark, thin eyebrows.

It was the Viceroy.

"My Lord," Mavis said. "I was just on my way..."

The Viceroy glanced at Grif for a moment and frowned. Grif shifted uneasily under the Viceroy's gaze—a perfectly reasonable reaction for anyone caught in that stare, even Jobin Tax.

Finally the Viceroy turned his attention back to Mavis. "I am not angry," he said. "Simply impatient. I need to speak to you *now*."

Mavis nodded. "Very well, my Lord. If... I may... if I may introduce you to our guest. Captain Jobin Tax of the *Alo Minh*. The *Alo Minh* is a Maximilian-class trading ship from the Nyst Trade Barony. Captain Tax, this is the Viceroy. He is a Sword of the Radiant Throne."

Grif didn't dare look the Viceroy in the eye. He bowed formally, looking at the floor. "I am honored, sir."

He felt the Viceroy study him for a moment. "The ship?"

"Passed inspection hours ago," Mavis said.

Time slowed to a crawl. Grif stood and summoned every ounce of willpower he had to look at the Viceroy directly.

I can't look like I'm trying to avoid him, Grif thought, *or he'll suspect. I have to look afraid but not specifically afraid. I'm afraid of him because he's a Sword, and no other reason. If he suspects... how can he not? How can he not know?*

But the Viceroy turned away. "I apologize for interrupting your dinner, Captain Tax. Mavis, I must speak with you privately. Now."

Mavis bowed his head, excused himself, and followed the Sword out of the room.

The three remaining officers relaxed slightly. Ando Fargus smiled at Grif apologetically. "I'll take you back to the flight deck, Captain," he said, "and see that you get back to your ship."

Grif nodded wordlessly, thinking only of the force of the Viceroy's mind as it had sifted through his on Tyrelos station. They were, it seemed, hopelessly and utterly screwed.

Chapter 30

WHEREIN Our Hero and His Employer Have a Disagreement Over Matters of Procedure

When Grif returned to the *Fool's Errand* he found Cyrus and Amys waiting for him in Bay One.

They remained in character until the transport decoupled from the hull and returned to the *Centurion*. At that point all three let out a long sigh.

Amys grinned at Grif. "They didn't find a goddamn thing."

"That's right!" Cyrus laughed. "They went through Bay Three with a fine-tooth comb and still couldn't find the door! And you were right about the search party—some of those marines had been through here before. They didn't recognize the Wardroom, they didn't recognize our living quarters, and one of them kept asking me for directions the entire time. Nobody could tell it was the *Fool's Errand*, Grif. If they couldn't find anything now, I don't think they're ever going to find anything ever."

"Good," Grif said.

Amys frowned. "You don't seem too happy about it. How'd it go with you?"

Grif stared at the seal to the nadir lock and didn't answer.

Amys' frown deepened. "Grif? Talk to me."

Cyrus' good mood vanished as he looked from Amys to Grif. "Oh, *hell*," he said. "Something bad happened."

"Yeah..." Grif snapped out of it and turned toward them. "Just us on board, right?"

Amys nodded.

"Right." Grif headed toward the door. "Meeting in the Wardroom, one hour."

"What's *wrong*?" Amys asked.

"We're screwed," Grif said. "So very, very screwed. Round up the others. One hour. I need a drink."

Grif was barely aware of his surroundings as he made his way to the Wardroom. When he entered the Wardroom, he stood in shock: for a moment he didn't know where he was. He hadn't seen it since Cyrus had remodeled it.

The faux wood paneling on the walls had been painted an off-white color. Digital frames displaying random images hung on the walls. The tiles on the floor were gone, replaced with thick, dark-red carpet. The light globes were gone, simple, brighter lights took their place. The tables and chairs had been replaced with strange, minimalist furniture. For a moment, in a fit of panic, Grif couldn't find the bar—they'd moved it over by the panoramic viewport, and painted it metallic silver.

"Sorry, Grif."

Grif turned and saw Cyrus shrugging apologetically.

Grif sighed and walked over to the bar. "Well, I did want it unrecognizable. Is any of it salvageable?"

"No." Cyrus followed him into the room. "We had to work pretty fast. We weren't being careful."

"Yeah." Grif looked behind the bar and took out a bottle of Stellis Blue. "Glass?"

"Sure," Cyrus said. Grif pulled out two and filled them to the top.

"It's a good job," Grif said. "I *hate* it. But it's a damn good job."

He raised his glass. "To the ugliest damn Wardroom I've ever seen on a ship," he said.

Cyrus chuckled and raised his glass in kind.

Within the hour the crew—all save Ktk—had assembled in the Wardroom. With them were Velis, Bennet, and a few other agents. Everyone could tell something was bothering him.

"The dinner," he said finally, "went rather well." Most of his crew relaxed slightly. Amys and Cyrus didn't, and neither did Velis.

"*After* dinner," Grif continued, "I learned that we have a new problem. Actually, it's an old problem. A problem I'd hoped we'd resolved on Tyrelos station."

"Grif," Amys said, "get to the point. What are you talking about?"

"I'm talking about that damned Sword," Grif said, trying to sound cheerful and sounding bitter instead. "He marched right into the dining room, grabbed Mavis by the ear and pulled him out to have a *very important talk*."

The tension in the room rose considerably.

Grif smiled bitterly. “He didn't recognize me. Not yet, anyway. He looked right at me, and just when I was *positive* he was going to tear my heart out, or melt my brain, or something like that, he apologized for interrupting my dinner and pulled Mavis out of the room. We can thank the new face for that. But... damn it all. We don't need this.”

“Are you sure it was him?” Velis asked. “I thought Amys killed him.”

“He looks really good for a corpse. But I'm sure. The ‘Viceroy.’”

Velis grew thoughtful. “That is inconvenient,” she admitted. “But it's not necessarily the end of the world. We all suspected a Sword might get involved eventually.”

“Maybe so,” Grif said, “but I hoped it would be someone other than him. He might actually know what our plans are.”

Bennet and Velis exchanged glances. “How so?” Velis asked.

Grif sighed. He reached for the bottle of Stellis Blue, thought better of it, then pushed it away. “I came up with the idea of using the robots in Ur Ados while he was going through my head. He *reacted* when I thought it up.”

“How much did he learn?” Bennet asked.

“I don't know!” Grif rubbed his temples in irritation. “I couldn't follow what was going on particularly well. I kept fading in and out of consciousness. Then I kicked him, which didn't work out particularly well for me, and then Amys shot him. A lot.”

“So he doesn't know the specifics of the plan,” Velis said.

“*I don't know*,” Grif repeated. “Maybe not. But he knows that I'm coming here and that I'm going to try and steal it... and he might know more.”

An uneasily silence settled over the room. Grif stared out the panoramic viewport, glaring at the ugly blotched surface of Varkav.

Finally Velis broke the silence. “We need to know what the Viceroy saw. *Exactly* what he did and didn't see. Then we'll know how much danger we're in.”

“That would be very useful,” Grif agreed. “How the hell do we do that?”

“We have a telepath, too,” Velis pointed out. “Mr. Tosk. We revive him.”

“Ebur?” Grif shook his head. “What can he do? He's powerful, but I don't think he'd be able to read the Viceroy's mind from here. And I'm damn sure he couldn't do it without the son of a bitch noticing.”

"Not his mind," Velis said. "Yours." Grif stared at Velis in shock.

"The same way the Viceroy did. Mr. Tosk will reconstruct the memory of the Sword going through your mind, and will experience what you experienced. He may be able to determine exactly what the Sword saw."

"Absolutely not," Amys growled.

"What she said!" Grif shouted. "Are you *crazy*?" Velis didn't raise her voice. "It's the only way to know for sure," she said firmly.

"You don't get it," Grif said. "It takes a week for the medicine to wear off. Then it takes a week for the new medicine to kick in. At that point he can't do anything on his own—you have to give him instructions. Considering how painful it was when someone who *knew what they were doing* tried to do that to me, I don't think I'd survive!"

"Then we don't put him on the new medicine," Velis said. "We let him do all the work."

"How is that a better plan?" Cyrus demanded. "Ebur's a lunatic when he's not on his meds. He'd kill Grif anyway, and probably the rest of us."

Velis' voice hardened. "Then we convince him it's in his best interest to help us."

"This is *idiotic!*" Grif shouted. "When Ebur is off his meds, his best interest is whatever it is he happens to be thinking about at the time. He's not *rational* when he's like that. He is *I-n-s-a-n-e insane*."

Velis' voice rose slightly. "Have you ever dealt with a Sword before? Other than your *very brief* encounter on Tyrelos Station. I'd think that would be enough for you."

"Look," Grif began, but Velis cut him off sharply.

"I have." She looked at him steadily, betraying no anger, no frustration, only a fierce, single-minded intensity. "I have lost many agents due to Swords. I have failed missions due to Swords. They are *insane*, but they are rarely *stupid*... and they are *very committed* to getting the job done. The only way to succeed against that kind of dedication is to match it with your own."

Grif shook his head. "Not like that."

"To exceed it."

"No, Velis, not like that."

"To want to win *more*, and to be willing to do what it takes."

Grif slammed his fist on the table. "There are limits, Velis!"

Velis smiled ever so slightly. "You know me better than that. And before you say anything else, I'd like to remind you how very outnumbered you and your crew are on this ship, *Captain*."

Grif tensed. So did his crew. The agents in the room, on the other hand, *relaxed*. It was the same basic reaction: both sides were awaiting orders.

Grif glanced at Bennet. Bennet stared back, expressionless, as relaxed as the rest of them.

Well, Grif thought, *this moment came a bit sooner than I'd expected*.

"The Throne has already searched this ship," Grif warned. "Think you can explain away all the casualties if you take it by force?"

"I'm willing to take that risk," Velis said. "Are you?" Grif considered his options. "No," he said. "You win. When Ebur comes off his meds we'll—"

"No need to wait that long," Velis said briskly. "Lieutenant Jax, please collect Dr. Lyle, and tell him to arrive at Bay Three with one of the psi kits." Bennet nodded and headed for the door.

"One of the what?" Grif asked.

"We studied Mr. Tosk's medicine to try and find a way to speed up the detox and transition process," Velis said. "We didn't find a safe alternative, but we came up with something we could use in an emergency. I'm declaring this an emergency."

"For once we agree," Grif said. "This is definitely an emergency. But something tells me we don't agree on what the emergency is."

Grif saw Amys nod slightly.

"Mr. Tosk will probably survive," Velis said. "And you will probably survive too. And once we're finished we'll know exactly what the Viceroy knows and what he doesn't. And everything goes back to normal."

Grif set his jaw.

"Or," Velis added, "you can decide to do this the hard way. I won't use force unless I have to... but I want to *win*, and I won't let your squeamishness get in the way."

Grif glared at Velis, feeling nothing but hatred. Velis stared back at Grif apparently feeling nothing at all. He was nothing but a resource to her... an expendable one at that. "Fine. Let's get this over with."

"Grif!" The disapproval in Amys' voice was plain.

Grif shrugged. "What else can I do, Amys? We have to appreciate the *gravity* of the situation."

"Good boy," Velis said.

Grif ignored her and turned to his crew. "As for the rest of you. Don't be *stupid*. What I said to Amys goes double for the rest of you. Things are going to get pretty heavy for a while. Just... go with it."

The crew said nothing, but Morgan sighed.

"I'm glad we understand each other," Grif said dryly. "Amys, go up to the bridge and monitor ship systems. I don't want Ebur flipping out and making the ship do something that makes the Throne curious. We're going to have to be light on our feet."

Amys nodded.

"Go with her," Velis ordered one of her men. "Make sure she doesn't try anything funny."

"Cutter, go to the Medibay. I don't care how good a physician Doctor Lyle is, we'll need you on hand when we wake Ebur up."

"OK, Skip," Cutter drawled. As he left, Velis ordered another agent to follow him.

"Now if you will excuse me," Grif said, "I'll be in Bay Three."

Grif stalked out of the Wardroom. Two of Velis' men followed.

"I know the way," he growled.

"I'm sure you do," one said. The other said nothing.

Grif stepped into the lift, his 'companions' taking positions on either side.

"An honor guard!" Grif said, forcing himself to sound cheerful. "I'm touched. Really."

He keyed in the command for the cargo deck, and the lift began to descend.

"Which one are you again?" Grif asked the one to his right, voice casual.

"Carsons," the man said.

Grif looked at the other expectantly.

"Laris," the second man said.

Grif nodded. "Well, Carsons, Laris, congratulations. You guys are officially running the show."

"Just open up that room," Carsons said, sounding bored. "Everything will turn out just fine."

The lift opened, and they stepped out into the deck.

"Hold on a moment," Grif said, and went to an intercom panel set into the wall.

"Quit stalling," Carsons said, reaching into his jacket.

"Not stalling," Grif said. "We need to let Ktk know we're coming."

Carsons considered it. "All right," he said. "Make it quick."

Grif punched the intercom. "This is the Captain," he said cheerfully. "Ktk, just letting you know that something's up. How's Ebur?"

Ktk replied that Ebur was currently locked in a stasis chamber.

"Glad to hear it," Grif said. "Look... We have a situation, so don't be surprised when we show up."

Ktk asked what was going on.

"Oh, about what you'd expect," Grif said. "Velis wants to make a few modifications to the org chart. We'll all have to adapt to the new environment. Vindh out."

All the interior lights in the ship went out. As the auxiliary lights kicked in, gravity reversed itself, and Grif launched himself across the room.

Chapter 31

WHEREIN Our Hero, Upon Reaching an Impasse, Finds it Necessary to Assert His Authority

The *Fool's Errand* used a parallel-plate system to generate artificial gravity: beneath the flooring on each deck were gravity plates, and just beyond the ceiling were nullifier plates. This allowed each deck to have customized gravity settings, if necessary, and the nullifier plates ensured that the gravity well never extended beyond the deck itself, or outside the ship. Each plate was also independently customizable, so it was possible, for example, to set one plate at half a standard gravity and its neighboring plate at two standard gravities, creating a startling and potentially dangerous gravity shelf where the two plates met up.

For the most part the granularity inherent in this technology remained unused; it was enough to turn off gravity while they were in tach, and turn it back on when they dropped back into normal space. However, when the ship was being boarded, the ability to wildly vary the gravity of each individual plate was extremely useful.

This was one of those times.

At the moment, all gravity in the ship was off. The auxiliary lights flickered on, off, on, off, as little-used circuits sluggishly came to life. In the strobe-light effect, Grif saw Carsons and Laris flailing, trying and failing to compensate for the lack of gravity.

Grif sailed past Laris, feet first, and snaked out an arm as he grabbed Laris' waist. The weight of the agent caused Grif's trajectory to change, pulling Laris along behind him. A quick twist and half-flip pushed Laris to the front, and Laris's face smashed against the bulkhead.

Grif let go, rolled up against the wall, and pushed off just as Carsons managed to steady himself, pull a weapon out from under his jacket, and fire at the spot where Grif had been moments before. But Grif was now on the other wall and pushed himself up to the ceiling, gaining momentum.

Carsons fired and missed a second time. This time, the shot unbalanced him, and he had to focus on keeping his balance. He tried to grab hold of a microgravity handle set into the wall to steady himself, but he drifted just out of reach, thrashing wildly instead.

Grif pushed off the ceiling, flipped in mid-air and kicked Carsons' face. He'd developed so much momentum that when his feet connected with Carsons' jaw he heard the jaw break. Carsons passed out immediately.

Grif flexed his legs, trying to dissipate as much momentum as he could against Carsons himself, and took the gauss pistol still clenched in Carsons' hand. Then he pushed away from Carsons in mid-air, causing the agent's unconscious form to crash against the bulkhead as he drifted in the other direction.

The lift opened, and two agents propelled themselves out of it. Grif fired. Gauss flechettes tore through an agent's arm, sending spherical drops of blood flying lazily through the air. The mild recoil from the pistol caused Grif to twist slightly in the other direction, but he managed to fire another shot, hitting the second agent in the chest.

The first agent released his weapon when his arm was wounded, but grabbed it with his other arm and fired, awkwardly. He missed.

Grif pushed himself out of the lift foyer and down the corridor.

"We have the bridge," Amys' voice said out of the intercom. "Intercom is linked directly here. No cross talk is permitted."

Grif turned and saw the agent push himself out of the lift and into the rec area.

"Amys, set the foyer on cargo deck to two gravities, now!"

Grif heard a grating sound as the grav plates underneath the foyer came to life. The agents yelped in surprise as they rammed into the floor at high speed. They did not move afterward. Carsons and Laris fell to the ground as well.

"Return to zero g, Amys. Four down."

"Instituting Boarding Pattern A in ten seconds," Amys said over the intercom. "Seven reported down so far."

Seven out of thirty, Grif thought. *Not bad so far*. He made note of what part of the ship he was in and pushed himself to the floor, bracing his legs.

"Three, two, one," Amys said, and the gravity plates shuddered as gravity returned to deck three. Grif's legs buckled but held, and he silently began counting down from fifteen.

Thirteen.

Grif was close to Bay Three, which housed Ktk's hidden room, and from beyond that door he heard a loud crash and some cursing. He ran to the door and keyed it to open, stepping to one side.

Ten.

Gauss flechettes burst through the door, impacting the wall on the other side, embedding themselves solidly in the metal.

Eight.

Grif glanced in the room and saw two more agents, each with rifles, standing atop a wall of cargo. He pulled back again, and more flechettes impacted against the far wall.

Four.

Grif took a few steps back and dove through the door, dropping into a roll...

Two.

...gauss flechettes burst around where his head had been as he came out of the roll and pushed off the ground...

Switch.

Deck three was weightless. Grif sailed up into the air, firing with his pistol. One of the guards clutched his shoulder and fell back. The other tried to swing the barrel of his rifle up too quickly and lost his balance, firing wildly into the air.

Ten.

Grif reached for a handle along the wall and grabbed it lightly as he passed, just enough to turn him in midair so he was facing the ground. He saw Dr. Evard Lyle hiding behind a crate, unarmed, a discarded laser torch burning into the wall.

They're cutting into my ship, Grif thought. *I just might kill every last one.* He searched the room trying to find the rest of them.

Five.

Grif reached the cargo bay ceiling and pushed himself over onto a catwalk. He lay down on the catwalk carefully, keeping a firm grip on the handle of his gun.

Two.

Flechettes tore through the base of the catwalk just in front of him.

Switch.

There was a squawk as someone fell. Grif leaned over and saw an agent exposed between a stack of crates. He fired quickly and missed, causing the agent to crawl back deeper into his cover.

"Ten casualties reported," Amys said over the intercom.

"Amys! Pattern C! Ten seconds!"

"Switching to Boarding Pattern C in ten seconds," Amys said.

Grif started to crawl forward, keeping his body close to the catwalk bottom, trying not to expose himself.

"Eight..."

The platform behind him was torn open by flechette fire. Grif reluctantly got to his feet and ran across the catwalk to the other side.

"Six..."

Flechette fire erupted behind him. The catwalk buckled dangerously. Grif almost lost his footing.

"Three..."

He felt the air move behind him. Below he saw two agents step out from behind the crates to get a better shot.

"One..."

Grif leapt off the catwalk into the open air, toward the nearest wall as gravity disappeared.

Thirty.

Grif had more momentum than he liked from his leap of faith and was descending too rapidly. He fired at the agents on the ground, who were again caught off guard by the change in gravity. He hit one in the leg. Better than nothing.

Twenty-seven.

Grif neared the wall and grabbed at a handle as it rushed past him. His arm jerked from the force of it. He let go of it before it broke his wrist, but he still felt a jolt of pain, and his left arm was numb. *Always the left arm...*

Twenty-five.

He could now control his descent. He landed on the floor behind the crates, taking him out of the agents' line of sight. He pushed off from the wall and glided across the floor, closer to the row where the agents were hiding.

"Seventeen casualties," Amys reported.

Grif smiled grimly. His crew was doing well.

Twenty.

Grif was gliding centimeters off the ground, propelling himself with his hands. He saw a pair of feet next to a crate not far from him. Looking up, he saw another agent scanning the ceiling.

Wrong direction, Grif thought. He smirked.

Fourteen.

The agent didn't notice him until Grif was less than a meter away. He shouted in surprise and lowered his rifle—again, as was all too common for them, too quickly, and he had to grab onto a crate to keep steady.

Grif grabbed the man by the ankles and pulled. The agent yelled in surprise, flailing his arms and losing his grip on his rifle. It flew across the room as the agent sailed straight up into the air, starting to tumble as he moved closer and closer to the ceiling.

"Happy landings!" Grif shouted.

Eight.

A shadow fell over him.

Grif moved just in time as a foot crashed into the spot where the small of his back would've been. He grabbed the foot and pulled, pushing himself over the surprised form of Bennet Jax as he pulled him under and smashed him into one of the cargo crates. Grif didn't let go, but used the man's weight to pull him back to the ground.

Bennet, unlike the other agents, knew what he was doing. He grabbed the side of the crate and kicked out with his feet, hitting Grif in the chest. Grif grunted as he flew back into the wall of cargo behind him. Air rushed out of his body from the force of the impact, but he kept his wits about him, steadying himself.

Six.

Bennet launched himself at Grif, hands-first. This was a risky maneuver. Hands-first also meant face-first, which left you exposed. Grif heard the hum of a vibroknife as it flicked into Bennet's left hand.

Five.

Grif pushed up, twisting as he reached the top of the crates, flipping over onto the top row. Bennet changed direction with practiced ease, but moving over the edge of the crate took a bit more effort, giving Grif the time he needed to lash out with his foot, striking Bennet's hand. The vibroknife tumbled uselessly across Bay Three.

Bennet shook his head, wiping away blood away from his nose and face. The blood spattered across the room like droplets of rain. "When the hell did you learn to fight?"

Three.

Grif didn't answer. He grabbed the edge of the crate and lashed out with his legs, hitting Bennet's shin. Bennet grunted in surprise and almost fell, but caught Grif's leg at the last second and held on.

Two.

Bennet pulled himself toward Grif, and shifting his weight, tore Grif away from his handhold. For a moment, the only thing Grif was connected to was Bennet's arm.

One.

Gravity returned, and Grif landed hard. Through the ringing in his ears he could hear the panicked shouts of the agent he'd thrown upward, who had managed to grab onto the catwalk and was holding on for dear life.

Bennet sprang to his feet, and Grif realized he was in trouble. Bennet was much better at fighting in standard gravity.

Five.

Bennet wasted no time and kicked Grif hard in the stomach. Air rushed out of his body and he tried to crawl aside.

Four.

"No you don't," Bennet said, and grabbed his arm, twisting it around his back with great strength.

Three.

"Twenty casualties," Amys reported.

Bennet placed a knee on each shoulder, and reached around to grab Grif's chin, placing another hand on the back of Grif's head.

Two.

"I've got your Captain," Bennet shouted. "Stand down or I'll break his—"

One.

Gravity evaporated. Grif pushed against the crates with his free arm. Bennet's weight had nothing to work against, and he let go of Grif's head as he tried to grab onto something to keep from flying away.

Thirty.

Grif grabbed onto Bennet and rammed his knee into Bennet's stomach. Bennet grunted in pain, and Grif followed up with a quick jab to the side. Bennet was dazed. Grif smashed his elbow into the side of Bennet's face, then twisted and drove it into the agent's gut...

The intercom crackled to life. "This is Velis Enge," a sullen voice said. "By my order, cease all hostilities against the crew of this ship immediately. Enge out."

Grif let go of Bennet, who grabbed the edge of the crate, breathing heavily. The agent who had been hanging from the ceiling dropped slowly to the floor.

"Gravity will return in one minute," Amys said over the intercom. "Please secure all loose-flying objects, including bodies, by that time."

Grif and Bennet stared at each other, each fighting for breath.

"Gather up your dead and wounded," Grif said coldly. "You may leave three men in the medibay to treat them, but you won't be one of them. The rest of your men—the ones who can still move—will report to the brig immediately."

Bennet nodded, still gasping for breath. "This... wasn't... personal."

"It was to me, you son of a bitch," Grif said. "I don't know what my sister might have told you about me, but I don't tolerate mutiny aboard my ship."

Chapter 32

WHEREIN Our Hero, Having Settled Matters to His Satisfaction, Considers the Relative Merits of Mercy and Justice

Eleven agents were dead, ten more were badly wounded. Carsons and Laris were both alive, though hurt from the two-G fall. Of Grif's crew, Cutter had been wounded in the arm by a gauss pistol and Morgan had taken a shot to the gut. Both would live. The others had only superficial injuries.

Ktk wanted to know what the hell was going on.

Amys explained the situation to Ktk as Grif and Cyrus ran a diagnostic to make sure no ship systems had been adversely affected by the fluctuating gravity. The ship was fine: aside from some scoring on the walls from stray gauss pistol bursts, there was no trace of the fight.

An hour later Grif, Amys, Cyrus and Hari were in the Wardroom reviewing the situation.

"Gurgan and Vod are guarding the brig," Hari reported, ridges on his face fully extended. "Armed to the teeth. They will shoot anyone who tries anything that looks even remotely suspicious."

"Good," Grif said. "How are Morgan and Cutter?"

"OK," Cyrus said. "I just came from the medibay. Morgan spent a little time in the autodoc while it fished flechette rounds out of his gut, and is now resting in his quarters. Cutter put his arm in a sling and claims he's fine."

"Good," Grif said. "Amys, excellent job. Just out of curiosity, how badly did you hurt your, ah, escort?"

Amys smiled. "He's in medibay now. He'll recover."

Grif poured everyone a glass of Stellis. "How is Ktk?"

Cyrus chuckled. "Ktk is upset that it missed the entire thing."

Grif laughed. "I think they might have surrendered sooner if Ktk had been involved. Nothing quite so disturbing as seeing a two and a half meter bug floating around the ship, wrapping tentacles around the necks of its opponents."

"I'm glad the ship came out OK," Cyrus said. "The grav plates are getting old, Grif, and we never did get around to upgrading them. We're going to need to do that soon or the next time we do this she'll hurt herself."

"Yeah," Grif agreed. "Some of the plates in Bay Three sounded like they were straining pretty hard. Well, that's something to worry about later. Right now I need to go talk to our prisoners and see if there's any reason I shouldn't kill them."

"I'll come with you," Amys offered, and they went down to the brig together.

"What are we going to do?" Amys asked as they made their way aft. "About this job, I mean? Scrap the whole thing and go home?"

"That's where I'm leaning right now," Grif said. "I don't see the point."

"Yeah," Amys agreed, then she frowned. "On the other hand... it means we'd have to deal with a very ticked-off Alef Halge."

"I don't particularly care," Grif growled. "Goddamn mutineers..."

The brig was on deck two and hadn't been used in some time. It was simple and effective, a single room sealed off with a plasteel door and wall, making it completely transparent to the jailers. It was set inside an outer room where Gurgan and Vod stood watch.

Six people sat in the brig: Velis, Bennet, three other agents, and one scientist. Three scientists were tending to the wounded in the medibay. The fifth scientist *was* one of the wounded in the medibay.

Velis sat on the floor, lost in her own thoughts. Bennet sat on one of the benches in the room, also staring off into space. The scientist and the three agents were sitting together, talking quietly.

When Grif entered the outer room, Velis and Bennet looked up at the same time. Velis scowled upon seeing him. Bennet looked a bit guilty.

"I suppose you've come to gloat," Velis said. "Not that it matters, since without our help you'll never get that—"

"I'm not here to gloat," Grif said, no emotion in his voice. "Amys is here to gloat... she has that luxury. She isn't the captain of this ship."

Amys knew that voice. She started to plan how they would dispose of the bodies, and how they would explain the reduction in crew the next time they were searched.

"I am here, Velis, because you organized a mutiny on my ship."

The word "mutiny" had an electric effect on all within the brig. Velis' eyes widened in shock. The four men talking together fell silent, and turned to look at Grif with worried expressions on their faces. Bennet seemed to deflate further and looked at the floor.

Mutinies were no laughing matter on any starship, and were usually dealt with on the spot. Even the Alliance considered the execution of mutineers as an act of self-defense under most circumstances.

Velis had the presence of mind to keep silent. Nothing she could say would have alleviated the situation—she and Grif both knew what she did. She raised her chin in defiance, however, which made one of the agents wince.

"Ten of your people are now dead, Velis," Grif said, voice harsh but calm. "Eleven are recovering from serious injuries. One of them, a scientist, I've half a mind to keep out of this, since all he was doing was trying to get out of the way when the gravity kicked back in. But the other half of my mind is in no mood to make exceptions. I need to decide what to do with you, and soon."

Velis kept her voice steady. "You will need our expertise to break into Ur Ados. Especially if that Sword is expecting you."

"Yes, well, this is the problem, Velis," Grif said. "I don't trust you. At all. We took back our ship because you didn't expect us to fight for it, and you underestimated how *good* we are at fighting for what's ours. But now you know, and you're all very good at your jobs. So unless I find some way to nullify the threat you pose, I have no way of knowing you won't try it again."

The prisoners were silent.

"So what should I do? If we weren't in orbit I'd be tempted to shove you all out an airlock and watch you swim before I hit tach. As it is, I'm half-inclined to break orbit right now to do just that. Fortunately for you, Varkav Orbital Command would have too many questions if I tried to leave so soon after arriving."

"We could just flood the brig with a toxin," Amys suggested.

Grif nodded. "I've considered it. But there is the matter of that artifact. We came all the way here to steal it."

Velis jumped on this thought. "Alef is expecting us to return," she said. "If we don't—"

"I will tell him about your attempted mutiny and explain that if he has a problem with the way I deal with mutineers on my ship he can take me to court."

Velis fell silent.

"So," Grif said, "here is what I'm going to do. I'm going to bed. It's been a rough day. I'll be back in the morning: when I arrive, you're going to give me a reason to trust you and your people. If it's a good reason I'll let you go, and we'll try to carry on with the job your boss hired me to do. If it isn't, then I'll deal with you in the manner all mutineers are dealt with on my ship."

With that, Grif left the room. Amys stayed behind, chatting a bit with Vod and Gurgan, watching the prisoners out of the corner of her eye. The four in the middle started to whisper amongst each other again. Bennet got up, looked at Velis, hesitated, and then sat next to her.

"Is he bluffing?" Bennet asked. He tried to ask the question quietly, but the microphones in the room picked his question up clearly.

Amys turned to the prisoners. "No," she said. You've got till tomorrow to convince him you can be trusted."

Velis snorted. "He's not going to kill us," she said dismissively. "He's just trying to put me in my place..."

Amys looked at Velis in disbelief. "Are you really that *stupid*?"

Velis glared at Amys.

"Velis, part of me hopes that you really ARE that stupid... just to see the look on your face when he pulls the trigger. But because some of your people *aren't* stupid"—she looked directly at Bennet when she said that—"let's make one thing perfectly clear: Grif won't hesitate to kill the lot of you, including your wounded, if you can't convince him you can be trusted. He'll do it and he won't feel a second of guilt. You tried to take his ship."

Velis didn't reply.

"I'll try this one more time," Amys said. "I don't care what you think Grif is or isn't, but understand one thing: when it comes to protecting his ship he is one of the most cold-blooded men I've ever met."

Gurgan and Vod nodded in agreement.

"If you want more proof," Amys continued, "just ask Vod about her brother. I'm going to bed."

Amys left the room. Bennet looked at Vod questioningly. "Your brother?"

"He was an idiot," Vod said, scratching her scalp irritably. The agents had given her hair, and she hated it. "He deserved what he got."

"They were never close," Gurgan explained.

* * *

The next morning, Grif came back to the brig, accompanied by Amys and Cyrus. He was wearing a sidearm.

"I'm listening," he said, and then leaned up against the doorway, arms folded.

Velis stood and walked to the plasteel wall. "Do you remember the last time we were all on Kinnar?"

Amys looked startled. Grif nodded.

"That is how I guarantee that, for the duration of this trip, I will acknowledge you as the captain of this vessel and, what's more, the leader of this mission."

Grif stared at Velis for a long time, saying nothing.

"It's the only pledge I can give," she said. "The only one that has any meaning to either of us."

Finally, slowly, Grif nodded.

He turned to Vod. "Let 'em out."

Vod shrugged, nodded, and keyed in a command at the jailer's station. The plasteel door hissed and unlocked. Gurgan slid it all the way open.

"Thanks," Grif said. "Get something to eat, and get some sleep. You look beat."

Gurgan and Vod nodded in agreement.

Grif turned to Velis. "You and your people can go back to your cabins," he said. "Get some sleep, take a shower, eat. Amys will stop by and collect all the monitoring equipment you've been using on us... that's going to stop."

Velis nodded.

"All right. Get out of here. See to your wounded."

Velis hesitated. "What about the dead?"

Grif thought. "Your call," he said finally.

Velis nodded again, then left. The other agents filed out behind her, including Bennet, who didn't speak.

After they left, Amys turned to Grif. "So you actually trust her now?"

Grif shrugged. "Kinnar."

"Kinnar," Amys muttered.

"What?" Cyrus asked. "What the hell does that mean?"

"Velis just told me she owed me, big time," Grif said. "I already knew that, but this is the first time she ever admitted it to my face."

Cyrus looked from Grif to Amys then back, exasperated. "Are you ever going to tell me what happened at that ruddy wedding?"

"I saved Velis' career," Grif said. "And probably the Alliance. Well hell, Cyrus, don't look at me like that. It was an accident!"

Chapter 33

WHEREIN Our Hero Wins a Wager in an Inconvenient Fashion

A day later they received word from Varkav Orbital Command that they were cleared to land on the planet's surface. They landed without incident and were searched once more without incident. That past, Grif decided it was time for Ebur to wake up.

Grif, Amys, Cyrus, Cutter and Bennet entered the secret hold in Bay Three to find Ktk had already assembled the bed where Ebur would spend most of his time. Cyrus and Bennet opened the stasis cylinder, and when Cutter turned it off Ebur shivered, then opened his eyes.

Grif grinned at him.

"Well come on," Ebur said, annoyed. "Quit toying with me. Turn the damn thing on already."

"Already did that. Welcome to Varkav. Now it's time to strap you to a bed and have Ktk shock you for a month and a half."

"Great!" Ebur said. "The best part of the job is when I get to be tortured by a bug."

Ktk replied, somewhat crossly, that it wasn't particularly fond of the experience either.

"What's the pool this time?" Ebur asked.

"Oh, no," Grif said. "That'd influence the outcome. We'll tell you after."

"What pool?" Bennet asked. "What are you talking about?"

"We always bet on who Ebur will get to first," Cyrus explained. "It's trickier this time around, because of the extra crew."

Ktk added that it had bet on Amys trying to kill Grif at some point.

"Stop giving Ebur ideas," Grif ordered. "But yeah, I've got money on that too."

"Hey!" Amys protested.

"Well I do," Grif said. "He's done it to you before. More than once. Must be some sort of secret urge."

"I stopped secretly wanting to kill you years ago," Amys insisted.

Cutter helped Ebur into his bed, and began applying the restraints.

"That doesn't look like much fun," Bennet observed.

"Better than what you lot had planned for him," Grif said. "Ebur's a trooper, though. That reminds me, Ebur, I have a question that needs your expertise."

Grif quickly told Ebur about the Sword, and the incident on Tyrelos station where the Sword read his mind.

"What I want to know," Grif explained, "is whether or not the Sword would have been able to read what I was thinking when I came up with the plan."

Ebur frowned. "Let me get this straight. The Sword was rifling through your mind, forcing you to remember specific pieces of information?"

Grif nodded. "Files and reports, yeah."

"And you came up with this idea while you were reliving one of those memories?" Grif nodded again. "That's right."

Ebur shrugged. "Then you're safe. There's no way he could have known what you were thinking at the time."

"But he was reading my mind!"

"Sure," Ebur said. "He was reading it in a very specific way. Trying to recreate a memory at that level of detail is very specific work, and it's a different part of your mind. He probably felt when you made that connection, but he wouldn't have known what it was. At most he knows you thought of something, but he wouldn't know what."

"Well," Grif said, "that's certainly a load off my mind. Now I can focus on all the other things that are very likely to get us killed."

"Glad to help." Ebur grinned. "Now could you all get the hell out? I'm trying to go insane here."

Grif spent the next few days playing Captain Jobin Tax, working through the mundane licensing and permissions issues needed to buy and trade cargo. He loathed doing it by the book—the last time they were in port Grif had simply bribed the man he was dealing with now—but it was necessary to maintain their cover. After a few days he received grudging permission to allow his crew to reach preliminary trading agreements with merchants on the planet. No transactions could occur until the paperwork was finished, but it allowed the crew out of the spaceport. Cyrus, Cutter and Vod went through the motions of talking to businesses and arranging for the sale of their cargo, as well as looking into buying new cargo. Meanwhile Bennet and some of his agents nosed around looking for a way into Ur Ados.

By the end of the week Jobin Tax had successfully navigated the treacherous waters of Varkavian Bureaucracy and won a license to trade on the planet. On the same day Ktk informed the crew that Ebur was starting to rant.

"He'll start trying to kill us soon," Grif explained to Velis. "That's the fun part. Found a way in yet?"

"I think so," Velis said.

"Really?"

"Maybe." Velis paused. "We may have an agent on the inside."

"Inside what? Ur Voys? Ur Ados? I thought they all died."

"So did I," Velis said. "We tried to use Ur Ados as a staging area to get a team into Ur Voys. The team was discovered and executed, but our first agent—the one who'd been assigned to scout out Ur Ados—was still in place. The team was never linked back to her. Everyone in Ur Ados was investigated, of course, but she kept her cover intact by destroying anything that might incriminate her, including all her communications equipment. She hasn't been able to contact us since."

"You didn't have a safe house on Varkav?"

"We did," Velis said. "It turned out to be... unsafe."

Grif shuddered.

"Bennet was able to make contact today," Velis continued. "We think she can get us in. But I'd like to extract her when we leave. Is that all right?"

Grif was surprised she asked instead of demanded. "Er... yes, I suppose."

Velis nodded. "Good. I'll have Bennet give you the rest of the details when they're all worked out."

That evening Bennet, Velis and Grif sat in the conference room, looking at a picture of a grim-faced young woman on a terminal screen. The name SYTHE, MEAGHAN appeared on the bottom.

"She'd be pretty, if she didn't look like she expected to be killed at any moment," Grif said.

"Deep cover work can do that," Bennet said. "You get twitchy after a while."

"So how is she going to help you get in?" Grif asked.

"There's not a lot she can do directly," Bennet said. "She was sent in ahead of the main group to look around, get a feel for security measures, that sort of thing. She works in the waste treatment and disposal plant at the facility. Hazardous materials are processed there, get turned into your basic sludge, and then get dumped into an artificial lake... of sorts."

"A lake 'of sorts?'"

Bennet wrinkled his nose. "I wouldn't call it a lake, exactly, because it doesn't hold water, exactly. What it does hold gets recycled. As a thickening agent to a lubricant, I think."

"So how is that going to get you in?" Grif asked.

Bennet hit a terminal key and the picture changed to a rough schematic of part of the facility and some of the nearby grounds. "We go in through the 'lake.' Travel up the slough and into the hazmat treatment facility."

"You're going to climb up a radioactive sewer?"

Bennet nodded. "It's the glamor of the job that keeps me coming back..."

"I assume you have something to protect you from the hazardous waste as you're, ah, wading through it?"

Bennet nodded again, and Velis said "we brought some equipment with us. Sneaking into places usually requires wading through something repulsive, these days... that's actually the easy part."

"Easy," Grif repeated. "OK, if you say so. When are you going to try to pull this off?"

"Sythe will be doing maintenance on the treatment systems in four days, so that's when we go in. Any alarms we inadvertently trigger will be written off as simulations. The tricky parts happen before, when we try and sneak into the 'lake' without anyone noticing us, and after, when we sneak around the base hoping nobody notices us."

"Well... can you do it?"

Bennet hesitated.

"Yes," he said finally. "It's our best shot."

Grif shrugged. "All right," he said. "You guys are the experts here. Tell us what we need to do on our end to help you—if there is anything—and we'll do what we can."

"Just give me an idea of what robots you want us to attach the receptors to," Bennet said. "We'll have to take care of the rest."

"Sure," Grif said. "I'll get you a list."

Over the next few days Grif felt uneasy, tense, and irritable. He kept running down the list of everything that might go wrong. It was a long list, and when he'd gone through it a second time it was nearly evening. He wasn't hungry, but he decided it was probably a good idea to eat something, and he made his way to the Wardroom.

As he neared it the door opened, and Hari flew through the air and smashed into the wall. Gurgan followed, bellowing in rage, fists clenched tightly.

Grif reached for the comm badge on his sleeve and clicked it on. "Ktk," he said. "Gurgan is trying to beat Hari to a pulp."

A second later Gurgan blinked, shook his head, and sheepishly helped Hari up off the floor, muttering an apology.

"The fun begins," Hari said, wincing as he massaged a spine running along the side of his head.

"Yeah," Grif said. "Yay for us."

Fights broke out continuously over the rest of the evening. Velis nearly killed one of her own people before Ktk shocked Ebur into submission. Afterward she placed herself in the brig.

On the fourth day Morgan, Cyrus, Bennet and four other agents hired a ground transport and loaded it with cargo. By all appearances they were getting ready to deliver it to one of Cyrus' buyers, but there were a few crates that held something else: the equipment Bennet and his men needed for their task. Late that morning, seven men drove out of the spaceport. That afternoon, only two returned.

"Nobody noticed them leave," Cyrus said. "Now we wait. Everyone still alive?"

"Yeah," Grif said. "Cutter tried to saw off Vod's arm with a surgical tool earlier today. I suspect she'll make him pay for that later."

Cyrus laughed in spite of himself. "How long till we can put Ebur on his other meds?"

"Two more days," Grif said. "But if you think about it, thing's have been going pretty easy so far—"

Cyrus hit him in the stomach. Grif doubled over, gasping for breath, then fell to the ground as Cyrus smashed him in the back. A heavy boot came down hard on his side, then again. He dimly heard Amys shout "Ktk!" into her Comm badge, and then Cyrus was picking him up, peering into his face.

"You all right there Grif? Er... sorry."

"I... need... a... drink..." Grif gasped.

"He's fine," Amys laughed.

The night passed without anyone else getting hurt. It was close—Cyrus saw Vod reaching for a laser torch while she and Gurgan were doing some work in the engine room, and contacted Ktk just in time to prevent Gurgan from losing his head—but by and large, people began to recognize the warning signs that Ebur was trying to pry into their heads. Night fell, and Grif returned to his brooding about Bennet and his men. Had they moved into Ur Ados yet? Had they been detected? Would they get out all right?

Bennet wouldn't return to the ship until tomorrow afternoon, when they would meet up with Morgan and Cyrus and come back in the ground transport they'd rented for the cargo. If all went well, the following morning they could start giving Ebur the new meds.

Grif spent that evening in his cabin, brooding and drinking in equal measure. Once again, he started to go through the List Of Things That Might Go Wrong. There were just too many...

The cabin door beeped.

"Who is it?" Grif asked.

"Sif, Amys," the door answered.

"Open," Grif said. The door opened, revealing Amys.

"Hey Amys," Grif said. "What's up?"

"Hello, Grif," Amys said softly, smiling slyly.

"What—?" Grif stopped and frowned. He glanced at the comm badge, dangling out of his jacket pocket, hanging from the back of a chair across the room. "Damn..."

Grif lunged for his jacket. Amys stopped smiling.

She leapt across the room toward him, face twisted into a mask of fury. She hit him in mid-air, sending him sprawling to the floor, then kicked him in the face as he tried to get up. He fell back and hit his head against the wall, hard.

In a haze of red and purple, Grif tried to force himself to think. Amys straddled him, snarling. All he could see was the comm badge hanging from her belt.

In desperation he grabbed at the badge and activated it.

"Ktk," he shouted, trying not to slur the words. "Gack!"

Something very sharp sliced through his body, and everything went dark.

Chapter 34

WHEREIN the Importance of Sewage Cannot be Over-Emphasized

Bennet tried not to think about what he was wading through as he and his men worked their way up through miles of slough tunneling, gradually nearing the hazmat treatment center.

"This is disgusting." Agent Nond, one of the four Bennet had chosen to go with him, was taking the forward position of the group. "There's a mass of... something, I don't know what it is exactly, just kind of sticking to the ground. It's not solid, it's just... goopy."

"Thank you, Nond," Bennet said. "That's more than I wanted to know."

The five agents were all wearing "flex suits," lightweight environmental suits designed for people who needed to do detail-oriented work in corrosive, radioactive, and high-pressure atmospheres. The suit was made of a special polymer that felt almost like rubber until current was run through it, upon which it stiffened and sealed the body completely from the environment outside. They were a little awkward to use sometimes, and their effectiveness lasted only as long as the power cells did, but the great advantage of the suits was that they were semi-collapsible and very easy to transport without arousing suspicions.

At the moment the suits were not powered up. They were walking up the slough where post-treated material was discharged into the 'lake' every two hours, and while unsettling, it wasn't particularly dangerous. The suits would be activated just before they reached the treatment plant.

Which was when the fun would really begin.

The five agents were tethered together by a single cable attached to their flex suits. It would keep them together when they were swimming "upstream" through the hazardous material, and it doubled as a solid-line comm link, allowing them to talk without fear of the transmission being picked up by anyone else. They were making the most of the luxury. Once they were in the station, they would spend most of their time communicating with hand signals, so station security wouldn't pick up unauthorized voice patterns and lock the place down.

"There aren't supposed to be any solids in this treatment line, are there?" Bennet asked, worried. "That might tangle us up. We might have to cut the line."

He heard Agent Dox swear over the line. Dox was taking the rear position, and if the line was cut he was the one most likely to get lost.

"I'd like to formally request we not do that, Lieutenant," Dox said.

Someone else chuckled. "That's OK, Dox, if we get separated you get to turn around and go home."

"Don't give him any ideas, Bera," Bennet said, which provoked a round of laughter from everyone, including Dox.

"Wait," Dox said, in a decidedly better mood. "I can feel... something... cutting through the line..."

More laughter.

"All right," Bennet said, "let's not get carried away. Sev, could you answer the original question?"

"No solids," Sev said. "This stuff comes from runoff from the reactor, various lubricants, that kind of thing."

"Lovely," Dox muttered.

"Here we are," Nond said. "I think we've reached the lock to the treatment center."

"OK." Bennet checked the chronometer on the heads-up-display on his visor. "2352—another eight minutes."

"And then at 0200 it does it again, right?" Dox sounded worried.

"Every two hours," Bennet said. "That's what Sythe tells us."

That produced an uncomfortable silence. No one was entirely sure that Sythe was "all right." She'd been in the field so long that even if a Sword hadn't brainwashed her there was always a chance she'd gone native just from trying to stay alive. No one was sure if she'd wind up double-crossing them.

"I know what you're thinking," Bennet said. "Stop thinking it. Start working."

The agents secured themselves to the side of the lock in preparation for the stream of treated waste that would come pouring out in eight minutes.

"Power up the flex suits," Bennet said, and activated his.

Power surged through his suit, and he felt the segmented plates placed all over the suit harden instantly. His helmet display indicated that all the miniature servo motors were online, meaning he could bend his limbs freely.

"Everyone working properly?" Bennet asked. One by one, the other agents replied they were.

A low rumbling sound came from the other side of the lock.

"All right," Bennet said. "Make *sure* you're secured to this wall. When the lock is open, we've got about twenty minutes to force our way upstream. Get started immediately."

The lock started to open. A trickle of brackish liquid streamed out of the center as the two plates separating the treatment plant from the outside world moved apart.

"Here it comes," Bennet said.

"Early," Nond muttered.

The trickle became a stream, and as the plates extended even further tons of treated waste roared down the slough toward the lake.

"Go!" Bennet shouted. He could hear the roar through his helmet, and it nearly drowned out the link. He wondered for a moment if the cable would hold against all the pressure.

Nond was the first in, using synthbond grips built into his suit to seal himself to the wall as the suit servos fought against the rush of liquid pouring out. Sev followed, then Bennet, then Bera, and finally, Dox. After the first ten minutes, the pressure had abated to the point where they could make their way more freely, though they were still forced to use the grips to keep themselves attached to the walls.

The treatment chamber was essentially a huge tank where waste entered one end and left the other. All around the tank were vents and spires and columns that emitted whatever it was that rendered all the hazardous material inert in only two hours. Bennet didn't know how the process worked. He did know they'd have to sit through the entire process on the way out, and he wasn't looking forward to it. He hoped these suits really could stand up to the crushing pressures and temperatures everyone claimed they could. He also hoped the energy cells didn't run out of juice before the process ended.

They were close to the other side when they heard the rumble of the external lock as it began to close.

"Let's hurry up," Bennet warned. "We have a bit of a climb."

The external lock—the lock that deposited the treated sludge into the "lake"—was located at the bottom of the treatment facility. The internal lock—the lock that provided the treatment facility with the hazardous sludge that needed to be treated—was located at the top of the treatment facility on the other end. This meant that the agents would have to climb up the side of the tank. Fortunately, the servo motors on the suits were strong enough to handle it, and the force of the sludge pouring in meant it would arc over them for the most part, but it was still psychologically daunting.

It was a large tank.

They were a quarter of the way up when the internal lock started to open. Bennet and his men were a little to the right of the lock itself, and they saw a stream of waste hiss down the side of the tank before the pressure caused it to arc into the room.

"I bet it smells really bad in here," Bera said.

They worked their way up to the lock and began the laborious process of fighting their way into the oncoming rush of waste. There was a single terrifying moment as Bennet pulled himself headfirst into the waste and realized he couldn't see anything at all.

He forced himself to remember that he liked his job. He forced himself to remember that over and over and over again.

Bennet crawled on slowly with others. Finally Dox announced that he was in, and they began to force themselves forward in earnest.

"You know," Nond said, after they'd worked their way in silence for a while, "I wondered why they didn't bother to put more security measures here... and now I know why."

"Why's that?" Bennet asked.

"Because only an idiot would try to get in this way," Nond said.

"That's what they pay us for," Bennet said.

"Is it?" Dox asked. "I thought they paid us to get shot at in a goddamn pirate ship."

That provoked dark mutterings from the other agents, and Bennet sighed. There was a fair amount of bitterness among the agents concerning that debacle.

"Focus," he said.

"It's all right, Lieutenant," Nond said. "It's all crawling through muck for the next half hour."

Bennet sighed again, but said nothing.

"How long do you think until the Major tries to take the ship again?" Sev asked.

"I hope never," Dox said. "I don't ever want to have to fight that woman again, *ever*."

Eventually the lock closed, ending the current and making it easier for the agents to move. They made more progress then, flowing "upstream" to the vats where the waste was deposited.

"Hold on," Nond cautioned. "I'm going to disconnect, check ahead, and see if she's waiting for us."

"Go on," Bennet said. "We'll wait here."

There was a click as Nond disconnected himself from the communications tether, and then silence.

"I hate being in the back," Dox said. "You can never see anything."

"I can't see anything, and I'm in the middle," Bennet said.

"Yeah, but you're the boss. You're not supposed to know what's going on."

Bera and Sev laughed.

There was a slight vibration and a click, and then Nond's voice reappeared over the link. "She's there," Nond said. "Coast is clear."

"Let's go," Bennet ordered.

They moved out of the sewage tunnel into a pool where waste was collected before being sent on to the treatment plant. They climbed up the side awkwardly and heaved themselves up onto a lip on the side of the pool. There was room for people to stand here; Bennet assumed there were things in this room that needed fixing from time to time.

Wiping the muck from his visor, he saw an observation room not far from the lip where they'd emerged from below. Standing in the window was Meaghan Sythe.

Sythe pointed to her left. Bennet saw a decontamination chamber.

"All right," he said. "We're going to remove the link. It stays off until we return. No speech unless Sythe tells us it's safe. Got it?"

Everyone agreed.

"I want Nond, Bera and Dox into D-Con first. Sev and I will follow. Unhook now, see you on the other side."

He unhooked the comm tether from his suit and let it fall to the ground. The others did the same, laying it carefully along the wall so it would stay out of sight from anyone in the observation booth. Then Nond, Bera and Dox stepped into the D-Con room. Sythe keyed in a command from the observation room, and the door closed behind them.

The room filled with foam, obscuring the agents briefly, then the foam was washed away with a chemical spray. The process took about ten minutes in all, and when the other door opened the agents moved into the next room.

Then it was Bennet and Sev's turn.

When the process had finished, Bennet deactivated his flex suit. His arms and legs felt unusually heavy, a side effect of servo-assisted motion. The other three agents had already removed their suits and were stowing them in a container.

Bennet removed his helmet and nearly gagged. His suit stank.

The door to the D-Con room closed behind him, and the door to the observation room opened. Meaghan Sythe entered the room, eyeing them warily. *She looks tired*, Bennet thought. *Not that I could blame her*.

“It’s safe to talk in here,” she said. “Too much noise from the sludge room for sensors to pick up voice patterns.”

Bennet nodded as he removed his flex suit. “How far are we from where they store the robots?”

“It’s the other side of the facility,” Sythe said. “But, as luck would have it, I need to drive across and pick up some extra parts for one of the machines in the observation room.” She smiled slightly—almost but not quite a smirk, tired but not defeated, still defiant. Bennet decided there was no way in hell that woman had turned on them.

Bennet nodded again. “Dox,” he said. “What’s the status of our equipment?”

“All here, Lieutenant,” he said.

“Get the harness hooked up,” Bennet said. “You’re getting us into the warehouse.”

Dox nodded.

“So you’re getting ready to go over there now?” Bennet asked Sythe.

She nodded. “About ten minutes. Look, you’re taking me with you, right? I’m getting out of here?” There was an edge to her voice that made

Bennet worry. She hadn't cracked yet, but she was only human, and all humans had limits. She'd nearly reached hers.

"Yes," he said. "We're getting you out. But we came here for a reason, and we're not leaving for a while yet. This is only the first part of a... a very complicated process. We can get you on board the ship, but if we do that too soon people are going to start looking for you."

Sythe shook her head. "I have leave I can take. A lot of leave. And my supervisor has been pressuring me to take it."

"All right," Bennet said. "That helps. When you get off your shift tonight, leave as usual and meet us where you met us before. We'll get you on board the ship. But we're going to be planetside for at least another month, and you'll be confined to the ship the whole time. All right?"

She took a deep breath and nodded.

Bennet looked at the others. "Are you ready?"

They nodded.

"All right—no more talking. Let's go."

Sythe led them out of the room, down a long corridor lined with doors, and into a garage with a ground transport. She motioned for them to get into the back.

Bennet waved the others in, and climbed up after them. Sythe looked up after them, gestured *fourteen*, then walked around and climbed into the driver's seat.

They were headed to building fourteen.

The ground transport started up and moved into the warm night air. Bennet couldn't see where they were going, but it seemed as if they were moving in a straight line across a well-paved road.

The transport slowed, then turned, then came to a halt. Bennet overheard Sythe talking with a bored guard.

"Hey, you," the guard said in a sleepy, familiar tone. "What brings you out here?"

Sythe betrayed none of the nervousness she'd exhibited earlier. "Doing maintenance on the sludge," she said, affecting an annoyed tone. "And we don't have half of our spare parts. We have an inspection in two weeks, if I don't have those parts..."

The guard laughed. "Yeah. Well, you need any help?"

"No, I'll just get the robots to load for me."

"All right," the guard said. "Number twelve, right? Go on." And the ground car started moving again.

About thirty seconds later, the car came to a halt. Sythe came around the back again, motioned for them to wait, then disappeared. A minute later she came back.

"Safe to talk," she said. "Security is disabled in twelve."

Bennet turned to Dox. "Your turn."

Dox climbed out of the back of the ground car and grinned at Sythe. "Which direction is fourteen?"

Sythe pointed.

Dox put on his helmet and headed out.

"How is he getting past the sentinels in fourteen?" Sythe asked Bennet as he climbed out of the truck.

Bennet nodded in Dox's direction. Sythe turned just in time to see him press something on his wrist, and he half-melted into the background.

"Chameleon net," Bennet said. "Best we could come up with. Dox has trained in it. He's pretty good, but this is going to take a while."

They waited. Time passed.

Everything was quiet, which was a good sign. Silence meant that Dox had not been detected, that he was moving slowly enough for the chameleon net to read his surroundings and correctly mask his presence from sensors and other electronic equipment. Assuming he didn't run out of power first, or get spotted by a human guard, he'd creep toward the door, get past the security there, and make his way to the building security hub.

Assuming he didn't run out of power first.

Thirty minutes passed. The power cell charging the chameleon net would only last about that length of time, which meant they were about to learn whether or not Dox had succeeded. After five minutes passed without any alarms, Bennet relaxed a little.

Ten minutes later, Dox crept back into twelve, and motioned for them to follow.

Bennet turned to Sythe. "Stay here," he said. Sythe nodded.

They followed Dox out of twelve, along the fence that separated twelve from fourteen, and into fourteen's front gate. There was no one else about—all the living security was focused on the perimeter of the storage compounds, not on the interior.

Dox led them around the side of the building through an open door. Dox took off his helmet and grinned.

"It's safe to talk," he said. "Took me a while to jimmy the locks, though. I ran out of juice just before the whole thing went down. I was afraid that was that..."

"Did you find the manifest?" Bennet asked.

Dox nodded and handed Bennet a slip of paper with model numbers and row locations written down on it. "I wrote down some good candidates. The cargo area is this way."

Dox opened a door and stepped through. The others followed, and they emerged into a cavernous room lined with robots of varying shapes and sizes.

"Here be robots," Dox said.

Bennet used the paper to find the four models Grif had suggested, and chose one of each. Nond, Bera and Sev set to work opening the chassis of each robot and inserting the receptor close to the central processor.

It didn't *have* to be close, Grif had said, but it made things easier.

Bennet turned to Dox. "How much time do we have?"

"Two hours," Dox said. "The external system thinks everything is still running normally. In two hours my little program is going to shut itself off, and it's going to look like a power outage—backup generators come on, systems recycle, they do a brief check, everything looks normal, life goes on."

"We've got one down," Bera said. "Starting the second."

It took them about an hour to finish. They hurried back to twelve and helped Sythe finish loading the equipment she needed for the treatment facility, then climbed into the back with the equipment and lay low as she drove the transport back to the treatment plant.

Ten minutes later, they were suiting up and preparing to return.

"See you tomorrow," Bennet said to Sythe.

She nodded, tightened her jaw, but said nothing else.

Bennet hooked up a fresh power cell to his flex suit and turned it on.

Again the plates went rigid, and power servos whirred.

On the other side of the D-Con chamber, they retrieved the comm tether and reattached it. Bennet looked up at Sythe, watching them from the observation room. He waved a final time, and then slipped into the hazardous sludge.

"Let's get out of here," Bennet said. "And let's hope this was worth it."

"They better appreciate this," Dox grumbled as they began to work their way down the sewage drain. "All this work while they stay on board that ship and get drunk."

"Slackers," Nond agreed. "The lot."

Chapter 35

WHEREIN Plans Previously Put in Motion Suddenly Bear Fruit

Grif opened his eyes. He wasn't in his cabin any more.

"I'm in the medibay, aren't I?" Grif turned his head and saw that he was, in fact, in medibay—and hooked up to a diagnostic monitor. Amys peered down at him, frowning.

"Hi Amys." Grif's face was numb and his stomach was on fire.

"How do you feel?" Amys asked.

Grif noticed that Cyrus, Hari, Cutter and Vod were also in the room.

"Like you tried to gut me with a vibroknife," Grif said, trying to grin.

Amys looked away.

"No, hey wait, I was only—wait a minute. You *did* try to gut me with a vibroknife..."

Amys nodded.

"Dammit, Ebur..."

"You know," Cyrus said, peering over the top of the diagnostic monitor to stare down at Grif, "we really should stop coming up with complicated plans that require the use of a psychotic telepath."

"I'm starting to agree," Grif said. "When can I get out of this thing?"

"Another hour or so," Cutter said. "Amys really did a number on you. Bruised your face up something fierce, put a big gash in your belly, broke your left shoulder—"

"Again with the left arm!" Grif shouted, exasperated. "What the hell is it with that arm?"

Cyrus, Hari, Vod and Cutter laughed, but Amys wouldn't look at him.

"Oi!" he said. "Hey, cut it out, you big softy. I'm OK, right? And you have no one to blame but yourself. If you'd waited another ten, fifteen seconds before dragging my ass down here you'd have field-promoted yourself to captain of this ship, and no one would be able to say anything about it. Teach you not to think ahead..."

Amys laughed in spite of herself. "You're a bastard," she said.

"Yep. Somebody get me a drink."

"He's back to normal," Hari announced. "I'm going to get something to eat."

"That'd be good, too," Grif said.

"You know you can't do anything while you're still hooked up to that thing," Cutter said, smirking. "See ya later, Skip."

"Wait! Hold on a second..."

"Glad you're OK, Grif," Vod said, and left with Cutter.

"This isn't right."

"Well, I gotta go, too," Cyrus said, laughing. "Morgan and I have to go out and buy some new cargo... and pick up the kids."

"What, now? How long have I—"

"Later Grif," Cyrus called, and walked out of the medibay, still chuckling.

Amys didn't leave. She looked at Grif and smiled a little.

"Those bastards!" Grif laughed in spite of himself. "Leaving me in my infirmity. What time is it, anyway? How long have I been out?"

"It's almost 1100," Amys said. "And for the record, I'm sorry..."

"Cut it out," Grif said. "If the only time I have to worry about you killing me is when you're being controlled by a bloodthirsty telepath, I figure I'm ahead of the game."

Amys chuckled and shook her head. "Well, I was worried for a second."

"So was I," Grif said. "The second I realized I was about two meters from that damn comm badge. After that, I was too busy to worry much..."

They fell silent, Amys looking relieved and Grif grinning like mad.

"That grin is a lot less charming on that face," Amys said.

"I'm hoping to get the old one back. Of course, with the agents as pissed off at us as they are, I might find out they've decided to make me look like Velis..."

"Which would be a marked improvement," Velis said as she entered the medibay. "I see you're not dead. Amys must be slipping."

"Hello, Sis," Grif said. "What can I do for you? Pardon me if I don't get up..."

"I just wanted to let you know that we haven't heard anything from Ur Ados," Velis said, "and that's a good sign."

"Oh. Good. So all we have to do is survive one more night."

"Actually," Amys said, "Ebur is being doped up as we speak."

"What?" Grif frowned. "That's not right. We had to wait..." Grif's frowned deepened as he tried to count out the days in his head. Then, a moment later, he laughed out loud. "That little shit."

Amys raised an eyebrow. Velis looked puzzled.

"What the hell are you talking about?" Velis asked.

Grif laughed again. "Ebur was completely weaned off the drug the day before yesterday. Ktk was just waiting until you attacked me before it started Ebur on the other set of meds."

Amys' eyes widened, then her jaw set. "So it could win the pool."

"That's right. That goddamn bug rigged the game."

Amys glowered. "I'm going to hurt that bug. A lot."

"I'm not," Grif said. "I bet the same thing. That means we split the pool."

An hour later Grif was declared fit. His belly was still tender and his arm was a bit sore, but mostly he felt better.

A few hours later, Cyrus and Morgan rolled up into the cargo bay with the rented ground transport, carrying a few dozen crates of good Varkavian whiskey and six very tired OIM agents. Once the cargo bay doors were closed, Bennet, Nond, Bera, Dox, Sev, and a very agitated Meaghan Sythe climbed out of the back of the transport. They all looked ready to collapse... Sythe looked ready to fall to pieces.

Grif walked up to her and grinned. "Hi, I'm—"

"Mavis!" she snarled, and lunged for him.

Grif stumbled back, just barely evading her grasp.

"What?" He said. "No, I—"

"Sythe!" Bennet grabbed her and pulled her back. "It's all right, he's not—"

"YOU BASTARDS, YOU SOLD ME OUT!" She shouted, thrashing wildly. "YOU SOLD ME OUT! BASTARDS!"

Nond and Bera had to help Bennet hold her down as Dox gave her a sedative.

"She's been through a lot," Bennet explained.

"I really need to get my old face back," Grif replied. "So... did it work?"

Bennet nodded wearily. "We did it. Put in the receptors, I mean. We weren't able to test them or anything, but..."

"You're exhausted," Grif said. "Which makes me an idiot. Go get some sleep. We'll have to wait a few days before we can test it out anyway."

Bennet shook his head. "De-briefing first," he said. "With the Major."

The other agents grumbled, but nodded, and they stumbled off to deck two.

The next few days were uneventful. Meaghan Sythe calmed down enough to be debriefed properly—which included explaining that Grif's uncanny resemblance to Mavis was a byproduct of surgery—and spent a fair amount of time to herself in a cabin they'd set aside for her.

"She's been under a lot of stress," Bennet said. "We didn't design her cover to last as long as it did, and she had to work pretty hard to make it stretch as long as it did. It was really wearing her down."

"She's not going to flip out and, uh, attack me again, is she?" Grif asked.

Bennet shook his head. "I doubt it. She's too tired, physically and emotionally, to do much of anything right now."

They set up the slave circuit equipment in the general mess hall—Grif would have preferred to use the Wardroom, but that would require opaquing the panoramic viewport and he thought that might attract attention. The rig consisted of an electronic device that allowed the remote operator to manually guide the object and a terminal screen that would allow the operator to view his surroundings from the remote object's perspective.

The rig also had a port where a proper computer could be hooked into it, allowing someone to interface with the remote machine. Bennet hooked up a portable unit of his that "did all kinds of interesting things."

Next, they had Ktk attach a device to Ebur's skull that would act as a receiver for the commands they sent to him.

"This thing works two ways," Grif explained. "We either send commands to him and he commands the object—that's usually what we do when we want to move it around—or we tell him to establish a link with the robot's programming. It's like having the highest level of access you need to interact with every system it has. After that, you need to spend a little time studying the thing, to see how it works, but then you can program it to do things when the receptor is gone."

"Interesting," Bennet said. "But will it work?"

Grif grinned. "One more day and you'll see for yourself."

Ktk was finally allowed out of the cargo hold, much to its relief. It was beginning to wonder if everyone had forgotten about it.

"Oh no," Grif said. "I haven't forgotten about you at all, bug! Nearly getting me killed just to win a bet..."

Ktk replied that Grif had in fact not been killed, so it had all turned out for the best.

"Using the Captain's own logic against him should be a crime," Grif said cheerfully.

Just then Meaghan wandered into the cargo hold, saw Ktk for the first time, and nearly fainted.

Ktk asked who she was.

"Ah... another agent," Grif said. "They found her on the planet. She's a little... twitchy right now, and probably didn't expect to see a two and a half meter bug standing in our cargo bay."

Ktk didn't understand why some humans seemed to react so violently to the presence of a two and a half meter bug.

"Don't feel so bad. She took one look at me tried to kill me."

Ktk noted that Grif often had that effect on women, but usually they had to have known him first.

"Quiet you," Grif said. "Just remember to check up on your patient, keep him medicated, and make sure he's not getting his tubes crossed. That would be... unpleasant. And if we get searched again get ready to scuttle back in there to hide."

The following day Grif announced it was time to see if the receptors worked. Ktk took its place with Ebur, ready to disconnect the link if it looked like anything was amiss, while Grif sat at the rig.

"Pull up a chair, Bennet," Grif said. "I'll need you on that computer when we start looking through the robot's programming."

Nearly everyone on the ship had gathered into the general mess to see if it would work. Velis was pacing at the far end of the room.

Grif turned on the pilot rig. The machine hummed to life, and various instruments lit up. The terminal screen, however, did not.

"It's blank," Cutter said, disappointed.

"We haven't told Ebur to link up with a receptor yet," Grif said. "Calm down. First we need to tell him which one, then we need to point him in the right direction... then he needs to find it, which could take a while. Establishing the initial link is sort of an imprecise science."

Grif keyed in something on the terminal keyboard. "This is the code Ebur gave me for the first receptor. He said he'd understand what it meant. I also need to give him basic directions... uh... anyone have the coordinates of Ur Voys? And our coordinates, now that I think of it. We need to figure this out in terms of 'this far north, this far northwest.'"

Velis stopped pacing across the room and shook her head. "Why?"

Grif shrugged. "That's the way he learned it. Which makes it a challenge when you're in orbit, by the way."

They managed to work out a rough location. Grif added that to the receptor identifier, and sent the entire thing through.

Ktk reported that Ebur twitched slightly. Other than that, nothing happened.

"Remember," Grif said. "Imperfect science."

The terminal screen remained dark. Everyone remained motionless, looking at the screen expectantly, but nothing happened.

"This might take a little time," Grif said. "I'm going to get a drink."

He got up and went into the galley. The crowd dispersed a bit, some still watching the monitor as others decided that a drink was probably a very good idea.

Grif reached for the whiskey, thought better of it, and poured himself a cup of coffee. Cyrus and Amys had followed him in, and he looked up to see Velis coming in after them.

"What do we do if this doesn't work?" Velis asked.

Grif shrugged. "It'll work. Ebur has never failed with this kind of stuff before."

"But what if it doesn't?" Velis persisted. "What if, for example, all those robots are in storage somewhere and haven't been deployed yet? Or what if all the receptors are malfunctioning?"

"Ah... I don't know," Grif said. "I guess we either come up with another brilliant plan, or we give it up and go home."

"I don't believe we have another brilliant plan, do we?" Velis asked.

"Well..."

"No," Amys said. "We really don't."

"I could try and think of another brilliant plan," Grif offered.

"Don't let him," Cyrus said. "Never, ever let him come up with Plan B."

"Hey!"

"Grif, I love ya like you were my own brother—the one I like—and you're a fine captain, but you have the worst backup plans I've ever been unfortunate enough to barely live through."

"It's true," Amys agreed. "Plan A is definitely your strength."

"Now, hold on there," Grif protested. "My Plan B's have always worked... mostly..."

"Last year—"

"OK, except for that one. That was, in retrospect, pretty bad..."

"Just that one?" Cyrus asked, eyebrows raised. "What about when we were trying to take off from Ventarii, and you—"

"Yes all right," Grif growled. "Not my finest hour."

Velis was looking at all of them with a bemused expression on her face.

"I don't really understand what's got into them," Grif said. "Usually they have absolute confidence in their Captain—"

"Usually," Amys said, "we don't have to resort to Plan B."

Cyrus nodded sagely. "Don't do Plan B," he said. "Ever..."

"Hey," Bennet yelled from the other room. "I think we have a picture."

Grif grinned. "Saved by Plan A!" He rushed back to the rig, spilling coffee the entire way.

Sure enough, the terminal was showing something that looked like a large white blob in the upper right-hand corner.

"What is that?" Bennet asked.

"I don't know." Grif sat in the chair and grabbed the controls. "Ebur doesn't know what it is either, so he can't focus on it. Let's swing the view around a bit and maybe we can let him focus on something that makes sense to him."

Grif moved the toggle around that controlled the view. The blob jerked off screen, and suddenly a number of lines appeared, crisscrossing each other to form a bizarre pattern on the screen.

"That's not much better," Bennet said.

"Hold on a moment," Grif said. "It's getting a little clearer."

The lines deepened into grooves, and other details began to fill in around them. They were tiles—floor tiles in a hallway. And then they could see the entire thing: a hallway lined with doors, and people in uniform moving hurriedly down it.

"Damn, Ebur, you are good," Grif said. "It's the security robot. We're in!"

A ragged cheer filled the room.

Chapter 36

WHEREIN a Potential Problem is Unexpectedly Resolved

They spent the next week familiarizing themselves with the robots under their control and learning the ins and outs of their programming. Grif practiced controlling them remotely while Bennet studied their code, in hopes of using that knowledge to infect other robots as well. Velis was often on hand, though not directly involved with work, in order to stay informed of the latest developments.

The four robots with the receptors turned out to be very well chosen. One was a security robot, and while it had a very limited area in which it was permitted to patrol, every night it linked to the central security system and loaded what it recorded that day into a data repository. Bennet thought it might be possible to use this link to get into the security computer itself, and was working feverishly to do so.

The second robot was a messenger bot. Messenger bots were used when people wanted to send messages directly to someone in an area where voice to voice communication was not permitted, which gave them virtually unrestricted access to the entire complex. Grif spent a lot of time observing it travel to get a rough familiarity with the layout of the complex.

The third robot was a maintenance bot—specifically, a diagnostics bot that assessed potential problems before human technicians or repair bots were sent in to fix the damage. This robot also had free access to nearly everywhere, and had the added advantage that people weren't surprised when it simply showed up and began to test hardware and computer systems.

"If we had enough time," Grif said, "we could wind up running the entire complex."

"How much time would we need?" Velis asked, clearly interested in the prospect.

Bennet shook his head. "A few years, probably.There are a lot of subsystems, hidden systems, secure systems. There are at least fifteen different secure areas, all of which require different kinds of clearance."

The fourth robot was responsible for loading and unloading cargo in one of the delivery bays, located near all the garages and hangars in the outside areas of the facility. It, like the security bot, was limited in the areas where it was allowed to go, but it had full run of the garages and some parts of the hangars. It was not the most useful robot as far as exploring the complex was concerned, but it did give them an opportunity to learn how cargo was loaded and unloaded from Ur Voys on a day to day basis.

By the end of the week, Grif had a fair idea where everything in Ur Voys was located. The external part of the facility contained the hangars and transports, as well as the facilities for loading and unloading cargo. There were also five levels set into the mountain Ur Voys was built against. The highest, which opened out into the external portion of the facility, had a wide hallway—wide enough for a ground car to drive through it—which led to a lift, and then descended into the lower levels. The only rooms in the first interior level were bureaucratic offices and monitoring stations manned by security personnel.

The second level consisted of mostly research and development work at the front, and station power generators and waste disposal stations at the back. Security on this floor was present but light. On the third level, security was very tight—this was probably where the anagathics were made, Grif guessed, though he never saw any proof.

The fourth and fifth levels were a mystery.

At the end of the week, Grif was familiar with all the routes the messenger bot usually took, and was taking the diagnostics bot around the first two levels of the mountain, looking for terminals to "diagnose." This gave Bennet a chance to nose around different parts of the Ur Voys network, to see what was there, and to gently probe for any gaps in the station's network security.

Meanwhile, Bennet made some progress breaking into the facility's security network. After analyzing a great deal of the security bot's programming he announced that it looked like customized work.

"They probably wipe the robot's programming clean, then install their own custom programming into it," Bennet said. "Probably the first thing they do when it arrives. If they do that with everything, that pretty much guarantees that their robots won't turn on them. Of course, they don't seem to have planned for these receptors."

"The Radiant Throne is arrogant," Velis said. "They believe they control the market where telepaths are concerned, and don't expect interference from other telepaths at all… and this ability of Ebur's is very, very rare."

"It's true," Grif said. "But the Swords *do* know about it, and they want it. They've tried to kidnap people like Ebur before. He's very careful about who he does business with."

"Odd," Bennet said. "That he insists on staying independent, that is. I mean, it's incredibly dangerous… has he ever thought about joining with any of the official groups that run about? The Trade Barons have a telepathic guild, don't they? And the Order of Charlemagne—I mean, I know you lot aren't terribly fond of the Alliance, but—"

"We like the Paladins even less," Grif said. "I believe whoever came up with the term 'goody two-shoes' was thinking of those jokers at the time. Ebur's not the kind of guy to convert to Catholicism just to get some protection from the Swords…"

"They're not all Catholic these days," Bennet countered.

"And," Grif continued, "they wouldn't take him anyway. None of them would. He's already psichotic… he needs his medication to keep it together, and he can't use his abilities when he's on his meds. The only people who would have any use for him at all are the Swords…"

"Not that I'm complaining," Bennet said, "but what does he have against the Swords, anyway? I mean, the Radiant Throne treats Swords like little gods, or, uh, prophets is probably a better word. And Ebur, well, he's pretty powerful. He'd do pretty well as a Sword."

"He's not what you would call a pious man," Grif explained.

During this time, Cyrus and Morgan slowly added to their cargo, playing the role of picky merchants to the hilt, and developing a very bad reputation with the businesses on the planet in the process. "This is the last time Migh Vox and Dobin Brans will ever be welcome on Varkav!" Cyrus shouted cheerfully one evening, as he and Morgan returned from another day of cutthroat negotiations.

"Good day?" Grif asked.

"You could say that. You know how last time we were here, there was that dealer in the Vodis district who got me steamed, and you guys had to pull me out of there before I said something I'd regret?"

"Yeah," Grif said. "I remember him."

"Well," Cyrus said, grinning wider, "today I said all of it!"

By the beginning of the third week, Bennet broke into the first layer of the security subsystem. After the initial breakthrough everything was easier: by the end of the third week, the entire security subsystem was at his disposal.

"I owe you a drink," Grif said, slapping Bennet on the back. "You pretty much just handed us the key to the station."

Grif and Bennet were working well together. Grif's exploration with the diagnostics bot allowed Bennet to get a fair idea of how the addresses on the network corresponded with the physical areas in the facility itself. And while Grif wasn't a programmer, he knew enough about the subject to understand what Bennet was talking about when he described the problems he was running into.

One of the first things Grif wanted Bennet to do was to find out where the artifact was being stored. This, Bennet explained, was easier said than done.

"There's something in here about that thing, I'm sure of it," Bennet said. "Problem is, the security system doesn't describe it as 'the artifact.' I don't know what the security system is calling it, so I can't tell you which room it's in, what level it's in, anything. I may have already seen it in one of the lists I was going through the other day. I just don't know."

"I see," Grif said. "Any thoughts?"

"Well, that Sword—you think he knows you're going after the artifact, right?"

"He..." Grif frowned. "Yeah, I think so. I'm pretty sure."

"All right," Bennet said. "I'll try this from a different angle. I'll look for any changes made to security that were authorized by the very top of the command chain. We can access the security monitor for each area until we find it."

"Well," Grif said, "it's not a *fast* plan. But it's better than the one I had."

"Which one is that?"

"Start hitting buttons at random until something interesting happens."

They found it the following day. It was late morning, after breakfast, and Bennet and Grif were the only two people in the general mess. Grif was watching the messenger bot deliver a message on level three when Bennet sat up in his chair, rubbed his eyes, and smiled.

"I think I've got it. Shortly after your dinner with Mavis they increased security in an area on Level Five."

"Promising," Grif said.

Bennet nosed around a bit. "The room has security cameras—want to see what's in it? I think I can patch us in."

"Hell yes," Grif said.

Bennet keyed in a series of commands. "I think this is it. If I understand what I'm looking at, this will give us access to about six feeds."

"All right." Grif leaned forward in anticipation. "Let's see the first."

The terminal screen flickered, and showed a picture of a doorway, with a guard on either side.

"I'm less than impressed," Grif said.

"Switching over to camera two," Bennet replied.

The monitor flickered and they saw part of the interior of a large room. A large, square table rested in the middle of the room. Something flat and dark sat on the table—Grif couldn't tell what it was. Hanging over the table was a large machine, a drill, or maybe a sensor. Figures in cleanroom suits moved around the table and worked on terminals set into the far wall.

"Hey," Grif said. "Hey, that could be it." He felt a rush of adrenaline as he leaned toward the monitor. "Can you get a better camera angle?"

The next three camera shots were the same angle, from different sides of the room. When they switched to the fourth side, Grif tensed.

"Stop." Grif stared at the monitor apprehensively. "Bennet. It's him."

"Yeah..."

Standing in the middle of the monitor, blocking their view of the table, was the Viceroy.

He was standing close to the camera. Unlike the other figures in the room, he was not wearing a cleanroom suit. He was dressed in an elaborately patterned robe, very similar in design to a monk's habit, but very expensive, high quality material. The hood was drawn back from his face, revealing his shaved head and dark, narrow eyebrows. His eyes were closed, his head bowed, as though lost in thought.

"Well," Grif said, "that's inconvenient, but at least we know where—"

At that moment the Viceroy's eyes snapped open, and his head swiveled to stare directly at the security camera.

"Er..." Grif said.

"*Hell,*" Bennet swore. He keyed a series of commands into the terminal. "I'm turning this off."

The Viceroy narrowed his eyes and cocked his head to one side.

"Any time now," Grif whispered.

"Working on it," Bennet said.

The Viceroy's expression hardened. He closed his eyes, and his brow furrowed in concentration.

"Bennet, *any time now*."

"It's not letting me do it." Bennet's voice was tight.

"What do you mean it's not—"

"I mean I key in the command and nothing happens. The connection doesn't break."

"Well switch to another camera!" Grif said.

Bennet keyed in a command, and the view immediately switched the camera across the room. They could see the figure of the Viceroy, hunched over and facing the camera on the far wall.

"Good," Grif said, relieved. "Now try to break the damn feed."

"What is he doing?" Bennet asked.

The Viceroy straightened, turned around, and gazed directly at the camera they were using.

"You don't think he—" Bennet began, but his voice trailed off as the Viceroy ran to the new camera.

"Switch it again!" Grif hissed, but Bennet was already in the act. The view switched to an adjacent wall, and for a moment the Viceroy couldn't be seen. A moment later, however, the Sword was in full view, staring directly at their camera, concentrating deeply.

"God damn it all to hell!" Grif shouted. "We've got to disconnect that feed!"

"You don't have to tell me twice!" Bennet shouted back. "Damned if I know how!"

Grif's comm link beeped. Ktk announced that Ebur was behaving strangely.

Grif looked at the Sword staring at them through the screen and activated his link. "Strangely how, Ktk? What's he doing?"

Ktk replied that Ebur was behaving as though he were having a bad dream. It added that Ebur never moved when he was operating as a slave circuit.

"It's got to be that Sword," Bennet said.

"Ktk," Grif said, "we need you to disconnect Ebur from his rig."

Ktk replied that Grif would have to end the connection first, or Ebur might be damaged.

"I'm changing the camera again," Bennet said, and switched to the opposite wall. Again they saw the Viceroy hesitate, turn, and move directly to the new camera.

Ktk reported that Ebur appeared to be whimpering.

"We're going to have to risk disconnecting him from the rig anyway," Grif said. "Ktk, we're viewing a room with the Viceroy in it. I think he's doing something that keeps us from—"

The camera view changed. It was the sixth camera—the last camera in the room. It was, apparently, mounted on the machine hanging over the table, and it gave a clear, unobstructed view of what was on the table itself.

"That's it," Grif whispered. "There's your damn artifact."

It was round and black. The surface was so dark it was difficult to make out any details, but it was disturbingly circular: he kept trying to find an imperfection in the edge, a slip that would make it less a circle and more a very slight oval, but he couldn't find one.

Suddenly it began to move.

The center of the circle *rippled*, then turned *white*, and tendrils of something like smoke seemed to dance over the part of the surface that was still black. The tendrils began to swirl in a clockwise direction around the center, making the disk look like the negative image of a black hole.

Over the comm link Ktk announced that Ebur was screaming.

Grif stared at his comm link, then back at the image of the artifact.

"Switch to another view!" he hissed.

The monitor blinked and switched to one of the side cameras. The figures were talking amongst themselves excitedly, pointing to the artifact on the table.

Ktk reported that Ebur had stopped screaming.

"Is he all right?" Grif asked.

Ktk said that it couldn't tell.

"Get Cutter to take a look at him," Grif ordered. "And Bennet, what the hell is that thing?"

"Got me," Bennet said. "I can tell you that 'tendency to turn white and get all swirly' wasn't in any of our reports."

"Whatever it is, it didn't make Ebur very happy," Grif mused. "I wonder what's going to happen when we get it on board this ship."

"When?" Bennet asked. "Not 'if'?"

"I'm a pessimist," Grif said.

"Shut up a minute," Bennet said. "Look over there. Looks like we have a casualty."

Grif looked to where Bennet was pointing and noticed a group of technicians crowded around someone lying on the floor. "Who is that? Can you see who it is? See if you can get us a better look."

The camera switched again, and they saw the Viceroy, writhing on the floor, clutching his head in pain.

Bennet and Grif stared at the image of the writhing man in silence.

"Couldn't have happened to a nicer guy," Grif said finally. "Can we disconnect the feed now?"

Bennet typed in a command and the screen went black. "Yes."

"OK... I vote we don't try to look at the artifact anymore," Grif said.

"Seconded," Bennet agreed.

A few hours later Bennet used the security system to access the Sword's medical records. They learned, much to Grif's delight, that the Sword had suffered extreme mental trauma and would have to be shipped off-planet for treatment.

"One problem down," Grif said.

Bennet looked unconvinced. "Is it? What's going to keep them from sending another Sword?"

Grif shrugged. "Nothing. But this one won't be telling anyone anything for a while. Now we just need to figure out exactly where those cameras were so we can hurry up and try to steal the damn thing."

"The good news," Bennet said, "is that I think I have enough information to find it on a schematic. I just need to find the schematics for level five."

A few nights later, Cyrus announced that he was almost done buying the cargo, and that they needed to hurry everything along. Grif and Bennet slept less, bathed less, shaved less and worked more. A few days later, Bennet announced that he'd gained access to all the schematics for the Ur Voys facility, and they now knew where the artifact was.

"Now all we need is a plan," he said to Grif cheerfully. "I reckon that's your department."

"What exactly does the security system access?" Grif asked.

"Almost everything, indirectly. Directly, it accesses everything that has to do with security."

Grif snorted. "Thanks."

"Well, there's more to it than you might think. I mean, aside from the security monitors, locking and unlocking doors, generating security keys and validation codes—all of which we'll probably find useful—there's a database of protocols, regulations and procedures for things security has to do in the event of an attack on the station, or if there's a fire, or..."

"Wait! Hold on a minute." Grif was standing in front of the rig, staring at Bennet excitedly. "There's a database of procedures and protocols?"

"Sure," Bennet said. "There are a lot of them. Some of the procedures aren't general knowledge, they probably change them from time to time, so that if an old procedure is leaked it won't pose as much of a risk..."

"So stupid," Grif said, laughing. "I am so *stupid*, Bennet—I should have thought of this before."

"Well I'm not sure what that makes me," Bennet said, slightly irritated, "because I have no idea what you're talking about."

"It's *brilliant*! This is going to put the artifact right in our laps. Think about it—they have security protocols that cover emergencies. Procedures that tell you what to do when, say, a moon crashes into the planet. Step by step instructions on how to evacuate the building in the event of mutant rat attacks... in short, procedures they don't even know they have!"

Bennet's eyes grew wide. "Or procedures they know they have but don't look at until they're needed."

"Right." Grif started to pace. "Look through those protocols and see if there are any that deal with the artifact—cross reference them with that number you mentioned earlier."

Bennet typed furiously. “I’ve found a few. Mostly they’re guard shifts, how new members of the science staff will be screened... hold up. Here’s one we want, I think—what to do if the artifact needs to be transported off site.”

“That’s it,” Grif said.

“What do we do with it?”

“We’re going to change it a bit,” Grif said. “Add a few instructions, leave out a few instructions... a little shaping and fitting. Then we’ve got to get to work setting up all our, ah, decoys. That’ll take a while.”

“Then?” Bennet asked.

“Then,” Grif said, eyes gleaming, “we steal ourselves an artifact, and get the hell out of here.”

Chapter 37

WHEREIN Our Hero Saunters Casually to the Exit

Ur Voys had a definite rhythm to the way it was run. People who worked there long enough developed a feel for when the cargo shipments came in, when the doctors and scientists arrived, when the shifts changed over... a general sense of who was supposed to be doing what, and where, and at what time.

Hallek Andros had been the overseer at Ur Voys for thirteen years. He knew how everything fit together, and he knew most—though not all—of the secrets within the complex.

He'd been placed in charge of Ur Voys because he served his Emperor with distinction. This stewardship had been validated when, after a common smuggler had stolen a large shipment of anagathics, the Viceroy poured God's wrath upon him, and his soul had been found blameless, and he was deemed worthy of his position.

A month ago, when he was summoned before the Viceroy and was informed that someone was going to try and steal Special Project 51273, Andros could scarcely believe his ears. This was Ur Voys, after all—the Alliance had tried for years to infiltrate this facility, and had failed every time. But Andros was an obedient and faithful man, and he trusted in the wisdom of the Swords. When this one told him the facility was in danger, he increased the guards on Level 5, added more security measures to the rooms where Special Project 51273 was stored, and warned the security forces that specialized in that project's defense to be on the alert, and to inform him of every irregularity.

When he reported his steps to Commodore Mavis—a man he respected, and whose authority he did not begrudge—Mavis was satisfied. He later informed Andros that the Viceroy, also, was satisfied, which pleased him very much. He was certain that any attempt to steal Special Project 51273 would be discovered and neutralized well before it got to the additional security measures, but he didn't question his superiors for insisting on them. It was a rarity, after all, and paranoia was healthy in these matters.

For weeks everything went smoothly. It wasn't until nearly a month had passed that things began to go wrong.

On that day one of his subordinates entered his office, looking concerned. This was enough to make Andros cautious. This particular subordinate was a very calm and confident man.

"Sir," his subordinate said, "I believe we have a security breach."

For a moment, Andros didn't understand what the man was saying. "A what?"

"Security breach," the subordinate repeated. "I very strongly feel there's been an intentional and deliberate attempt to disable or sabotage equipment on our facility."

Andros motioned for the man to close the door behind him. "Explain."

The subordinate took a deep breath. "Security for Special Project 51273 became aware of a message bot near the entrance to the main room. Message bots aren't often used on Level 5, so that was unusual... but not unheard of. What made them suspicious was that it was *wandering aimlessly*. A message bot is programmed to deliver its message and immediately return to its queue. This one... wasn't."

Andros nodded. "That is strange."

"Yes," the subordinate said. "What's even stranger is that when one of the guards approached the message bot, she noticed its message carrier was empty."

Andros blinked. "Empty?"

The subordinate nodded. "In short, there was no reason for it to be there. The guard promptly deactivated the bot and alerted the shift commander, who ordered the bot sent to maintenance to have its programming studied."

"That was properly done," Andros said. "See that the shift commander is given a commendation on his or her record."

"I will," said the subordinate, "but it doesn't end there. When the maintenance crew attached the bot to a diagnostics station and restarted it, the bot deactivated itself immediately."

Andros stared at the subordinate in disbelief. "What?"

The subordinate nodded. "It had wiped its own programming, sir."

Andros' eyes widened. "It's not supposed to do that."

"No sir."

"Could the programming be recovered?"

"Maintenance attempted to use the standard recovery tools, but determined that the programming could not be recovered. They've classified the wipe as 'deliberate and thorough.'"

Andros sighed. "It is a breach," he agreed. "The question is, how did someone—"

The terminal on his desk beeped.

"Excuse me a moment," Andros said, and turned the terminal on. "This is Hallek Andros."

It was another subordinate, looking just as worried as the first. "Sir, we seem to be having a problem with the diagnostic bots in the Special Project 51273 areas."

"What?" Andros' eyes narrowed. "What do you mean, a problem?"

"Sir, there are at least ten of them in the room housing the item. They seem to be running diagnostics checks on various terminals but no one is quite sure why they're all doing it at once."

"Turn those damn things off!" Andros roared.

"They're trying, but the diagnostic bots are actively interfacing with the equipment in the room and—"

"Do what you have to do! Shut down the equipment if you have to! Consider those bots a security risk!"

He turned to the first subordinate, listening to the exchange in alarm. "Go below and assist in the investigation," Andros commanded. "Tell me when you learn what's going on."

Just as that subordinate left, another came in, wearing a sickening familiar expression of worry. "Sir..."

"Is this about Special Project 51273?"

The subordinate looked confused. "Er, no sir..."

"Good!"

"We had to disable a workbot in Hangar 5. It was tearing a hole in one of the grav sleds."

"It... what?" Andros kept waiting for someone to wake him up.

"Yes sir... when maintenance tried to run a diagnostics check on it..."

"Let me guess. It erased its own programming."

The subordinate looked surprised. "Yes sir, that's it exactly. And we've had reports of other workbots leaving their authorized work zones, and having to be deactivated by security."

Andros breathed deeply. "Have any of these workbots attacked any station personnel?"

"No sir. They stop moving as soon as anyone comes within two meters, and don't react when deactivated."

Andros scowled. "This makes no sense."

At that moment, an alarm sounded.

"That's a security alarm," Andros shouted. He opened a desk drawer, pulled out a pulse pistol, and turned on his monitor. "Get me security!"

The chief of station security appeared on screen.

"Chief, what in God's name is going on?"

"One of the security bots attempted to leave its patrol route," the Chief said, looking troubled. "It seemed to be heading for the lower levels."

"Did it attack anyone?"

"No..." The Chief hesitated. "It came close. A technician tried to deactivate it, and the security bot trained its weapon on the man. One of our guards deactivated it."

"Have you run diagnostics on it?"

"We're sending it to maintenance now."

"DON'T. Do not run any form of diagnostics on it at all, until I give the order. Do you understand?"

The Chief nodded. "Understood."

"All right." Andros sighed. "Turn off the siren, but stay on alert." He turned to the subordinate still in the room. "I am going to authorize a kill command for all bots on the facility grounds," he said. "Ten minutes."

The subordinate gulped, nodded, and turned to spread the word.

***

Commodore Hu Mavis stood on the deck of the *Centurion*, worrying about things he could not control.

The Sword had pulled him out of what had turned into a very agreeable dinner to tell him that Grif Vindh was planning to steal something Mavis knew very little about. Since then, Mavis had been trying to rack his brain to determine how.

He coordinated the increase of security measures in Ur Voys with that facility's commander, a competent man who put every available resource at his disposal. And he'd kept a careful eye out for Captain Vindh and that ship.

The problem was, the Maximilian class was a very popular model, even in the provinces of the Radiant Throne. On Varkav, at this moment, there were no fewer than ninety-seven Maximilian class starships visiting the planet. This didn't include those Maximilian class ships that were owned and used by agencies local to the planet itself.

Of the ninety-seven Maximilian class starships visiting the planet, none of them appeared to be the *Fool's Errand*. Or, rather, while none of them *appeared* to be that ship, they all had the *potential* to be that ship, even the *Alo Minh*—but there was nothing definitive about any of them that gave it away. Destroying all of them was out of the question. The Viceroy had suggested that very course of action, but Mavis cautiously reminded him that the Emperor required far more compelling circumstances for such a display of divine wrath, and the Sword, upon reflection, had agreed.

So a month had passed, and Mavis was at an impasse. There was nothing in the facility that suggested anything untoward or out of the ordinary, and there were no ships on the planet that appeared to belong to Captain Vindh. There was, at the moment, nothing more he could do.

And then the Sword had been grievously injured by the very thing they were trying to protect. He immediately informed his superiors of the event, but had received no reply as of yet. He hoped they would send another Sword to investigate, but it appeared that, at least for the moment, no more aid was forthcoming.

"Commodore." Katryn Valdyrs stood up from her comm station on the deck below, calling up to him in a clear voice. "Hallek Andros is on a secure channel and wishes to speak with you immediately sir. He says it's important."

Mavis nodded, and pointed to the direction of his private office. Valdyrs nodded in return, and routed the communication there.

Mavis sat down at his desk and turned on his terminal. After recognizing his retinal scan, the terminal shifted, displaying a picture of an unusually agitated Andros.

"Commodore," Andros said, "we have trouble. Ur Voys security has been compromised."

Everything Mavis had been thinking the moment before was instantly cleared away: the only thought in his head was about Andros, and what he was saying. "Go on."

"It's the robots, sir," Andros said. "They're... they're going crazy. It seems like they're trying to get into where Special Project 51273 is being held. So far the breaches have been mostly minor and non-lethal, but there have been a lot of them, and one was nearly lethal. Some of the security bots are affected by whatever is going on.

"The security bots?" Mavis' voice didn't betray the alarm he felt.

"Yes sir. A few started moving toward the lower levels. They don't resist when security personnel deactivate them, but if other personnel get too near they train their weapons on them."

Mavis steadied himself. "Is anything else affected?"

"Other bots," Andros said. "Some worker bots, some diagnostics bots, and at least three messenger bots. Some of the diagnostics bots actually got into the room itself."

"Strange," Mavis muttered. "Do you know why?"

"No sir," Andros replied. "Whenever we try to run a diagnostic on the robot, it immediately wipes its own programming. Deliberately, from what little we can determine."

"I see," Mavis said. "What is being done?"

"I've ordered all the robots on station deactivated, sir. But it's obvious security has been breached. I intend to activate the transport protocols, if you agree it's proper. We will move all our classified material—including Special Project 51273—to secure areas in other facilities."

"That may be what they want," Mavis warned.

"May be," Andros said. "But we don't know the extent of the breach here. We've shut down all the robots, Commodore, and some of them do things we can't. Especially in our reactor. If we can't guarantee they're not a security risk, we may have to bring the reactor off line..."

"Yes, I see your point," Mavis said. "It seems wise to proceed. Mavis out."

The picture of Andros nodded, then disappeared.

Deeply troubled, Mavis walked out of his office and on to the deck of his ship.

***

Sgt. Mollaek Firs gripped his pulse rifle tightly as he sat on the back of the ground transport, watching the rest of his platoon as they raced through the barren Varkavian landscape. It was a small contingent of men, considering the rumored importance of the cargo they were guarding, but they were well armed and armored.

Armed well enough to fight off an ambush, Firs thought. *Especially here, so close to the light of the Throne.*

The only deviation from protocol had been the order to leave the robotic gunner behind. Firs felt uneasy about this—they'd trained with it and would be off balance trying to work without it. Still, what with all the problems they were having with robots lately he supposed it was a good idea.

One of his corporals waved to get his attention. Sergeant Firs leaned forward, so he could hear the man over the roar of the wind.

"Where are we going?" The corporal shouted.

Sergeant Firs looked at the instructions the lieutenant gave him before they set out. "A rendezvous point, somewhere," the Sergeant shouted back. "My protocol doesn't give a location—that's for the driver to know, and the LT."

The corporal nodded. "What are we supposed to do?"

Sergeant Firs pointed at the long, thin, sealed box lying on the base of the transport. "Guard that. We hand it off to another team when we reach the destination."

One of the privates pointed into the sunlight. Sergeant Firs looked, and saw something metallic gleaming beneath the sun. He pulled out his magni-visor and zoomed in on that location. He saw another ground transport—civilian model, it looked like—and a number of heavily armed soldiers in unmarked commando uniforms.

Civilian transport. Odd.

Sergeant Firs put his magni-visor away and frowned, staring at the speck as it grew larger and larger until, finally, he could see the group on his own. They certainly carried themselves like the military, but they weren't wearing proper uniforms, and that civilian transport was fishy.

The Corporal leaned forward again. "You reckon they're special ops?"

Sergeant Firs shrugged.

Their ground transport slowed to a halt, and the Sergeant ordered the men to take their positions on the ground. They jumped off and staggered themselves, watching the dark-clad soldiers in front of the civilian transport warily.

One of them—an officer, Firs guessed—stepped forward. "Who is in command here?"

The LT got out of the passenger seat and walked toward the man. "I am," he said.

The stranger nodded, and produced a datastick.

"Sergeant," the Lieutenant called out.

Sergeant Firs ran up next to the Lieutenant, who was also holding a datastick.

"The key, sergeant."

Sergeant Firs held out a fist-sized cylinder. The Lieutenant put his datastick in one end, and the stranger put his datastick in the other.

A second passed, then the light on the cylinder turned green.

"It's approved," the Lieutenant said. "Sergeant, have the men load our cargo into their transport."

"Aye, sir." Firs turned to the platoon. "You heard the man," he roared. "Get OFF your asses and MOVE THAT CARGO, NOW!"

* * *

"They're all on board, Grif," Amys said.

"Do they have it?" Grif asked.

"Yes," Amys said, grinning. "Went off without a hitch."

"Hell," Morgan muttered, "we actually did it."

"Not yet we didn't," Grif said. "We have to get out of here first." He punched the intercom. "Ktk, is Ebur back in stasis?"

Ktk replied that he was, though he still needed to purge the medication from his body before he could get back on his standard meds.

"I know," Grif said. "We'll deal with that later. I just don't want him awake with that thing on board."

Grif hit the intercom again, this time broadcasting to all decks. "This is your captain speaking. Cargo has been secured, and we are now getting ready to lift off. All crew, man your stations."

A minute later, Bennet appeared on deck, still dressed in a simple black commando outfit, and sat at the comm station.

"Welcome back, Bennet," Grif said. "I hear you had a nice trip."

"Very nice," Bennet replied. "Trouble free. The locals were cooperative."

"Excellent. Radio Port Authority and tell them we are ready to take off."

Bennet began negotiating their clearance as Grif ran down the pre-flight checklist.

"Uh... Grif," Bennet said, "there might be problem."

Grif froze. "You're killing my mood, Bennet."

"Sorry," Bennet said, "But Mavis is hailing us from *Centurion*."

Chapter 38

WHEREIN the Woods, Learning Something is Amiss, Endeavor to Pursue

Commodore Mavis sat in his office and waited for word from the planet below.

Someone was making a play for something on the station. If the Viceroy was right, and Mavis suspected he was, then it was for the mysterious artifact sitting on level 5 in Ur Voys. Only now, the artifact was not in fact sitting on level 5 in Ur Voys, it was being moved to another location. One that wasn't compromised.

Someone had compromised the security at Ur Voys.

The breach was, in truth, clumsy: the robots had moved too brazenly, too openly, and were deactivated before anything was accomplished. Still... the very idea that someone had managed to cause a breach on such a scale... incredible.

"Commodore." Katryn Valdyrs' voice emanated from the intercom. "Station commander Hallek Andros, on a secure channel for you."

"Very good. Patch him through here."

Mavis' terminal blurred, and Andros' face appeared.

"Commodore," Andros said, "I have good news." "

Report."

"We've just received word from the last of the transports. All shipments have been handed off to their second convoys without incident. All security codes were validated."

Mavis relaxed slightly. "Very good, Andros. When will we receive confirmation that the items are secure in their new locations?"

"I estimate within the next six hours."

"Good. Very good..." Mavis drifted off into his own thoughts.

"Sir?" Andros peered at him through the terminal screen questioningly.

Mavis blinked, eyes refocusing. "Have you made any progress as to the cause of this breach?"

Andros shook his head, frowning. "Not yet. But I'll let you know the minute I find anything at all."

Mavis nodded. "Thank you Andros. Keep me informed. Mavis out."

He turned off the terminal and sat back in his chair, drumming his fingers on his desk. This was good news. It meant that the artifact was out of the environment the thieves had planned to compromise. That said, Mavis was deeply troubled. His instincts told him this wasn't over, not yet. And, despite all evidence to the contrary, his instincts told him that Vindh was behind it.

Mavis shook his head and tried to dismiss the notion. It made no sense. Captain Vindh was a clever man, perhaps even ingenious in his own way, but he simply didn't have the resources to do something on this scale. His crew was competent, but they didn't have the skills or the equipment to reprogram the robots of Ur Voys en masse.

Mavis pressed the button for his private intercom. "Ando."

Ando Fargus, Mavis' first officer, responded on the other end. "Aye, sir?"

"Is there any speculation as to how the security in Ur Voys was compromised?"

"Well..." Fargus hesitated. "Nothing we can pin down, sir, but there are some irregularities."

"Oh? What are these irregularities?"

"Well sir," Fargus said, "I did a little checking and spoke with the commander of Ur Ados. Ur Ados is the facility that services the robots that work in Ur Voys. A few weeks ago there were a few irregularities in station security. None of them were irregular enough to raise suspicion at the time, but they're being revisited now."

Mavis leaned forward, interested. "Please go on, Mr. Fargus."

"Well sir, there are records of some unusual power readings detected by sensors in the hazardous waste sewage pipes. No one thought anything of it at the time, because those systems were undergoing maintenance."

"Maintenance?"

"It's fairly common," Fargus explained. "Every time the system is cycled and reset the readings spike."

"Was that the only irregularity?" Mavis asked.

"No sir," Fargus said. "One of the warehouses had a shipment of robots slated to be sent to Ur Voys the following day... the security for that warehouse performed an unscheduled cycle and reset."

Mavis found that very interesting. "Did it now?"

"Yes sir..." Fargus took a deep breath. "The official cause was logged as a temporary power failure. There was no reason, at the time, for anyone to think otherwise... but..."

"But you believe you have found a link between them," Mavis finished.

"Yes sir... a few hours before the power cycle, the technician conducting the maintenance on the hazardous waste treatment system accessed warehouse twelve, located right next to the warehouse holding the robots."

"So this technician is responsible for tampering with the robots," Mavis concluded.

Fargus hesitated. "Well... we can't say. There's no evidence she was ever in that warehouse. She was in twelve to get some equipment she legitimately needed for the maintenance. She is on record for going in there, and she did take the equipment from that facility. The only irregularity was that she disabled the security in that warehouse, but a lot of the personnel on the base do that when they're loading or unloading equipment..."

"I see," Mavis said. "Where is this woman now?"

"That's what makes this more suspicious," Fargus admitted. "She hasn't been seen since. She took leave immediately following her shift, and we haven't been able to contact her."

"Did she now..." Mavis drummed his fingers on his desk, thinking. "It appears we have our saboteur."

"Aye sir," Fargus replied. "Although... there weren't enough robots in storage that day to do what Ur Voys is reporting, sir. And we found no record of similar irregularities on previous shipments. There was an attempt to breach Ur Voys through Ur Ados about six months ago, but the attempt was very different... and in no way connected with Miss Robis."

"Robis?"

"The specialist who disappeared."

Mavis frowned. "I am coming to the bridge," he said. "And we will discuss this further. Mavis out."

He strode out of his office onto the bridge of *Centurion*, standing next to his command station. Ando Fargus was climbing up the stairs from the lower tier, heading in his direction.

When Fargus approached, Mavis asked "do you have an image of Miss Robis?"

Fargus nodded, moved to an empty terminal and keyed in a command sequence. The terminal screen blinked, and the picture of an attractive young woman with red hair appeared.

"She was last seen on her shift?"

"No," Fargus said. "She was last seen in a bar the following afternoon."

"Was she seen talking to anyone unusual?"

"She was talking to someone," Fargus said. "No one knows who he was. We're looking into it."

"Commodore." Katryn Valdyrs called up from the lower tier of the bridge. "You asked to be informed of all Maximilian-class ships attempting to take off."

Mavis peered down at the woman. "Yes, I did. You have news?"

"Sir, the *Alo Minh* is asking for clearance from the tower."

Mavis hesitated. "Hail the *Alo Minh*. I wish to speak with her captain."

"Yes sir."

Mavis turned to Fargus. "I want you to listen to everything Captain Tax says, and make sure it checks out properly."

Fargus nodded. "Yes sir."

The terminal screen at Mavis' command station flickered, and the aristocratic face of Jobin Tax appeared on screen.

"Captain Tax." Mavis forced himself to keep his voice casual, conversational. "Leaving so soon?"

Jobin Tax smiled, a weary yet courteous smile that suggested he'd gone through many trials to get to where he was right now. "Soon is hardly the word... I logged my request to leave nearly two and a half weeks ago. I'm afraid we were quite unprepared for the bureaucracy involved..."

Mavis smiled. He glanced at Fargus, who began to access the Port Authority database to search for Tax's clearance records. They would have a log of every misstep made. It wasn't an implausible excuse: many outworlders were unprepared for the exacting nature of the clearance process on Varkav. He'd thought Tax would do better...

Fargus looked up. Mavis switched off the sound on the transmission and nodded slightly for him to report.

"His story checks out," Fargus said. "He filed two and a half weeks ago—one of his crew did, actually. Looks like he tried to rush the process, and it cost them quite a bit of time. Also looks like Captain Tax had to go down there and straighten it out himself. His ident authorized the last round of documentation, not his crewman's.

Mavis nodded again, and switched back on the audio. "I regret you ran into so much trouble, Captain Tax."

Tax sighed, shrugging slightly. "It is my fault for hiring the man I did. He has done nothing but try to cut corners the entire time we were on this planet. I believe there are three or four suppliers in this district who will have nothing whatsoever to do with me when I return."

Mavis smiled again. "I trust you will be able to mend those fences, given time. Well, have a safe trip, Captain. I look forward to your return..."

"Thank you," Captain Tax said. "Tax out."

With that, the terminal screen went blank.

"Miss Valdyrs," Mavis said, "Tell the port authority they may clear the *Alo Minh* for takeoff."

"Aye, sir," Valdyrs said.

"Fargus."

Fargus looked up at him. "Aye, sir?"

"We need to learn more about this incident."

Fargus nodded. "I'll get right on it, sir."

"Very good. I will be in my office."

Mavis returned to his office and thought about the events of the day. The attempt to steal this mysterious artifact had, by all appearances, been foiled. So why didn't he believe it? Could the memories the Viceroy read in Vindh's head have been nothing more than a ruse? Not likely... how would they have known the Sword would be hunting him? And why would Vindh submit to a process that would most likely kill or seriously harm him? Perhaps Vindh had been placed there under duress? If so, Mavis felt little sympathy for him.

And none of this explained why Vindh was nowhere to be found.

As the hours passed, Mavis grew impatient. He could not act until he had useful information to act on, and at the moment there was little he could do to facilitate that.

Eventually Mavis' desk terminal beeped. "Commodore, Hallek Andros is on the secure comm channel and insists he speak with you immediately."

"I will take it here," Mavis said. "Patch it through."

The image of Hallek Andros, Station commander of Ur Voys, appeared on screen. Andros looked tired and gray, as if he'd aged ten years.

"Commodore," Andros said. There was a note of defeat in his voice.

"What?" Mavis said.

Andros took a deep breath. "I regret to inform you that Special Project 51273 is missing."

"What?" Mavis stared at the man incredulously. "What happened?"

Andros shook his head and shrugged. "I don't know. It must have taken place on the other leg of the journey, after we handed it off in mid-point. Their access codes were up to date, and their authorization key was perfect..."

The intercom beeped again. "Sir," Fargus said, "I have more information about our possible saboteur. One of the locals said he saw her talking to offworlders."

"Report, Fargus," Mavis said. "And be quick about it."

"Well, sir, it was some of the crew from the *Alo Minh*."

Mavis closed his eyes and counted to ten. "The *Alo Minh*."

"Yes, sir."

The time for speculation had ended. It was now time to act.

Mavis stood up, pushing back his chair carelessly. "I will handle this myself," he said, straightening his uniform. "Fargus, I'm entering the bridge. Tell whoever is at helm to prepare to leave orbit. Immediately."

Chapter 39

WHEREIN the Woods are Led Down the Garden Path

Tracking down the *Alo Minh* would prove to be a difficult task, especially if—as Commodore Mavis now suspected—her captain didn't wish to be found. She had a six- or seven-hour head start, which meant that she was probably out of the range of standard sensors. Even with sensor beacons placed throughout the system there were more blind spots than not, which meant that finding a single ship in an entire system required a fair amount of coordination.

Mavis paced the bridge, delivering orders in a crisp, clear voice. "I want the location of every one of our ships in this system. If they are planetside, I want them in orbit and standing by. I want all available communications relays listening for the *Alo Minh's* signature key. I want that information triangulated as soon as possible. If the *Alo Minh's* key isn't confirmed within the next three hours, we'll assume it has ejected the key and it will be classified as a rogue ship."

Katryn Valdyrs replied with an "aye, sir" and began relaying orders. Twenty minutes later, various forces around the system were standing by and the communications beacons were listening for any sign of the *Alo Minh*.

Once again Mavis found himself waiting. It seemed to be the most significant part of any crisis—the time when most mistakes were made, he reminded himself. Wait for the information, act on the information you get.

Mavis waited.

An hour and a half later a comm relay reported receiving the *Alo Minh's* signature key. Twenty minutes later, a second reported receiving the same. It took another forty-five minutes for the third, and then they triangulated the ship's last known position.

The presence of the beacon was a promising sign.

"We have projected their course, sir."

Mavis shook himself out of his thoughts and turned to Ando Fargus. "Report."

"There is a fair amount of delay between the *Alo Minh* and the third beacon, and between the beacon and us, but even taking that into account I think we know where they are." Fargus pointed to the large holographic tactical map hanging over the bridge.

Mavis frowned. "That's not as far away as I expected."

"Yes," Fargus agreed. "They're moving slower than we thought."

"What is the closest ship to their position?"

"The *Damascus*," Fargus said. "But not by much... and we could reach their position before Captain Ison if we opened up our engines."

"Good," Mavis said, nodding. "Order navigation to lay in a course to intercept the *Alo Minh*. I want all possible speed."

"Aye sir," Fargus said. "We estimate it'll take about four hours." Information, decision, action—and then, as always, more waiting.

Three hours later, the *Centurion's* communication and sensor arrays picked up traces of the *Alo Minh's* signature key... but there was no trace of the *Alo Minh*. This made Mavis very unhappy.

"Where is she?" Mavis demanded.

"I'm... not sure," Fargus admitted. "We should be picking up signs of their fusion drive, at the very least. Unless they're running with their shields up..."

"No," Mavis said. "Their screens would block their signature key."

The signal grew stronger as the *Centurion* closed the gap, but there was still no trace of the *Alo Minh*.

"I don't understand," Fargus admitted. "Their signature key is transmitting, but we can't see them. I don't know how they're doing it, but we can't detect them with our sensors."

"Do we have the correct position?" Mavis asked.

"We're still getting triangulation data from the communications relays," Fargus said, "and it points here. That information should be reliable."

Mavis sighed in frustration. "The ship is either there or it isn't."

"We'll know soon," Fargus promised.

Twenty minutes later, they knew.

* * *

Grif waited until the *Fool's Errand* was four hours out of Varkav before he gave the order to dump the *Alo Minh* signature key.

They were on the cusp of a dead patch of Varkavian space—just beyond the basic sensor range of the closest planet's sensor array, though they were still visible to anyone watching for their fusion drive.

Grif punched the intercom. "Ktk, get out on the hull and bring the sig key beacon into the cargo bay."

Bennet looked up from the communications station in surprise.

Grif grinned.

Ktk's race could survive in vacuum for nearly two days without the need for extra protection. This job took two hours to finish. Ktk claimed to enjoy the work—it was preferable, it claimed, to baby-sitting a middle-aged telepath in the throes of psichosis. When it reported it was in Bay One with the sig key beacon, Grif ordered Cyrus to go help with the "refit."

"Come on," Bennet said, exasperated, "give me a hint."

Grif grinned again. "We have an old-model planetary probe sitting in Bay one. Nothing useful compared to today's technology, but it can be programmed to follow a preset course. Cyrus and Ktk are going to put the beacon on the probe, and we're going to give Mavis something to chase down for a bit. We'll probably get an extra day out of it."

Bennet smiled. "A decoy."

Grif nodded. "I figure we've got an hour or so before they realize this artifact isn't where it's supposed to be. And a few more hours after that before they figure out we're the ones who took it. Six to eight hours before they start to look for us, maybe twelve if we're lucky."

"Right," Bennet said. "I'd assume closer to six than twelve."

"Killjoy," Grif said. "Now if I was Mavis, I'd want to find me—er, Jobin Tax, that is—as soon as possible. So the first thing I'd do is stay put and listen to see if we're still emitting a signature key, and triangulate that position."

"I see," Bennet said doubtfully. "And what would stop Mavis from knowing you as well as you know him, and suspecting that you've done all this?"

"On, come on," Grif said dismissively. "He doesn't even know it's me. And let me tell you what, de-coupling a signature key from a ship is *hard*. You're not supposed to be able to do it outside a shipyard, you know."

"Impractical, too," Morgan said. "It's easier to just mess with the beacon so you can switch signature keys at will."

Bennet didn't look convinced. "If it takes shipyard facilities to decouple one of those things, how is it that Ktk can pull it off all by itself?"

Grif looked nonchalant. "Trade secret."

"Figures," Bennet muttered, which just made Grif grin all over again.

The intercom beeped, then Cyrus said, "it'll be about half an hour."

Grif punched the intercom. "Get to it. We're on a schedule here!"

He turned to Amys. "In about forty minutes we're going to send the beacon on its merry way. Plot in a course to take us out of the system in a nonstandard route. We'll be flying blind, so try not to map a path through any rocks."

Amys smirked and started plotting courses.

"So what's the plan?" Bennet asked.

"It's pretty simple," Grif said. "We send Mavis in one direction, we go the other direction—screens up to mask our engines. We're going to be just another point of light in the wash. With any luck they won't notice us until we're so far out that it won't matter..."

"What if they notice us before that?"

"Well," Grif said, "there's always plan B..."

Morgan swore under his breath.

Bennet raised an eyebrow. "What is...?"

"Don't ask," Morgan said curtly.

Half an hour later, Cyrus reported that they were finished.

"We've set a rudimentary course," he said. "Nothing fancy, but it'll fly straight, and fast enough to look like a ship."

"Good," Grif replied. "Launch it."

They waited in silence as Morgan monitored the sensor station.

"The probe has launched," Morgan announced.

"Excellent!" Grif said. "Amys, tell me you have a course worked out."

"I have a course worked out," Amys said. "Transferring to your station now."

"Excellent! Screens up."

The view ports went dark as the ship's screens powered up, blocking all energy—including light—from passing through them.

"Morgan, extend the passive sensors if you please."

Morgan keyed a command into his console that extended a small array of sensors past the ships screens, allowing them to collect a limited amount of data without emitting much detectable energy. "Done."

"Right." Grif pushed his seat forward, so that it locked into the pilot's station, and reached for the controls. "My turn."

The ship shuddered slightly as Grif entered a sharp course correction and then opened up the engines, allowing the ship to gain speed. "How fast do I need to push her to get out of here in four days?"

"Hell, Grif," Amys said, "just leave it alone. Five days is plenty fast."

"Hmph." Grif thought it over, then shrugged. "I suppose so. There, done." He pushed his chair back out and turned to face the rest of the bridge. "Now it's just a matter of waiting."

"Great," Bennet said. "My least favorite part of an op. So what are we supposed to do while we wait for the ship to leave the system... or for Mavis to find us, and squish us like a bug?"

"Oh, there are plenty of ways to kill time," Grif said. "Drinking for one... though probably not a good idea till we know we're safe. But hey, I have an idea... how about you guys give me back my face?"

* * *

When Fargus came to report to Mavis, he was clearly frustrated.

"We found the signature key," Fargus said. "But not the *Alo Minh*. Somehow they managed to decouple the signature key, put it into a standard probe, and launch it into space. I'm sorry, Commodore, we've been following a decoy."

Mavis stared at a tactical map of the system, thinking. "Inform all ships in the area that there is a Maximilian-class vessel using a falsified signature key, or else not using one at all. All Maximilian-class vessels are to be stopped, and their signature keys verified, before being permitted to continue."

Fargus nodded. "Aye, sir. Any other orders?"

"Yes," Mavis said. "We're going to have to find the *Alo Minh* the hard way, I'm afraid."

Fargus nodded again, shifting uncomfortably. He was a man of action, Mavis knew, and didn't like waiting.

This, unfortunately, would require waiting. Lots of waiting.

Mavis was unsure whether the Terran phrase "looking for a needle in a haystack" was appropriate for what he and his people were trying to do. On one hand, a haystack was considerably denser than the space that the crew of the *Alo Minh* was moving through. On the other hand, a needle was sufficiently different from straw to make it obvious whether you were looking at a needle or at straw.

The *Alo Minh*, Mavis assumed, was moving through space with screens up, effectively masking most of its energy emissions. It had about a day's head start, moving it well beyond short-range sensors, and was most likely traveling through one of the vast regions of "dead space" in-system—areas where no tactical sensors could reach. The only useful technology in those instances was the use of communications beacons and visual scanners, which were able to provide detailed visual images of things very far away. The most logical course of action was to look at an object in the sky, confirm that it was a Maximilian-class vessel, confirm that it wasn't transmitting a signature key, and go after it.

The only problem was figuring out where to look.

Even with her screens up, the *Alo Minh* would be reflecting some light: like all technology, screens were not 100% efficient. Still, visually she would be no more distinct than a distant planet, a large asteroid or a very distant star. Visual scanners would confirm she was a ship if they happened to look in the right place at the right time, but the further an object was, the more precision they would need to capture its image.

The only way to find the ship was to sit in one place and look at all the points of light in the sky, figure out which ones were moving, and look at each in turn to see if it might be the *Alo Minh*. This involved more waiting, and although Mavis was a very patient man he was getting more and more frustrated as the search continued.

The *Centurion* sat motionless in space, taking visual snapshots of all the points of light in the sky at various intervals and various magnifications, comparing them to see which points were moving. Other ships and stations across the system were doing the same thing. The ones that didn't move were discarded; the ones that did were examined in more detail. This was a laborious process: there were many moving objects to investigate. Even the objects that were already entered into star charts—asteroids, comets and the like—had to be examined, in the event that the *Alo Minh* was using that object to mask her own course out of the system.

It took time to record the first batch of images, and it took more time before the second batch of images could be recorded in order for the movement to be significant enough to be detected. It took even more time for those differences to be processed, and even more time for a rough estimate of each object's current position to be extrapolated from the images. And even then, looking at each object required a certain level of *luck*—the data collected was enough to give the sensor crews a general idea of where to look, but not enough to give them precise locations. Two days passed. About a third of the objects had been viewed and dismissed, and they were quickly running out of time.

In the middle of the second day, they found it.

"It is a starship on a non-standard course," Fargus confirmed, "and heading out of the system very quickly. It's the right size for the *Alo Minh*."

"Can we intercept?" Mavis asked.

"Unfortunately not. None of our forces will be able to intercept it in time, though we have two ships that are close. In another day or two—we haven't been monitoring it long enough to determine its actual velocity—it will pass far enough out of the star's gravity to enable activation of their ATID."

"We can't have that," Mavis said. "Set a course to intercept, maximum speed. All ships in the vicinity are to do the same. I want estimates—accurate estimates, Mr. Fargus—on how close each ship will be by the time the *Alo Minh* reaches her break-free point."

"Aye, sir." Fargus turned and began shouting orders. Mavis sat down in his command seat, nursing a half-empty cup of now lukewarm coffee.

Centurion's engines opened up, and the ship gathered speed as it aimed for the *Alo Minh*. It wouldn't be close enough to engage her directly, but if Divine Providence held, it or another ship would be able to prevent the thieves from making the jump to tach.

If they made the jump to tach, Mavis knew, that would be the end of it. According to the two ship inspections, the *Alo Minh's* ATID was powerful enough and had enough fuel to take it deep into Trade Baron space. Even into Alliance space, if necessary.

"Sir, we have that data—I'm routing it to your chair," Fargus said.

Mavis looked at the data carefully. There were two other ships—a frigate and a scout—that would be able to intercept the *Alo Minh* fifteen minutes before *Centurion* arrived. There were many other ships in *Centurion's* space at present, but none could reach the speeds she could, so she would arrive well before they did.

"Order the two ships at the top of the list to engage," Mavis said. "The other ships may stand down. We will be joining the fray as well."

"Sir, the *Alo Minh* will be able to activate their ATID—"

"I am aware of that, Mr. Fargus," Mavis said. "Our job will be to counteract that. Please inform me when the *Alo Minh* is half an hour away from their break-away point."

"Aye sir."

"It seems we have another day before we engage," Mavis said. "All crew not on duty should take this time to sleep. All crew currently on duty will be relieved before we engage so they can do the same. Everyone has performed with admirable efficiency—let's keep it up."

"I will pass that on," Fargus said.

"Very good." Mavis stood, stretched, looked at his coffee and yawned. "I will be in my quarters. Mr. Fargus, you have the bridge."

Chapter 40

WHEREIN Our Hero, Lacking Compelling Alternatives, Resorts to Plan B

Grif ran his hands over his newly restored face carefully, examining his reflection in a mirror.

"It looks like me, right? I mean, it is my face, right?"

"Yes, Grif," Morgan said. His voice was muffled from the bandages that still covered his face, but it was obvious he was tired of the question. "It looks just like you."

Amys peered at him and frowned.

"What?" Grif looked at his face again. "What? What's wrong?"

"I don't know, but it's not right."

"Dammit!" Grif swore. "I knew it."

"Oh, that's what it is," Amys said. "No stubble."

"What?" Grif ran his hand across his chin. "Oh. You're right. Well, that's a relief." He peered at his chin worriedly. "It will grow back, right? They didn't, ah, do anything to damage it, did they?"

Amys rolled her eyes.

"Christ, Grif, you are so damned vain," Morgan grumbled.

"Hey," Grif protested. "You didn't wind up looking like Hu Mavis for more than a month... actually, I'm sort of surprised you want your old face back..."

Morgan muttered darkly.

Grif grinned. "I'm going to the bridge," he said.

Amys fell in step beside him.

"How soon till we can jump to tach?"

"Soon," Amys said. "I need to check, but I think an hour, hour and a half."

They entered the lift, and Grif keyed the sequence for the top deck. "And those ships?"

"Only three moving to intercept, it looks like. A frigate, a scout ship... and *Centurion*." Amys grinned. "They're not going to make it in time."

Grif laughed. "It's a shame... you know, he's never going to know for sure it was me. So unfair."

The lift door opened, and they stepped out onto the bridge. Bennet was there, manning communications, and Cyrus—his head wrapped in bandages, just like Morgan's—was sitting up at the pilot's station.

"Any news?" Grif asked.

Cyrus pushed the pilot's seat back into the bridge proper and got up. "Nope."

Grif sank into the chair and pushed it forward, sighing happily. "My face, my ship. Life is good."

Amys sat down at her station and checked their position. "We can jump to tach in 30 minutes," she said.

"Excellent."

"Guess I'll head down to the main gun," Cyrus said. "Just in case Mavis pulls a fast one. Grif, I want you to know that I've put down quite a bit of money on us getting away with this."

"You bet we will get away with this, or we won't?"

Cyrus grinned. "You know me."

"Good man. And may I hazard a guess as to the identity of the poor fool who bet against me?"

"Not much point in guessing," Cyrus said. "Same two and a half meter tall bug that always does."

Grif shook his head and punched the intercom. "Ktk, you realize that if you actually win this latest bet with Cyrus, we're all going to die, right?"

Ktk replied that every time it had lost a bet it had also survived, and that it really considered the process less of a gamble, and more of a tax to ensure its survival.

Grif laughed. "How long till we jump, Amys?"

"It's still thirty minutes, Grif."

Grif sat back in his chair and drummed his fingers against one of the arms impatiently.

Time stretched on.

Grif distracted himself by tracking the progress of the three Radiant Throne ships that were bearing down on them. The frigate and scout would engage in forty to forty-five minutes—it looked like the scout would probably edge out the frigate in terms of speed. The *Centurion* was another fifteen minutes behind, though it was presently moving faster than either of the other two ships.

It was going to be close.

"Funny that they only dispatched three ships to intercept us," Grif noted.

"Not that funny," Amys said. "We've got too much of a head start. Why dispatch half the fleet sitting in-system when none of them can reach us?"

"And *Centurion* could handle us on her own," Cyrus added.

"True enough," Grif agreed. "It just seems strange. We break into one of the most secure facilities in Throne space, make off with some kind of weird artifact from an advanced civilization, and at the end of it all, three lousy ships are sent after us."

"*Centurion* is hardly a lousy ship," Cyrus said.

"Well, all right—one lousy ship, one middling ship, and one admittedly grand and imposing ship. My point is, well, we've had bigger crowds chasing us over smaller matters. It's almost, I don't know, anti-climactic."

"I'm all for anti-climactic," Bennet said. The rest of the bridge crew agreed heartily.

"I suppose," Grif sighed.

"We're outside the gravity well," Amys reported. Grif heaved a sigh of relief.

"Good," he said. "Now we can get the hell out of here."

Amys smirked. "What happened to 'anti-climactic?'"

"That was just talk. I prefer it when people don't shoot at us."

"Speaking of which," Cyrus said, looking uncomfortable, "I really am going down to the gunnery bay now."

Grif nodded. "Good idea, though we should be jumping to tach in about ten minutes. Amys, you have that course laid out?"

"Feeding it to your console now."

Grif saw coordinates flash across his screen, and he began setting everything up.

As Cyrus headed out the bridge door, Grif turned on the intercom. "This is your captain speaking. We'll be jumping to tach in ten minutes, and disabling ship's gravity in five. Please secure everything in that time, including yourself. General countdown to zero-G begins in four minutes. Vindh out."

With that, he shut off the intercom and returned to laying in the course. "Morgan, they're not going to get close enough to shoot at us, are they?"

Morgan ran a few computations on his station. "No."

"Just what I want to hear," Grif said. "Then we sit in the bubble for a few hours, and poof, Tylaris System. Drop off the cargo, get paid, and with any luck never see Velis and Company again—no offense Bennet."

"None taken," Bennet said. "But how do you know the Major isn't going to double-cross you?"

There was a brief but uncomfortable silence.

"Well," Grif said finally. "You know how to throw water on a perfectly cheerful fire. But I'm pretty sure she won't."

"Oh?"

"Well first of all, despite the fact that under many circumstances you're a fairly decent chap, you work for her... if she was planning another coup you wouldn't be asking that question. And second, she wouldn't go back on the guarantee she gave me when you lot were in the brig. Not her style."

"If you say so," Morgan muttered.

"Don't mind him," Grif said, "he just has more reason than most to mistrust her."

"Oh?" Bennet looked at Morgan curiously. "You two have a history?"

"You could say that," Morgan said. "I almost married her."

Grif punched on the intercom. "Zero G in one minute. All hands strap in." As he spoke, he began to fasten himself to his chair. The other members of the crew did the same.

Cyrus, Cutter and Hari reported in that they were secure. A few seconds later, Ktk, Vod and Gurgan did the same. Half a minute later Velis called up to announce that her people were secure as well.

"Excellent," Grif said. "Zero G in twenty seconds." The countdown continued, then at zero there was a strange shifting sensation, and the hum of the gravity plates fell silent.

"Gravity off," Amys reported.

"Good," Grif said. "Let's get ready to jump."

The next five minutes were spent going over the course in excruciating detail, running down all ship systems and making sure that it would be safe to activate the ATID. The ship began to slow its velocity, so that when it hit tach it would achieve the best possible superluminal speeds.

At one minute to go Morgan swore loudly. "Gravity just jumped up a tick in our vicinity."

"What?" Grif looked at his instruments and swore in turn. "I'll be damned, it did. It just went up a hundredth of a G."

"And it's climbing," Morgan reported. "Slowly but surely."

"Dammit." Grif looked at Amys. "Are we ready yet?"

Amys shook her head. "It's too dangerous now."

"The hell it is," Grif said. "At a hundredth of a G there's a little bit of risk, but not nearly as much as waiting for those ships to get close enough to open up with their guns."

"A hundredth of a G is pushing it, Grif," Amys said. "I don't want to be crushed like a grape when we turn that thing on."

"Me either," Grif said. "I also don't want to be blown out of the sky by an ion canon. Or anything else for that matter. We've done a hundredth of a G before–it's not fun and we'll have to fix up our ship after, but I'd rather do that than—"

"Grif..." Morgan was staring down at his console, shaking his bandaged head. "We have a fairly significant problem."

"We're talking about that right now, Morgan..." "No, Grif, shut up a sec. Do you know why gravity just jumped up a tick?"

"Uh..." Grif thought. "Now that you mention it..."

"It's the *Centurion*," Morgan said. "They've activated their gravlock." Grif felt his face go slack and his jaw drop.

"That bastard. That sneaky, sneaky bastard."

Bennet looked at the others on the bridge in confusion. "What? What just happened?"

"Mavis just screwed us," Grif said. "Morgan, what's the ETA on the first two ships?"

"How?" Bennet asked. "I don't understand. What about the gravlock?"

"About ten minutes before they can start missing us close enough for us to notice," Morgan said.

"Ten? You said fifteen earlier."

"Hello?" Bennet was obviously confused. "Sorry, I don't mean to play the ignorant farmboy here, but my experience on a starship is strictly limited to working a com station."

"We weren't slowing down then," Morgan said. "We slowed down to jump to tach. They didn't."

"Son of a bitch," Grif swore, and opened up the fusion drive. "Can we outrun them?"

"The frigate, yes," Morgan said. "The scout ship, no. The *Centurion*... no."

"Dammit." Grif sighed and turned to Bennet. "Mavis has activated his gravlock. Normally, this would be no big deal because *Centurion* is too far away for the tractor beam to be strong enough to actually pull us in. But it is apparently close enough to create an artificial gravity well."

"Which is bad," Bennet finished.

"Oh yes," Grif said. "Very bad. Because we can't outrun her."

Grif activated the intercom. "This is your captain speaking," he said. "Red alert. Battle stations."

Ktk, Cyrus and Velis immediately responded, each wanting to know what the hell was going on.

"It's just a little setback," Grif said, trying to sound unconcerned. "It seems that Commodore Mavis has hit upon the brilliant idea of using a gravlock to set up a little gravity well around us—we can't jump to tach, and we can't outrun him."

"What?" Cyrus sounded aghast.

"Is there anything we can do?" Velis asked.

"Afraid not. Just sit tight. Uh, well, belay that—any of your people with shipboard experience, send them to engineering. Ktk can set them up to deal with damage control, if necessary."

"You're going to fight the *Centurion*?" Velis asked in disbelief.

"Well it's not what I'd *like* to do," Grif said.

Ktk replied that this was a terrible time for it to win a bet.

"You haven't won yet," Grif snapped. "We're going to engage the enemy in..."

"Nine minutes," Morgan said.

"Nine minutes. Get ready. Vindh out." Grif switched off the intercom.

"What are your orders, Grif?" Amys asked.

"I'm thinking."

"Captain," Bennet broke in suddenly, "*Centurion* is hailing us."

"Great," Grif said, "just what we need. Morgan, set up our tactical map."

Morgan keyed in a command and a battle map appeared above the fore view port.

"Uh... about the *Centurion* hailing us," Bennet repeated.

"Not now," Grif said. "Just ignore them. However, if you would be so kind as to patch the intercom to the gunnery bays and the engine room. We're going to need them on all the time now."

Bennet nodded and hit a few keys. "Done."

Grif nodded in return. "Cyrus, Ktk. Can you hear me?"

"Yes," Cyrus said. Ktk replied that it could.

"Good," Grif said. "Cyrus, we think the scout is coming in first. We're going to forgo formalities and try to take it out first thing. The frigate is going to be more of a problem, and I don't want to deal with both at the same time if I can avoid it."

"All right," Cyrus said. "What about *Centurion*?"

"We have another..." Grif looked at the data scrolling past his screen. "... fifteen minutes or so before we have to worry about her."

"That's your plan?" Amys asked, incredulous. "You're going to fight?"

"My plan was to jump out of here before they caught us," Grif said. "Mavis sort of screwed that up. Now I'm forced to improvise. We can't go anywhere as long as that gravlock is fixed on us, we can't outrun the *Centurion*, it's going to catch up with us eventually, and the closer it gets, the stronger the gravlock... until eventually it will be able to tear us apart, if that's what Mavis wants to do. So basically we're going to have to take it out."

"What, the *Centurion*?" Cyrus clearly didn't like the sound of that.

"No, not the *Centurion*," Grif said crossly. "What do you think I am, an idiot? No way we can take out *Centurion*. Hell, I doubt an Alliance *battleship* could take out *Centurion*. We do need to disable its gravlock, though."

"How are we going to do that?" Bennet asked.

"No idea," Grif said. "It all depends on what Mavis does when the *Centurion* gets here. But I think we might be able to give it a little nudge in the right direction... Ktk, we may need to, ah, misrepresent ourselves a bit. Smoke and mirrors, if you get my meaning."

Ktk replied that it understood perfectly, and would get the men Velis had sent down to engineering to set everything up.

Grif sighed. "Well, I suppose it was too much to ask to keep you guys in the dark as far all my dirty tricks are concerned," he said to Bennet. "But it's annoying. There are only so many ways to make a secret hold, and the Radiant Throne knows one arrangement, and the Alliance knows another."

"Look at it this way," Bennet said. "If we die, your secret will be safe."

"Hm," Grif said. "When you put it that way, I don't mind sharing. Cyrus..."

"Aye."

"Do we have any slugs on board?"

"We should."

"Get Cutter or Hari to load 'em up."

"The scout ship is coming into range," Morgan reported.

"All right," Grif said, "let's get this over with. Amys, man the screens."

The stars lining the view port began to blink in a strobe effect as the ship's defense screens started to pulse, affording the *Fool's Errand* some protection all over the ship while still allowing the ship's sensors to collect some information. As they closed in on the craft Amys would begin to manipulate the screens with more precision, activating some shields on full and leaving others down, moving the shields around to protect critical systems while leaving untargeted parts open. It was risky, but allowed Morgan to collect as much information as possible.

"The scout vessel has activated her screens," Morgan reported.

"And *Centurion* is still hailing us," Bennet said.

"All right," Grif said. "Put them through. But audio only—no picture on our part, and no return audio—just let them know we're listening."

After a short delay, Mavis' voice came through loud and clear.

"Captain Tax," Mavis said, "this is Commodore Hu Mavis of the *RTS Centurion*. You will lower your shields, power down your weapons, and consent to be boarded. If you do this, if you surrender now, I give you my word that no harm will come to your crew."

Grif rolled his eyes.

"If you don't, however," Mavis continued, "I give you my word we'll disable your ship and execute the lot of you."

"Such a diplomat," Grif said. "Morgan, what are they doing?"

"*Centurion* is still closing. The frigate is still closing. The scout is hanging back. Waiting, I guess."

"Right... Cyrus, the scout in range?"

"For our main gun, yes," Cyrus said. "But it's got screens up on the side facing us."

"It's a scout ship," Grif said. "Its screens are nearly useless. Don't target it yet, they might pick that up. But get ready to do so when I give the order."

"Captain Tax," Mavis continued, "I must insist that you acknowledge this transmission. Failure to do so will be taken as a declaration of hostility."

"Oh, I'll give you a declaration all right..." Grif snarled. "Bennet, Amys needs to use your station for a moment."

Bennet looked surprised, but stood up and backed off. Amys got up and sat in the comm station.

"Are we doing what I think we're doing?" she asked.

"You bet," Grif said. "Transmit the Jolly Roger on all channels."

Chapter 41

WHEREIN Desperate Times Call For Desperate Measures

Commodore Hu Mavis stood on the bridge of the *Centurion* and watched the battle with interest.

The *Alo Minh's* response had been savage and unexpected—not that Mavis had expected her to go quietly, but he hadn't been prepared for the potency of her guns. How the presence of an ion cannon had escaped the Radiant Throne's inspections was beyond him, but somehow the crew of the *Alo Minh* had managed to conceal it. It was a fairly powerful one, considering the size of that ship, and while it wasn't enough to penetrate *Centurion's* screens it had nearly incapacitated the scout ship after the first shot. Mavis ordered the ship to pull back, and the *Alo Minh* had left it alone after that—it wasn't interested in the kill, it just wanted the ship out of the fight.

It made a beeline for the frigate next—a more evenly matched fight, in Mavis' eyes. Normally, he would assume the frigate would have the advantage, since it was designed with combat in mind, but he was no longer confident of this where the *Alo Minh* was concerned. And it seemed that the crew was very competent and combat ready.

A very dangerous brand of pirate indeed.

Mavis stared at the skull and crossbones staring back at him from the terminal at his station. They'd long since ceased transmitting that damnable signal, but he'd kept it on his terminal to remind him who he was dealing with.

He doubted they were actually pirates. Privateers perhaps... they were almost certainly working with the Alliance, considering what they'd gone to incredible lengths to steal. Mavis frowned in anger. He'd thought Captain Tax a reasonable and civilized man. This was, in hindsight, precisely what Jobin Tax had wanted. He wondered again who Tax actually was, and again the same name floated to the top of his mind. He dismissed the name angrily, refusing to believe that Vindh was capable of such a well-orchestrated heist.

When he saw the ship in combat, though, his doubts were themselves plagued by doubts. The pilot of the *Alo Minh* was exceptional, making it do things that would be difficult even in smaller vessels. The frigate was attempting to engage it as a larger ship—plotting an attack course, locking in guns, firing as it passed. The *Alo Minh* was behaving like a gunboat, or even a fighter craft. It was "dogfighting," always altering course at the last minute or attempting to move in a way that would give it a shot somewhere the frigate's screens were not.

Mavis kept in constant communication with the frigate, trying to advise her captain during the course of the fight, but the captain was clearly having difficulty adjusting to this style of fighting.

"Captain," Mavis said, trying to remain patient. "You must try to adopt the methods the *Alo Minh* is using against you, or you will lose this fight."

"Acknowledged, Commodore," the captain replied, "but this ship isn't built to do that. I've never even *tried* that before—we might just break into a—hold on a moment."

The *Alo Minh* was advancing on another strafing run. The Captain barked orders to intercept, and then shouted more orders as the *Alo Minh* abruptly changed course so that it was beneath the frigate, firing at her belly. Damage was minimal—it was an attack from one of the smaller guns—but it made Mavis wince regardless.

"Captain, you must change your tactics to accommodate theirs," Mavis insisted.

"With all due respect, Commodore, it's not that easy," the captain replied. "We weren't trained to do that. We don't know how much stress we can put on our ship before she cracks."

Mavis was forced to admit the captain had a point. Most ship captains didn't try to fly their ships as if they were fighter pilots...Tax did.

"No," Mavis said softly, "not Tax. You know very well who this is."

He stared at the skull and crossbones sitting on his monitor, and then at the battle map.

"Vindh."

Mavis wondered why Vindh was working for the Alliance. It wasn't his style. "When will we engage the target?"

"Two minutes," Ando Fargus replied.

Mavis nodded. "I want screens up around the gravlock. Everything else should be pulsed as usual. Ready weapons, launch fighters."

"Aye sir!"

Mavis raised his voice so that it would be picked up and transmitted to the frigate. "Captain, I am about to strengthen our gravlock. It should affect the target's mobility. Take advantage of the opportunity, and shoot to disable."

"Understood," the captain replied.

"Mr. Fargus, when we are within range..."

"Aye, sir."

The captain changed tactics, fighting defensively, never letting the *Alo Minh*—or, as was very likely, the *Fool's Errand*—close in, but never trying to go for the kill himself. It was a smart tactic, though Mavis half-feared it would make Vindh suspect something was amiss.

"Open a channel to our target, please," Mavis commanded.

"Aye, sir." Katryn Valdyrs keyed in a command. "The channel is open."

"This is Commodore Mavis. Captain Vindh, this is your last chance to stand down."

Ando Fargus looked up at Mavis in surprise when he said Vindh's name.

"Sir," Valdyrs said, "we're getting a reply."

"On my terminal, please."

The skull and crossbones shifted, and was replaced by the smirking face of Captain Grif Vindh.

"Hello Mavis," Vindh said brightly. "Been a while."

"Stand down, Captain, or I will destroy your ship."

"Much as I'd like to continue this discussion," Vindh said, "I'm kind of busy. Trying to escape, you know. Vindh out."

With that, the terminal screen went blank.

"They've killed the transmission," Valdyrs said.

"So it seems," Mavis agreed. "Mr. Fargus, are we within range?"

"Twenty-eight seconds to go," Fargus reported.

"When we are within range, I wish that ship immobilized."

The *Fool's Errand*—for he was *quite* certain that Vindh was piloting his own ship—was getting more and more aggressive in its attacks on the frigate. Mavis suspected that Vindh was becoming more and more desperate. The *Centurion* was only seconds away from entering the fray, after which the fight would be most assuredly finished.

Suddenly the *Fool's Errand* began to list and move erratically.

"We hit her," the captain of the frigate reported. "I thought we only grazed her, but we set something off. She's definitely having difficulty maneuvering."

"Good work," Mavis replied. "Now disable her completely."

"Commodore," Fargus said, "our sensors are picking up massive explosions coming from the underside of the *Alo Mi*—er, the *Fool's Errand*."

"What?" Mavis walked over to Fargus' station and peered at his terminal.

"We're still studying it, but it looks like the hit triggered a chain reaction of some sort. Possibly damaging the fusion drive. There's some structural damage, and a lot of radiation pouring out the side."

Mavis stared at the readout on Fargus' terminal and thought quickly. "Are they trying to hail us?"

"They're not doing much of anything."

"Sir," one of the sensor techs reported, "It appears as if the power plant has been damaged. Their screens have dropped, their guns have no power, and they're not moving."

"Are you sure?" Mavis asked.

The sensor tech shook his head. "All that radiation is making specific readings difficult. We're getting heat readings but we can't find any people—the radiation is washing it all out."

"How fortunate," Mavis said. "Prepare a boarding party."

***

It was getting hot on the bridge of the *Fool's Errand*. Grif was sweating.

"Is it working?" Morgan asked yet again. As always, Grif shrugged.

"They haven't blown us out of the sky yet," he said. "Ktk, how's it going down there?"

Ktk replied that it was quite warm.

Grif drummed his fingers on the arm of his chair impatiently. "Come on, Mavis," he muttered.

"What's taking so long?" Bennet asked.

"Mavis," Grif said. "He's torn between pride and paranoia. I'm hoping pride wins out."

"We got something," Morgan said, sitting up straight in his chair. "Looks like *Centurion* is sending out a boarding party."

"Finally," Grif said. "And the gravlock?"

"Still on and pulling us closer."

"How close?"

"Pretty close at this point," Morgan said.

Grif nodded. "OK, let's get ready to move this thing. Cyrus, is Hari ready down there?"

Hari's voice came back over the intercom. "Ready to go. Just point me in the right direction."

"OK... Ktk, I'm going to count down from five... if you could release a nice bright wave of radiation out of that engine on 'one,' I'd appreciate it. Morgan, do a quick—*very*, *very* quick—scan at the same time, just to give us our position and basic targeting info."

Morgan nodded. Ktk said it was ready.

"Right... five... four... three... two... one."

"Scanning," Morgan said. "Information acquired, sending to you now..."

"I've got it," Grif said. "OK, let's get ready to move. Ktk, get ready to turn off the fireworks. Amys, after we take out the gravlock we're going to have to skip out. Ktk, do we have enough power for that?"

Ktk replied that they did, but it was worried about interference from *Centurion*.

"It's not *that* big," Grif said. "Anyway, we're not going to have much choice in the matter. Amys, you see where I've got to move this bucket to take out the gravlock. I need two courses from that point."

Amys nodded, frowning. "What about the screens? I can't do both."

"Just set 'em to pulse," Grif said. "When I give the order."

He looked around at his bridge crew. "Are we ready for plan B?"

Amys and Morgan groaned. Over the intercom, Cyrus swore loudly, and Ktk made a noise that was definitely a sign of distress.

"Don't call it plan B," Amys said. "Just call it... improvisation."

"The boarding vessel is getting closer," Morgan warned.

"Right," Grif said. "Then let's get started, on my mark."

He sat up in his chair and put his hands on the controls.

"They're pulling us in," Morgan said.

"Good," Grif said. "Now!"

The *Fool's Errand* shuddered as the fusion drives roared to life. The tactical screens blinked as Morgan began feeding Grif real-time information. The view ports flickered in time with the screens, and Grif felt a blast of cool air as the life support systems returned to normal.

The *Fool's Errand* was, fortunately, pointing towards *Centurion*. Mavis had used the gravlock to turn the ship around so that the radiation spewing out the engine was pointing away from the larger ship. Grif grinned as his ship streaked toward the larger vessel.

"The boarding craft is breaking off its intercept course," Morgan reported.

"Good," Grif said. "Now if I can just move us close enough so that—"

The fire of laser cannons impacted against the screens and the world went dark for a moment as they went to full strength in order to absorb the blast.

"Not good," Grif muttered. "We really need to see..."

The screens lowered momentarily as the ship moved out of the field of fire of those particular guns, and then the world darkened as others hit them.

"How are the screens holding up?" Grif asked.

Amys broke from her calculations and glanced up at another part of her console. "They're about half done in," she said.

"Great..."

And then the screens returned to normal.

"Excellent," Grif said. "We've flown under their field of fire. Mostly."

They were very close to the ship's hull, and Grif turned their own ship so they were flying along the hull as if it were a large, metallic planet.

"They're opening the fighter bays," Morgan reported.

"Bound to happen sooner or later. Amys, how about those courses?"

"Almost done," Amys said. "Ask me after you've taken out the gravlock."

"Hari," Grif shouted. "You ready?"

Hari's voice sounded relatively calm over the intercom. "Ready, Skip."

"OK, well, we're nearly there..." The *Fool's Errand* shook, and streaks of light arced past the starboard view port.

"We were hit," Morgan said. "Screens took most of it though."

"*Centurion*?"

"No, one of her fighters. There's a whole mess of 'em back there."

"Morgan," Grif said, clenching his teeth, "if you could be a bit more precise than 'mess,' I'd dearly appreciate it."

"Uh... twenty-five. But only a few are close enough to target properly... for the moment."

"That is a mercy..." Grif changed course sharply. "Hari, we're almost there, hold on, I'll get you in position."

Grif turned the ship over, so that the *Centurion* was now hanging over them. *Centurion's* screens pulsed on , and she looked like a large black blot in the night sky.

"Screens are up," Grif heard Hari mutter. "This will be interesting."

"Can you make the shot? The *Fool's Errand* is too big to fly under them..."

"Don't worry," Hari said. "I don't have to be too accurate with these..."

The *Fool's Errand* shuddered again as more laser fire impacted into the hull. Ktk chittered angrily.

"Amys, turn the aft screens on full," Grif said. Amys sighed, annoyed at the distraction, and hit a control absently. The shuddering stopped.

"We're almost there, Hari," Grif said.

"Don't worry about me, Skip, I've got it," Hari said. "Just keep us from blowing up!"

Grif grinned. "Well, all right. But only because you asked nicely..."

"We're almost there," Morgan said. "Twenty seconds. And it looks like they're trying to head us off at the pass..."

The tactical screen showed a contingent of fighters bearing down on them, trying to cut them off.

"We're not changing course, dammit." Grif snarled as a burst of cannon fire narrowly missed them.

"Ten seconds," Morgan said. "Eight, seven, six, five, four, three, two, one..."

"Slugs away!" Hari shouted.

The fighters were upon them.

Grif pushed down on the controls, and the *Fool's Errand* dove away from the *Centurion's* hull. The fighters swarmed after them, all jockeying for a position to fire.

"Amys I need that course now!"

"Sending!" Amys shouted. "Sent!"

Grif looked at the coordinates and changed course. "Ready—drop screens!"

The screens dropped, and view ports were filled by a swarm of angry fighters. Grif yelped in surprise and jammed his thumb down on the switch that activated the ATID.

The view ports went gray. The gray disappeared. They were hanging in empty space.

Grif sighed in relief.

"Pretty good skip," Amys said. "We're almost to the second set of coordinates."

"I'm slowing her down," Grif said. "Morgan, where's *Centurion*?"

"About ten minutes out," Morgan said. "And... no gravity wells."

Grif heard a whoop from the intercom.

"Good shot, Hari!" Grif said.

"You bet your ass it was a good shot," Hari said. "It was a *great* shot. It was a *fantastic* shot!"

"That's my crew," Grif said. "Humble to the end. OK, folks, time to go." Grif eased the ship into the proper course and heading, and activated the ATID. Once again, the view ports went gray.

A ragged cheer erupted from the bridge, and Grif sat back, sighing in relief.

"We made it," Grif announced. "We're on course for the Tylaris system."

"Then there's only one thing left to say," Cyrus said gleefully. "Pay me, bug!"

Chapter 42

WHEREIN Our Hero, Having Escaped Certain Calamity, Celebrates His Unexpected Survival

Grif Vindh, captain of the *Fool's Errand*, was very, very drunk.

They were in Dyorbid's, waiting out the repairs on their ship and celebrating the fact that they had, when all was said and done, not been killed.

By the time they reached Trade Baron space they all had their original faces back—Cutter even had his scars, much to Vod's satisfaction. They were greeted at the edge of the Tylaris system by an Alliance warship carrying none other than Alef Halge. The cargo was transferred quickly, and Velis left without so much as a goodbye, which suited everyone fine. Some of her people nodded briefly as they left, more acknowledgment than Grif had expected, and Bennet actually shook his hand.

"It was interesting serving on your ship," Bennet said. "On the whole. Despite the... ah... awkwardness."

"You'd be a good crewman," Grif replied. "Under normal circumstances. But I trust you won't be offended if I say I hope we never meet again."

Bennet grinned. "No offense taken," he said, and left.

Alef Halge was true to his word. As soon as he'd confirmed receipt of the artifact, he transmitted confirmation that Vindh was the owner of a freshly minted charter to trade within Alliance space.

"I trust," Halge said, "that such a valuable gift will be used properly."

"Of course," Grif said, voice non-committal. "Enjoy your, uh, alien thing."

After that, they took a week floating in deep space to take Ebur Tosk out of stasis and put him back on his meds. Ebur was more than a bit cranky to have missed everything, but he felt much better after taking a proper shower, getting a decent meal, and confirming that he had been paid.

All that was left to do was to repair the ship. Grif chose the Tyrelos system for that, since the *Fool's Errand* wouldn't be able to land on any planet with an atmosphere until the breech in their hull was repaired. That led to Vindh and his crew sitting in Dyorbid's, getting progressively more inebriated as the hours passed.

Eventually all their bragging and self-congratulation gave way to drunken speculation.

"I wonder what that thing was," Morgan said. "I would've loved to take a closer look at it."

Grif peered at Morgan over his drink. "What, the mysterious piece of alien technology that potentially proves all your views about the origin of life in the universe?"

"Yeah," Morgan said defensively. "*That*."

"I wouldn't waste too much time thinking about it. Let it go. It's probably sitting in some high-security scientific facility in Alliance space, waiting for the Radiant Throne to steal it back."

"But what *is* it?" Morgan persisted.

"It's the kind of thing that makes my sister show up," Grif replied.

Morgan thought it over. "Never mind," he said.

The crew laughed.

"I, for one, am happy to be rid of it," Grif said. "It's nice to pull off the impossible, but it's a lot more trouble than it's worth. Entangling alliances, and all that. The less I'm involved with politics the happier I am."

"The further away from your sister I am, the happier I am," Amys added, and there was a general round of agreement to that.

Grif stood and raised his glass. "A toast," he said. "To staying away from my sister."

The crew responded with an enthusiastic "here, here!" and everyone drank.

"What about you, Cyrus?" Grif asked. "What are you going to do now? Are you going to buy that ship?"

Everyone fell silent and looked at him.

Cyrus sighed and shook his head. "If it's all the same to you, Grif, I'm going to stay on for a bit."

Grif raised an eyebrow. "Why? Captaining a ship is what you want to *do*."

"I know," Cyrus said. "But you heard about Tylaris, right? Joining the Alliance?"

The rest of the crew grumbled at that. The official announcement had been broadcast just after they'd arrived at Tyrelos Station.

"Yeah," Grif said. "I heard."

Cyrus shrugged. "Well, the ship I had lined up to buy is on Tylaris, and I won't be going back there to do any business any time soon. The Baronies are going to be a rough place for a while, and anyone who goes into that system will be seen as taking sides. Anyway, a few more years on a ship with a charter to trade in Alliance Space and I'll be able to buy something better. Er... assuming you'll have me."

"Oi!" Grif protested. "Of course I'll have you on this ship. What do I look like, an idiot? You don't turn away one of the best gunners in the Baronies just because he has future plans."

Cyrus grinned. "Well some might."

"Hey Grif," Hari, said, facial spines settling into a pattern of curiosity. "Speaking of money, how exactly are we paying for the repairs?"

"Sorry?" Grif asked.

"Well we got pretty burned up in that fight with *Centurion*," Hari said. "And it's being fixed as we speak... but they didn't pay you in money, they paid you with a charter. Which is good! Don't get me wrong! But it's long-term good, not short-term good. So how are you paying to get the *Fool's Errand* fixed?"

"Now that you mention it," Cutter drawled, "that's a good question. Are you payin' for it out of pocket, Skip? Or did Alef give us some money to cover expenses?"

"Well..." Grif looked up at the ceiling. "I may have agreed to a job after the repairs are finished on the grounds that we were given an advance..."

The table fell silent. Grif looked at his crew and grinned.

Cyrus threw back his head and laughed, then reached over and hit Ktk on its carapace. "I told you, bug! It wouldn't be a month before he got us into something else!"

Ktk sighed and said it would pay Cyrus tomorrow morning.

They drank through the night, laughing and telling stories. As the night grew to morning, more and more of the group fell away, until eventually only Amys and Grif were left.

"I'm glad Cyrus is staying on," Amys said. "He's good for the ship."

"He is indeed," Grif agreed, raising his glass in a toast. "It'll be a bad day when he actually leaves for good."

Amys shrugged.

Grif stared at her in silence. Amys grinned, then frowned, then finally, in an agitated voice, said "what?"

Grif took a drink of Stellis, cocked his head to one side, and asked "so when are you leaving?"

Amys blinked. "When am I *what*?"

"I'm serious. Some day Cyrus is going to be the captain of his own ship. And he's going to be a good one. But why aren't you one already?"

"Trying to get rid of me?" Amys asked, smiling slightly.

Grif leaned forward. His expression was serious, mixed with curiosity, mixed with... something else. "You should do it. Why haven't you done it? It doesn't make sense. I'm not complaining... but it doesn't make sense."

Amys didn't reply.

"There's no reason you should be stuck in the number two seat, Amys. You keep your cool, you're an excellent pilot... you'd be hell of a smuggler captain. Or pretty much any kind of captain you wanted to be. Bottom line? If I had my way, you would always be XO on my ship. But why should you? Buy your own ship. Get your own crew. I'll help if you need it, but you won't—you've done it all before, only for me. Now do it for yourself."

Amys stared at Grif, trying to think of something to say. Grif stared back, afraid of what she would. Finally Amys smiled.

"You know I never take your advice," she said.

And that was it.

Grif grinned, relaxed, and settled back in his chair. "All according to plan," he said. "Reverse psychology. Works every time."

"You're a liar," Amys said.

Grif pretended he didn't hear.

About the Author

Writer, former musician, occasional cartoonist, and noted authority on his own opinions, C. B. Wright's weakness for tilting at windmills has influenced every facet of his adult life. He enjoys reading and writing fiction. He also enjoys writing about himself in the third person. He refuses to comment on whether writing about himself in the third person also qualifies as fiction. He currently lives in Alabama with his wife, daughter, dog, and his overpoweringly large ego.

Also By Author

Curveball Year One: Death of a Hero (eBook, Trade Paperback)

Curveball Year Two: That Which Does Not Dream (eBook, Trade Paperback)

www.ingramcontent.com/pod-product-compliance
Lightning Source LLC
LaVergne TN
LVHW030908080826
845145LV00010B/2809